BARE-KNUCKLE SURGEON

Nick Black

Grosvenor House
Publishing Limited

This book is published by
Grosvenor House Publishing Ltd
Link House
140 The Broadway, Tolworth, Surrey, KT6 7HT.
www.grosvenorhousepublishing.co.uk

This book is a work of fiction. Any resemblance to
people or events, past or present, is purely coincidental.

A CIP record for this book
is available from the British Library

Paperback ISBN 978-1-83615-473-0
eBook ISBN 978-1-83615-474-7

A stirring, highly imaginative, and – for all the fact that it is a novel – a convincing account of the early life of Thomas Wakley – the man who founded *The Lancet*, and thus paved the way for modern medicine. The battles, the setbacks and the occasional triumphs that led him to that are told with vim and vigour. If this is not quite what actually happened, it captures the spirit that was to instil *The Lancet's* early days. A cracking read.

Nicholas Timmins, *The Five Giants*

A meticulously researched and compelling tale, Nick Black brilliantly brings to life the unregulated and fascinating world of early nineteenth century medicine. This book is an enthralling look at a long-neglected medical hero. Such a fascinating story - really loved it.

Hannah Wunsch, *The Autumn Ghost*

Thomas Wakley was one of medicine's most important reformers – needling the pompous, exposing the corrupt, holding the mighty to account. *Bare-Knuckle Surgeon* animates this remarkable man and situates him in a vibrant medical world on the cusp of revolution. If you value well-researched, lightly worn scholarship or just enjoy a good story, this is for you.

Paul Craddock, *Spare Parts*

Nick Black transports us back to Georgian England, where medicine is unregulated and nepotism is rife. He weaves the story of Thomas Wakley's early years into this patchwork, bringing a very human face to the founder of *The Lancet*. For the first time, this book recognises his achievement in doing what no other doctor had ever done, initiating reform. I really loved it. It's extraordinary Wakley isn't better known.

Ellen Welch, *Why Can't I see My GP?*

Nick Black is emeritus professor of health services research at the London School of Hygiene & Tropical Medicine. He's spent many years studying health care, helping students understand how to improve its quality, and advising national policymakers.

He is the author of *Walking London's Medical History,* which won awards from the British Medical Association and the Society of Authors, and his first novel, *The Honourable Doctor,* was long-listed for the Page Turner Book Award in 2023.

He lives in London and Herne Bay with his wife, Pippa, and two black cats.

"Reformer indeed! Thomas Wakley... was more than a reformer, he was a revolutionary."

Vic Feather, General Secretary of the
Trades Union Congress (1969-73)

"Wakley, ...one of the magnificently angry men of his age."
A N Wilson, novelist and biographer (2002)

"A champion is someone who gets up when they can't."
Jack Dempsey,
world heavyweight champion (1919-26)

"It is a bore to study, and if we can but manage the trick of passing at the Hall, we obtain a licence to cut, hack and slay, any, or all of his Majesty's subjects."

The Hospital Pupil's Guide through London (1800)

Chapter 1

1811

All he could see were blades of wet grass. He struggled to breathe. Men were shouting and jeering. Then Incledon's face, inches from his, spittle dripping from his mouth, screaming.

"Get up. Now. For God's sake, don't let the gypsy beat you. On your feet."

His whole body ached but Thomas managed to haul himself up. The icy water Incledon splashed over his face stopped his head spinning, bringing the crowd into focus. He could sense their anger and hostility. As the referee called time, Incledon turned him round to face his adversary who was leering at him, goading him to fight. Light from the flares at each corner of the makeshift ring made the man's gold tooth sparkle. The referee retreated and the crowd grew even louder. Thomas took some deep breaths and raised his fists.

He stepped forward, letting fly a volley of punches. His opponent's expression had triggered memories of being taunted by his brothers. Until that moment he'd never understood what people meant by fighters becoming possessed but, as he landed punch after punch, he felt himself taken over. His adversary was reeling, looking scared and had resorted to just defending himself. Time after time Thomas floored him until he finally landed the decisive blow. Immediately he knew his opponent wouldn't recover in the half minute allowed. The crowd pushed the rope aside and poured forward to congratulate him.

Those who had backed him soon headed into the inn to celebrate their winnings and gloat over those who'd bet on the gypsy. He could hear Incledon claiming it was all down to his coaching. Thomas lowered himself, gingerly, onto a stool, waiting for the last of the crowd to disperse. In the flickering light, the smell of burning pitch filled his nostrils. Looking across the now deserted yard, his opponent was sitting alone on the ground, leaning against an outhouse. He'd even been abandoned by his waterman. Thomas went over and crouched down. The man's eyes were so swollen Thomas wondered how much he could see. Dark bruises were starting to appear over his bare torso. The man tried smiling but it clearly hurt.

"For a young un, you got a punch on yer." He pointed a finger at Thomas. "You know what? You can go far."

"Will you be all right?" asked Thomas.

"Ah, nothing that won't fix itself. Don't you go worrying, lad. Fair fight. Go on… get yourself a drink."

Thomas hesitated. "I don't drink."

The man tried to laugh. "Is that so, then? That's a first."

Thomas was about to ask him how he'd get to his bed when the man's head slumped down onto his chest and his eyes closed. A gust of wind made Thomas shiver and he felt the first drops of rain on his bare back. He slowly stood up and went and retrieved his coat. As he was pulling it on, Incledon appeared.

"Wakley. What a fight. Come on, everyone wants to see you."

Thomas had lived in Incledon's house for over a year but had never before realised how much the man looked like a terrier. Short and wiry, his deep-set eyes framed by dark hair, wet and bedraggled.

"No. Enough. I'm exhausted."

Incledon was taken aback, not used to being refused by his young apprentice.

"But they paid for the purse. You've got to."

"They've had what they wanted."

As Thomas was walking away, he stopped and pointed to his defeated opponent slumped on the ground.

"Reckon he could do with a drink, though."

Incledon sneered and turned away.

*

The grand sounding *Chemical & Medical Hall* was just a small shop, tucked in between a bakery and an ironmonger in the middle of Taunton. On arriving the previous year, Thomas had been puzzled by the lack of a workshop. How could Incledon be an apothecary? On the first night, when he'd asked, the man he was to be apprenticed to for five years had just smirked.

"Proprietary medicines. Jewels, my boy. Gold nuggets. *Hallam's Anti-bilious pills, Cornwell's Oriental Cordial, Wessell's Jesuit Drops.* No-one else in Taunton is allowed to sell 'em."

Pausing only to knock back more whisky, there was a glint in his eye, clearly proud of what he was doing.

"I tell you, Wakley, it's the future. People can rely on what they're getting. Same every time. Not like these damn apothecaries, compounding their own medicines... you don't know what you're getting."

Thomas had said nothing, needing time to decide what to do. Incledon's advertisement clearly stated he was an apothecary and druggist but Thomas could see all he'd learn would be how to sell drugs, not the doctoring skills of an apothecary – diagnosing complaints, deciding on treatments, making up medicines. He was stuck. He couldn't look to his father for more help, as when he'd first announced he wanted to be a surgeon, his father had scoffed at the idea. Told him he should get a proper trade or maybe military service. But having been persuaded by his older sister, Anne, to pay for this apprenticeship, Thomas couldn't possibly abandon it. Incledon would never return the fee his father had paid.

As long as his indenture document at the end of his five years stated he'd completed an apprenticeship with an apothecary, even if it wasn't true, it would allow him to enrol as a medical pupil in London and go on to fulfil his dream of becoming a surgeon.

Thomas soon discovered another part of Incledon's advertisement also wasn't true. It had said the apprentice would be treated as a member of the family. But there was no family, only a kitchen maid.

"Just the way newspapers like to phrase things," Incledon had said when Thomas questioned him.

Thomas doubted that was true but as he liked his own company, he didn't mind. Being alone meant there was little to distract him from his other ambition, to build himself up physically. After all he'd endured at home, at school, and his time at sea, he was determined to be able to defend himself. So, every evening he exercised in the small back yard, building up his stamina and strength. The speed with which his muscles had developed had delighted him, a change not lost on Incledon.

"Big lad like you. Should try bare-knuckle fighting," Incledon had said after Thomas had been there some months. "A fine sport. Bet you can handle yourself in a fight. You've got the height, the reach and, if you don't mind me saying, the looks. Punters like a good-looking boy – your long golden locks, blue eyes."

Thomas had been taken aback. He had no desire to fight. He was just determined never to be bullied or intimated again.

"Sport of Kings'!" Incledon had said. "Your aristocracy and nobility indulge. You could end up fighting a lord or duke!" He'd smiled obsequiously. "Make a pretty penny to boot."

It was the prospect of no longer being dependent on his father for money that persuaded him to give it a go. And after watching some bouts in the back courtyards of pubs, he reckoned he would do all right. He could see how fighters were often so drunk they could be outwitted. Although he lost the first few fights, always withdrawing to avoid being seriously hurt, he persevered. Now, after a year, he went into the ring expecting to win. It was something he'd discovered. However big or strong an adversary might look, you had to believe you'd win.

The morning after his fight with the gypsy, his whole trunk ached from the pummelling it had taken and the bruises on his face had swelled up, partly occluding his left eye. Fortunately, he'd suffered no cuts so hadn't needed stitches.

"God, you're a sight," said Incledon, when Thomas appeared for breakfast. "Best the customers don't see you. Not a great advertisement for me. I'll give you some *Godfrey's.*" Smirking, he added, "Won't charge you."

The maid reappeared with a pot of coffee. As she collected up the dirty plates, Thomas asked Incledon for his winnings.

Incledon pulled some bills from his waistcoat pocket. "Here. Two pounds."

Thomas noticed the maid pause for a second, narrowing her eyes. He took the money and sat turning it over in his hands.

"Was that all? There were so many there, I'd imagined the purse would have been bigger."

"No. Mean lot that crowd at *The George.* Four pounds. Half for you, half for me, like we agreed."

Thomas saw the maid glance at him before leaving. Incledon tipped some snuff into his hand and, sniffing it, emitted a satisfied sigh as he breathed out.

"Don't know what I'd do without this," he said, offering Thomas the snuffbox. "Still sure you won't indulge?"

Thomas shook his head. As for the fight purse, he needed time to decide what to do.

*

Every morning there'd be a trickle of customers, most wanting more of what they'd bought before. Sometimes Incledon tried tempting them to try some new concoction his suppliers had sent from London.

"Thing to do," he told Thomas, "is tell them the new products are being used by the most fashionable members of society in the capital."

What galled Thomas most was Incledon's contempt for his customers. He'd turn on the charm, convincing them he understood and sympathised, but once they'd gone, he ridiculed them.

Once it was clear to Thomas he'd learn nothing from Incledon, he'd taken to studying the labels on the products to see what he could teach himself.

"What do you want to do that for?" Incledon had asked when he found Thomas making notes.

"So I know what's in them and why they work. Some customers ask."

"You don't want to be bothering them. Just tell them it'll work."

"But when people ask what medicine they should take, I need to know."

"You know, Wakley, you're going to have to learn to fit in if you want to succeed."

Gradually, over time, Thomas had worked out which medicines were best for each of the commonest conditions people complained about. That very morning he'd been able to advise a man complaining of indigestion and flatulence to take a medicine that dislodged acrid bile.

*

"Just realised why I recognise you," the man said as he was about to leave the shop.

Clutching his bottle of *Daffy's Elixir*, he came back over to the counter. "You beat that huge gypsy fellow. Wouldn't put myself through that for ten pounds."

"Ten pounds?" Thomas blurted out. "I'm sorry, sir. Didn't mean to be rude. But I thought you said ten pounds."

The man looked puzzled. "I did. Have to say, you deserved every penny of it."

As he'd suspected, Incledon had lied. For the rest of the day Thomas wrestled with what he should do. If he confronted his master he risked being dismissed and losing all hope of becoming a surgeon. To give himself time he started turning down fights by feigning injuries. Initially he enjoyed the power and control this gave him, gaining satisfaction from Incledon becoming angry but unable to do anything.

After a few weeks of refusing to fight, Thomas was missing pitting his wits, strength, and stamina against other men. He'd come to love the thrill of winning, the adulation of the crowd, a feeling unlike anything he'd ever experienced. To be the centre of attention, even if it was only for a few minutes, was glorious. He'd developed a range of different stratagems – when to hold back and tire an opponent, how to duck under punches, ways to control his breathing and ensure he could outlast his opponent. The key, he'd discovered, was to think, to be clever. Keen to resume, he decided to confront Incledon about the winnings.

He waited until the end of dinner one evening when Incledon had had plenty to drink. He'd decided to start by winding him up just to annoy him.

"A woman from The Crescent wanted more *Dalby's Carminative* for her child," Thomas said, reporting on the day's customers.

"Ah! *Dalby's*. Turns us a nice profit," chuckled Incledon.

"She'd run out and couldn't afford anymore. Told me that without it, her child got a fever, was shaking and not eating. Never wants to run out again."

"Stupid woman," he scoffed. "Told her she mustn't stop giving it."

"She wanted to know what was in it."

"Who knows?" laughed Incledon. "Doesn't matter, does it? That'll have taught her a lesson."

Thomas waited till the maid had left the room.

"A gentleman who saw me fight at *The George* a few weeks ago said the purse had been ten pounds."

Incledon looked up from his plate, sat back and sniffed.

"What are you suggesting? Do you think I cheated you, is that it?" He refilled his glass. "Yeh, it was ten pounds but I had to pay the inn and to keep the law away. All costs money. Only leaves four for us."

"This gentleman said the purse is meant entirely for the winner."

Incledon narrowed his eyes, his cheeks getting redder as he breathed deeply. It reminded Thomas of a bull about a charge.

"I know I agreed to getting only half," continued Thomas, "but it doesn't seem fair. I'm the one fighting."

"Fair? Fair? What do you know about fair?" Incledon shouted as he rose from his seat and stood, looking down at Thomas. "Some of us had to struggle, pull ourselves up without any help. There's you, son of a rich farmer. Never known what it is to go without food. Sent to grammar school. And you tell me it's not fair."

He walked over to the fireplace and took his snuffbox off the mantelpiece. Having filled his nostrils, he came and sat down again, his outstretched hands flat on the table.

"My father were a carpenter, small village in Devon. If he had no work, we didn't eat. As for going to grammar school, no chance. Somehow he bought me an apprenticeship with a Mr Weeks, a druggist in Barnstaple. He were a good man but there just wasn't much trade. Not many down there could afford fancy medicines. Couldn't compete with herbalists. When my time were up, made my way to London, doing odd jobs along the way. Even harder to survive there."

As he talked, Thomas was relieved Incledon had calmed down.

"But your advertisement said you'd been apprenticed to an eminent practitioner."

Incledon was toying with the knife lying on the table.

"Come on. Grow up. That's just newspapers exaggerating. Helps their circulation."

"So, it's not true?"

"Who's to say? I went to lectures in the hospitals. Worked out that if I went in after they'd started, didn't have to pay."

"What I don't understand then," asked Thomas, "is how you set up the shop."

"Questions, questions. You never stop, do you?"

Incledon sat forward, still playing with the knife.

"London wasn't a complete waste of time. It's where I came up with my plan to sell proprietary medicines. Sought out the manufacturers and offered to sell their wares. Pretended I already had a shop here in Taunton. That there was a huge market waiting to be satisfied. Did deals with lots of them. Had to make them good offers. Once I had enough, I headed here and set up."

Thomas couldn't stop himself admiring the man's ingenuity. Incledon drained his glass and sat back. Bleary-eyed, he stared at Thomas.

"I'll level with you. I offered them manufacturers too generous a deal. So, need to find other ways to make money."

Thomas narrowed his eyes. "Like getting me to fight. That's what this has all been about, isn't it?"

They sat in silence. Incledon refilled his glass, staring into it as he swilled the wine around. Eventually he looked up at Thomas.

"All right. Half the purse."

In the course of his short life Thomas had seen bad men do unforgiveable things. He didn't think Incledon was bad; just foolish and struggling to make a life for himself. But what he couldn't forgive was the way his father had been deceived, hoodwinked into paying for a bogus apprenticeship. He could feel his heart racing as he took a deep breath.

"The whole purse. Otherwise, I won't fight."

That night, lying in bed, he couldn't sleep. He kept replaying the conversation, amazed he'd had the courage to stand up for himself. It had been as exhilarating as landing a final blow in a fight. What had surprised him was how Incledon had acquiesced, as if he'd known he'd met his match.

*

With the start of spring, Thomas hired a horse one Saturday and rode to Land Farm. It had been over a year since he left home. His mother made such a fuss, wanting to know all about his life in

Taunton. His father spent most of the weekend in the stables, trying to decide on his mount for the Easter hunt. He barely spoke to Thomas, which was a relief as he'd feared being questioned about Incledon.

After church on Sunday morning, Thomas and his sister, Anne, decided to walk the two miles back to the farm rather than go in the family's carriage. As a child, Anne had always taken his side when his brothers picked on him. It was only now, at sixteen, he'd come to realise how much he owed her. She'd been like a mother to him, teaching him to read and always ready to listen and protect him.

After climbing the hill out of Membury, they stopped and leant on a gate, looking across the Yarty valley. The Blackdown Hills were dotted with cattle and sheep.

"It's so calm here," mused Thomas. "How life is meant to be. And the air. Taunton always smells of coal fires."

Anne laughed. "I always suspected beneath that serious face lurked a romantic."

He smiled. Thomas felt so at ease with Anne. He told her about Incledon's dishonesty and how he wasn't an apothecary.

"I don't know what to do," ended Thomas, staring out across the fields. "I so want to be a surgeon, so I've got to complete my indenture with him."

She put her hand on his shoulder, rubbing it slowly. "Knowing you, you've told him what you think of him."

He frowned. "Well, I can't bear seeing him hoodwink customers. The other day I served a woman who'd been buying a medicine for ages but I could see she couldn't afford it and it wasn't doing her any good. When I suggested she stop, Incledon accused me of undermining him, wanting to ruin his business and worse. I wasn't going to let him speak to me like that when I'd done nothing wrong."

"Ah, same old Thomas," she said, shaking her head. "Never could stay quiet when you believed you were right."

"But I was right."

She took his hands in hers. "Must be hard being you. And even harder for others."

"It's like being held captive. I'm stuck there for another four years."

She let go of his hands. "I'm sorry. When I told Papa about the apprenticeship, I thought it was perfect for you. Let you pursue your dream."

"No. You weren't to know he was a scoundrel. And I won't let it stop me becoming a surgeon."

As he held out a bunch of grass, some of the bolder lambs approached but their mothers came and nudged them away.

Anne pushed a lock of her hair back behind her ear. "I wish I knew what's best to do but something tells me you'll work out a way. Come on, they'll be wondering where we've got to."

Walking along they pointed out flowers to each other, naming them. "You taught me those," said Thomas. "Made me learn the Latin names."

She laughed. "Only Latin I knew. Not like you now."

"You must promise not to tell Papa about Incledon. You know what he's like. Chances are he'd go and horsewhip him!"

*

Thomas spent hours thinking of how he might escape and still pursue his dream. The best he came up with was to irritate Incledon so much he'd want Thomas to leave. As Incledon wouldn't or couldn't afford to return the apprenticeship fee his father had paid, Thomas would only agree to go if Incledon signed his indenture document certifying he'd completed his apprenticeship.

An opportunity to aggravate Incledon soon presented itself when an elderly doctor visited the shop.

"Strangest thing," said Thomas over dinner that evening. "A doctor came in this morning."

Incledon grunted and carried on eating.

Thomas, watching him closely, continued. "Works in East Street. Explained how he was both an apothecary and did some simple surgery. Described himself as a general practitioner."

"That'll be old Braithwaite. What did he want?"

"Interested in seeing what we're selling, though he called it 'peddling'."

That had the intended effect. Incledon stopped eating.

"These damn doctors. All the same. General practitioners, surgeons, physicians. They look down on us. You know why? It annoys them that people come to us for treatment."

"He was quite friendly," said Thomas, ignoring Incledon. "Wanted to know what was in some of the cordials but I explained the makers kept that secret, else people would copy."

"That must have pleased him," scoffed Incledon.

"He asked if we'd be going to the Medical Society meeting on Thursday. Apparently, they meet twice a year – spring and autumn. All the doctors are there."

"Ha. Like hell we would. He sounds like a troublemaker. Have nothing to do with him." He leant forward, waggling his knife at Thomas. "Doctors like Braithwaite think they're so superior. You know why they sneer at us?"

Thomas shook his head, encouraging Incledon to go on.

"'Cos the real surgeons look down on them. Worst of all are the physicians who think going to university and speaking Latin makes them the best doctors. Ha!"

Incledon put down his knife, pushed his plate away and wiped his mouth with the back of his hand.

Thomas finished eating and sat back. "Well, I'm going. Might be interesting."

Incledon, red in the face and sweating, got up and fetched his snuffbox.

"You know, Wakley, you can be so damn obstinate. You spend your whole time buried in a book or making notes on God knows what. If you go on doing what you want, no-one will employ you. Not everyone is as easy going as me."

He spilt snuff on his jacket sleeve as he snorted some up each nostril.

"Probably won't be able to make any sense of it. Don't be surprised if they ignore you."

*

The Taunton Medical Society met upstairs in the *Black Horse Inn*. There were twenty or so there when Thomas arrived. One or two glanced over but most ignored him. He wondered if any of them would recognise him from his fights. He felt awkward and out of place, just as Incledon had predicted. He could see Braithwaite on the far side of the room talking to two other elderly men. He didn't dare go over so started looking at the pictures on the wall near him. Mostly hunting scenes.

"Wakley."

He turned to see Braithwaite.

"Glad you came. Think you'll find it interesting. Woodforde's speaking about dyspepsia. You know him?"

"No," said Thomas. "I don't know any of the doctors."

"Really? Well, we need to put that right." He took a sip from the glass he was holding. "You know, you're a puzzle, Wakley. Don't take you for a druggist."

Without hesitating he said, "I want to be a surgeon."

As he heard himself, he couldn't quite believe he'd said it. And to a stranger. Maybe that was what had emboldened him.

Before Braithwaite could speak, there was the sound of a gavel and a call for everyone to be seated. Thomas found it hard to concentrate during the talk, so lost was he in wondering what possessed him to tell Braithwaite. Then it dawned on him. By telling a doctor, he had in some way crossed over into their world. By doing so, he'd signalled to the medical profession his intention.

*

The following morning Thomas said nothing about the Medical Society, knowing Incledon would be desperate to know but pride would stop him asking. It was only when Thomas was leaving the breakfast table that Incledon cracked.

"Any of it make sense?" he asked, fiddling with his snuffbox.

Thomas stood looking down at him.

"Some of it." He paused. "Had never realised how many doctors there are around here."

Incledon scoffed but said nothing. Delighted by the effect he'd had, Thomas turned and left.

They spoke little in the shop that morning. Around midday, a fine carriage pulled up outside and an elderly man was helped out. Not like their usual customers. Incledon was at his most obsequious, feigning concern about the man's condition.

"Dr Francis, my physician, recommended this," he said, handing Incledon a piece of paper.

"Ah, yes," said Incledon. "One moment. Let me see if we have it."

With that he headed into the back room, telling Thomas to come, too.

"What does it say?" asked Incledon in a hushed voice, passing him the prescription.

It was in Latin. In two years, Thomas hadn't noticed Incledon couldn't read Latin. It dawned on him that was why he'd sought an apprentice with a classical education.

"You deal with him," said Incledon, ushering Thomas back out to the shop.

"Mr Wakley here will be able to assist you, sir," said Incledon, before disappearing back into the office.

Thomas read the prescription. "Dr Francis wants you to take a water tablet."

Looking along the shelves behind him, he selected a box.

"*Guy's Hospital Pills*. Very good at clearing fluid from the body."

"Good, good. Give me enough for a week. If they work, I'll be back for more."

As soon as the man had left, Incledon reappeared, beaming with delight, slapping Thomas on the back.

"That, Wakley, is just the sort of customer we need. Sort of man who'll tell his wealthy friends about us."

1812

As the months went by, his sense of being trapped, unable to escape, built up. He learnt that whenever he found himself clenching his fists and raging inside, time in the backyard exercising vigorously and lifting weights would calm him down. Afterwards, sitting panting and sweating, he racked his brains for new ideas, ways of achieving his goal that had eluded him so far. But he could think of nothing.

Meanwhile, he knew that if he succeeded in engineering his escape, he'd need more money than he'd saved so far. That meant more fights, ideally against richer, more upper-class men. Fighting local labourers and tradesmen was all very well, but the son of some aristocrat, out to show off to his friends, would attract a much bigger purse and attract a bigger crowd. As for Incledon, Thomas didn't need him, as a few pence was enough to get himself a waterman. He was well enough known locally to attract an opponent if he just let a few pub landlords know of his interest. And a bonus of setting up a fight without Incledon was it would annoy him further.

By the time of the Medical Society's spring meeting, Thomas was starting to question whether provoking Incledon would prove sufficient to bring things to a head. His low spirits were immediately lifted by Braithwaite's wholehearted welcome.

"Wakley. Good to see you. Want you to meet this young man. New apothecary at the hospital. Just completed his studies in London."

A tall, wiry man with ginger hair, not much older than Thomas, bowed his head.

"Rodspear. I hear you've got your heart set on surgery."

As they moved to take their seats, Rodspear took his arm. "Come and see me. Maybe I can help."

Thomas wasted no time in taking up Rodspear's invitation. A few days later, standing outside the new four-storey building in East Reach, he read the words emblazoned on the grand façade. *Taunton & Somerset Hospital. Supported by Free Contributions.* He doubted his father had contributed. Devout churchgoer though he was, he didn't agree with charity. One of his favourite sayings was, "people should stand on their own two feet".

Steps led up to a grand portico over the main entrance. Inside, in the marble hallway, a beadle asked him his business.

"Workshop in the basement at the rear," he said, directing Thomas to a flight of stairs.

Rodspear, who was busy compounding, looked up and smiled.

"Wakley. Come on in."

He put down the large pestle and wiped his hands on a cloth hanging from his apron.

Thomas gazed around the room. Shelves of pots lined the walls. Three large stone mortars sat on the bench in the centre, and in the far corner was a stove under a metal hood.

"Looks chaotic but it's not," Rodspear laughed. "I know where everything is, just as long as no-one comes and helps themselves. So, what do you want to know?"

Thomas was captivated listening to Rodspear's accounts of being a medical pupil in London, of the lectures he'd attended, the anatomy demonstrations, the operations.

"Happy to help a fellow traveller," said Rodspear. "Now, you picked a good day to visit. Mr Liddon's amputating a leg at noon. I can get you in to watch if you think you can handle it."

They made their way upstairs. A dozen men surrounded the table on which the patient lay. Above, a skylight augmented the light from the large north-facing window at the foot of the table.

Liddon and his two assistants had donned aprons, blood-stained from previous procedures.

Although barely conscious, the patient managed one more brandy before Liddon got to work. Without hesitating, Liddon made a sweeping incision down and then over the front of the man's thigh. The assistants then raised his leg so he could complete the cut round the back. They clutched the incised flesh with towels to control the bleeding, but with only limited success. Meanwhile, Liddon was cutting through the underlying muscle to expose the bone. Without having to ask, he was handed a saw and set about sawing through it. The rasping sound was mixed with cries from the patient, now roused from his slumbers. The bone was bleeding so much, Liddon couldn't have seen much, relying instead on feel. It took no more than a minute before an assistant carried the severed limb away, placing it in a waiting bucket. Liddon rapidly wrapped a flap of skin over the exposed stump, securing it with several stitches. As he stood back and wiped sweat from his brow, his assistants wrapped the stump tightly to prevent further bleeding. Four-and-a-half minutes.

"That was so impressive," said Thomas, when they got back to the workshop.

As Rodspear perched on a stool, Thomas paced around, too excited to settle.

"The confidence with which he did it, never pausing, knowing exactly what he was doing."

Rodspear chuckled. "Liddon's one of the best. I've seen surgeons take half an hour or more!"

"Half an hour? How do patients cope? Even that man today, from his cries and struggling, was in agony as Liddon was sawing the bone."

"Indeed, but he must have known he had little choice. The gangrene in his leg would have killed him soon if Liddon hadn't operated. Five minutes pain, or death. Not a difficult decision."

Thomas stood thinking.

"What's the matter? Suddenly not so keen on being a surgeon?"

"No, not at all. I was just wondering how Liddon managed to ignore the distress he was causing, to concentrate. He must have to cut himself off, not hear the cries."

"Never really thought about it but I suppose you're right." Rodspear stood up. "Right, I must get on. Tell you what, if you want, I'll let you know whenever there's a capital operation."

"Would you? I'd love that."

＊

From then on Thomas spent as much time as possible at the hospital. He loved the theatricality of operations. The audience's anticipation beforehand, wondering how straightforward it would be, how long it would take, how the patient would cope. And at the centre, the surgeon. The way everyone fell silent as he took up his instruments. Then, as he cut, people whispering to their neighbours, pointing things out while the surgeon, unaware of those watching, remained absorbed in his task, a picture of calm concentration. What he'd give to do that. To feel the adulation, to be held in awe. To be a hero.

With the end of summer, Incledon announced he'd be visiting patients in Devon and so would be away overnight. He'd done this the two previous years, always returning with several game birds, said to be presents from grateful customers. Thomas would hear him instructing the maid to take most of them to the poultryman and ensure she got a good price.

Then, in early October, he returned from a trip empty-handed. He said nothing but was agitated, walking around the house, slamming doors and shouting at the maid. At dinner, Thomas enquired if everything was all right but Incledon just grunted and dismissed the inquiry with a wave of his hand.

All became clear the following week when *The Taunton Courier* reported he'd been charged with poaching. Thomas read the report several times. Caught shooting pheasants in Nettlecombe by a tithingman.

Thomas felt so stupid. It was like his failure to realise Incledon didn't read Latin. How had he not seen what had been going on. Gifts from grateful patients! He was angry with himself for being so gullible. It was just another way Incledon had been making money. It was at times like this Thomas was glad his father was dependent on Anne reading the paper to him. He could trust her not to read that particular item to him.

Thomas chose to say nothing, as did Incledon for four days.

"You don't want to believe all you read in the paper," Incledon suddenly said at dinner. "Just a misunderstanding. Went for a walk after seeing patients and met an old friend who was out shooting. Didn't occur to me he was poaching."

Thomas was barely listening, having suddenly realised that Incledon's arrest could pave the way for his escape. If Incledon was found guilty, surely he couldn't carry on as master to an apprentice? It took all Thomas's self-control to conceal his excitement.

"Damnable business," said Incledon. "There's to be a hearing at the *Hare & Hounds* in Nettlecombe. Magistrate should have better things to do. Plenty of reprobates out there need catching."

Despite the hope that Incledon's demise offered Thomas, he felt sorry for him. To see anyone brought low saddened him. Though nothing had yet been proved, there were fewer customers and those who did come were less friendly. Incledon stayed upstairs, drinking. When he did appear, it looked as though he hadn't shaved in days.

The following week when he returned from the hearing in Nettlecombe, he was pale and dejected. He slumped down in an armchair in the parlour, clutching a glass of whisky, staring into the fire.

"Didn't stand a bloody chance."

Thomas knew there was no point in saying anything.

"Luxton. Supposed to be a man of the cloth. Not an ounce of Christian mercy." He drained his glass. "It were a joke.

Can you believe it? Magistrate's the parish council clerk, for God's sake. And who is the parish beholden to? That man Wyndham on whose estate they claimed we were poaching. Well, I may be naïve, but he's hardly going to displease his rich master, is he? Always the same. Maybe those French had the right idea after all. Off with their heads!"

Although Thomas knew he didn't mean it, he was still shocked that Incledon would say that. He'd read of people being imprisoned or transported for siding with the French.

Incledon sat forward, reached for the decanter and refilled his glass. He waved the decanter at Thomas. "What's wrong with you? Can't take a drink?"

He slumped back in his armchair and was quiet for so long Thomas thought he'd fallen asleep, until he muttered, "Fined me five pounds."

As he looked up, his eyes were watering. "It's not the money."

He looked at Thomas imploringly. "It's my good name – been besmirched. And I was to be wed."

*

Incledon rarely spoke to him over the following few weeks. He was so withdrawn, the maid started asking Thomas about what she should cook. Thomas was convinced it was only a matter of time before he could get what he wanted and leave but wasn't sure how to make it happen.

Dinners had become even more desultory. Incledon showed no interest in hearing about the customers, waving away Thomas's attempts to tell him. Then, one evening, to Thomas's surprise, Incledon put down his fork and looked across the table.

"Wakley. Need to let you know. We'll be joined soon by my wife."

Startled, Thomas was lost for words. He'd dismissed Incledon lamenting the consequences of his conviction for his chances of marrying as drunken nonsense.

"Well, what have you got to say?" asked Incledon.

"Sorry. Congratulations. It's just, you've taken me by surprise. Is she someone in the town?"

"No. Lives over in Martock. Ann, Ann Hamlyn. Father was a soap boiler, but he's been dead these past four years."

If this was just Incledon's latest attempt to acquire money, it didn't sound like it would prove fruitful. Thomas wondered how well she knew him. Did she know about the poaching? Maybe she wouldn't care.

*

With Ann's arrival, Incledon was even less inclined to talk at dinner than he had been in the past. Ann rarely smiled, seemingly anxious not to annoy her husband. Thomas felt sorry for her. When he asked her about Martock and her family, Ann would look nervously at Incledon and say little. It all made Thomas even more determined to get away. He dreaded the prospect of staying there for another Christmas.

With a week to go before the holiday, a man wearing dark, sombre clothing and top hat came into the shop. As was now usual, Thomas was there alone.

"Good morning, sir," said Thomas.

The man just nodded, placed his case on the counter and took out a wallet of papers from which he selected a page.

"Incledon here?"

"He's out, I'm afraid," said Thomas.

"Give him this," he said, handing Thomas the sheet of paper. "Tell him it's no good him ignoring it like the letters we've sent. Payment by the end of the month or we claim what is ours."

Glancing down, Thomas saw it was from *Shaw & Edwards*, one of their suppliers. The man looked around the shop, even poking his head into the storeroom, then left without saying anything more.

As soon as Incledon returned, Thomas handed him the letter and passed on the message.

"Oh, that old rogue," he said, tossing the paper onto his desk. "Always making life difficult for us. Doesn't realise how things work down here in the provinces. Londoners... always been the same."

"What will you do?" asked Thomas.

"Same as usual. Pay him something to keep him quiet until next time."

After a pause he added, "And, Wakley, not a word to Ann. Do you understand? Don't want her worrying over nothing."

Over the following days, other London suppliers called in, demanding payments. After each visit, Incledon tried to dismiss it as a minor inconvenience, that he had everything in hand. But Thomas knew this wasn't true. Sales had dried up; the business was dying. He tried not to get too excited but at last he could envisage getting away.

Incledon looked sallow and said little. When he stood up, he was bent over as though trying to hide. Even his anger about the unfairness of the world ceased.

Then, on Christmas Eve, two men appeared and announced they were closing the shop and seizing all the contents. Incledon was made to hand over the key. Like a shattered fighter, he offered no resistance. He and Thomas went upstairs where they found Ann seated at the table, clutching a handkerchief and dabbing her eyes.

"That's it, Wakley," he said, staring out of the window, unable to look at Thomas. "You'll have to go. Nothing for you here now."

"Then I want half of my father's payment returned."

Incledon just stared at the floor and said nothing. Just when Thomas wondered if he'd heard, he looked up.

"Haven't a penny to my name. Those men took everything."

Having rehearsed this scene so many times, Thomas was prepared.

"In that case, my indenture document showing I've completed my apprenticeship."

Incledon managed a slight smile. "My own fault, turning you into a fighter."

"No," said Thomas. "You encouraged me, but I've always been a fighter."

Incledon pushed himself up out if his chair and shuffled over to a small corner cupboard.

"Here you are," he said, returning with the document.

"You'd already signed it? You knew?"

Incledon wearily sat back down but said nothing.

Upstairs, Thomas packed his few possessions. As he left the house, the two men were loading boxes from the shop and storeroom into a cart. He turned south and set out. The walk home to Membury would give him time to work out what he'd tell his father. He felt the paper in his inside pocket. Only he knew that it had been two-and-a-half years with a druggist, not an apothecary, who'd taught him nothing.

Chapter 2

1813

"If a man doesn't work on the land, he loses his bearings," Henry Wakley pronounced, sitting back in his chair at the end of the long dining table, staring into the distance.

Winter sunshine, boosted by the snow-covered ground outside, streamed through the stone mullioned windows into the oak-panelled room. Thomas had just finished telling his father what had gone on in Taunton and why he'd returned to the farm halfway through his apprenticeship.

Henry shook his head and sighed. "The man's clearly a scoundrel. Good mind to go and demand my money back." He loosened his neckerchief and looked at Thomas. "You say he'll be in Martock by now?"

"That's what he said. And he's bankrupt, so couldn't pay you."

His father grunted his disapproval. Thomas, unsure what to say, sat looking down at his hands, clasped together on his lap. The smell of cooking drifted in from the kitchen.

Having filled his pipe, his father walked over to the fire and bent down to light a taper. He returned to his seat amid clouds of smoke. Clean-shaven, he still had a fine head of hair, although the earlier blond locks had turned grey. He seemed even more distant than Thomas had found him when a child.

"So, what's to become of you?" he asked. "Everything you try, you come back telling me it wasn't for you. First, it's not wanting a life at sea, now this. You can't keep giving up, you know."

Thomas closed his eyes for a moment. That was so unfair. It took all his determination not to retaliate and defend himself. But he knew it would be pointless.

"Well, there's the army. They're recruiting. Expecting to be sent to France to put an end to Napoleon. Pay's not bad... you could do worse."

Thomas had to stall. He needed time to work out how he could make best use of the next two-and-a-half years. No London hospital would admit him as a pupil until he'd been registered as an apprentice for five years.

"Would do you good," continued his father. "Teach you to obey orders. Put a stop to you thinking you know best. Question your officer and you'd find yourself in trouble."

"I'll think about it," said Thomas, though he had no intention of doing so. "While I'm here, I could help with the lambing."

"You may as well. Earn your keep."

Thomas was relieved to see him smile. "Go on then. And I don't want any trouble with your brothers." As Thomas got up, his father looked him up and down. "Mind you, looking at you, they'd be daft to try taking you on now. Not like when you were younger. You were such a wisp of a boy."

Thomas narrowed his eyes. "Well, that was a fair few years ago."

"Hmm. Don't know what you've been up to, but it's turned you into a man."

*

With snow still thick on the ground and lambing several weeks away, there was little for him to do. During the short daylight hours, he often went walking. If he set off early, he could make it over to the River Otter and back. Out on the Blackdown Hills it was bitterly cold. The only sound was his footsteps, crunching the snow as he picked his way through the woods. Standing on the bank of the Otter, ducks slipped and slid on the frozen backwaters. Eating a sandwich – his favourite, tongue and mustard – he tore off some crust and scattered it on the bank. With the low sun shining through the lifeless, skeletal trees, his time with Incledon already seemed so distant.

Every evening, his brothers would ride to the *King's Arms* in Stockland. They didn't bother inviting him, knowing he rarely drank. Later, lying in bed, he'd hear them return, the younger ones singing and shouting despite the best attempts of his oldest brother, Charles, to stop them. Although now grown men, they hadn't changed. He couldn't understand how they were content just working on the farm and, in the evenings, drinking. Maybe he would have been the same if his father hadn't sent him to grammar school. He'd never understood why he'd been the only one to go but would be eternally grateful he had been.

Thomas preferred to spend his evenings in the parlour, reading. He'd bought some history, science, and medical books in Taunton, knowing the only books in the house were romances – much loved by his sisters but of no interest to him. He couldn't see the point of novels.

It was difficult concentrating with Anne reading the newspaper out loud to their father. As a child, he'd just accepted that, like lots of men, his father couldn't read. It was only now that it occurred to him how much his father's success in becoming one of the biggest landowners in the county and running a stud farm had depended on Anne and his two other sisters. They must have handled all the crucial paperwork, recording the pedigree of the horses sired in their stables and managing the accounts.

One morning, it was snowing so heavily Thomas stayed indoors, settling himself in the window seat in the parlour to read the weekly newspaper. It reported there had been a frost fair on the Thames in London and the London-Exeter stagecoach, which passed nearby the farm, rarely managed to get through. He could hear Anne talking to the kitchen maid in the dining room, organising what they'd have for dinner that night. She always had so much to do, so he was surprised when she came and joined him.

She took the small armchair by the fire, leaning forward to warm her hands. As usual she had her hair tied back.

He couldn't recall the last time he'd seen it hanging free. In profile, he could see she had the same high forehead he and their father had.

She looked round and smiled. "Hard to believe that years ago I had golden hair like you."

"I don't remember that."

"Course not. It was before you were born."

Thomas carried on looking at her. "Papa and Mama really depend on you, don't they?"

Anne sighed. "They do. Mama struggles with her arthritis, particularly in winter."

Thomas nodded and rubbed his chin. "What would happen if you left?"

"I dread to think. I don't think I can." She was speaking so quietly, Thomas left the window seat and joined her by the fire.

"But Charlotte and Catherine, they both did," he said.

Anne smiled. "That's why I can't." She suddenly added, "Do you imagine I haven't dreamt of it?"

Thomas was taken back. The way she'd said it was so heartfelt. He could see there were tears in her eyes.

"I'm sorry," she added, "it's not your responsibility." She tried to smile, reaching out and placing her hand on his arm. "You go out in the world and make something of yourself."

"Oh Anne, what's the matter?"

She blew her nose. "You're not to breathe a word of what I'm going to tell you. Not to Papa, Mama, and certainly not to our brothers. Promise."

"I promise," said Thomas, wondering what was coming.

"I've met someone." She paused and swallowed. "I went into Axminster one day last summer. This man held the door open for me as I was going into a tea shop in Trinity Square. There was only one table free. Although he'd been ahead of me, he insisted I take it. I know it might sound improper but it seemed churlish not to offer to share it." She laughed. "I could

27

see ladies at other tables watching and muttering to one another but I didn't care. I was strangely excited."

Thomas had never seen his sister like this before.

"He was very polite. Told me he was visiting from Bridgewater. Had been in the navy for thirteen years but was now looking for a post on land." She had to pause to take a deep breath. "We've been writing to one another ever since. Papa and Mama don't know. Then, in his last letter, he asked me to marry him."

She started dabbing away the tears on her cheeks.

"Dear Anne, that is wonderful. What have you said?"

He waited while she regained her composure.

"I don't know what to do." She looked up from the handkerchief she was clutching in her lap. "I'm worried about asking Papa. How would he and Mama manage? I'm all they have now."

"They'd cope. They could get a housekeeper. Papa can hire a bookkeeper. It's not your problem. You've got to think of yourself."

"Oh, Thomas. Something I've always admired in you – certainty. Even if it makes you so difficult at times," she added with a laugh.

"If it's what you want, you must accept him. Trust me, it's a wonderful world out there. There's so much to discover."

"You're so persuasive. I can see Taunton at least taught you how to sell!"

"So, tell me. What's his name? What's his trade?"

"Richard Phelps." She looked at Thomas and smiled. "He was a naval surgeon but wants to be a country doctor."

Thomas grinned from ear to ear, lost for words for a moment.

"I'm sorry," he said. "It's just, that is the best thing I've heard for so long. I'm so happy for you."

*

By April, with lambing underway, Thomas spent nights in one of the huts out on the hills. He felt a twinge of guilt that he was

2 8

pleased when a sheep got into difficulty as it allowed him to do something. Although he'd seen it many times, he still found joy in watching a newborn lamb being licked clean by its mother.

He'd avoided asking Anne if she'd made a decision, not wanting to hear she'd turned Phelps down. On Sundays, in church, he prayed she'd accept. Then, on Easter Sunday, sitting round the large dining table, Papa made the announcement.

Thomas was overjoyed. He'd convinced himself that Anne wouldn't have the courage. He was so pleased he'd been proved wrong. They were to marry in Bridgewater, then move to Beaminster, a small town in Dorset where Phelps had bought a practice.

That afternoon, Thomas found Anne alone in the front garden cutting roses for the house.

"Just the person I need," she said. "I can't reach the lilac."

Thomas stretched up and cut several blooms of the white and blue flowers.

"You looked so anxious as Papa was telling us," he said, as he handed them to her.

"Did I?" She put down her trug and brushed some locks of hair off her face. "I can't stop worrying about them. Mama tried so hard to be pleased when I told her but I could see her disappointment. Her last daughter leaving. And going so far away."

"Fifteen miles. It's not so far."

Thomas thought of the thousands of miles he'd once travelled.

"So that's my future," she said. "What about you? What will you do?"

He frowned. "No idea yet. I can't become a pupil in London for over two years and I can't ask Papa to pay for another apprenticeship. I've some savings but not enough."

"Wait a minute. You're the one who's always telling me anything is possible." She linked her arm in his. "You'll find a way. I know you will."

*

29

The day after the wedding, Anne and Richard broke their journey from Bridgewater to Beaminster to stay overnight at the farm. Knowing they were coming, Thomas had decided he'd seek his new brother-in-law's advice. In a lull before dinner, he asked Richard if he'd like to see the sunset from the hill above the farm.

As they climbed to the top, he was about to raise the topic when Richard pre-empted him.

"Anne tells me you want to be a doctor."

Thomas relaxed. "Yes, a surgeon."

"You know it's a long slog?"

"That doesn't bother me. I've been apprenticed for almost three years, not that I was taught much. But I've read a lot and can catch up."

"Have you found a new master?"

As Richard was now family, he decided he could confide in him. "Papa's paid once; I can't ask him to pay again."

They'd reached the summit and stood watching the sun disappear. In Taunton, Thomas had met several men who had served as officers in the Royal Navy. Like them, Richard had the same upright bearing, shoulders pulled back. Thomas liked the way he talked. Simple, clear, and direct, with none of the flowery language he'd heard from doctors at the Medical Society meetings.

Richard gazed at the far horizon. "How would you like to come and help me?" He turned to Thomas. "I've never had an apprentice, not taught anyone. So, I wouldn't charge you anything. Being a small town, it'll be a mixture of apothecary and surgery. What they're starting to call general practice."

Thomas's heart was racing. It took all his self-control not to shout his excitement across the hills.

"I don't know what to say."

"How about, yes?" said Richard, smiling.

"Oh, thank you, thank you," he said, grasping his brother-in-law's arm. "I'd like nothing better."

"Whoa, steady," said Richard, laughing. "That's settled then. And I know how pleased Anne will be."

*

When Thomas broke the news to his parents, his father's relief that he wasn't being asked for more money was abundantly clear. The following week, walking to Beaminster, he felt he was leaving his misfortunes behind. He'd read how people thought facing adversities and surviving them made you stronger, but he wasn't sure. What he was sure about was there was no point in dwelling on the past.

In Beaminster, Richard and Anne were already settled in the house they'd taken over from the previous doctor. Richard had a steady stream of his predecessor's patients.

"I don't compound or dispense," Richard told him. "Don't want to put Hine, the druggist, out of work."

The wagon-load of furniture and goods Anne had brought from Land Farm was already spread around the house, making it look as though they'd lived there for ages.

Thomas had an upstairs room overlooking the kitchen garden at the back. He'd never been so content. He was up before first light, ready to work. After a week, Richard had to ask him to slow down as he couldn't keep up and, in the evenings, Anne had to force him to stop reading and have dinner.

Thomas accompanied Richard on his visits. Although Richard had only been there a few weeks, lots of his patients seemed to know him.

"I thought you said you'd never lived here," queried Thomas, as yet another person greeted them as they made their way through the town.

Richard chuckled. "They must have heard stories about me. This is Phelps country, always has been. The vicar told me a widow Phelps received twenty shillings from someone's will in 1627! Come on, got to visit Mrs Birley."

Down an alley, off Church Street, they found a small, thatched cottage that seemed to be sinking into the ground.

Bending to get through the low doorway, the front room was dark and smelt strongly of wood smoke. As they entered, a small black cat scarpered into the back room.

"Good morning, Mrs Birley," said Richard who, like Thomas, was barely able to stand upright. "I hear you're not feeling so good."

"Oh, Doctor, it's my legs again. Dr West used to give me some medicine, but it doesn't seem to do nothing no more."

"Would you mind if Mr Wakley asks you some questions and has a look?"

She looked at Thomas. "Seems awful young." Then a smile broke out across her face. "Go on then, I don't mind. Bit old for minding."

Thomas had assumed he'd just be watching for some time so was taken aback. He cleared his throat and stepped forward.

"What's the problem with your legs?" he asked.

Mrs Birley wasn't going to be rushed. She recounted how her husband had died fifteen years earlier, how she easily became breathless, and how she rarely saw her children. It took Thomas some time to get a clear picture of her problem. When he then examined her, he could see how swollen her legs were. Pressing on them with his thumb, as he'd seen Richard do, the indentation remained for several minutes.

He turned to Richard. "I think she has dropsy."

"Good. And what would you recommend we do?"

Buoyed by his success in diagnosis, Thomas relaxed. "A diuretic? It'll reduce the swelling and help her breathing."

"Excellent," said Richard.

Over the next few weeks, Thomas couldn't believe how quickly he gained confidence. To his delight, much of what he'd taught himself in Taunton about drugs was proving useful.

While he enjoyed diagnosing and deciding on the best medicines to give patients, he longed to do some surgery. There was a table in Richard's consulting room but most people preferred to be operated on in their own homes. Over the following weeks,

Richard let him carry out small, simple procedures – draining abscesses, suturing incisions, immobilising broken bones.

As the nearest hospital was in Taunton, several hours away by carriage or wagon, many serious cases had to be dealt with by Richard, with Thomas's assistance. As he operated, Richard would explain each step.

One evening, they had to go to an isolated farmhouse to amputate a man's arm which had been crushed in a threshing machine. Even though it was past ten o'clock by the time they got home, Thomas was determined, over the rabbit pie Anne had kept hot for them, to discuss the operation.

"I want to understand everything," said Thomas.

"Very well," said Richard, "but something's puzzling me. Right from the start, the first time you assisted an amputation, you seemed to know what to do. I hardly needed instruct you. How come?"

"Well, I watched several in the hospital in Taunton. Could see what needed to be done, what an assistant had to do."

"No. It's more than that. It's more like you've actually helped out before."

Thomas looked at him and then at Anne. He wiped his mouth with his napkin, knowing he couldn't evade the question.

"All right. You're right. I have," he said quietly.

"What?" said Richard, stifling a laugh. "How come?"

"When I went to sea." He glanced at Anne who was listening intently. "I helped the surgeon."

"I knew you'd been to sea, but not that you'd been a surgeon's mate."

"No, I was only a midshipman, but I helped the surgeon."

"So, I'm not the first naval surgeon you've worked for. As you can see, we're a fine band of men, not that those bigwigs in London think much of us."

Thomas looked at Anne and, to his relief, she curtailed the conversation by asking if they wanted dessert. "There's strawberry tart."

"Splendid," said Richard, "then it's bed for me." He looked at Thomas. "Up at four bells. We've got our monthly visit to the workhouse over in Powerstock."

*

One evening, their dinner was disturbed by frantic knocking on the front door. They could hear voices and then the maid came in.

"It's a boy, sir," she said. "Says to please speak to you."

When Richard returned, he put his napkin on the table.

"A lad from Netherbury. Midwife sent him as his mother's in difficulty. I must go. The stable boy's preparing my horse."

He turned to Thomas. "Pack the saddlebag while I get my coat."

"The roads will be icy," said Anne. "Do be careful."

"Don't worry, always am," he laughed. "Don't wait up, could take half the night."

After Thomas and Anne finished eating they moved through to the parlour and settled down. Candles on the side tables added to the light from the fire. They picked up their books – the French Revolution for Thomas, a family saga for Anne. Every so often he got up to stoke the fire before immersing himself in his book again. After a while, Thomas became aware his sister was looking at him.

He looked up. "What is it?"

"Oh, I was thinking," said Anne, "how I'm not surprised you chose medicine. You always were fascinated by doctors."

"Was I? I don't remember that."

"Dr Allbright? You don't remember him?"

"Who was he?"

"*Keeper's Travels*. You made me read it to you repeatedly. Until you could read it for yourself. Then I couldn't get you to put it down."

Thomas gazed into the distance. "Hang on. I do remember. Keeper was a dog that searches for his lost master." He looked back at her. "I loved that story. Dr Allbright was kind and helped Keeper when men threatened him. I'd forgotten all about that."

"Mind you, your absolute favourite was *Sandford and Merton*."

"Oh yes. One of them was a spoilt rich boy. Tommy Merton." He laughed. "Couldn't stand him."

"And Harry Sandford," said Anne, "taught Merton what really matters in life. I think you saw yourself as him."

"It all seems so long ago." He stared at the fire. "So much has happened since then."

"It has for you," said Anne.

"Well, look at you. Married, living in a town."

Thomas got up to trim the wick on one of the candles which had started guttering. He could see Anne watching him.

"Thomas. There's something I've often thought about. Something that still troubles me."

He sat back down and waited.

"When you came back from your time at sea, you wouldn't tell us anything. And you didn't have your sea chest. I've never stopped worrying about what happened."

Troubling images, long buried, flooded his head. He could feel his eyes filling up and his heart pounding. He'd always known the day would come when Anne would ask him. And he'd always known she would be the one he would eventually tell. On several occasions he'd sensed she was about to ask but each time he'd managed to avoid the question by diverting her onto some other subject. He knew in his heart that after all she'd done for him, he owed her an account of what had happened.

He leant forward, his elbows on his knees, tracing the Paisley pattern in the rug with his eyes. When he looked up, he saw her concern, as if fearing what she was about to hear.

"What I tell you, I don't want you ever to tell anyone."

*

"I didn't know going to sea was going to be like that. I remember how excited I was. Every boy's dream. How I pestered

Papa all through that winter to let me go and how eventually he'd asked his old friend, Captain Smith, if he'd take me on his East Indiaman."

"Mama was set against it," said Anne. "She thought you should stay at school. You were only eleven and smaller than other boys."

Thomas smiled. "That was the point. I'd had enough of being teased and bullied. Our brothers were always goading me, and fighting back was no use. I had to get away."

"Oh, I knew what they did," said Anne. "So did Papa and Mama. That's why they sent you to board in Honiton. To protect you."

"Really?" said Thomas, sitting forward. "I thought it was because I was missing so much school in Chard, not being able to get there on days the weather was bad."

"Well, that was true as well. Riding alone all that way when you were only seven. You might have been small, but you were always intrepid." She paused. "There was another reason, too."

"Another reason? What?"

"You may as well know, as it's all in the past now. Papa got a letter from the teacher in Chard. He said that you were disrupting his lessons, making it impossible for him to teach with your constant questions. And you sometimes refused to do as you were told."

"Only because he told us to do ridiculous things like copying out ancient texts which taught us nothing."

"Oh, Thomas." She smiled at him. "I can imagine how difficult you made the poor man's job. Anyway, he told Papa he didn't want you back. So, we found you a place at All Hallows Grammar."

He rather liked the idea he'd been thrown out of school for standing up for his principles.

"Well, I'm glad they sent me to Honiton, otherwise I'd not have heard Admiral Cochrane speak. Do you remember him? Fought with Nelson."

She nodded, waiting for more.

"My second summer there, there was a Parliamentary election and Cochrane stood for the Whigs. They held hustings in the High Street. He looked so heroic in his uniform, addressing the crowd, his medals glittering in the sun. I'd never heard a Scotchman before. He talked of how, as a boy, he'd been a midshipman, and he pointed at me and said, 'Like that lad.' I remember thinking he was telling me that's what I should do."

Thomas took a sip of water from the glass on the side-table.

"It sounds ridiculous now but not to an eleven-year-old. I'd never seen the sea. It sounded so exciting."

He glanced at her and saw he had her full attention.

"The *Lord Hawkesbury,* that was the ship. I couldn't believe how large it was when I first saw it moored on the Thames. There were six of us midshipmen. I was the youngest. We were told we'd sail to Portsmouth first, where we'd wait until our convoy was complete. I enjoyed those first few days. Captain Smith chose me to run errands for him. Trouble was, the other midshipmen resented it. Started calling me 'Captain's pet' and worse. One day I found my bunk was soaking wet. I knew they'd done it, but they just laughed at me. That was just the start. Before long, things went missing from my sea chest. I couldn't say anything as they were bigger than me."

"Couldn't the Captain stop them?"

"If I'd told him, I feared things would get worse."

Thomas sat staring at his shadow, cast on the wall by the candle beside him. Vivid images of the ship filled his head.

"And they did get worse. Before we reached Portsmouth, the quartermaster fell overboard and drowned. I was so shocked that someone could die so easily. What made it worse was no-one seemed bothered. They just accepted it."

Thomas ran a hand through his hair. "We were there for a couple of weeks before sailing for St Helena. There were ten East Indiamen and some navy ships to protect us from pirates and foreign navies. Three months we were at sea. It was dreadful. Some of the sailors and the men who worked below deck found out I was serving at the Captain's table and told me to steal food. That if I didn't, I'd regret it. They didn't see why the officers ate so well while they had miserable rations. Told me I had to decide whose side I was on."

"Why didn't you report them?"

"I did eventually. Told the Captain about one man who'd half-throttled me until I said I'd get him some food. The next day everyone was summoned on deck. The man I'd named was in chains, tied to a post. After the charge was read out, he was flogged. We were made to watch. When they'd finished, he slumped onto the deck, covered in blood. Buckets of sea water were thrown on him before he was taken below deck."

Thomas took some deep breaths. Anne leant over and put her hand on his arm.

"Don't go on. I can see how upsetting it is."

"It's all right. I want to tell you everything. I need to."

He blew his nose and took another deep breath.

"I spent days trying to decide if I'd done the right thing. The rations the men got were awful, whereas the Captain and his officers ate handsomely. The cook baked bread every day for them and they had fresh meat. Can you believe it? There were livestock on board for them. Didn't seem fair."

"But that man had no right to threaten you," said Anne. "It wasn't your fault."

Thomas got up and put some more logs on the fire. As he sat back down, he smiled at his sister.

"We had to watch more floggings before we reached St Helena. All for theft, we were told. I suppose the Captain thought it would be an example to others. I decided the best thing to do was keep out of the way, avoid the other midshipmen who were still stealing things from my chest. To be fair, one of them, a boy called John Hodgson, wasn't too bad. I could see he just went along with it to avoid being picked on himself. We tried to help one another. He even made me a card for my birthday just before we reached St Helena.

"Before we got there, the Captain stopped giving me tasks to do for him. I think it was because I told him I didn't like having to watch the floggings, that I thought it was cruel. He was furious. I was to do as I was told, or he'd put me on a ship back to England and he'd inform Papa."

"Thomas," said Anne, looking horrified. "Did you really think you could question the Captain?"

"I suppose not, but those men suffered dreadfully. They almost killed one of them."

"Go on."

"We were in St Helena a month, unloading cargo and taking on fresh water. It was so hot in the cramped, smelly quarters we had. The others slept because they went to bed much the worse for drink. So, I'd slip out and find somewhere on deck I could hide and enjoy the cooler air. For those few hours each night, it was like I had dreamt going to sea would be. The stars seemed so much brighter than here, as if you could reach out and touch them. Some nights I saw whales and flying fish.

"Then, like most on board, I developed a fever. I was sent to the surgeon, Mr Davis. He was kind and gave me some medicine. Even instructed the quartermaster to give me some fresh food from the officers' table.

"When I was better, Davis started getting me to run errands for him. Asked me to help him in the sick quarter. I'd clean his instruments and keep the place tidy. The Surgeon's Mate, Greville, wasn't happy about the attention Davis was paying me. I don't think Davis thought much of Greville. For one thing, unlike me, Greville couldn't read Latin. I soon worked out that if I did the menial tasks Greville was meant to do, like mopping the floor, he'd put up with me.

"I really enjoyed spending time with Davis. He showed me how to make up medicines and then let me help him. And when there were no patients, I could look at his medical books.

One day he announced he had to amputate a sailor's leg and would need two assistants. Warned me it would be nasty. For some reason, I assured him I'd be fine. Told him I'd seen lots of blood, lambing.

"Greville and I had to hold the man still. Of course, it was nothing like lambing. It was horrible. Worse than the man's screams was the sound of the saw on the bone. Afterwards Davis congratulated me. Said he'd never seen a first-timer cope so well. What he said next stuck with me. 'You'd make a good surgeon, lad.' From then on, he always got me to assist him."

They were interrupted by the maid wanting to know if they needed anything else before she went to bed.

Thomas was too lost in memories of the Indian Ocean to respond.

"We'll have some hot chocolate, please," said Anne.

"Have you heard enough?" he asked after the maid had left the room.

"No, I want to hear everything," said Anne.

"All right. Everyone knew I was helping the surgeon. Those same men who told me to steal food now demanded I steal medicines, especially laudanum. Their threats were dreadful, and I believed they would carry them out. I regretted it then and still do, but I started removing small amounts of drugs. Enough to keep those men from harming me but not enough for Davis or Greville to notice. To this day, I'm ashamed I took advantage of his trust in me."

"Anyone would have done that," said Anne. "You had to protect yourself."

"It wasn't only that. I'd seen how dreadful the seamen's lives were. Poor food, overworked, flogged if they did anything wrong. What made it worse was the difference from the lives of the officers in their fancy cabins and good food. It didn't seem right.

"Things got even worse for the sailors and deckhands as we neared Calcutta. A navy ship came alongside and some armed ratings boarded. They demanded men and the Captain agreed they could press gang eleven. Though I have to say, I was glad to see they took the two who had threatened me the most."

The maid came in with the cups of chocolate. She asked if she should light some more candles but Anne said it wasn't needed. Thomas watched the steam rising from his cup.

"Did you go ashore in Calcutta?"

"Yes. The Captain sent me to deliver letters." He drank some chocolate and sighed. "You wouldn't believe how awful it was. People living and sleeping on the streets amid mounds of filth, picking scraps of food out of waste heaps, they were so hungry. And the smell was so overpowering I had to tie a handkerchief over my nose and mouth, not that it did much good. Couldn't wait to get back to the ship.

"A few times Davis took me ashore with him to collect drugs. One time he told me to wait in a teashop and was gone for hours. When he returned he was having difficulty walking. I'd never seen him so jovial. Kept telling me what a good young man I was. If I hadn't been there, I'm not sure he'd have found his way back to the ship."

Thomas stopped, staring into the fire. "It was strange. He was different after that. Spent a lot of his time in his cabin sleeping. Told Greville to deal with the men, even though he'd never trusted his mate before. I wondered if he was sick, some strange tropical illness."

"Good job you weren't at sea," said Anne.

"Well, we soon were. Set sail for Madras, fully loaded with cotton, pepper, cinnamon, and saltpetre. We were to anchor off the coast awaiting the rest of our convoy of East Indiamen to assemble. Then something strange happened. Davis disappeared. Captain Smith sent a search party ashore but there was no trace of him. He must have hidden on a boat taking cargo ashore and then run away. Rather than try and find a replacement in Madras, the Captain told Greville to take over."

"But you said Greville didn't know much," said Anne. "Did the Captain not know that?"

"Don't know. My fears for anyone who might fall ill on the voyage home were soon realised. And it was the Captain himself. Greville had no idea what to do. Just gave him any medicine, pretending to know what he was doing. The Captain's fever worsened and he became delirious. I was so frightened as there was nothing anyone could do. I prayed at night but to no avail. After six weeks he died. They wrapped him in a sail cloth and, after a blessing, he was slid overboard. Burial at sea, they called it."

"How dreadful," said Anne, clutching her handkerchief. "The poor man. And his wife and children don't even have a grave to grieve over."

"Harmsworth, the chief mate, took command. I kept out of everyone's way as much as I could. All I wanted was to get home. Occasionally a sailor threatened me if I didn't steal food for him. I wasn't going to risk getting caught stealing, so I'd give him my rations. Thankfully it worked and he left me alone.

"The voyage home seemed to last forever. I'd never felt so relieved and excited the morning England was sighted. Couldn't wait to get ashore when we anchored. All I'd taken with me had disappeared. My sea chest was empty. If I'd brought it home, I'd have had to explain what had happened, so I decided to leave it and say nothing. I wanted to forget how I'd felt humiliated, abused, unable to standup for myself."

"Oh, Thomas."

"I vowed that day, as I made my way to the farm, that I never wanted to feel vulnerable again. No-one was ever going to bully me or humiliate me again."

He looked at Anne, his eyes filled with tears. "You must never tell a soul."

"I won't," said Anne, getting up and taking his hands. "Thank you for telling me. I've worried so much, fearing all manner of things."

Thomas looked up at her, tears in his eyes. "When I was young, I don't know what I'd have done without you. The times you looked after me."

"Don't think I need to now," she laughed. "Look at you. Tall, strong… Can't imagine anyone trying it on with you. Least if they did, more fool them."

Thomas managed to smile. He thought about telling her about his boxing matches but decided he'd revealed enough for one night. Maybe another time.

1814

Richard was in his consulting room when Thomas got back from visiting patients one afternoon. It was so dark and gloomy outside, some candles were already lit.

"How d'you get on?" he asked, as Thomas put down his bag and took off his outdoor coat.

"Fine." Thomas sat down on the other side of the desk and unbuckled the bag. "Mr Graham in Hogshill is feeling better. Says the gout isn't as bad. Managed to get to church on Sunday. First time since Christmas. Said he wasn't keen about going on with the medicine. Means he's up and down all night, passing water. Apparently, his wife's been moaning, says she can't sleep properly. But he agreed it was for the best for now."

"Well done. What about old Keddle? How's his ulcer?"

"His house was so cold. Says he can't afford any more logs this winter. Had hoped for an early spring. I don't know how some of these people survive. Despite that, the ulcer is clean and slowly healing. He can't praise you enough. Said 'that Dr Phelps, he's a fine doctor'."

Richard smiled. "Quite right. Wise man!"

"Only problem, he said, was costiveness. Hasn't passed stool for a week. So, I administered a clyster. Will check on him next week."

Thomas took some papers out of his bag, sorted them out, and put them down on the desk.

"Can I ask you something?"

Richard stopped what he was writing and looked up. "Anything."

"I've learnt a lot since being here. But I've been wondering how you keep up to date. I mean, there must be new ideas and treatments all the time. How do you learn about them?"

Richard put his pen down and leant back. "With difficulty. Chance really. On the odd visits to Yeovil or Dorchester, I've made a point of visiting the doctors there. We talk, tell each other what we've heard." He sat forward, leaning on his desk. "I know what you're thinking, and you're right. Could be missing lots of important advances."

"I'm not criticising. Just wanted to understand."

Richard looked troubled. "Don't know what else I can do. You'll see, when you get to London, you'll hear all the latest in the lectures. But once you leave and start practising, you hear nothing. Unless you're in London, of course. There, you can go to the lectures year after year. And there are the societies. But for all of us outside London, there's nothing."

Thomas sat forward. "So, doctors who trained years ago are practising what they learnt years ago?"

"Afraid so." He laughed. "Best you consult a newly qualified one if you're ill."

Thomas went to get up, but Richard asked him to stay.

"Don't look so worried. I've been thinking about your training. You've learnt a lot, not that I claim the credit. Never known someone read so much, all hours of the day. Trouble is, I don't know how much more help I can be. This is a small place. As you've seen, not a lot goes on. You might be better off somewhere bigger, with more doctors. I don't want to lose you. But I'm thinking what's best for you."

Thomas hadn't expected this. He'd imagined staying here for two years before going to London, if he could find the funds.

"What would I do?" asked Thomas. "Where could I go?"

Richard picked up a letter. "I've heard from Dr Coulson in Henley. He's highly respected. A general practitioner like me.

After twenty-five years there's nothing much he hasn't dealt with. Anyway, he's looking for an apprentice. I wrote and told him about you, and he's keen to have you."

Thomas didn't know what to think. The past months had been some of his happiest. But he knew Richard was right. Working somewhere larger, he'd see so much more.

"How do you know Coulson?"

"Ah, long story, but gist of it is he was a pupil in London at the same time as my master in Bridgewater, Mr Henley. They'd kept in touch, and Coulson visited a couple of times when I was doing my apprenticeship. It was Coulson who suggested I join the navy as a surgeon. Helped get me a posting."

Thomas sat thinking.

"Take your time," said Richard. "Coulson doesn't need an answer until the end of the month."

"Did he say how much I'd have to pay?"

"He said if you're as good as I told him you are, he'll only charge sixty pounds a year. I think he's been known to charge a hundred."

"Right," said Thomas, wondering how on earth he'd be able to take up the offer.

As he made his way up to his room, he knew the time had come when he'd have to confront his father. And he knew exactly how to persuade him to help.

*

"Thomas, that's wonderful," said Anne, hugging her brother when he got back from Land Farm. "You must be getting more diplomatic!"

Thomas took the knapsack off his back and sat down. The smell of baking mixed with the scent of freshly cut flowers on the table was so welcoming.

"You must be tired... and hungry. Walking all that way."

"Didn't really notice. I was too distracted. Flowers in the hedgerows, fields full of lambs, trees coming into leaf. And the view from the top of Blackdown Hill. Could see for miles."

"So how did you persuade Papa?"

"Wasn't difficult. Papa could see how happy Mama was to see me, and although he tried not to show it, I think he was pleased, too. I told him I was still determined to become a surgeon, whatever it took. To show him I meant it, I said I only wanted him to pay half. I'd pay the other half."

"Pay half? How can you? That's thirty pounds a year."

He smiled at her. "I've already got it." He paused. "Don't look so alarmed. I didn't steal it. I got forty pounds from my time at sea and when I was in Taunton, I took up fighting."

She gasped. "No."

"Became good at it and won a lot of fights. The purses weren't large but I saved everything I won. Whole reason for doing it was for a time like this."

Anne looked aghast, her eyes wide open. She reached out, grasping the edge of the table to steady herself. "Didn't you get hurt?"

"Sometimes but never seriously. Few days to recover and I was right as rain."

"Sorry, but I'm shocked to hear this."

"Anne, lots of men do it. It's a sport. Even nobility indulge."

The colour was gradually returning to her cheeks.

"The main thing is, it means I can carry on. I can pay Coulson and then go to London. And if it reassures you, I'm not planning any more fights."

Two weeks later, on a bright spring morning, with all his possessions in the bag on his back, he set out to walk to Henley.

Chapter 3

1814

"The doctor's out. Said you were to come in and wait for him," said the maid.

Thomas had to stoop as he entered the hallway. She showed him into the front room which, from the furnishings, he assumed was Coulson's consulting room. He removed the heavy bag from his shoulders and sat down. Despite the rattling of wagons passing the window, he could make out the sound of a piano from somewhere in the house.

"I'll bring you some tea, sir," said the maid.

As he looked around, he could imagine that patients would find the wood-panelled room safe and comforting. The bookshelves were packed with medical tomes and on the desk was a periodical, the *Medical & Physical Journal*. Against the far wall was a table, long enough for even someone of his height to lie down. He'd just started looking at the journal when he heard the front door closing and a well-dressed, portly man carrying a leather bag came in. Thomas leapt to his feet.

"Ah, Wakley, you're here. Splendid." He put his bag down and they shook hands. "Coulson, Luke Coulson. Welcome to Henley."

His thick head of hair was starting to go grey, and he had a rather florid complexion, probably heightened by hurrying home.

"Can see Hannah has looked after you," he said. "Could do with one myself."

He rang a small bell and Hannah reappeared with another tray of tea.

"She knows me too well," laughed Coulson as he slumped into his desk chair.

He picked up his pipe and lit it. "Ah. That's better."

Thomas sat back down and watched a cloud of smoke float up and spread across the ceiling.

"How was the stage?" asked Coulson. "Wretched way to travel, stagecoaches. Luckily got my own carriage now."

"Actually, I walked," said Thomas.

Coulson froze, his pipe halfway to his mouth. "What! All the way from Dorset?"

"I enjoyed it. There's so much to see at this time of year."

Coulson smiled, a twinkle in his eye. "Phelps said you were from farming stock. Well, good for you. Getting to the top of West Hill is my limit."

Thomas could see he was clearly a man who enjoyed his food and drink. At that moment, the piano became louder. Coulson raised his eyebrows and shook his head.

"My eldest daughter, Caroline. Plays all the time. You'll get used to it."

"It's no trouble," said Thomas. "Only piano I've ever heard was in our church and at school."

"Well, this is a bit livelier, I can assure you," he said, laughing. "Now, it's getting late. We'll get you started tomorrow."

He rang for Hannah, who showed Thomas to his room at the top of the house.

"Dinner is at seven, sir," said Hannah, as she left.

The room was small, with large heavy wooden joists and sloping ceilings. Apart from the bed, there was a washstand, a small desk and a chest. Ducking his head, he made his way to the window from where, looking down, he could see the back yard and stable. Away to the left was the Thames, with small wharves lining the bank.

He unpacked his clothes, hanging some on the back of the door, placing the rest in the chest. His few other possessions, some books and his chess set, he put on the desk. He pulled off his boots and lay back on the bed, his hands behind his head. The smell of cooking made him realise how hungry he was. Closing his eyes, he could hear bargemen working on the nearby wharfs.

*

"Sorry. Am I late?" asked Thomas, entering the dining room to find the family already seated.

"Not at all, Wakley, come in," said Coulson, getting up. He held out his arm, encouraging Thomas to step forward. "This is my dear wife, Elizabeth, and over here my daughters, Caroline and Louisa. And that rascal is my youngest, Richard."

"Good evening," said Thomas.

"And this, my dear," Coulson said, turning back to his wife, "is young Wakley, my new apprentice."

She indicated the vacant chair. "Mr Wakley. Please, come and sit down."

Hannah placed a tureen of mulligatawny soup on the table. As Mrs Coulson served, Thomas looked around the room. The pictures of hunting scenes reminded him of the dining room at Land Farm but the atmosphere couldn't have been more different. At home his father had discouraged conversation whereas here there was constant chatter.

"Can you believe it," said Coulson to his wife, "Wakley walked all the way here. Must be, what, a hundred miles?"

"About that," said Thomas.

"How long did it take?" asked his wife, looking quite anxious.

"Four days, but please, I enjoyed it. Met lots of people, and I got to see Stonehenge."

"Really?" said Richard. "I'd love to see it."

"Well, maybe we'll go one day," said Coulson. "Come on, eat up. I'm ready for that pie I smelt cooking earlier. Rabbit, I hope."

Over dinner, Thomas was asked all about his family and home, his school days, and his time in Beaminster. He carefully skirted over his time at sea and in Taunton. On two occasions, he noticed Caroline looking at him, but as soon as he caught her eye, she looked away.

After dessert of apple pie, they all went through to the parlour. Although the weather was finally warming up after the long harsh winter, a fire had been lit. Candles on the mantelpiece and on two side tables bathed the room in soft yellow light. In the corner stood the piano.

"Caroline," said Mrs Coulson, "will you play for us? I'm sure Mr Wakley would like to hear you."

After some encouragement, including Thomas confirming that indeed he would, she agreed. Although he knew nothing about music, Thomas could see how accomplished she was. He couldn't stop himself clapping when she finished, which amused the younger two children, sending them into fits of giggles. Caroline smiled sheepishly and thanked him.

*

Thomas didn't sleep much that first night. Too many thoughts were whirring around in his head, not least the way Caroline had returned his smile. As soon as it was light, he got up and crept downstairs, not wanting to wake anyone. He was letting himself out the front door when Hannah appeared.

"Morning," he whispered. "Going out for a bit."

The street was already busy with men unloading wagons outside the inn on the other side of the road. Walking towards the river, he had to shield his eyes from the sun which had now risen above the nearby hills. He stood on the stone bridge watching the river racing beneath him. Tree branches had lodged in the stone arches, struggling to free themselves and go on their way towards London. On the far side, the river had burst its bank, flooding the fields. The cries of pheasants could be heard from the distant woods.

The wharves were already a hive of activity. Men were hoisting huge sacks onto the waiting barges. A sweet, rather sickly smell filled the air. Looking across the town, he could see the tops of malthouse kilns dotting the skyline.

He took the track behind the wharves before heading away from the river. The smell of malt drying was even stronger here, forcing him to cover his nose and mouth with a handkerchief. Shops were opening and the streets were now clogged with wagons and carriages. Back at the house, he went through to the dining room where Coulson was sitting, reading a newspaper.

"Morning, Wakley. Been out and about already I hear."

"Yes, sir. Such a beautiful morning, thought I'd explore a bit."

"Well, have some breakfast. There's rolls, honey and we seem to have marmalade as well at the moment. And there's plenty of coffee."

Coulson had to push on the arms of his chair to lever himself up. "I'll be in the front room when you're done."

Thomas was so keen to get started, he wolfed down his breakfast.

Coulson, at his desk writing, looked up. "Got a few visits to make this morning. You stay here and see those who call in. Phelps tells me you're used to visiting, so we'll get you out there soon. I imagine you're used to riding."

"Had to ride six miles to school when I was seven."

Coulson raised his eyebrows. "Really? Didn't let my sons start that young. Suppose you had to, living on a farm."

He pushed his chair back from the desk. "Our horse is getting on a bit so might not be as lively as you're used to. Robert, my eldest, rode her while he was my apprentice. You'll meet him at Christmas. Pupil at Guy's and Tommy's now."

Over the road, the bells of St Mary's sounded eight as Coulson packed some surgical instruments in his bag.

"Hannah will answer the front door. Anything you need, just ask her. And if you don't know what to do with a patient, ask them to come back later."

After Coulson had gone, Thomas sat behind the desk wondering how different it might be to Beaminster. In the event, the seven patients he saw had only minor problems, no different from the conditions he'd been used to diagnosing and treating.

Around midday, just when it seemed there'd be no more, Hannah knocked on the door to say a Mr Nugent was outside.

"He's not in a good way, sir."

The man limped in, mopping his brow as he sat down. "Hello, Doctor. It's my leg."

"Let's have a look," said Thomas, moving the long table away from the wall. "Lie yourself down."

Even without touching him, Thomas could see he was feverish. Nugent pulled his trouser leg up, revealing the cause. A large abscess. Having watched Phelps lance abscesses, and given the pain the man was in, Thomas decided he needed to deal with it straight away. Incising it brought forth a satisfying amount of pus. After Thomas had cleaned and dressed the wound, Nugent sat back up, smiling.

"Thanks, Doctor. Already feels better."

Thomas felt so fulfilled. Nugent was still limping slightly as he left but no longer in pain.

Just before one o'clock, Coulson returned.

"What's this I hear?" he said. "A fine new doctor in town."

He put down his bag, hung his jacket on the back of the door, and sat down. Thomas wasn't sure whether Coulson meant it or was teasing him.

"Met Nugent as I was coming down Bell Street. Told me how you'd operated on him."

Thomas relaxed. "Yes. Lanced and drained a large abscess."

"Did you indeed? Well, fortunately for you he's happy. But look here, Wakley. You have no right to undertake operations without me."

"But you said yourself, Nugent was grateful."

"That's not the point. You're my apprentice. This time it went well but if anything went wrong, I'd be liable." Coulson wiped his mouth with the back of his hand and sat forward. "Maybe I didn't make it clear. You're not to operate without me in future."

"I'm sorry," Thomas said quietly.

As he made his way up to his room, he felt Coulson had been unfair. His diagnosis and treatment of Nugent had been correct. He couldn't understand why he should be criticised.

*

Their altercation was soon forgotten. Coulson never referred to it again, and Thomas always sought his advice if he thought surgery was needed.

Thomas soon fell into the pattern of life in the house. He liked its regularity, especially knowing the time of each meal. He developed his own daily ritual. He'd head out soon after sunrise and walk by the river. The church bells ensured he got back in time for breakfast. His mornings were spent in the consulting room, but after a month Coulson started sending him out to visit patients in nearby villages. He loved being up high on horseback, able to see over the hedgerows and across fields. The sight of pheasants scurrying around made him wonder what had become of Incledon and his poor wife.

With the start of summer there were fewer patients. On hot afternoons, it was too stuffy to stay in his room. He'd taken to finding somewhere quiet by the river to read. His favourite place was on the far bank, a few hundred yards downstream from the bridge. Dragonflies hovered over the water and swans glided by, the parents protecting their cygnets. In the distance, the town shimmered in the heat.

He was soon so absorbed in his book, he didn't hear people approaching.

"Mr Wakley. So, this is where you get to."

He turned and looked up, shielding his eyes from the sun. Caroline and Louisa stood holding parasols. Their light, floral dresses seemed so much more vibrant in the bright light than in the gloom of the dining room.

"Good afternoon, Miss Caroline, Miss Louisa," he said, quickly standing up, brushing grass off his shirt and pushing his hair back off his face. Louisa turned half away, trying to stifle a giggle.

"Louisa, your manners," said Caroline. "Please ignore her, Mr Wakley. I'm sorry, we shouldn't have disturbed you."

"No, not all. I was only reading. It's such a beautiful day, and it's so peaceful here."

"May I ask what you're reading?"

"Oh, it's physiology. How our bodies work."

As he talked, he noticed how she didn't take her eyes off him. Louisa had wandered off, picking flowers. Caroline twirled her parasol slowly.

"Sounds rather dry and difficult."

"Oh, I don't find that." Then, without thinking he said, "Not as difficult as playing the piano. That looks much harder."

For a moment, he couldn't tell what she was thinking. Then she smiled broadly and laughed.

"You're very kind to say that but I can assure you, it's not as hard as it may look." She looked around and saw Louisa was getting restless.

"We must let you read and we must finish our walk. Until dinnertime, Mr Wakley."

Thomas slowly sat down, feeling flustered. As he gazed across the river, all he could see was Caroline's face, her blue eyes, the freckles on her cheeks, the ringlets of strawberry blonde hair and her smile. He lay back, looking up at the sun-dappled trees above, wondering what she'd been thinking.

*

At the end of each day, Coulson set aside time to discuss patients with Thomas.

"Best way to learn," he'd said, "reviewing your own cases."

The cases that intrigued Thomas were those in which the diagnosis wasn't clear. A history and symptoms that didn't fit with any known condition.

"Do you think it's because diseases can vary a lot," Thomas mused, "or is it that there are diseases still to be discovered?"

"There's always new things to discover, always will be. You'll learn the latest when you go to London next year."

Thomas sat for a while thinking.

"What's bothering you?" asked Coulson, filling his pipe.

"Something I talked to Phelps about. How do you manage to keep up to date?"

Coulson leant back, exhaling great clouds of smoke.

"I'll be honest. I don't. Only way would be to go to London and attend lectures."

Thomas grimaced. "Does that mean most doctors are out of date?"

"Pretty much, apart from those in London. The rest of us are kept in the dark."

"But what about this?" said Thomas, pointing to the *Medical & Physical Journal*.

"Well, you'll have seen for yourself," said Coulson. "Just descriptions of cases and their doctor's account of how clever they've been! Who's to say if any of it is correct?"

"Why don't they include the lectures? Then you'd know the latest science."

"Ah, that's one of your easier questions," he chortled. "Lecturers earn a fortune from pupils' fees. They'd never let journals publish them."

"But they must know doctors like you can't find out their discoveries and new ideas."

Coulson smiled. "Oh, they know all right. But once we've been their pupils and they've had our fees, that's that."

Thomas picked up the latest copy of the journal and thumbed through it.

"The other thing I've noticed is people don't question what's published. Why don't they have debates?"

"Think about it. Doctors wouldn't submit reports if there was a risk of being questioned, perhaps ridiculed. Then the journal would lose the few subscribers they have. Other problem is, it only comes out once a month. Most people have forgotten what was in a previous issue."

"What about that new periodical you've started getting? Is that any better?"

"*London Medical Repository*. Just the same. If anything, even duller and staler than the *Journal*. Hoped it would be useful, as one editor, Burrows, advocates reform. According to him, the Society of Apothecaries they're setting up will be as corrupt as the College of Surgeons."

Thomas ran a hand through his hair. "Doesn't sound like you think things will change."

"I wish they would but can't see how. It'd take a special person to do that. Still, we can live in hope. Meanwhile, can't wait for Christmas when Robert will bring me news of the latest ideas. Best present he could give me!"

✳

"It's such a beautiful day," said Mrs Coulson, "why don't you girls go boating?"

They were just finishing lunch.

"Oh, Carrie, can we?" pleaded Louisa, putting down her spoon and standing up.

"I'm sure Mr Wakley would row for you," her mother added, smiling at Thomas.

He glanced at Caroline who, despite not looking up from her plate, was smiling slightly.

"Of course," said Thomas, "if I'm not needed here."

Coulson, whose mouth was full, waved his hand affirming he could go.

An hour later they were floating down the river beneath overhanging willows. Caroline and Louisa lay back, holding their parasols to keep the sun off their faces, trailing their free hands in the water. Thomas sat facing them, the oars resting in the gunwales, clear of the water. Every so often he gently dipped one in the river to keep from running into the bank.

"This is glorious," said Caroline. "I adore summer afternoons."

Thomas watched as she took her hand out of the river and let the water drip from her fingers. She saw Thomas looking at her and smiled. He could feel his heart racing and was glad when Louisa broke the spell he was under.

"Look, Carrie. Over there. There's a teahouse. Do let's take tea."

Thomas smiled at Louisa, dropped the oars, and rowed them over to a small wooden jetty.

"Wait while I tie up," he said, but before he could, Louisa had jumped out and was heading up the path. As Caroline took his hand to steady herself disembarking, he could feel how small and soft it was. He was convinced she held on longer than necessary, tightening her grip slightly. She unfurled her parasol and started making her way up to the teahouse. Thomas retrieved his jacket from the boat, giving him a moment to compose himself.

"You're always reading," said Louisa. The three of them were sitting at a small metal table drinking from bone china cups.

"I have to," said Thomas. "Got a lot to learn to become a surgeon."

"Don't you ever read novels?" asked Caroline.

Thomas detected a reproach in her question. "Not since I was a boy. What would you suggest?"

"I know, I know," said Louisa. "That new one by Jane Austen." She turned to Thomas. "It's my most favourite book."

Caroline smiled at Thomas. "*Pride and Prejudice*. Yes, perfect. I have a copy. And you must tell me what you think of it."

Thomas wondered what he'd let himself in for but if it provided an opportunity to spend time talking with Caroline, he was prepared to read it.

*

Summer ended abruptly. Waking one morning in early September, Thomas felt cold for the first time in weeks. As he closed his bedroom window, he was struck by how strong the smell of malt and brewing was, held back by the low cloud and lack of any breeze. He rummaged among his clothes to find something heavier to wear.

"Wakley. We're off to the workhouse this morning," said Coulson at breakfast. "Likely to need both of us."

Being market day, they had to wind their way through the crowds, between the barrows that filled the main street. With stallholders shouting their wares, heavily laden trolleys clattering on the cobbles, and people calling to one another, Thomas and Coulson gave up trying to talk.

When they reached West Hill, Coulson stopped in front of a fine two-storey redbrick building.

"Wasn't always this grand," said Coulson. "Only had a small poorhouse, overcrowded and barely fit for farm animals when I arrived, but managed to persuade the overseers we needed a proper building. I'm sure it helped put an end to smallpox. Never had to use the pesthouse since."

As they approached the central gateway, Coulson lowered his voice. "You need to understand. We can only do the basics, given what the poor law overseers pay me."

The workhouse master greeted them, doffing his cap. "Morning, Doctor."

"Morning, Smithells."

In the work rooms, emaciated women were sitting on the stone floors, sewing or weaving, while a few thin, wide-eyed children sat or lay beside them. The stench was so strong, Thomas's eyes watered. He was glad to get back into the open air in the back courtyard where men were chopping logs. There were dozens of them, thin and weak, struggling to carry out their tasks. Some were limping, others only able to use one of their arms as they bent double to carry their loads.

"So, who've you got in the infirmary?" asked Coulson.

Smithells led them into a small room in which a man sat on the floor clutching his arm, wrapped in a filthy cloth.

"Unwrap it," said Coulson. "Let's have a look."

Thomas was aghast. There was a deep cut, at the bottom of which, clearly visible, was the radial bone.

"Axe slipped," the man said. "Weren't his fault. He'd been chopping logs all day. Could barely stand he were so tired."

"Why hasn't it been cleaned?" asked Coulson, turning to the master.

"Well, Mrs Smithells hasn't been that well herself of late," he said, shuffling his feet and not looking at Coulson. "I'll get her to do it presently."

"Make sure you do," said Coulson, "then she needs to dress it with a clean cloth, else he'll lose his arm."

Thomas wanted to get a bucket of water and wash the wound himself but knew he mustn't. In the adjoining room were two heavily pregnant women. Another woman, who Thomas took to be another inmate, was bustling about doing her best to make them comfortable.

"She knows what she's about," whispered Coulson. "Delivered dozens over the years she's been here."

Lots of the inmates wanted to be seen. Most had long-standing coughs and breathing difficulties. Thomas suspected a hearty meal would do more good than any medicines.

When he and Coulson got back out into the fresh air on West Hill, Thomas took some deep breaths.

"You'll get used to it," said Coulson. "If they weren't here, they'd probably have already starved to death."

Thomas looked at him. He knew Coulson was a compassionate man but even he seemed to have accepted this state of affairs.

"I was thinking of the pregnant women," mused Thomas. "What chance will those babies have?"

"Believe me, it's a lot better than it was."

"I'm sorry. I wasn't criticising you. It's just, it's so unfair."

"Few years back it wasn't this bad," said Coulson, "not when it was first built. Only had about seventy inmates. The enclosures have a lot to answer for. Lots of the families in there used to get by fine with their plot of land and grazing some livestock on the common ground. But the big landowners have put paid to that."

"How were they allowed to?" asked Thomas.

Coulson shook his head. "Enclosure Act. Doesn't just allow it. Encourages it. The wealthy reckon they can make better use of the land, produce more corn for the country. Which is just what the Tory government want."

"Can't the farmers stop them?"

"They can complain as much as they like but at the end of the day, it's the enclosure commissioners who decide."

"Who are they?"

"Other big landowners! Convenient, eh?"

Thomas was shocked that he hadn't known this was going on.

"As the good book says," said Coulson, putting a hand on Thomas's shoulder, "'to those that have shall be given'. Matthew, I think."

Back at the house, they unpacked their bags and sat down.

"I was going to send you over to Badgemore House this afternoon," said Coulson, "but perhaps visiting one of our biggest landowners today is not such a good idea."

Thomas sat with his elbows on his knees, staring at the floor, wondering if his father was guilty of taking land in the way Coulson had described.

"Sorry," said Thomas, looking up. "Miles away. Badgemore? That's fine. I'll go."

"All right. But keep to medical matters. Owner is Joseph Grote, a banker. He's not long for this world. His butler said he was in some pain. Doesn't think he should summon his physician all the way from Oxford just for that. He wondered if we could give him something. Take some laudanum with you."

That afternoon, as he rode up the steep tree-lined drive, the old manor house came into view on the brow of the hill. When he reached the top, a stable boy appeared to take his horse. The front door was opened by a man in uniform who Thomas took to be the butler. From the way he looked Thomas up and down, clearly Coulson had been expected.

"This way," he said, leading Thomas upstairs and into a bedroom. With the drapes closed, Thomas struggled to make out Grote. He lay buried amid several pillows, his small frame almost lost from view. He was barely conscious.

"How are you?" asked Thomas, but as he said it he realised how fatuous that sounded. Grote turned his head slowly, lifted his arm slightly and tried to smile. Thomas took his hand. His skin was dry and thin. The pulse, barely perceptible, was slow and irregular. His mouth was parched, his lips cracked.

He struggled to speak, his voice weak and croaky. "Lot of pain."

"Right, sir. Some laudanum should help."

He gently laid Grote's arm back down. As he handed the butler a bottle of the dark tincture, he stressed, "Small amounts only. And try to get him to drink more water."

"Dr Simpson, very eminent I believe, recommended avoiding water," said the butler. "Would tax his kidneys."

What nonsense, thought Thomas. But remembering his promise to Coulson, he simply nodded.

"Let Dr Coulson know if you need anything more," said Thomas, doubting that Grote would survive for long if his physician continued to, in effect, kill him through dehydration.

He couldn't wait to get out of there. Riding back, he took in nothing of the passing countryside. His visit had been as upsetting as the trip to the workhouse.

*

"Have you finished it yet? The Austen novel?" Caroline asked.

Thomas looked up from the medical book he was reading. "I have. Yesterday."

They were sitting alone in the parlour. Louisa, who would usually hang around, was out at her elocution lesson. The late afternoon light was starting to fade.

Caroline put down her embroidery. "So, what did you think?"

He wasn't sure how to answer. He could talk with confidence about physiology or *materia medica,* but a novel. What could be said? He was flummoxed, unable to find the right words.

"I enjoyed it."

When he glanced up from looking at the fire, he could see she knew he was struggling.

"What did you think of Mr Darcy?" she asked.

"Darcy?" He paused. "He irritated me, the way he mistreated Elizabeth."

Relieved she wasn't laughing at him, he was emboldened to carry on.

"To be honest, I didn't like any of the men. They were all so rich and privileged but behaved so badly."

"But men do behave like that," she said, "only concerned about how women look."

"Some do, but not all, surely? And the women weren't without fault. Look at Elizabeth Bennett."

She sat forward in her armchair. "Go on."

"Well, she chooses to believe everything she's told about Darcy. But she doesn't know about the good things he's done."

"Yes, because he keeps those secret, so how could she?"

Thomas nodded. "I suppose so."

"What's bothering you?" she asked.

"I had no idea there could be so much to unravel." He paused. "I'd thought, at first, it was just a simple story. But there's so much going on."

She smiled. "Oh, indeed. Just like real life." She raised her eyebrows. "You must try another of Miss Austen's books."

He got up to light some candles then knelt down to put more coal on the fire.

"I've got a suggestion of something new for you, Miss Caroline."

When he glanced round, he saw she furrowed her brow and narrowed her eyes.

"I'd like to teach you chess."

"Chess? I wondered what you were going to say."

"It's all about strategy and planning, attack and defence."

"Not so different from Austen's novel then."

It took him a moment to realise she was serious. "Yes, I suppose it is. I hadn't seen it that way, but you're right."

As he lay in bed that night, he thought about the warmth of her smile, the way she'd held his gaze as they talked, but most about the way she saw the world so differently. He'd never met someone who saw a similarity between chess and a novel. And on top of everything, on one occasion that evening, he was sure she had deliberately brushed against him as she passed.

*

Christmas was almost upon them. The house was festooned with greenery and Robert had arrived. After dinner on his first evening, Coulson announced that he, his son and Thomas were adjourning to the front room to talk medicine. A whisky decanter and glasses were on the desk. Although it wasn't as comfortable in there as in the parlour, they'd be able to talk freely. Coulson banned medical talk elsewhere in the house.

"Right, young man," said Coulson, having poured the drinks. "Tell us all about it." He turned to Thomas. "Listen and learn. This will be you next autumn."

As Robert regaled them with a litany of hardships and complaints, his father looked increasingly anxious. Robert told them of how difficult it often was to hear lecturers or get a good view in anatomy demonstrations. How physicians and surgeons turned up late for ward rounds, then spent little time teaching the pupils and offered no opportunity to ask questions.

"Was it the same in your day?" he asked his father.

Coulson sat gazing into the distance, speaking quietly. "I'd hoped by now things would have improved. But it sounds like nothing has changed."

"But, Papa, don't worry. I've still learnt a lot. Some lecturers are so inspiring. Sir Astley Cooper. He's not like the others. He talks about scientific surgery and how we must improve what we do."

Feeling this was a private conversation between father and son, Thomas had kept quiet but eventually he couldn't contain himself.

"If lots of pupils feel like you," asked Thomas, "why don't you say something, try and change things?"

Robert snorted. "Impossible. We'd be thrown out, barred from lectures. Then we'd not get our attendance certificates."

Thomas looked at Coulson. "If St Thomas's and Guy's are so bad, why are you suggesting I go there?"

Coulson sighed. "As ever, a good question. Trouble is, the five other hospital medical schools are, by all accounts, no different."

"Don't worry," said Robert. "There are ways to cope. Get to lectures early and get near the front. Only go on ward rounds with the doctors who take time to teach. And learn from each other. Share your notes with friends to check you understood properly."

"Ah," said Coulson, "I can see I've taught you one thing. Enterprise! Good for you."

He refilled his and his son's glasses. "Now, I want to hear the latest thinking on a whole number of conditions."

He brandished a piece of paper with a list of topics. Robert proceeded to regale them with the latest ideas about gout, aneurysms, headache, rashes, syphilis, and jaundice. Each time Thomas thought they were finishing, Coulson raised another disease. It was Robert who brought proceedings to an end.

"Papa, we can talk more tomorrow. But now I think we should rejoin the others."

"Yes, you're right. Sounds like Caroline's playing."

1815

As they stepped down from the carriage, music could be heard coming from upstairs. Thomas had had mixed feelings when the family insisted he join them at the New Year ball in the Assembly Room. Delighted to be treated as one of the family, but worried as he'd never danced and was sure he'd make a fool of himself. Caroline had brushed his worries aside, assuring him that she and Louisa would show him what to do.

As he walked in, Caroline took his arm.

"Got to do this properly," she laughed.

He'd never seen her so animated. She seemed to know everyone, smiling and greeting people as they made their way to a table at the far end of the room. As Caroline and her mother sat down, the band struck up and the floor filled with dancers. Overhead, the two chandeliers, each with dozens of candles, bathed the dancers in yellow light. Robert and Louisa had already joined in. Thomas stood behind the table with Coulson, watching, trying to make out what the dance involved.

"Used to love a Scotch reel," said Coulson, over the noise of the band. There were cries of delight as people spun round and found their partners again.

Thomas envied the way Robert was so at ease. It made him even more anxious, as he knew he wouldn't be able to avoid dancing. Caroline was tapping her foot along with the music. Mrs Coulson caught his eye and beckoned him over. He had to bend down to hear her.

"I think Miss Caroline would like to dance," she said quietly.

He knew he had no choice. When the next dance was announced, he braced himself and asked Caroline.

As they took to the floor, she squeezed his hand gently and whispered, "Just follow me. You'll be fine."

Watching, it had looked so complicated. But after the first few stumbled attempts to keep in line and cross over at the right time, he realised the same moves just kept repeating. By the end he'd relaxed and wondered why he'd been so fearful. Best of all had been seeing how happy it made Caroline.

As they returned to their table, she laid her hand on his arm. "Please ask Louisa to dance."

The next couple of hours flew by. He hardly took a break, no longer bothered about making a fool of himself when he got the steps wrong. He loved sweeping around the room, working out how to arrive back in the right place, and the way the ladies' skirts swirled as they turned.

Returning to the table after a particularly lively dance, Caroline announced she needed some fresh air and asked him if he'd accompany her.

Standing outside on the small balcony, they could hear coachmen in the courtyard below, talking. The crisp night air enhanced his senses. As she stared up at the night sky, he couldn't stop looking at her. The curve of her lips, her slender neck, the ringlets covering her ears. He reached out and stroked her cheek with the back of his hand. She turned, took hold of his hand and gently lowered it.

"I'm sorry," said Thomas, "I thought…"

"Oh, Thomas. I'm sorry." He lowered his head, unable to look at her. "It's just, you've become like a brother to me. I love the time we spend together."

He was crestfallen. How had he got it so wrong? He had been sure she felt the same as him.

"Thomas, please don't be sad. The last thing I want is for us to fall out." She paused. "Least not until I've learnt how to beat you at chess."

When he looked up, he saw she was smiling. From inside, the sound of the next dance being announced was met with cries of delight.

"The cotillion," she exclaimed, grabbing his hand. "The grand finale. Come on."

*

It took him several weeks to accept that nothing was going to happen. At first, he hoped Caroline would admit she'd been confused and had made a mistake. When that didn't happen, he started blaming himself, wondering what he'd done wrong, what he should have done differently. Painful though it was, he realised how, over the previous few weeks, he'd got ahead of himself. He had been so sure she felt the same as him. He felt so stupid. How had he got it so wrong?

He immersed himself in work, filling every moment seeing patients, reading, and talking with Coulson. He found if he kept busy, he could go the whole day and not think of her. As ever, he'd be up and out of the house before daybreak, walking beside the river as the sun rose. He loved seeing the first rays of sunlight catch the turrets on the tower of St Mary's and then the cupola on the town hall.

Most mornings, he was already at breakfast when Coulson appeared.

"No visits this morning," said Coulson. "I need your help cutting for stone."

"Really? How exciting."

Coulson frowned.

"Well, not for the patient, of course," Thomas quickly added.

Coulson shook his head. "You know, at times your enthusiasm gets the better of you. Patient is Trent, a maltster in Caxon Terrace. Classic symptoms of bladder stone for several weeks. Poor man can't work, so whole family face losing their home and ending up in the workhouse."

Coulson and Thomas were joined by Pope, another general practitioner. At Caxson Terrace, Trent had already drunk a fair bit. His wife had prepared their dining table for the operation and despatched their children to neighbours. Having helped Trent onto the table, lying on his back with some pillows under his head, Coulson produced a bottle of brandy from which Trent took several swigs.

"Right," said Coulson. "Strap his legs."

Pope and Thomas stood on either side, each holding a leg bent double, pushed right up against his chest. A long strip of material was placed round the back of his neck and tied to each ankle, before tying his wrists to his ankles. They were all set.

Coulson successfully slid a metal staff up into his bladder which Pope was to hold, to act as a guide for the scalpel as the perineum was incised. Coulson then inserted a pair of forceps through the incision into the bladder, and within a minute he'd successfully grasped and extracted the stone. As a dressing was applied to the wound, Pope and Thomas released the man's legs. Coulson held up a smooth, grey one-inch stone.

"He'll be wanting that," Pope told Thomas. "They always do."

It had taken three minutes, and Trent had only cried out occasionally. Back at the house, Thomas couldn't contain himself.

"You did that so expertly. Where did you learn to do it?"

Coulson smiled. "Same as everyone. By watching as a pupil. Anatomy lectures and dissection help, but in the end it comes down to having a go yourself. You learn by doing it, gradually getting better."

"But what if it goes wrong? There's no-one here to help."

"True, but the nearest hospitals are in Oxford and London. So, for someone like Trent, it's me or no-one. Like other general practitioners, I don't operate often, but with ten thousand of us across the country, we're the ones who do most of the operations."

*

He was on his morning walk, a mile out of town, when he heard the bells of St Mary's start ringing incessantly. Intrigued to find out what was going on, he hurried back. When he reached the bridge, the main street was packed as if it was market day. People were cheering and singing.

"What's going on?" he called to a man passing by.

"Wellington. Beaten Boney and them Frenchies."

He had to push his way through the crowds to get to Coulson's house but found it deserted. He rejoined the throng and made his way towards the Town Hall. All around him people were chanting, 'Waterloo', 'Wellington'. Drummers had gathered in front of the Town Hall. When the mayor and aldermen appeared on the balcony, a huge cheer went up. A Union flag was draped over the balustrade. The drumming stopped, and the mayor announced that the English army, led by the Duke of Wellington, had won a great battle at Waterloo. The war with France was over. Bonaparte was defeated. The crowd went wild, cheering and hugging each other.

It was several days before the town returned to normal. Then the consequences of the war started to become clear as men, returning from the battle, started appearing. Discharged with a derisory payment, they had been left to find their own way home. Men appeared seeking help for wounds that the army hadn't treated.

"How some of them have made it back here," said Thomas, "is a wonder."

"I know," said Coulson. "Saw one this morning with a gaping leg wound, tendons and muscles severed and just wrapped in filthy rags."

"I've noticed," said Thomas, "some men just seem to be survivors." Coulson looked puzzled. "What I mean is, it seems some people will survive come what may. Whatever happens, they have the willpower to overcome adversity. Others succumb, give up without a fight."

Coulson nodded. "I've been lucky. Never had to face anything like a battle. Don't think I'd cope with what these men have been through."

*

"Can't believe your time here is over," said Coulson, resting his elbows on his desk. "Don't be put off by what Robert said at Christmas. You'll manage fine."

Thomas had no worries about the training. His only concern was living in London.

"Not sure how I'll find being in a city."

Coulson smiled. "I think you might come to like it. And if you want to be a hospital surgeon, you'll have to get used to it." He chuckled. "After all, that's where the hospitals are."

"I suppose so."

"Now," he picked up a letter on his desk, "I've heard from your brother-in-law, Phelps. Seems like he's still looking out for you."

"What do you mean?"

"He was in London to get some breeches made, and it turned out the tailor," he looked back at the letter, "Thomas Wiltshire, has a son, Sampson, who's also starting as a pupil at the Borough hospitals. Taken lodgings nearby in Dean Street and needs someone to share it with. What do you say?"

"That's wonderful. Yes, please thank him."

Coulson put the letter down.

"Wakley. I've had several apprentices, but I have to say, none have been as keen and hard-working as you. And I include Robert! I won't pretend it hasn't been a job keeping up with you at times. But a word of advice. Don't forget to enjoy yourself as well. Life isn't just work."

"I know. It's… I find it hard to stop when there's so much I want to know."

"Well, remember. Not everyone is as committed as you. Doesn't mean they don't care."

"I've been thinking about what you said about these," Thomas said, picking up a copy of the *Medical & Physical Journal,* "and how much you learnt from Robert at Christmas. What if there was a way you could read about all those things he told us?"

Coulson smiled. "It would be wonderful, but that's not going to happen."

Thomas put down the journal. "I don't understand why the hospital physicians and surgeons don't think you and all the other general practitioners aren't important. That you can just be ignored."

Coulson sighed. "Look. Of course there's lots wrong with the way things are, and maybe one day they'll change. But for now, just concentrate on your studies. Don't try changing the world."

Thomas stared out of the window, watching the clouds passing the church tower. After a while he turned back to see Coulson studying him.

"Not sure I've convinced you," Coulson chuckled.

Chapter 4

1815

Every seat in the large, elliptical theatre in Guy's Hospital was taken. Even the gallery was packed, latecomers being forced to stand at the back. In the centre stood the revolving table that Thomas had been told about by Coulson, and to one side, on a low podium, the lecturer's chair. Overhead, through the handsome skylight, he could see rain clouds scudding across the night sky, lit up by a full moon.

He was glad he'd persuaded Wiltshire to get there early. Even so, as they'd climbed the flight of stone steps from the hospital quadrangle, it was clear other pupils had the same intention of getting a place near the front. Despite this, they managed to get into the third row. Thomas sensed the anticipation. Suddenly it went silent, but it was a false alarm. Just a demonstrator checking all was ready for the lecturer. Finally, as the bells in St Thomas's church sounded eight, Sir Astley Cooper entered to hearty applause, which he acknowledged with a slight smile and a bow of his head as he took his seat and arranged his papers.

From the moment he started lecturing, Thomas was transfixed. Tall and muscular, Sir Astley's presence filled the theatre. Everyone hung on his every word. Thomas was in awe, loving the clarity of what he was hearing.

"The principles of surgery," he said, leaning on the lectern and looking round the audience, "are learned from observation of the living when diseased, by dissection of the dead, and by experiments made on living animals." He wagged a finger. "You should entirely discard hypotheses. Instead, sound theory should be derived from your observations and experience. This is the basis of scientific surgery."

Thomas had to stop himself applauding. As Sir Astley listed all the topics he'd address over the coming weeks – inflammation, injuries, hernias, birth deformities, cancers, aneurysms – Thomas wanted him to get started right away. He'd gladly have stayed all night to listen, but all too soon Sir Astley was gathering up his papers, preparing to leave.

Thomas turned to Wiltshire. "That can't be it. It hasn't been an hour."

"It has," chortled Wiltshire. "Come on. I need a drink. *The Ship & Shovel.*"

"It'll be packed," said Thomas. "All this lot will be going. How about *The Chequers* on Hay's Wharf. They do a fair pigeon pie."

He'd only been in London a week but, on the advice of Preston, their landlord, Thomas had already learnt where to eat and, more importantly, where to avoid. As they crossed the hospital quadrangle, light from the wards on the first floor made the wet paving stones shine. Moonlight picked out the white stone pilasters adorning the red-brick walls. Thomas still couldn't quite believe that he was here.

Out on the street, he pulled up his collar and bent his head against the cold drizzle. He had to keep stopping and waiting for Wiltshire.

"Can't walk as fast as you, Wakley," said Wiltshire, when he caught up, gasping, his plump face quite red.

"Sorry," said Thomas, "just don't want to get soaked."

The inn was packed with men dressed in coarse, filthy clothing. Having found a table, Thomas sat looking around. It was a world away from the genteel dining room in Henley.

"Finest porter," said Wiltshire, returning from the bar with two tankards. "Large for me, small for you."

Wiltshire filled his pipe and lit it from the candle on their table.

"You never smoked?" he asked.

"Never," said Thomas.

"I don't know. Don't drink much, don't smoke. Bit of a monk, aren't you?"

"A monk?" puzzled Thomas. "I thought they indulged heavily."

A maid appeared with two huge plates of pie and mash, which they devoured in silence.

"Hadn't realised how hungry I was," said Thomas, wiping his plate with a chunk of bread.

He sat back and pulled out his lecture notes which he had to hold up to the candle to read. When he looked up, Wiltshire was smiling.

"Do you never stop?" asked Wiltshire.

"But it was so good. Didn't you think so?"

Wiltshire shifted in his chair and put down his pipe. "To be honest, I got a bit bored. He went on rather."

"How can you say that?" said Thomas. "He was so damning of much of medicine. How did he put it?" He looked through his notes. "Here it is. 'I do not believe a single correct idea has emanated from conjecture alone.' That can't make him many friends."

Wiltshire looked puzzled. "Why?"

"Can't you see? He's as good as saying doctors don't know what they're doing. He's questioning if any of it is any use. Damning those who just do what they believe, regardless of science."

"That's as maybe," said Wiltshire, standing up, "but I need another drink. No point asking you, I suppose."

Thomas continued to scrutinise his notes until Wiltshire got back.

"You know," said Wiltshire, "you make me realise how little interest I really have in medicine. I wish I could get as excited as you, but I can't."

Thomas put his notes back in his pocket. "Maybe you will. Give it time."

*

Their lodgings were on the second floor of a terraced house in a narrow road off Tooley Street. At first, Thomas didn't think he'd be able to put up with the stench and filth in the street. It brought back memories of Calcutta. But the landlord, who lived with his family on the ground floor, had been so welcoming, and upstairs the smell wasn't too bad. He did wonder, though, how it would be in summer, when he'd want to open the window.

The bed took up most of his room, leaving barely enough space to store his few clothes, let alone to wash and dress. In the sitting room there was a desk and two armchairs. From the size of the grate, he doubted it would provide much warmth once winter set in.

Every morning, at about seven, Preston's maid brought jugs of hot water and mugs of tea. The bedroom was so cold the mirror over the washstand misted up when he filled the bowl, making shaving hazardous. Not having many shirts or underclothes, he was thankful that Mrs Preston did the laundry so quickly.

Although Wiltshire was proving to be an amiable companion, Thomas couldn't understand his lack of interest in medicine. Several times in lectures he'd noticed that rather than taking notes, Wiltshire was sketching. Sometimes it was the whole scene, sometimes a portrait of the lecturer. He managed to ignore it until one morning, sitting together in a coffee shop in Borough High Street, he could contain himself no longer.

"For God's sake, Wiltshire. What's your problem with medicine?"

Wiltshire, startled, put down his cup. "What do you mean?"

"I'm sorry," said Thomas. "Didn't mean to blaspheme." He paused. "It's just, I can't understand why, if you're not interested, you're here?"

Wiltshire looked down, fiddling with a spoon that lay on the table.

"You don't have to tell me if you don't want to," added Thomas.

"No, it's all right." Wiltshire looked up. "Truth is, it's my father. Always wanted me to become a doctor."

Thomas was at a loss. "You're only doing it to please him?"

Wiltshire said nothing, just gazed at the spoon he was holding.

"Can't you tell him?" asked Thomas.

Wiltshire leant forward, his elbows on the table. "You've not met my father." He looked at Thomas. "Being an apprentice was sheer drudgery. Treated like a servant. Wasn't taught much. But from what I hear, that's not unusual. Trouble was, my father had paid for it, so I was stuck. Wasn't it like that for you?"

"No," said Thomas, recalling his time with Phelps and Coulson. "I must have been lucky." Then he thought of Incledon and added, "Though my first master turned out to be a rogue. Wasn't even an apothecary, just a druggist. He ended up in court and bankrupt."

"What!" exclaimed Wiltshire, so loud that people looked over at them.

Thomas smiled. "At least it meant I could escape halfway through, and I got my indenture certificate!"

"Well, that was something."

"So, what would you rather do?" asked Thomas.

"Paint. It's all I've ever wanted to do. Father scoffs at the idea, says I'll end up penniless, begging on the street."

Wiltshire relit his pipe from the candle.

"What will you do?" asked Thomas.

"Oh, I'll see out the year but not sure I'll take any exams." He smiled. "No point, as I don't want to practise."

Thomas felt sorry for him. He looked so downhearted.

"I don't know anything about paintings," said Thomas. "At home all we had were some hunting scenes, horses and dogs and all that."

Wiltshire laughed. "Well, would you like to see more?"

"Never thought about it. I did once see some portraits in a manor house I visited in Henley, but the place was so dark, couldn't make them out. And there's that portrait of Cheselden in the operating theatre."

"Right," said Wiltshire, sitting forward, suddenly animated. "We'll go and look at some this weekend. I know just the place."

*

Guy's and St Thomas's, the Borough hospitals, were neighbours. Thomas soon discovered that Tommy's dealt with the emergency patients while Guy's cared for those with chronic conditions. What he didn't understand was why half the pupils, like him, registered with Guy's, and half with Tommy's. Not that it seemed to matter, as they all took the same lecture courses.

That autumn, he attended morning lectures on the theory of medicine, chemistry, and *materia medica*. The highlight, though, was Sir Astley's lectures on surgery on Wednesday and Friday evenings. He spent the rest of the time in the museum studying preserved preparations of dissected parts of the body. When he wasn't there, he was in the library of the Guy's Physical Society, which, on Coulson's advice, he'd joined in his first week.

He'd never missed a lecture until one Thursday, having been awake all night thinking about what Sir Astley had said the previous evening, he decided to skip chemistry. Getting up at dawn, he found Wiltshire already huddled in front of the fire, drawing.

"Fancy going for breakfast?" Thomas asked.

A big grin appeared on Wiltshire's face. "Missing a lecture? Ha. So even you have your limits."

As they walked along Tooley Street, the smell of rotting flesh and excrement wafted up from the alleyways that led down to the river. The fog was so dense, they could barely make out people on the opposite pavement. They picked their way across the muddy pot-holed road, avoiding passing carts. From the dark courtyards at the end of each side passage came the sound of babies crying, dogs yelping, and the squeals of pigs. They turned onto Borough High Street and found a coffee shop.

Ensconced in a booth, they were soon sitting over steaming cups of coffee. Between mouthfuls of bread dipped in honey, Thomas couldn't stop himself talking about Sir Astley's lecture the previous evening.

Wiltshire shook his head. "And where did you get to afterwards?"

"Nowhere. Just stayed behind to ask some questions."

"You really can't get enough, can you?"

Thomas thought for a moment then smiled. "You're right, don't think I can." He paused. "Thing is, if I'm to be selected for a dresser-ship, I've got to get noticed, to stand out."

"Well, I hope you do. Can't imagine there's anyone keener."

"Anyway, you must admit, Sir Astley's much more interesting than the others."

"I'll grant you that. Ten times better than Curry."

"That's not difficult," said Thomas, starting into a second roll. "He seems to think all diseases are caused by dysfunction of the liver."

"And so everyone gets prescribed calomel."

Thomas finished chewing. "Ah, be fair. Sometimes its calomel and opium!"

"True," said Wiltshire, chuckling.

Thomas finished eating and pushed his plate away.

"You know the other thing about Sir Astley?"

"I can see you're going to tell me."

"He's prepared to say that sometimes it's best to do nothing, best not to operate, if you're not sure. He's so unlike the others."

All around them, the booths had filled up with men on their way to their offices.

"Wonder if we'll ever have the money to dress like them?" mused Wiltshire.

Thomas glanced around. "Would you like to?"

"Of course. Wouldn't you?"

"I suppose so, though not if it meant compromising my views."

Wiltshire shook his head. "You really are an awkward puritan, you know."

Thomas ignored him and went and got the newspaper left lying on a nearby table. As he scanned the pages, Wiltshire interrupted him.

"Never seen you miss a lecture before."

Thomas put the paper down. "I know, but chemistry last week was awful. Yet again, it wasn't Marcet. Sent his assistant who, poor man, stumbled through it, just reading Marcet's notes. Not sure how much he understood."

Wiltshire guffawed. "Wakley, you're incorrigible."

"But we've paid to hear these great men and then they don't turn up."

As the young serving maid was handing them two more cups of coffee, Wiltshire joked with her, making her blush.

"Were you flirting with her?" asked Thomas, after she'd gone.

"Of course," said Wiltshire. "Pretty little thing, don't you think?"

Thomas shook his head and sighed.

"What?" said Wiltshire. "Too proud for a little dalliance?"

"It doesn't matter," said Thomas. "Forget it. Do what you like."

"You're quite a prude, aren't you, Wakley? You know, one Saturday I'm taking you out on the town. You might not drink much, but that doesn't stop you enjoying other pleasures."

*

"Those seascapes," said Thomas, "were so realistic. I could almost feel the spray."

"And what about the *March of the Guards*?" asked Wiltshire. "Hogarth. What an artist."

It was Sunday afternoon, and they were in one of the back bars at *The White Hart* enjoying roast venison after their visit to the Foundling Hospital.

"And you say the artists donated them?" asked Thomas.

"They did. The hospital was cunning. They knew paintings would attract the well-to-do. Once in the door they could show them the little orphans and ask for donations."

"Makes you wonder why others haven't thought of doing that."

"Ah. Those that have great ideas shall be rewarded," chortled Wiltshire.

Thomas stared into the distance. "You're right. But it's not just about having an idea. You've got to be bold and brave and follow it."

"True. Same in art. Look at Turner."

"Turner?"

"Our most radical artist. He's like the Sir Astley of painters."

"What?"

He wasn't sure whether Wiltshire meant it or was teasing him.

"Next May," said Wiltshire, "I'm taking you to the biggest exhibition of the year. You're in for a treat."

They were distracted by the sound of raised voices in the outer bar, and a moment later five men, fellow pupils, came in and settled round a nearby table. They were all talking and no-one was listening. Apart from one, who sat slightly apart and seemed to be in his own world. Thomas had noticed him at lectures because he was so different, almost childlike. He couldn't have been more than five feet, and he dressed in a way no-one else did. His white shirt dwarfed him, billowing about his small frame. Despite being so small, Thomas was fascinated by the extraordinary presence he had. When he spoke, the others stopped talking and listened, treating him with reverence.

Thomas leant forward and beckoned Wiltshire closer. "Who is he?" he whispered.

"Keats," said Wiltshire.

"How do you know?"

"Wakley, if you spent less time studying and more time enjoying yourself, you'd know. He's often in here or round at *The George*. Gets into more brawls than anyone."

"What! Looking at him, I can't believe that. He's so slight."

Thomas sat back, trying to ignore the group, but couldn't resist surreptitiously glancing over every so often. Unlike his friends, Keats was drinking claret.

"So, this Saturday," said Wiltshire, "I'm taking you over the river to a tavern in East Cheap."

"Saturday? No good. It's Phys Soc."

"You could miss it for once."

"Sorry, not even for you. Especially this week. It's Lawrence on vitalism."

"Wakley, do you never stop? Life's for enjoying yourself."

"I enjoy Phys Soc! You might, too. Come as my guest. Last week some doctor really took on Hodgkin when he was talking about how to treat tumours. Got quite heated."

"All right. Here's a deal. I'll come with you, but after we go to East Cheap."

Thomas sighed. "Just this once."

*

On Saturday evening, it was snowing as they made their way past the statue of Thomas Guy and through the colonnaded passage into the inner courtyard of the hospital. Thomas had learnt to slacken his pace when walking with Wiltshire, aware how quickly his friend could get out of breath trying to keep up with him.

"Can't believe I've let you bring me to another boring lecture," said Wiltshire, "and in this weather."

"Just you wait and see. Come on."

The room was already half full, and by six o'clock there was standing room only. At the front Thomas spied the Society president, Sir Astley.

"There's even more here than usual," said Thomas.

An elderly man with a large grey beard approached the lectern, tapping it repeatedly to get attention.

"Gentlemen, if you please."

The audience gradually quietened.

"Tonight's subject is controversial," said the chairman. "You may find the views of our speaker difficult to accept, but I ask that you listen patiently. There will be time to challenge and discuss what he has to say at the end."

Thomas had never heard such a request before.

"Told you it was different from our lectures," he whispered to Wiltshire.

"Mr William Lawrence, Fellow of the Royal Society and Professor of Anatomy at the College of Surgeons," announced the chairman.

There was polite applause as a tall, round-faced man in a maroon velvet jacket and waistcoat rose and approached the lectern. He brushed his tousled brown hair off his forehead and smiled. Over the following half hour, he criticised the established medical view, shared by the church, that life was due to vital spirit. He ridiculed the notion that living things were pervaded and animated by this vital spirit.

"Life can be explained through science, through physiology and anatomy. Our thoughts and mental processes," he claimed, "arise from our brain function, not from some supposed mystical spirit."

The doctors and pupils in the audience mostly stayed quiet, though occasionally people could be heard talking to their neighbours. Thomas saw heads shaking and some men clearly getting angry.

"We must set aside our moral and theological convictions and not let them obstruct scientific advances."

With that, Lawrence bowed slightly and sat down. Immediately hands shot up trying to attract the chairman's attention. Someone sitting near the front was the first selected.

"What you've said contradicts scripture, sir. Are you saying what we read in Genesis is wrong?"

From the cheering and booing, it was clear how divided the audience was.

"We cannot take what is written in the Bible literally," said Lawrence, standing up again. "It was never meant to be read that way."

This just inflamed his opponents. Some leapt to their feet accusing him of blasphemy and demanding he apologise. Thomas loved the way Lawrence ignored them, maintaining a dignified serenity, politely addressing each criticism and concern, and avoiding personal insults.

As the debate continued, with Lawrence citing scientific observations to support his view, those opposed just dug in deeper, resorting to denouncing the idea rather than offering counter arguments.

Thomas's delight at seeing Sir Astley rising to speak quickly turned to disappointment.

"Gentlemen. I have no religious objection to Mr Lawrence, but given that the father of surgery, Hunter, believed in vitalism, I cannot countenance its rejection."

Thomas couldn't believe what he was hearing. How could the great advocate of scientific surgery take such a stance?

By the time the chairman called the proceedings to a close at eight o'clock, the two camps seemed even further apart.

"So? What did you think?" asked Thomas, as he and Wiltshire left.

"It was splendid. If all our lectures were like that, I'd never miss any."

"It's not always that lively," said Thomas. "Lawrence is a brave man. Can't imagine he's got many friends in the College of Surgeons."

"Or in the church," added Wiltshire.

Outside, it was no longer snowing though the wind had got up, so flurries of snow swirled around the courtyard. Thomas tied his scarf tightly round his neck and turned up his collar.

"Right," said Wiltshire. "Let's see if I can match that with my half of the evening. Come on."

*

Next morning, when Thomas got back to their lodgings from attending the service in the hospital chapel, he found Wiltshire sitting, wrapped in a blanket, in front of the fire.

"What a morning," said Thomas. "The sun on the snow is breathtaking."

Wiltshire peered up at him. "How can you be so bright? Did God raise your spirits?"

"For one thing, I didn't drink so much that I had to be helped home."

"Oh, yes. Sorry about that." Wiltshire smiled. "That was some evening. Debunking of vitalism and then the pleasure of a lady-bird."

Thomas took off his coat and warmed his hands in front of the fire.

"Which was best?" asked Wiltshire. "Come on now, don't pretend you didn't enjoy yourself."

Thomas sat down and stared at the flames, recalling their adventure. "All right. But I'm not making a habit of it. Apart from anything, I can't afford it."

Wiltshire was chuckling. "You know, Wakley, you're not as strait-laced as you make out. Bit of a dark horse, I reckon."

Thomas ignored him and announced he was off out again.

"Going to see someone I knew at school." He pulled a letter out of his pocket. "Says he lives above a piano shop of all places."

A bitterly cold wind was blowing as he crossed London Bridge. Large lumps of ice in the river buffeted against the arches, trying to get through. At least the freezing temperature had dampened down the smell. Going up Fish Street Hill, he had to reach out and steady himself against the buildings as the pavement was treacherous in places. At Lombard Street, he headed west to Cheapside.

Being Sunday, Clementi's piano shop was closed. Thomas pulled the bell and soon saw a tall, stooping figure making his way through the shop. On seeing Thomas, he beamed with delight.

"Thomas. Come in, come in."

"Freddy, so good to see you."

They shook hands and Freddy led him past the pianos to a door at the back. Two flights up, they came to a small sitting room.

"Let me take your coat. Sit yourself down," said Freddy, "and tell me, what are you doing in London?"

"I'm living here. A pupil at Borough hospitals." Thomas couldn't stop staring at his boyhood friend. "You've changed, hardly recognised you."

"It's just the clothes. Anyway, so have you, though I can see you've still got your mane of hair and kept your Devon accent."

Thomas leant forward, rubbing his hands together in front of the fire.

"Still thin as a rake," said Thomas. "Are they not feeding you?"

Freddy laughed as he brought a tray of tea over and sat down in the other armchair.

"It's so good to see you," said Thomas. "Who'd have thought it, all those years ago when we were in Wiveliscombe, that we'd both end up here?"

"I know. I still can't believe my luck."

"So, what happened?"

"It was all because of my uncles, William and Frederick. They'd left Wivey before your time They took me on as their apprentice. I must have pleased them because I'm still here."

"Who'd have thought you'd end up selling pianos?"

"I know. Only piano I'd ever heard was Mr Haskell thumping out hymns at school."

"Do you play?"

"First thing I had to do, learn to play. You're no use selling pianos if you can't demonstrate them." He put down his cup. "But what about you? When I last saw you, you were off to Taunton, to an apothecary."

Thomas told him about his time with Incledon, about how his sister, Anne, had rescued him, not for the first time, and then his time at Beaminster and Henley.

"So, soon it will be Doctor Wakley," said Freddy. "Wonderful."

"Of course, your Papa is partly to blame," said Thomas. "I loved those two years I boarded with your family. Became so interested in what your father did."

Freddy nodded. "I remember. Couldn't keep you out of his workshop."

"He'd tell me all about the drugs he was compounding and what they did." Thomas paused. "Never occurred to me, but did you mind me spending all that time with him?"

Freddy laughed. "Goodness, no. Medicines didn't interest me."

"Me neither, now."

Freddy stopped as he was getting up to put more coal on the fire.

"What do you mean? I thought you were set on being a doctor?"

"Oh, I am, but a surgeon. From the first time I saw an operation, that's all I've ever wanted to do. Happy to leave drugs to general practitioners and physicians. It's the scalpel for me!"

While Freddy stoked up the fire, Thomas went over to the small window. Down below, an elderly man was struggling to pick his way past piles of rubbish in a cramped courtyard to get to an outdoor privy. Even here in Cheapside, away from the river, he imagined the miasma must take its toll.

"As I remember," said Freddy, as they both sat back down, "when you came to live with us you were just back from being at sea."

"Do you still play chess?" asked Thomas, changing the subject.

"When I get the chance. No-one here plays. It's one of the few ways my uncles aren't perfect." He shook his head. "They can't see the point of games."

"Then we must play. One of my few possessions is a chess set."

"You're on. I'm a bit rusty, but it will soon come back."

"So, what do you do when you're not selling pianos?"

"Listen to them. Signor Clementi gets lots of invitations to concerts from people who want to impress him, but often he can't attend or doesn't want to go. Apart from the shop, he composes. In fact, these days that's mostly what he does. That's why he made my uncles his partners. Lets them run the business."

"How wonderful, going to concerts. In Henley, my master's daughter played the piano. I got so used to hearing it every day, I've missed it since being here."

"Then you must come with me to some concerts. And not just pianos but full orchestras."

"I've never heard an orchestra. Nearest was an army band."

"Bit different from that," laughed Freddy.

He refilled their cups. Through the window, Thomas could see that it had started snowing again.

"I must head back soon before it gets too deep."

"Before you go, there's something that's always puzzled me," said Freddy. "I never understood why your father sent you to school in Wivey, so far from your farm."

"They wouldn't have me back at Honiton."

"What? Why not?"

"Ha. Recently found out from my sister. Reverend Lewis found me difficult, always questioning him, not doing what I was told."

Freddy grinned. "I can believe it. I remember Mr Clarke getting irritated by you. 'A disruptive influence', that's what he called you."

"Not proud of it, looking back."

"Well, I hope you've not stopped being disruptive. World needs people like you. I'm no use. Not in my nature."

Thomas smiled. "Well, right now I just want to study and pass my exam."

❊

It was the quietest Christmas he'd ever spent. On Christmas Eve, Wiltshire went home to spend a few days with his parents in Lambeth. In the hospitals, no senior doctors appeared the whole week. As he was one of the few pupils around, Thomas took advantage of it and spent lots of time examining patients on the wards. Twice he went to services in the hospital chapel, and he joined a crowd singing carols in one of the courtyards.

On Christmas Day, he pictured his family round the dining table at Land Farm, his father carving a huge goose that one of his brothers would have butchered in the long barn. They'd be discussing the Boxing Day hunt and which horses they'd ride. The hunt was the only part of Christmas he really missed. He wondered when he'd ever get the chance to ride to hounds again.

1816

"It's not fair. It's always the same. Deceit and favouritism," shouted Thomas, storming into their lodgings.

As he tore off his coat and scarf, he could see how startled Wiltshire was.

"What's happened?" asked Wiltshire, putting aside his sketch pad.

"Cline operated on a hernia tonight, and we weren't told."

Thomas slumped down into an armchair.

"I know what they're up to," he said. "Last week I was lucky to overhear that there was to be an operation so went along. Discovered only the pupils apprenticed to the hospital's surgeons were there."

"That's terrible," said Wiltshire. "We've all paid the fees."

"Waste so much time hanging around the operating theatres at noon in case a capital operation is done."

"You could pay a dresser to let you into the secret."

"I'm damned if I'm going to do that," thundered Thomas. "It's bad enough having to bribe the dead room porters to find out when *post mortems* are taking place."

"Come on," said Wiltshire standing up. "A drink at *The Grapes*."

The pub was packed with pupils, but they found a couple of stools at the end of a long table, and Thomas went to get drinks.

"Managed not to spill too much," he said, having had to push his way back through the crowd.

The sound of a piano and raucous singing filtered through from the other bar. Although they were so different, Thomas had warmed to Wiltshire. He liked his honesty and plain-speaking.

Wiltshire glanced up from filling his pipe and gestured with it. "You should try one. Might help calm you down."

"I don't want to be calm," said Thomas. "We're being cheated. Not told about operations and *post mortems*. Lecturers sending their assistants." He took a swig of beer and slammed his tankard back down on the table. "Why can't they all be like Sir Astley? Not only turns up but stays afterwards to answer questions."

Wiltshire leant forward and put his hand on Thomas's arm. "You know I agree."

"And the ward rounds," continued Thomas. "You were there on Wednesday. Forster kept us waiting, in the rain, for best part of an hour. Wasn't even worth waiting for. He sped round, barely saying anything. Could only hear if you were at the front."

"They know we'll put up with anything to get our attendance certificates."

"So why doesn't someone do something about it? There are scores of us."

"But do what?" said Wiltshire, sitting forward, cupping his tankard in his hands.

They sat in silence for a while.

"Been meaning to ask," said Wiltshire. "Where did you get to on Friday evening?"

Thomas smiled. "It's no secret. The big fight in Lewisham."

"What? Bare-knuckle? Didn't know you liked that."

"Local man, Jeffries, took on this Irishman, Mahoney. Big brute, covered in seafaring tattoos. They went twenty-three rounds. Must have been a thousand there."

"Well, let me know next time."

"All right. What about cockfighting? Interested? Discovered a place in Shad Thames that has some of the biggest birds you'll ever hope to see. Gets quite bloody, so may not be for you."

"Wakley. Just because I didn't grow up in the backwoods doesn't mean I haven't the stomach for a good fight."

Thomas clapped him on the shoulder. "Then next time, we'll go."

*

Even though the weather was still bitterly cold, Thomas was relieved to get outside after spending several hours dissecting. Although he'd got used to the smell of the preservative, fresh air was a welcome relief. He took some deep breaths before heading down Borough High Street to a pub where there was a sparring room out the back. It was never crowded in the daytime. He'd exercise a while on the bars and lift some weights before finding someone to spar with.

Back at their lodgings, Wiltshire was sitting with a sketch pad on his lap. As Thomas unwound his scarf, he saw it was a drawing of their sitting room.

Wiltshire sniffed. "Been dissecting again, haven't you?"

"Can you smell it?"

Wiltshire laughed. "Always can. So, what was it today?"

"The forearm. Didn't make much progress, as Walton and Stotterforth turned up late. Then when I complained they weren't pulling their weight, they stormed off."

Wiltshire put down his charcoal and stared at him. "You're a tough taskmaster, Wakley."

"What do you mean? If they're serious about learning anatomy, they should arrive on time and help."

"They're fellow pupils. You can't go ordering them about."

Thomas sat silently, furious that Wiltshire was admonishing him.

"I'm sorry," said Wiltshire, after a while. "It's just, you'll get on much better if you tolerate others more. Least, that's what I think."

Wiltshire picked up a stick of charcoal. "Have you heard about Keats?"

Thomas shook his head.

"Lucas has appointed him a dresser."

"What! How can he? He started with us in October. He's only done six months."

"It's odder than that. Apparently, he was promised it at the end of October, after three weeks."

"That makes no sense. Why would Lucas do that?"

"Word is that it was Sir Astley's doing. Turns out Keats attended his lectures over the past two years before becoming a pupil. Seems like Sir Astley took a shine to him. God knows why. He's forever drunk and getting into brawls."

"So, when did he do his apprenticeship?"

"Even more mysterious. I asked around. Apparently he only did two years, with an apothecary-surgeon in Edmonton. It's said he walked away with an indenture saying he'd completed five."

Thomas said nothing, thinking of his own document from Incledon, carefully stored in his bedroom.

"Why was it terminated?"

"They had a big falling out. It's said Keats objected to being treated like a servant. Wasn't allowed to live in his master's house and felt humiliated when he was left standing in the street holding his master's horse, right outside his old school." Wiltshire smiled. "There's even a rumour he punched his master."

"What! But that doesn't explain why Sir Astley favours him."

"Some are saying Sir Astley heard of his plight and took pity on him. Others that Sir Astley sees him as a fellow radical who needs supporting."

Thomas sat back, shaking his head. "Keats, a radical?"

"You know how he often looks detached, lost in his thoughts? Turns out he spends his time writing romantic poems."

"Poetry?" Thomas paused. "Have to say, the more I hear about Keats, the more intrigued I am."

"I just think he's odd," said Wiltshire, resuming his drawing. "Not sure I'd want him as my surgeon. Mind you, it's not all good news for him." He looked up, grinning. "He's got to work for that cack-handed butcher, Lucas."

"Yes, but if it meant getting a surgical dresser-ship, I'd take it," said Thomas.

*

April had come and gone, and there had been no sign of the sun. It was constantly dark and gloomy. Then, one morning in May, it snowed. There was disbelief and fear. Preachers appeared on the streets beseeching people to mend their ways, that this was God's judgment and the sun wouldn't appear until people renounced sin.

"Not what it says here," said Wiltshire, looking up from the newspaper.

They were sitting in a small coffee shop after that morning's *materia medica* lecture.

"Says it's all because of a volcano in the Dutch East Indies. They reckon the price of corn will soar if the harvest fails."

"As if it wasn't bad enough already with the Corn Law," said Thomas. "Heard there'd been riots up in Ely."

Everywhere the air was thick with acrid dust. Countless people hobbled into outpatients, struggling to breathe. There was little that could be done for them, as there was no escaping the foul air. Thomas feared the miasma would carry off many weak and old, impoverished people.

It didn't stop him visiting Freddy in Cheapside most Sundays. Their chess games were becoming more sophisticated as both of them spent time preparing, learning new moves. When they took a break from playing, they'd go downstairs to the shop where Freddy would play the pianos.

"Why are there so many different ones? Why not just decide which is best?" asked Thomas.

"Ah. People want different things. Listen carefully," said Freddy, getting up from playing one and repeating the same piece on another. "Hear the difference? This one has a much richer sound, stronger bass tones. That other one is lighter, more coquettish," he laughed.

Gradually Thomas started to discern these subtle differences. He was fascinated by the ease with which Freddy played. His long, slender fingers seemed to take on a life of their own, as if they themselves knew where to move. His own fingers were thick and muscular from bare-knuckle fighting.

"I haven't forgotten I promised you a concert," Freddy said. "Next month there's one at Hertford House. Signor Clementi is abroad and asked me to represent the firm."

"Really? Will it be all right for me to go?"

"Of course. There'll be over a hundred there. You'll need to dress up a bit. Nothing grand!"

"Just as well," said Thomas, "these are my only clothes."

"There'll be some Haydn, and the latest works by Beethoven and Schubert."

Thomas, who had heard of Beethoven but not the others, could see how excited Freddy was.

Later, as he made his way back over London Bridge, he marvelled at how his life had changed. Five years earlier he'd been fighting in the backyard of a pub in Taunton and now he was going to a concert in the Earl of Hertford's palatial home in Manchester Square and the Royal Academy exhibition.

*

Carriages queued along The Strand waiting to enter the central arched gateway of Somerset House. As Wiltshire led him in, Thomas stared at the finely dressed men and women being helped down from their carriages by flunkies in uniform.

"What a crowd," said Thomas.

"Of course," said Wiltshire, guiding him towards the door. "It's the biggest exhibition of the year."

Going up the steep semi-circular staircase took some time. Many of the older people needed to take a rest on each landing as they made their way to the third floor. There, the walls of the Great Hall were festooned with paintings, bunched up against each other. Not an inch of wall was visible. It was hard to make out the darker canvases, as the only light came from windows high up around the edge of the arched ceiling, and not helped by the lack of sunlight.

"Why do they hang paintings so high up?" asked Thomas. "You can't see them."

Wiltshire laughed quietly. "Artists are so desperate to exhibit here they'll accept anything. The more well-known you are, the lower down your work is hung."

They were forced to shuffle, squeezing past people who had stopped to greet those they knew. Wiltshire had to crane his neck and stand on tiptoe to see the paintings. It wasn't helped by the flamboyant hats many were wearing.

Thomas leant close to Wiltshire again and whispered, "All anyone seems interested in is looking around to see who else is here. Hardly looking at the paintings."

"That's society people for you."

"There are so many portraits," said Thomas. "They all start to look the same after a while."

"Not to the sitters who have paid a fortune to have them painted."

"Suppose so. And so many battle scenes."

"It's the first exhibition since Waterloo. Lots of generals want to ensure their exploits aren't forgotten. Times like this, artists are valued."

"And I thought I was the sceptical one," laughed Thomas.

"Come on," said Wiltshire, gripping his elbow. "Not all artists are so reverential."

They forced their way through and stood looking at a huge canvas of a Greek temple set in a sunlit, rural landscape.

"*The Temple of Jupiter Panellenius*," said Wiltshire. "Turner's latest. No boring soldiers for him but vibrant landscapes. A true romantic."

"What? Because of all the young maidens cavorting?" asked Thomas.

"Not just that," said Wiltshire, smiling. "Turner's always refused to paint in the old established manner. Look at that sky, the colour, the light. So uplifting. The way he sees the world is radically different. He's disrupted all the conventions. Said to paint outside in all weathers."

As they walked back to Borough, Thomas felt he was returning to a more familiar world. He found mixing with rich people unsettling. Standing beside them in the exhibition, he'd felt a barrier, of being an outsider. By the time they were crossing back over the river, with the sound of waterwheels steadily turning, he felt comfortable once more. For all that the streets were crowded and oppressive, and the air was fetid, Borough felt like home.

By June, the lecture courses ended, and the Physical Society meetings were over for the year. Thomas knew that the dresser-ships would soon be announced.

Still the sun hadn't appeared. People had given up hope, calling it the year without summer. Fears for the harvest were growing, and there were stories that riots had spread from rural areas to the city. Thomas wondered if there'd be unrest back in Devon, and how his father and brothers would behave. It would be tenant farmers and labourers who'd suffer. With Anne no longer living there, he couldn't imagine those worst affected getting much help from his father. Knowing him, it was more likely he'd see it as an opportunity to swallow up yet more land on the cheap.

*

The next day, as Thomas was passing St Thomas's gatehouse, the beadle stopped him.

"It's Mr Wakley, isn't it?"

Thomas nodded.

"Treasurer left this for you," said the beadle, handing him a letter.

What on earth would the hospital treasurer want with him? Had he done something wrong? Standing in the cloisters that ran round the inside of the quad, he broke the sealing wax. It was a summons to see him.

"Why would Chapman want to see you?" said Wiltshire that evening.

"No idea," said Thomas. "Sooner I see him, sooner I'll know."

He'd never been into the Counting House. He made his way to the first floor, where a clerk showed him into Chapman's room. The treasurer, an elderly man, was sitting behind a large oak desk, covered in piles of paper which he could only just see over.

"Ah, Wakley. Thank you for coming. Please, take a seat."

He put down his pen and peered at him over his spectacles.

"Probably wondering what this is about. As you know, the hospital depends on subscriptions from our governors. Some of them are very generous, others not so much. Of course, many of them get something in return. One of our benefactors is a Mr Joseph Goodchild. Runs a manufactory round in Tooley Street. Fenning Wharf. May have seen it."

Thomas shook his head and mumbled he hadn't.

"No matter. But you've probably seen some of his men. Forever coming with cuts and burns, what with working with glass and molten lead. I've been looking at the outpatient records. We're seeing more and more of them. Now, in confidence, I don't think Mr Goodchild's subscription of one hundred pounds a year begins to meet the demand he puts on the hospital. Some of these men need surgery and have to be kept in."

Chapman paused, took some snuff and blew his nose, while Thomas sat watching, still wondering why he was being told all this.

"I can see you're puzzled," he said, smiling. "Goodchild knows we want him to increase his subscription but has asked I send a couple of pupils, people who have helped treat his men. So, I want you to take along another pupil and go and ask him to double his subscription."

Overnight, Thomas had come up with all manner of explanations for having to see Chapman, but this wasn't one of them.

"Do you have any questions?"

"Is there any reason why you're asking me rather than other pupils?"

Chapman smiled. "I can't tell you who advised me, but he said you were inquisitive and enterprising."

Thomas felt his heart racing. That could only have been Sir Astley. No-one else could have noticed him. He'd hardly spoken to any other senior doctor. He quickly concentrated again as Chapman was giving him more instructions.

"Soon as possible. I'll write to Goodchild, explain you'll be coming, and ask which day suits him."

A visit to Tooley Street wouldn't take up much time, thought Thomas, and he could ask Wiltshire to accompany him. Might be interesting.

"It'll need to be at a weekend," said Chapman. "And we'll pay for the stagecoach."

"Stagecoach? I thought he lived in Tooley Street."

"Ah, didn't I say? Being summer, not that we've seen the sun, he'll be at his residence in Mill Hill at weekends."

Chapter 5

1816

"Ah! Smell that air." Thomas had to shout to be heard over the rattling wheels and horses' hooves. "Can breathe again."

Wiltshire was concentrating on clinging to his seat as the mail coach swayed from side to side. Pale and grey, he grimaced. "Sorry, not used to it."

Having reached the top of Haverstock Hill, after the long climb out of London, the coach now sped up as they headed across Hampstead Heath. Thomas was so relieved to be out of London. Willow warblers and chiff chaffs were dipping in and out of the yellow gorse, and a woodcock suddenly took off, alarmed by the noise of the coach, bringing back memories of days in Devon spent shooting game. *Could have had that*, he thought, then wondered if, after so long, he was still a good shot.

An hour later, they drew into the stable yard at *The White Bear* in Hendon.

"Thank God that's over," said Wiltshire, as Thomas helped him clamber down.

Wiltshire made a great show of brushing himself down. "Chapman could at least have paid for seats inside."

"Go and sit on that bench. I'll get you a drink."

By the time he returned clutching a tankard, the colour had returned to Wiltshire's cheeks. As Wiltshire drained his drink, Thomas stared up at the escarpment behind the pub.

"It's like a cliff."

Wiltshire was still trying to brush dust out of his curly hair. "What on earth is Goodchild doing here?"

"It's what rich merchants do. Build themselves a house up there, on the ridge. Somewhere to escape to in summer."

"But they've got businesses to run."

"Oh, they don't stay here," Thomas said, taking a seat beside Wiltshire. "It's for their wives and children. Protect them from the filth and smells of summer in the city. The men only come on Saturdays."

Wiltshire chuckled. "Ah! Very convenient. Left to their own devices all week."

"Come on," said Thomas. "We need to find a carriage."

The lane wound back and forth through the trees, allowing only glimpses of the valley they had left behind. But when they reached the top, the view was spectacular.

"Well, you've got to agree, this makes it all worthwhile," said Thomas.

"Suppose so," said Wiltshire. "Anything's better than that mail coach."

As they went along the ridge, they passed a string of houses. While some were small weather-boarded residences, others were large stone and stuccoed mansions set in extensive grounds, with grand ornamental gateways.

"Some of these are grander than Kensington," marvelled Wiltshire.

They passed a large pond into which a couple of herdsmen were driving cattle.

"Drovers," shouted their driver over his shoulder. "Get 'em looking good before 'eading to Smithfield to sell 'em."

They stopped outside a fine two-storey house, set back from the road. "Merton 'ouse, gentlemen. Be back for you at three."

A York stone path led up to the front door. With the lack of sun that summer, the rose growing up the side of the doorway had produced only a few forlorn half-open blooms.

Wiltshire pulled the bell and soon a maid appeared.

"Mr Wiltshire and Mr Wakley to see Mr Goodchild," said Thomas.

She stood back, holding open the door. The grandfather clock in the hallway started chiming twelve as she ushered them into one of the front rooms.

"Please, sir, the master said you were to wait in here."

The walls were lined with books, and a small piano stood in one corner.

"I'll tell him you're here," she said, closing the door as she left.

"This is all right then," whispered Wiltshire. "This stuff doesn't come cheap."

There were oriental rugs on the floor and a fine brass fire guard in front of the white marble fireplace.

"Did you see how she curtsied to us?" Wiltshire chuckled.

Thomas didn't want Goodchild to find them huddled together so went over to the bookshelves. His eyes immediately alighted on the Jane Austen novel he'd read. As he was looking along the shelf, the door opened and a stout man with rugged features, somewhat shorter than Thomas, strode in. His dark, hard-wearing jacket and breeches seemed out of place amidst the gentility of the furnishings.

"Goodchild," he announced, nodding to each of them in turn before gesturing to them to take a seat. Light from the window highlighted a long scar on his left cheek.

"Nothing to do with me, those books," said Goodchild, waving his arm at the shelves. "Can't stop my daughters buying them."

Thomas smiled but Goodchild remained stony-faced. He could see getting anything out of him was going to be difficult and wondered if that was why the hospital treasurer had acquiesced to Goodchild's request and passed the responsibility to them.

"Right, gentlemen. Gather Chapman thinks I should pay the hospital more. Convince me."

From the look of panic on Wiltshire's face, Thomas knew he'd have to take on the challenge.

He cleared his throat. "Mr Chapman and the surgeons wanted you to know how grateful they are for your support."

"Young man. Save me the flannel. Just answer my question."

Thomas narrowed his eyes. Goodchild stared back, expressionless, waiting.

"We're seeing a lot of men from your works. Some are so seriously injured they need surgery and have to spend time on the wards." Goodchild's expression still didn't change. "You can't go on expecting the hospital to provide all this care without paying more."

"What about all the waste? People lying around for weeks, then dying. Chapman should make better use of what we give him."

Thomas, determined not to be the one who looked away, could feel his fists clenching. Damn it, who did Goodchild think he was? Just because he was rich, Thomas wouldn't let him get the better of him, even if it meant their journey had been in vain.

"Those who seek our help have nowhere else to turn, Mr Goodchild. They can't afford to pay the way you can."

"Well, maybe if they spent less on drink, they could."

Thomas was about to hit back when he heard Wiltshire, quietly, trying to join in. "It's true, many do drink a lot..."

"That's irrelevant," snapped Thomas, glancing at his friend. He was mortified to see Wiltshire visibly shrink back into his chair. He turned back to Goodchild. A slight smile seemed to fleetingly appear on the man's face.

"Sir, you've got to understand, those seeking help are hardworking, like your own men. An occasional drink is one of their pleasures. You've seen the state of the alleys and courtyards where they live."

Goodchild said nothing, slowly standing up and walking over to the mantelpiece, where he picked up a pipe, filled it, and lit it. He stood peering down at Thomas through clouds of smoke.

"I like a man who doesn't mince his words." As he sat down, Thomas could see Goodchild had spotted his clenched fists.

"Just testing you. It's my way. Hospital's lucky to have you."

Thomas wasn't sure if he meant it or if it was a ploy to disarm him.

"I like to think I'm a fair man. Got to look after your men if you want to succeed. Something my father taught me." He pointed with his pipe at a portrait hanging to the right of the fireplace.

"So important," said Wiltshire, sounding mighty relieved.

"Right. I've heard enough. Time for lunch. Hope you've got a good appetite. Venison, I believe. And no more talk of money. Not allowed in front of the ladies. Come on."

*

Goodchild led them through to the dining room where a large table was laid for six. Through the open French doors, the smell of freshly cut grass drifted in.

"Ah, there you are, my dear."

Thomas turned to see a woman, who he took to be Mrs Goodchild, entering followed by two young women.

"Let me introduce our guests," said Goodchild. "Mr Wakley and Mr Wiltshire."

Mrs Goodchild smiled. "You're most welcome." She turned to the two younger women. "My daughters, Miss Sarah and Miss Elizabeth."

Thomas bowed his head slightly and smiled. While Miss Sarah returned his smile, her sister barely looked at him.

"Sit yourselves down," said Goodchild, taking the chair at the head of the table.

Thomas waited till the women were seated, unsure where he and Wiltshire should sit.

"We're God-fearing folk but don't bother with grace," said Goodchild. "Hope it doesn't offend you?"

Goodchild was studying him again, making Thomas feel obliged to respond. He wondered if it was another test.

"Not me," he said, unable to gauge from Goodchild's face whether that was the right answer. To his relief, Mrs Goodchild smiled.

The maid appeared carrying a large plate of meat, which she placed in the centre of the table alongside two covered serving dishes.

"Forgetting myself," said Goodchild. "Would you take a drink, gentlemen? We have wine," he said, pointing at a carafe on the sideboard.

"Not for me, thank you," said Thomas.

"Don't drink?" asked Goodchild.

"Only occasionally."

"Quite right. No good ever came of it. Seen good men throw their lives away. No use in a factory. Hazard to themselves and others."

Thomas imagined Wiltshire would have gladly enjoyed some fine wine but couldn't possibly accept now. Mrs Goodchild finished serving herself and passed the spoons to one of her daughters.

"So, you're going to be doctors?" she asked.

Wiltshire shifted in his chair, raising his napkin to dab his mouth.

"Yes," said Thomas. "I want to be a surgeon." Her smile encouraged him to carry on. "Always wanted to, ever since I first helped at an operation."

Glancing round the table he saw the two daughters were staring at him. "I'm sorry, perhaps I shouldn't talk of such things at the table."

"Goodness, no," said Goodchild. "Don't worry about them. Tough as nails, aren't you?"

Thomas could see his daughters were used to their father's forthright manner.

"Surgeon. Good living to be had, I shouldn't wonder," continued Goodchild, "given how much they charge us. Only got to look at their fancy carriages to see how well they do for themselves."

"But, my dear, think of the lives they save," interposed Mrs Goodchild. "They deserve it."

Her husband grunted. "Maybe. Certainly better than all those quacks with their concoctions."

Thomas was struck by how like his own father Goodchild was. A man who knew his own mind and wouldn't easily be swayed in his convictions. Although he said little, Thomas could tell he was listening carefully as his wife enquired about where he and Wiltshire had grown up and their families.

Several times, when Thomas glanced down the table, he caught Miss Elizabeth looking at him. Sitting bolt upright, she displayed a distinct elegance that seemed more appropriate for a grander setting. Even the way she served herself and handled her silverware was precise. He suspected she had spent time learning how to deport herself. On one occasion, Thomas had smiled at her as he was talking about his time in Beaminster, but her lack of response inhibited him from doing so again.

"There may be no sun," announced Goodchild at the end of the meal, "but for once it's not raining and warm enough to take tea on the terrace."

This was clearly taken as an instruction, not a suggestion, by his family.

*

Mrs Goodchild led them outside, where some white metal chairs were arranged around a table. Thomas walked over to the edge of the terrace. Beyond the lawn, gently rolling hills, heavily forested, stretched to the horizon. Here and there, a church tower could be seen poking up through the trees.

"Lost in thought, Mr Wakley?"

He turned, discomposed for a moment at seeing Elizabeth standing nearby. "Just imagining there must be good hunting to be had out there."

"Do you hunt?"

"Little else to do where I grew up," said Thomas. "Nothing quite like the thrill of a chase, outwitting a deer."

She looked at him but said nothing as she walked past, out onto the grass. He followed, sensing she wanted to move away from the others. Slender and only a couple of inches shorter than him, her dark brown eyes were matched by the cascade of brown ringlets that framed her face. He was struck by her questioning countenance.

"Past years this was a blaze of colour," she said, standing in front of a long border.

"Do you garden?"

For the first time, she smiled. "It's one of the joys of spending the summer here."

She knelt down to look closely at a plant. "Now look at it. So much rain and no sunshine." She looked up at him. "I know I shouldn't complain when the weather's causing hardship for so many, but for me, this garden is all that matters. One of the few things I thought I had control over, but it seems not."

Behind them, Thomas could hear Wiltshire holding forth.

"It's so quiet here after London," said Thomas.

She stood up, brushing a ringlet off her face. "That's the other reason I love being here."

"So, how do you spend your days?"

"Reading, mostly."

"I saw you have a piano. Do you play?"

"No. Ann, our other sister, is the pianist. Do you like music?"

"I think so."

She laughed. "You think so? Don't you know?"

"Sorry. It's just, I've not heard much." He paused. "I'm going to an orchestra concert soon."

"Really? And where's that?"

"Hertford House."

Elizabeth's mouth opened a fraction as she leant her head slightly to one side, scrutinising him more closely.

"Hertford House? I believe it's more of a palace than a house."

"I don't know. A friend's taking me."

They fell silent, Thomas desperately trying to think of something to say.

"May I ask how you like to spend your time in London?" he asked.

"The theatre. Nothing I like more. The magic and the make-believe."

He was relieved to hear Mrs Goodchild summoning them for tea.

Thomas remained standing on the lawn a moment, watching Elizabeth saunter slowly back to the table. Wiltshire was finishing an account of their visit to the Royal Academy exhibition which, from his audience's laughter, he'd managed to extract much humour.

Thomas had just joined them when Goodchild appeared and handed him an envelope.

"Letter for Chapman. He should be pleased with the two of you."

On the coach going back, Thomas's wish to sit quietly, thinking about Elizabeth, was constantly interrupted by Wiltshire regaling him with how he had amused Mrs Goodchild and Sarah. He beamed with delight and, unlike that morning, seemingly not bothered by the discomfort of the journey.

"You know what, Wakley," he shouted to make himself heard, "I think Miss Sarah took a bit of a shine to me."

*

Next day, Thomas had to force himself to get up for the morning's midwifery lecture. The theatre seemed drab and dull after the excitement of their adventure. Later, sitting in a coffee shop, Wiltshire was as bumptious as he had been on the journey home.

"Can't quite believe that was all for real. Keep thinking it was a dream, didn't really happen."

Thomas pulled Goodchild's letter from his inside pocket. "There's the proof. Must take it to Chapman."

Wiltshire leant forward. "Come on then. What did you think of Miss Elizabeth?"

"Oh, she was charming."

"Just charming? Is that it? Come on, I could see you were taken by her."

Thomas drained his cup and sat staring at the coffee grounds left behind. "All right, she did intrigue me."

"I knew it," chortled Wiltshire.

"At first, she was quite scary. Didn't smile and seemed rather critical and distant. But once we'd been talking a while, she changed. She seemed really interested I was going to a concert."

Wiltshire was smirking. "And you wonder why? Come on, of course she was. You're going to the grandest house in London. That will have thrown her. She'll be perplexed. How does a medical pupil get to mix with high society?"

"It's not like that. It's just a concert."

Wiltshire laughed. "I know that but she'll be wondering if there's more to you than meets the eye." He leant back, raising his left hand, his thumb and index finger touching. "Perfect."

"Perfect? What do you mean?"

"Wakley. Trust me. Even as we speak, I'd wager she's grappling to make sense of this pupil who cavorts with the rich." He laughed. "That's when he's not with his friend at the Royal Academy!"

Thomas couldn't stop himself smiling. "Right, enough of this. Let's see if there's an operation today."

As they entered the inner quad in Guy's, they spotted Lucas's new dresser hurrying across the square, head bent against the rain.

"Keats," Wiltshire shouted.

Keats stopped, peering in their direction to see who was hailing him. They hurried over, worried he'd head off when he saw it was just them.

"Any operations today?" asked Thomas.

Keats looked from one to the other, his brow furrowed. Eventually he confided, "Lucas is amputating a leg at noon." As he turned to go, he added, "If you can stomach it."

Thomas and Wiltshire stared at one another.

"No great loyalty to his master," said Wiltshire.

"Admirable honesty, I'd say."

"Probably still resentful he was saddled with working for Lucas."

※

Despite the difficulty finding out when operations were taking place, a few dozen pupils had learned of this one and were already in the theatre. The patient was being helped onto the table while Lucas's assistant was laying out the instruments. The surgery man came in with a bucket of sawdust which he scattered on the floor around the table.

Just after noon, Billy Lucas shuffled in awkwardly and was handed one of the blood-stained gowns hanging on the wall at the back of the theatre. He barely looked up at his audience as he mumbled, "An amputation this morning, gentlemen. Left leg. Below the knee."

As he stood over the patient, an assistant handed him a scalpel.

"Surely he's on the wrong side?" Thomas whispered to Wiltshire.

"What do you mean?"

"For the left leg he needs to stand on the other side of the table."

By now, from the muttering in front them, the dressers had also spotted Lucas's mistake. Whether Lucas himself had realised or his assistant had been brave enough to speak up, the surgeon stood back and changed sides. The patient, barely conscious – having been plied with large amounts of brandy and opium – remained unaware of what was happening.

As if to cover his initial mistake, Lucas immediately started incising the skin. With his view now partly obscured, Thomas had to lean in front of Wiltshire to get a clearer sight.

Thomas straightened up, shaking his head. "Those cuts. It's the wrong way round."

By now Lucas was sawing through the bones. There were muffled cries from the patient, who pulled against the straps restraining his torso and arms. Blood dripped onto the sawdust, some landing on Lucas's shoes. With a mix of relief and glee, Lucas straightened up and his assistant placed the amputated leg in a bucket. As the surgeon stood back, sweating profusely, Thomas at last got a clear view of the stump.

"Oh God," said Thomas, louder than he had intended. Some pupils standing nearby looked at him. He lowered his voice. "The skin flap. He's left it on the amputated limb. There's nothing to cover the stump."

The assistant and dresser were doing their best to stem the bleeding. Lucas, having realised the dreadful mistake he'd made, looked lost, unsure of what to do. Sir Astley, who'd been sitting watching, stood up and came over to take a closer look. Thomas could see him talking quietly to Lucas but, try as he might, he couldn't hear what was said.

"What can he do?" asked Wiltshire.

"Only one thing. He'll have to amputate again, higher up, and get it right this time."

"You mean, above the knee?"

"Nothing else for it."

Wiltshire was shaking his head. "How could he have done that?"

Thomas leant back against the railing behind them. "It was when he changed sides. He didn't alter the position of the leg."

"So, he did the operation upside down?"

"In effect, yes."

Lucas started amputating above the knee. Sir Astley, who had taken off his frock coat and donned a surgeon's gown, stood alongside, offering advice. Only a few pupils remained, most no longer able to watch what had turned into a fiasco. Lucas kept hesitating, Sir Astley having to cajole him to keep going.

When they'd finished, the few remaining pupils left the theatre in silence. As soon as they got outside, Wiltshire could no longer contain his distress.

"That was awful, Wakley. Can see why he's called the hospital butcher."

Thomas stood staring into space. "How does the hospital allow him to operate?"

"They say he only operates if Cooper or Cline are here," said Wiltshire.

"That poor man. Two amputations, and higher than it needed to be."

"What will Lucas tell him?"

"If he survives, some nonsense about surgical necessity, disease more extensive than imagined. Nothing the man can do about it."

"Meanwhile Lucas will go on operating," mused Wiltshire.

"Who's going to stop him?" shouted Thomas.

"Shsh. People are staring. Calm down."

"It's not right. It shouldn't be allowed."

*

Thomas always looked forward to seeing Freddy. The peace and calm of the piano store was a welcome respite from the noise, smells and bustle of the hospitals. Freddy wanted to know all about the Mill Hill trip, repeatedly interrupting, asking the make of the piano, what paintings they had, and even how the venison had been cooked.

"Freddy. These things don't matter," said Thomas.

"That's where you're wrong. I need to build up a complete picture."

"Why? I'm never going to see them again."

Freddy stared at him. "That's also where you're wrong."

"What on earth makes you say that?"

"Come on. You were quite taken by Miss Elizabeth."

Thomas was speechless.

"There," said Freddy, clapping his hands together. "That confirms it. If I was wrong, you'd have denied it."

"Well, even if I was, I won't be seeing her again. She lives miles away in Mill Hill."

"Only for the summer. Few weeks' time, she'll be back in London."

"But that doesn't mean I'll see her."

"Well, that's up to you. Anyway, I think you're going to hear from Goodchild soon enough."

"Nonsense. No reason for him to contact me."

"Thomas. Think about it. Why did he invite the two of you to Mill Hill for lunch when he could have seen one of you in his works in Tooley Street?"

"I don't know, though I agree, it was strange."

"Plain as day," laughed Freddy. "He's got two daughters of marriageable age. His wife is probably pestering him. He's ambitious, wanting to see his daughters go up in the world. What better than a couple of aspiring doctors with prospects?"

"Steady. You're getting carried away."

"Am I? Well, you come up with a better explanation."

The more he thought about it, the more Thomas could see there was something in what Freddy suggested.

"Still doesn't mean that Goodchild will do anything."

"Thomas. If Miss Elizabeth is as curious about you as your account suggests, she'll insist her father invite you again. And as likely as not, Miss Sarah will want to see Wiltshire again. Thought you said they both enjoy painting?"

Thomas sat mulling it over while his friend went and made tea. Freddy was still smiling when he returned carrying a tray.

"Seeing how much you enjoyed the Hertford House concert, how about some Mozart piano sonatas? A recital at the King's Theatre next week."

"Be delighted. But I must find a way to repay you. Don't suppose you want to come and watch a gory operation."

*

Lying in bed the following morning, Thomas couldn't get Freddy's explanation out of his mind. At the time, he'd assumed Mrs Goodchild's enquiries were her just being polite. But he could see now that his and Wiltshire's prospects were being assessed. His annoyance at not having seen this for himself was mixed with excitement. He imagined Goodchild questioning his daughters after their visit, gleaning their views.

Sitting up and rubbing his eyes, he told himself to stop getting carried away. He'd allowed Freddy to plant a wild idea in his mind. After all, he hadn't been there. It was just fanciful guesswork.

In the sitting room, Wiltshire was at the table, drawing. Thomas went and gazed out the window.

"Do you think it was odd the Goodchilds asked us so much about ourselves?"

Wiltshire stopped drawing and pushed his chair back from the table.

"No. They were just being friendly."

"What did you talk about with Mrs Goodchild and Miss Sarah?"

"Nothing much. How awful it is without any sunshine, the coach journey, and what I plan to do." He looked at Thomas. "Now I come to think about it, Mrs Goodchild did ask quite a lot about what sort of practice I hoped to have and where it might be." He paused. "Yes, particularly where I hoped to set up. Of course, I didn't let on I don't plan to practise."

Thomas sat down, lost in thought.

"Why are you suddenly asking?" asked Wiltshire. "It was two weeks ago."

"Something Freddy said. He thinks the Goodchilds deliberately invited us to see if we might be suitable husbands for their daughters."

"What! Where did he get such an idea?"

"Think about it. It explains a lot. Insisting on us going to Mill Hill, interrogating us, enabling us to meet his daughters."

Wiltshire looked down, rubbing his mouth with the back of a hand.

"It's possible. Sort of thing rich people do."

"That's exactly what Freddy said. I'd never thought about it before. Back home, everyone knew everyone, mostly through going to church. Not a lot of choice. But here, there are so many possibilities."

"We're men of the world now, Wakley... or you will be," laughed Wiltshire. "Me, I'll be a penniless artist, unless I marry a rich daughter!"

*

"Well done, Wakley. Whatever you said worked," said Chapman.

Thomas had been making his way back from the anatomy theatre in St Thomas's when he'd met the treasurer clutching a bundle of papers.

"Even Sir Astley was pleased when Goodchild's generous new subscription was read out at the Weekly Board meeting." He moved closer to Thomas and lowered his voice. "Between you and me, it takes something to please Sir Astley."

He nodded at Thomas and chuckled to himself before turning and heading off to his rooms. Thomas so wanted to ask him if Sir Astley knew which pupils had persuaded Goodchild. If he did, it would enhance Thomas's chance of being selected for a dresser-ship. He'd come to realise that was all that mattered. If he didn't become a dresser, it was unlikely he'd achieve his ambition of becoming a hospital surgeon one day.

Back in the lodgings, Wiltshire showed little interest in Chapman's comment. Having abandoned even pretending to study, he was spending his days at the Royal Academy making sketches of famous paintings and sculptures.

As the days went by, Thomas came to accept Freddy's conjecture so wasn't that surprised when an invitation to a party at Mill Hill arrived.

"Embossed," said Wiltshire, running his hand over the surface of the card. "Never thought I'd receive one like this."

Thomas sat at the table, his head in his hands.

"What's the matter?" asked Wiltshire. "Thought this is what you were hoping for."

"I was, and I'm pleased, but what will I wear? All right for you with your fancy coat and breeches."

Wiltshire jumped up. "My Papa. That's who you need. We'll go and see him tomorrow. He'll run you up a fine outfit."

"Wiltshire, I've no money. Need all my savings to last till Christmas."

"Don't worry. For a friend of mine, he'll do it for next to nothing. And you can pay him later."

*

As they approached Merton House, they could hear a hubbub of voices. A flunkey in a red jacket bowed his head slightly in welcome. From the hallway, Thomas could see both the parlour and the dining room were full of people. He and Wiltshire made their way through the house and out onto the terrace where a maid stood holding a tray of drinks.

"Mr Goodchild and I are so pleased you were able to come."

Thomas turned to find Mrs Goodchild.

"Thank you for inviting us."

"And I know my daughters will be pleased." She moved a little closer to them. "Not many young people here, I'm afraid. Hope you don't find it too dull."

With that she went on her way, greeting those who had just arrived. Thomas made his way out onto the lawn. The evening air was humid after the recent rain.

"Mr Wakley."

He hadn't heard her footsteps on the grass. She was a few feet away, her face half hidden by her fan.

"Miss Elizabeth. I'm so pleased to see you again."

"Really?"

As she fanned herself, her ringlets moved in the breeze.

"Your mother said she holds a party every year."

"She does. Seems to be a requirement if you live here on the Ridgeway." She moved closer, lowering her voice. "I suspect there's a greater being who assigns everyone their Saturday."

Thomas wasn't sure what to make of that.

"Don't look so shocked," she said. "I'm joking."

After hesitating, he smiled. "But parties must be a welcome relief from the quiet life the rest of the week."

"For some, I suppose, but I find them tedious. Same people every week, saying the same things."

"Yes, I can see that."

"Now, you were going to a concert. How was it?"

"Ah, you remember. It was wonderful. I couldn't believe how everyone in the orchestra knew when to join in. At first, I couldn't see why so many different instruments were needed but came to realise each added something."

"Has it given you an appetite for more?"

"I've already been. Piano sonatas by Mozart."

She reached forward and picked some white fluff off his sleeve. "Willow seeds. It's been getting everywhere this past month."

She looked up, holding his gaze for what seemed like ages.

"So, Mr Wakley, apart from concerts, what do you like doing when you're not cutting up bodies?"

He smiled, wondering if she was teasing him again. "Watching operations. Best theatre there is."

She narrowed her eyes, then burst out laughing, raising her fan to cover her mouth. "All right. I deserved that."

Thomas was struggling to know what to say. "When we came for lunch, I couldn't believe how many books you have."

"Oh yes. I love reading, but I don't expect they're the sort of books you'd like."

"Novels? I've only read one."

She leant her head slightly to one side. "And what was that?"

"*Pride and Prejudice.*"

She furrowed her brow. "I didn't think men read Miss Austen."

"I got quite involved with the characters. Felt as though I was there with them."

She was nodding, her mouth slightly open.

"You're full of surprises, Mr Wakley."

They might have gone on looking into each other's eyes if Sarah hadn't appeared.

"Here you are. Been looking all over for you," she said, taking Elizabeth's arm. Looking at Thomas, she blushed slightly. "Sorry, I didn't mean to interrupt you."

"It's all right," said Elizabeth. "We ought to rejoin the party."

Before walking back indoors, she turned to Thomas. "I hope we can talk more about books another time."

Thomas bowed his head. "I'd like that."

He stood there for some time, watching a pair of bats flit across the garden. He couldn't face mixing with strangers and making polite conversation, telling people who he'd never see again how he was training to be a surgeon. So, he was relieved Wiltshire appeared.

"Thank goodness," said Thomas.

"What's the matter?"

"Absolutely nothing. Quite the opposite, but I'd really like to get away."

"Have you eaten?"

"Not got much appetite."

"Nonsense. Come on, you must eat. I could do with more, and afterwards we can leave."

Thomas had never seen such a vast array of dishes - Dutch turbot, calves' liver, jugged hare, ox tongue.

"No need to choose," chortled Wiltshire. "Least I didn't. And when you're done, the best apple pie I've ever tasted."

As they ate, Thomas could see Elizabeth being the dutiful daughter, talking with her parents' friends. At one point she caught his eye and smiled.

"We must thank Mrs Goodchild before going," said Wiltshire. "She's in the parlour."

"I do hope you've eaten well," she said, smiling.

"We have, thank you," said Wiltshire.

She moved closer to Thomas. "Mr Wakley. If you have any intentions towards Miss Elizabeth, I advise you to speak to Mr Goodchild." She put her hand on Thomas's arm. "I believe you impressed him."

As he and Wiltshire made their way along the Ridgeway to *The Three Hammers,* where they'd taken rooms, he couldn't work out why Wiltshire kept looking at him and laughing gleefully.

"Come on, Wakley. Tell me. What's going on?"

"I'm not sure."

"Well, I can see what's afoot even if you can't. Be wedding bells before you know it."

Thomas stopped. "What? What are you talking about?"

"Come on. It's clear as day. You're made for one another. She's even tall enough for you."

Wiltshire put an arm round Thomas's back and started frog-marching him down the road, singing.

"*When young and thoughtless, Elizabeth said, 'No-one shall win my heart…'*"

"Sshh. Everyone will hear," implored Thomas, but to no avail.

Wiltshire had now broken away and was dancing a jig as he sang even louder.

"'*…But little dreamt the simple maid; Of love's delusive art.*'"

Try as he might, Thomas couldn't stop himself laughing.

"You're mad, you know that?"

Wiltshire turned and clasped Thomas's hands. "And you, my friend, are in love."

*

A few days later, Thomas was in the museum when Wiltshire bounded in.

"They've been announced," he said.

People looked up and scowled. "Shh, keep your voice down," said Thomas.

"Just as we thought," he whispered. "All Sir Astley's dresser-ships go to his own apprentices."

"I guess if you've paid five hundred pounds to be his apprentice, it's the least you deserve. What about for Lucas and Forster?"

"Sorry, not you." He got a bit of paper out of his pocket. "Haynes, Carter, Hempson, Monez, and Gossett."

It felt as though he'd been felled by a vicious uppercut. He sat staring at the book he'd been reading, unable to speak. Then he felt Wiltshire's hand on his shoulder.

"Wakley. Are you all right?"

Thomas gathered up his notes and let Wiltshire lead him out. In *The George* it was quiet, as the morning stagecoaches had long since departed and passengers from the overnight arrivals had dispersed. Wiltshire ordered them plates of oysters and mash but Thomas couldn't touch his.

"You should eat something," said Wiltshire. "Always best after a shock."

"Not hungry." He pushed his plate aside. "What a fool I've been. How could I have thought I stood a chance."

"Don't say that. You're better than all of them. We know it's nothing to do with how good you are."

"Been kidding myself." He paused and looked at Wiltshire. "I'm not going to let this stop me. I'm determined to be a surgeon."

"But how, without a dresser-ship?" asked Wiltshire.

He stared at his friend for some time. "Don't know. Need time to think." He paused. "My registration lasts till Christmas. Chance to learn more. I'll go to Bell's lectures in Great Windmill Street. He's said to be as good as Sir Astley. And I'll attend operations and *post mortems* here. Then, membership exam at the College in February."

"And after that?"

Thomas managed to smile. "Haven't a clue. But I've never let that put me off."

Wiltshire laughed. "Wish I was like you. I don't know if I'm brave enough to do what I want to do."

Thomas reached out and gripped his friend's arm. "If you want something enough, it'll work out."

*

It was already autumn. Charles Bell's lectures were proving to be as good as Thomas had been led to believe, but on Sir Astley's ward rounds he couldn't stop wondering if the great man had even considered him for a dresser-ship.

With no lectures to attend, most mornings he and Wiltshire took breakfast in *The Borough Coffee House*. Since abandoning his studies, Wiltshire seemed so much happier.

"Still got to break the news to my father," said Wiltshire, slowly stirring his coffee. "But now I know there's no alternative, I don't feel so fearful of telling him." He put his spoon down and sat back. "It was meant to be. Not something I could control."

"You sound like a vicar. Pre-destination. That's what clerics and the government and the King want us all to believe. Keeps people in their place."

"So, are you telling me that your falling for Elizabeth was your decision?"

"That's different."

"Oh, really? It's like me giving up medicine. It's something I have to do. I never chose to be a painter. And I've got my first commission. Least I think I have."

"That's wonderful. How did you get it?"

"The fateful party!" laughed Wiltshire. "While you were courting, I was busy. Miss Sarah introduced me to her uncle. Trouble was, she told him I was an accomplished portrait artist."

"What!"

"I know, but I suppose I'd been trying to impress her. Anyway, this gentleman wants his portrait painted, and if he likes it, one of his wife."

"There you are," said Thomas, sitting back. "Just as I said. You took control, shaped your destiny. So much for leaving things to fate."

*

The highlight of his week remained the Physical Society. Thomas always came away with ideas swirling around his head. But also frustrated that, once again, he hadn't joined in and voiced his opinion. He knew why that was. Reluctance to speak until he had sorted out his thoughts, which often took him hours or days. This didn't seem to be a problem for others, who were quite happy, even proud, to spout nonsense with no foundation. He preferred to write down his thoughts. He'd already filled several notebooks and, as he perused them, he could see his views had developed and changed.

"I'm sorry. I shouldn't go on about it," said Thomas, as he and Freddy sat over the chess board. He'd been talking at length about the previous evening's meeting.

"Not at all," said Freddy. "I like to learn about something other than pianos!"

They continued playing in silence for a while.

"The thing is," said Thomas, "you have to be famous to get heard or read. Like William Lawrence. He's just had his College lectures ridiculing vitalism published. It's already causing a furore."

"Hardly surprising," laughed Freddy, "if you go around blaspheming."

Thomas sat back. "It must be so exciting. To lock horns with all these grand men who think they know everything."

"Sounds like you should be a politician."

"Well, if I can't be a surgeon, who knows?" said Thomas.

Freddy was looking at him. "I did mean it as a joke."

Thomas shot him a look which made Freddy wipe the smile off his face.

"Publishing's all changing, you know," said Freddy. "Steam presses. We're selling sheet music for a tenth of what we were charging last year."

"But medicine's different," said Thomas.

"Is it? They said that about politics until Cobbett started his *Register*. Now look at him. His *Tuppenny Trash* sells tens of thousands, much to the annoyance of the government."

"Well, maybe things will change in medicine. Certainly need to."

"Meant to tell you. Signor Clementi has moved back to the continent, so there'll be lots more concerts if you want to go."

"Are you trying to distract me from our game?" asked Thomas, scrutinising the board.

"Would I do such a cunning thing?" said Freddy, moving his queen. "Checkmate."

"I knew it. You were."

"All's fair in love and chess. Talking of which, you've not mentioned Elizabeth."

Thomas leaned back, stroking the rounded ends of the arms of the chair.

"Oh, Freddy. That's because I don't know what to do. I wonder if she's thinking of me as much as I am of her. I might have just imagined the connection I sensed."

"I'm not experienced in matters of the heart, but it seems clear to me what you must do. See her and ask her."

"It's not just that. I can't go on pretending I'm going to be a surgeon when it may never happen."

"Listen. It's you she's interested in, not your job."

"Well, even if you're right, when will I get the chance to talk to her? I can't just turn up at her house unannounced."

"Write to Goodchild. Ask if you might pay them a visit. What's the worst that can happen?"

＊

Each attempt he made to compose a letter sounded wrong. He was on the point of giving up when an invitation to a New Year's Day party at the Goodchilds' arrived.

"Divine intervention," said Thomas, "or just the next step in Goodchild's strategy?"

"You really are a cynic, aren't you?" said Wiltshire. "Just be grateful. I am. Might find some clients."

"What about all those you told me about?"

"Ah. Promises, promises. Haven't heard from most of them."

"I'm sorry. Can only be a matter of time. It's this uncertainty. Those riots last week in Spa Fields have rattled the rich."

"Maybe." He paused. "I have to say, Wakley. Never met anyone as hopeful, as optimistic, as you."

"Hm." Thomas smiled. "Don't be taken in. It's often an act. Something I learnt fighting. If you believe in winning, you stand more chance of succeeding."

"So, what do you believe you'll do?"

"Thought of little else. Only thing possible. Find a surgeon who needs an assistant."

1817

On New Year's Day, they made their way along Tooley Street, avoiding wagons heavily laden with goods from the riverside warehouses. The Goodchilds' home was part of a terrace of yellow-brick townhouses, so blackened the yellow was barely visible. Opposite the house, the family's glass and lead premises in Fenning's Wharf was locked up and silent.

"Give them the day off and they'll work all the harder the rest of the year," said Goodchild as he welcomed them. "Simple economics, though precious few seem to understand it."

The drawing room on the first floor was packed. The air was so heavy with scent, Thomas held the bridge of his nose for a moment to stop himself sneezing. As he turned to speak to Wiltshire, he saw Sarah had already whisked him away to meet someone. *Hopefully a commission*, thought Thomas as, with some difficulty, he picked his way through the crowded room looking for Elizabeth. He spotted her near the piano, her back towards him. She was talking to an elderly woman who, on seeing Thomas looking at them, must have said something, as Elizabeth turned and came over.

"Mr Wakley. With all the New Year's Day concerts, I thought you might be distracted elsewhere."

He was sure Elizabeth was standing closer to him than even the crowded room necessitated. Despite being hemmed in on all sides, he felt they were isolated from those around them.

"Have you finished your studies?" she asked.

"I have. I take my exam next month."

"And then what?"

"I must find a job, assisting a surgeon for a few years, before taking on my own practice."

"In London?" she asked.

"That's my intention. Now Christmas is over, I'll start looking."

She nodded slowly, never taking her eyes off him.

"How have the theatres been this autumn?" he asked.

"Oh, as wonderful as ever. So many interesting plays. You should go yourself."

"On your recommendation, I will."

She blushed slightly and looked around, checking to see if anyone was watching. He knew at any moment she may move away. It was now or never. He may never get another chance. She held his gaze, seemingly encouraging him to step out onto the ice, to risk it. He leant even closer to her.

"Miss Elizabeth, would you do me the honour of being my wife?"

His heart was pounding, convinced he'd misread the situation and she'd be offended. For what seemed like ages she didn't react, then as she smiled, tears welled up in his eyes.

"I'd like nothing more."

*

Two weeks later, Thomas was back at Tooley Street to meet with Goodchild. The maid showed him into a small ground floor office, with piles of papers on the desk and the walls covered in charts.

"Ah, Wakley," said Goodchild, as he came bustling in and dumped a sheaf of files on the desk. "Sit yourself down."

Goodchild slumped into his well-worn leather chair.

"So, what can I do for you?" he asked, lighting his pipe and blowing great clouds of smoke across the room.

Although Thomas had rehearsed what he would say, now it came to it he'd forgotten what he'd planned.

"I've been talking with Miss Elizabeth."

Goodchild continued to look at him, offering no help.

He decided to launch straight in.

"Would you let me marry her?"

Goodchild sucked on his pipe, blew out another cloud of smoke, and pushed himself up out of his chair. Thomas felt cold sweat running down his back, fearful he was about to be shown the door. Still saying nothing, Goodchild came out from behind his desk and held out his hand.

"Wakley. I most certainly will. Delighted."

Thomas thought he detected a smile, something he'd never seen before.

"Have to say, you've impressed me from the start. I like a man who is serious about his trade and not frightened of hard work."

He returned to his seat. "Just so we're both clear. I can't let you marry until you've got a decent income. You need to be able to keep her in the manner to which she's been accustomed."

"Of course. I'd want nothing less for her or myself."

"Afraid Borough's not for her." He raised his eyebrows, seeking Thomas's affirmation. "But I can see you're ambitious. We live in difficult times, Wakley. These riots are worrying. Wasn't a problem when they were up north, but now, on our doorstep. Government needs to do something."

Goodchild gazed out of the window as if expecting rioters to appear in the street at any minute.

"If we can deal with Napoleon, I'm sure the army can deal with these troublemakers."

Thomas was unsure whether Goodchild was expecting him to concur; if he was being tested.

"Anyway," said Goodchild, turning to look at Thomas. "What are your plans?"

"It's the College exam next month. I'm hoping to be an assistant to a surgeon until I can afford to buy a practice."

"And what if you don't find a job?"

Thomas had been trying not to think of that eventuality.

"I'd have to go back to Devon. My family's well-known, so I should be able to set up a successful practice there. As soon as I've saved enough, I'll be back."

"I see." He fell silent, studying his pipe. "Tell you what. Best we don't announce your engagement until you've got your own practice. We'll keep our understanding to ourselves."

Thomas could see no problem with that. Nothing was going to alter his desire to marry Elizabeth.

"And a word of advice," continued Goodchild. "Elizabeth isn't one to wait around. Can be rather impatient. Admirable quality in many ways, but damn demanding."

This time Thomas was sure Goodchild smiled as he stood up and offered his hand again.

"Welcome to the family."

Upstairs, he found Elizabeth in the drawing room.

"Don't keep me waiting," said Elizabeth. "What did Papa say?"

Thomas smiled, taking her hands in his. "He agrees, but he won't announce it until I've got my own practice."

Her smile vanished, and there was a look of anguish. "When will that be?"

"Soon. Working hard, I can save enough as an assistant in a year or two. And we can see each other regularly."

*

As the days passed, Thomas's initial optimism faded. No surgeons were advertising for assistants. Time was running out. The prospect of having to return to Devon looked more and more likely.

An icy wind was blowing the morning he made his way over London Bridge to Lincoln's Inn Fields. At the front door of the College of Surgeons, under the grand colonnaded portico, a beadle redirected him to the back door in Portugal Street.

"Only Council members and Fellows allowed in here," he said, with what Thomas sensed was some pleasure.

Inside, he was made to wait with several others in a small wood-panelled room. Every half hour, a bespectacled clerk came in and called a name. It wasn't until mid-morning he was summoned. Entering a large, ornately decorated room, there was a long, dark oak table, behind which ten surgeons were seated, including Sir Astley. The man in the centre who, from the large sash and medallion round his neck, Thomas assumed was the College President, cleared his throat as he peered at the papers in front of him.

"Wakley?"

"Yes, sir."

The clerk leant over to speak to the president, but Thomas couldn't hear what he said.

"Seems like your papers are in order. Tommy's and Guy's, eh?"

The president looked along the table. "Mr Abernethy."

All Thomas could think was how Lawrence's denunciation of vitalism had been targeted in particular at Abernethy.

"Costiveness," said the surgeon. "Nine possible causes."

With no difficulty, Thomas reeled off the answer. Sir Astley looked like a proud parent. When Thomas finished, Abernethy grunted his approval. The president invited further questions from the examiners. Three seemed to be dozing. Only two had questions, neither of which taxed Thomas.

"Well, Mr Wakley," said the president. "Welcome to the College."

As no-one said anything more, Thomas assumed it was over so, tentatively, he got up and left. Outside, he was both pleased to have passed but angry at how lackadaisical it had been. He couldn't understand how any pupil could fail.

He was still fuming about it when he got back to his lodgings. Wiltshire, who was busy packing, showed little interest.

"Sorry, no longer my world," laughed Wiltshire. "But I'm not surprised. Sounds as woeful as most of our training."

"True," said Thomas. "So, where are your new lodgings?"

"Just off East Cheap. Not the finest, but it's near the works."

A few days earlier, Wiltshire had told him how, until his portraiture work built up, he'd make a living as a paint-stainer.

"The demand for wallpaper's growing by the day," he'd said. "I'm told there's a good living to be had for successful designers and stainers."

Thomas had detected disappointment in his voice but was pleased he wasn't completely abandoning his dream.

"At least I'll be working with paints," he'd said. "Sarah's going to carry on trying to get me commissions. If the paint-staining goes well, I'll be able to ask for her hand in marriage. Just imagine, Wakley, we could be brothers-in-law!"

Thomas now had nothing to keep him in London. He couldn't put off having to tell Elizabeth. As he made his way round to Tooley Street, he grew increasingly fearful of how she would react. As soon as Mrs Goodchild left them alone in the drawing room, he lost no time in telling her.

"I won't be away for long. Once word gets round, I'm sure patients will come my way, as I can offer the latest treatments from London."

Elizabeth said nothing for a while. "How long?"

"A year, maybe two. I'll work all hours."

It seemed an eternity as he waited for her to say something.

"As long as it's not longer."

"I promise I'll not stay a day longer than necessary. And I'll write every week."

The following morning, he packed his few possessions in the bag he'd arrived with. The only addition was the set of surgical instruments and selection of plaisters and bandages he'd purchased with his last remaining funds. As Wiltshire headed over the river to his new lodgings, Thomas set out to walk to Devon.

Chapter 6

1817

"Oh, Thomas. What happened?"

His mother reached up, pushing locks of hair off the large bruise on his forehead.

"It's nothing, Mama. Don't worry. Took a tumble and hit my head on a branch. Shouldn't have tried going through the woods. Thought it would be quicker."

He had no intention of telling her about his bare-knuckle bout in Shaftesbury two nights earlier and how much worse he'd looked then. The fight had gone well. Still had it in him. Together with the one in Andover a few days earlier, it meant he'd not have to ask his father for money.

"Come and sit down," she said, pulling a chair out from the kitchen table. "I'm going to get some arnica."

As she was leaving the room, she turned and laughed. "Don't know what I'm doing telling a doctor what's needed."

Could it only have been four years since he'd last sat here? Nothing had changed. Every pot and plate were where he remembered from his childhood. The comfort and reassurance he felt was mixed with a disconcerting sense of being dragged back to his childhood. It was as if all he'd experienced and learnt since leaving home was dissolving away, as if it had never happened.

"Here we are," said his mother, bustling back into the room holding a jar. As she gently rubbed the ointment onto the bruise, he felt guilty that the only reason he was there was because he had no other option.

"Now, I want to hear all your news before the men get back. Let's go through to the parlour."

His mother settled in her usual armchair. Having knelt down to put some more logs on the fire, Thomas stood up and turned to her.

"I'm going to be married."

"I knew it. Come here." He went over to her, and she flung her arms wide to hug him. "I could tell there was something. Oh, Thomas, that's wonderful. Who is she?"

"Elizabeth. Father's a merchant in London. Trouble is, we can't marry till I've a good income."

"So, come on. What's she like?"

He'd spent much of the past week puzzling over how he'd describe her. While he knew she was the one for him, he struggled to put into words why, what it was about her. It had annoyed and frustrated him. He could describe a patient's condition in detail but when it came to this, he was at a loss. Until, that is, the night he was staying in Salisbury. Sitting alone, eating dinner, it had suddenly dawned on him that it wasn't just not knowing the words, it was because he barely knew her. They'd talked for no more than a few hours and then only about the things they each liked doing. But her interests weren't what fascinated him. So, what was it?

It took another two days to work it out. As he was striding across Cranbourne Chase, a blustery wind in his face, everything became clear. He'd stopped and gazed out across the hills, the immensity of the sky reminding him of Turner's landscape. There wasn't a soul in sight. The light covering of snow muffled the sound of any animals that might have been foraging in the gorse.

"That's it," he'd heard himself say as he realised what it was that captivated him.

His mother was patiently waiting for an answer.

"What's Elizabeth like?" said Thomas, staring into space. "She sees things so differently to me. It's as if she's opening doors to worlds I didn't know existed." He looked at his mother. "She doesn't just accept what people say. I love the way she questions everything."

His mother had been nodding as he spoke. "Just like you."

"What do you mean?" He frowned but she just smiled. "Is that how I seem?"

"Thomas. You've always been like that. It's why you couldn't go back to the school in Chard or in Honiton. The teachers had had enough of your constant questions: 'Never accepts what I say,' that's what one of them told us."

"Do you think that's what attracted me to her?"

"Peas in a pod," laughed his mother. "You sound well-suited."

Mama had seen in minutes what had eluded him for months. It was just like Freddy fathoming Goodchild's motive for inviting him and Wiltshire to Mill Hill.

"Son," said his mother, leaning over and taking his hand. "It's always easier for others to see things about ourselves. Now, tell me more."

He spoke of Elizabeth's love of reading, gardening and the theatre. About her family and their summer house in Mill Hill. And how they had met, maybe because her father had engineered it.

"I'm so happy for you," she said. "Perhaps I can stop worrying about you, though mothers never stop worrying about their youngest."

Thomas got up and hugged her again. "It's good to be home."

At that moment, he really felt it.

*

It took him a few days to recover from his walk. It was only now that he realised how much it had taken out of him. That and his two fights. His sparring sessions in London had helped maintain his strength, but the fights had pushed his stamina to the limit.

When he came to write to Elizabeth, there was so much he had to tell her about his journey, the people he'd met along the way and his mother's delight:

"Mama wanted to know all about you. She thought we sounded rather similar. Are we? Maybe it was the way I described you. Whether we are or not, I love you the way you are."

Each week, as soon as he'd consigned his letter to the London-bound mail coach at *The Longbridge Inn*, he'd start imagining her reading it.

It was several days before his father showed any interest in talking to him about his intentions. When, finally, they sat together at the vast oak table in the dining room, it reminded Thomas of the time he'd returned from Taunton years before.

The room filled with clouds of smoke from his father's pipe. Papa sat staring at him for some time. As a child, Thomas had found that so disconcerting but now it seemed more like a weakness than a show of strength. As if his father didn't know what to say.

"So, what brings you back? You couldn't wait to get away."

As forthright and blunt as ever, thought Thomas. "Papa, I left to train to be a surgeon. I'll always be grateful for your help."

His father grunted, waving smoke away from his face. "Suppose you want more money."

"Not at all. I plan to practise here. With you being well known and respected, it should help me attract patients."

His father pushed on the arms of his chair to adjust his position and get comfortable.

"You reckon there's work round here, do you? We've got doctors down in Axminster and over in Chard. Should have thought that's enough. There isn't a war going on here, you know."

"I know but I can offer the latest ideas of how to treat people."

"Not sure people here want to be experimented on. They like the old ways."

"You may be right. But I intend to try."

*

133

Despite the incessant rain and sleet, Thomas spent much of the next fortnight riding round all the nearby villages, introducing himself at the largest farms and houses. He knew he couldn't expect to survive just offering surgery but would have to use his apothecary knowledge as well to treat medical conditions.

Three weeks passed and no-one requested his help. How could he have imagined people would want his service? How arrogant he'd been, thinking that because he'd come from London with the latest knowledge, people would flock to him. It was on market day in Axminster, when he fell into conversation with an elderly farmer, that all became clear.

"Young man. Jenkinson might not be the best doctor in the kingdom but I know him, trust him."

Thomas felt so stupid. Of course. It wasn't just about competence. Far from it.

It was the letters from Elizabeth that kept his spirits up. Four days after writing to her, he started anticipating her reply. On those days, he'd ride home from trying to drum up interest in his practice, convinced there'd be a letter. When there was, his excitement compensated for all the days of disappointment. He'd rush upstairs to his room, settle in the small armchair and carefully break the sealing wax. She wrote in a way he longed to be able to. Her descriptions of plays were so vivid, he felt he had been there. Her latest letter had tantalised him, promising to send him something special next time.

While he loved her letters, they made him more anxious about his failure to establish a practice. He'd even started thinking of what else he might do. The navy was always looking for surgeons, though the thought of going back to sea filled him with dread. Then, one evening, a young boy appeared at Land Farm.

"My Pa's not well. Can the new doctor come and see him?"

Thomas grabbed his bag of instruments and dressings and rode back with the boy to a small farmhouse a mile away. Inside, the only light came from a single candle and some meagre embers in the grate. The boy's mother was distraught, pacing around, clutching an infant on one hip.

"Thank you, Doctor. It's Pullen, my husband. Been taken dreadful bad."

She handed the baby to the boy and, carrying the candle, led Thomas upstairs. The man was lying in a darkened room. From the fetid smell, Thomas knew what to expect. He pulled back the filthy sheet and saw Pullen's right arm was red and swollen, with a large abscess engulfing his elbow. Feverish and dehydrated, the man was barely able to speak.

"Good job you called me, Mrs Pullen," said Thomas. "Open the window and bring a bowl and bucket of water, as warm as possible."

From what he'd seen, boiling water was out of the question. While waiting, he laid out his instruments. When Pullen's wife returned and he had all he needed, he told her to wait downstairs.

He placed the bowl under the abscess. As he pierced it with his scalpel, he had to hold his breath to stop himself retching. He enlarged the incision to ensure all the pus was out. The weak, flickering candle made it difficult to see, so he had to rely on his sense of touch and feel. Once satisfied, he removed the bowl, washed the arm, and wrapped a plaister over the wound. Pullen's breathing had settled and he looked more comfortable.

"He'll be all right, won't he, Doctor?" implored Mrs Pullen, when Thomas went back downstairs.

"I hope so," said Thomas. "He must drink plenty. And try and get him to eat. He needs to build up his strength."

Looking around, there was little sign of food. He looked back at her.

"How long has he been unwell?"

"All week. Said his arm hurt something dreadful if he moved it. All started when he cut himself."

"So why didn't he seek help earlier?"

She started crying and wiped her tears away with her apron. "He said not to. Said it would sort itself out. Couldn't afford to pay a doctor."

"What? But you've got a farm."

She said nothing, lowering herself onto a stool. It was only then that Thomas realised she was with child.

"We don't have a farm. Not no more. They took it away."

"Who did? Why?"

"Them commissioners. Said they could make better use of the land."

He could feel the anger rising in his body. She reminded him of a boxer who'd given up, accepted defeat.

"Mrs Pullen, let me know if you need me to come again."

"We've troubled you enough, Doctor." She was fumbling in her apron pocket, and he saw her clutching a couple of coins.

"Put those away," he said. "There'll be no charge tonight. Remember. Get him to drink and eat. It may take some time, so be patient."

Pullen proved to be the first of a steady trickle of patients seeking his services, as word of his skills circulated. He set up a rudimentary consulting room in an outhouse. As his reputation spread, it pleased him that he was proving his father wrong.

His spirits were lifted further when the surprise Elizabeth had promised arrived. Her letter was larger than usual, tied with cord, with several wax seals. As he unfolded it, he found himself looking at her. He gasped, astonished at the likeness. And there, in the bottom corner, a familiar name – Sampson Wiltshire.

*

Just as spring was turning to summer, his hopes were dashed. He knew something had happened from the anger on his father's face.

"We need to talk. The dining room, now."

With the door firmly closed, his father remained standing, looking down on Thomas who had taken a seat at the table.

"It's got to stop. Quite out of hand. I can't show my face in Chard. Fellow Commissioners wouldn't deign to speak to me last night."

"What have I done?"

"What have you done? Don't try and be clever. The doctors are furious. You're stealing their trade. They insist I put a stop to it."

"And you agreed? You put them before your own son?"

"This isn't London. Here, everyone knows their place. That's how we all get along. It's what everyone wants."

That was it. Thomas decided he had nothing to lose. He rose and approached his father.

"Was it what the Pullens wanted? To have you and your cronies take his farm away?"

"How dare you! What are you talking about?"

Thomas moved even closer to him. He wasn't going to let him treat him like the schoolboy he once was.

"You know," said Thomas. "You seized his land and gave it to some large landowner."

As his father looked away, unable to look him in the eye, Thomas realised the full horror of what had happened.

"It was you, wasn't it?" he said, speaking slowly. "You got given Pullen's land."

"And what if I did?" thundered his father, the veins in his neck standing out. "It's already producing more corn than it ever did in his hands."

Thomas stood staring at his father, speechless.

"This country's going to the dogs," his father continued. "It's bankrupt after the war. You should be grateful that some of us are prepared to help turn things around. Boost our farming. Reduce our imports. What do you think pays for your fancy lives in London?"

"But do you not see what it's doing to people like the Pullens? It's broken them. Reduced to living in squalor, not enough to eat, can't afford the doctor."

"Nonsense. They afforded you."

"Do you think I took money off them?"

"Well, there you are. In your world there'd be no economy. Wake up, son. There have always been winners and losers. Always will be. You have to decide which you want to be."

With that he stormed out. Thomas slowly sank back down onto a chair and put his head in his hands. He couldn't stay there any longer. He had to accept what he'd known from the day he arrived back. He no longer fitted in there, not that he ever had. He had to get back to London and find some way to survive there.

✳

"What a surprise. How wonderful to see you," exclaimed Anne, hugging him. "You should have let me know you were coming."

Thomas put down his bag and pushed his hair off his face. "I would have done but I only decided this morning."

The true explanation could wait. He needed to sit down. He'd set off from the farm at such a pace that after several miles he'd been out of breath. The last five miles to Beaminster had been a slow trudge.

"Sit yourself down. I'll get some tea."

When she reappeared, she was smiling broadly. "Can't tell you how happy I am to see you. And I want to hear everything about Elizabeth."

"Everything, I promise."

"Richard expects to be back before nightfall. So, if you can survive, we'll have dinner when he gets here."

Thomas was relieved that all his sister wanted to talk about that evening was Elizabeth, so all mention of what had prompted his sudden departure from Land Farm was avoided. Anne's excitement and her enthusiasm was the tonic he needed. By the time he went to bed, that morning's events seemed quite distant.

The next few days were bliss. After no summer the previous year, there were now endless days of hot, sunny weather. While

Richard worked, he and Anne walked through the countryside, pointing out flowers and birds to one another, reminiscing. One afternoon, they climbed up to Beaminster Down and lay on the grass, closely cropped by sheep, watching swifts soaring above them.

"You still haven't told me why you left the farm so suddenly," said Anne.

He sat up, shielding his eyes from the sun as he gazed out over the rolling hills.

"Papa and I argued. I knew he was pretty unforgiving and that he loyally supported the King and the government but I hadn't realised just how far he'd go. Do you have any idea what he and the other big landowners are doing?"

"Well, I knew he was involved in enclosures, to make better use of the land."

"Anne, for goodness' sake." He turned to her. "You sound like him."

Anne's face dropped. "Thomas."

"Oh, God. I'm sorry. You're the last person I want to upset. But can't you see? Men like Papa are seizing the common land and robbing small farmers of their livelihoods. Worst of all is that Papa doesn't care. Not sure he even knows the poverty and despair he's creating."

"Come on. He's only carrying out his responsibility. It's the law."

"It may be but it's wrong."

He told her of the Pullens' plight and how he'd confronted their father.

"I want nothing more to do with him. I'm never going back."

"Don't say that. You can't mean it."

"I'm sorry but I do."

They sat in silence for a while.

"You'll feel differently in time."

"Not this time, I won't."

"I'm not going to condone his behaviour," said Anne, "but try and see it from his point of view. You don't live there. He's worked the land for years, ever since his father passed. Always making sure Mama and the ten of us had all we needed. He can only see what's in front of him – common land, uncared for, and farmers failing to use their land properly. So, of course he gets frustrated and wants to do something. He's only trying to do what's best as he sees it."

"Anne, he's doing great harm. And he didn't care, even when I told him."

"Oh, Thomas. I know you're right but you've got to compromise. We all do throughout our lives. Do you think I haven't put up with things I didn't like?"

Thomas said nothing, feeling as upset as the morning he'd left the farm.

"I don't want to argue with you," he said quietly. "Let's leave it. Maybe I'll think differently one day. But for now, I can't forgive him."

They walked home in silence, both lost in their own thoughts.

That evening, he was about to tell them he intended leaving the next day, when Richard asked if he'd run the practice for a few days while he visited his parents in Bridgewater. After all Richard had done for him, Thomas was pleased to be able to repay the debt he owed him.

Each evening Thomas told Anne about his day.

"Everyone is so friendly," he said, as they sat in the small garden enjoying the last of the sun. "So many remember me from when I was here before. Can't walk down the High Street without people stopping me, wanting to talk."

"Of course. What did you expect?"

"I don't know. It's so different in London. No-one speaks to you in the street unless it's to harangue you or to try and sell you something."

"Sounds like you're more suited to rural life," Anne said, laughing.

The sky had turned red as the sun disappeared behind the hills.

"It's tempting... and maybe there was a time I'd have been happy somewhere like this." He looked at her. "But to be a surgeon, I have to be in a city. Don't get me wrong. What Richard does is so valuable but being a general practitioner isn't for me."

She smiled. "I know you too well to think I can change your mind."

"And Elizabeth would never countenance moving away from her family."

The morning after Richard returned, Thomas set off.

Anne hugged him. "Promise me you'll think about what I said about Papa. I'd hate to think you never spoke to him again. You must, for Mama's sake if nothing else."

After six months away, he was ready to get back to London. But before he did so, there was someone he needed to see.

*

Coulson leaned forward, resting his elbows on the desk. He was slowly shaking his head.

"Just like in my days."

Thomas had just finished recounting his time as a pupil.

"Sitting here, two years ago," said Thomas, "I thought Robert must have been exaggerating. If anything, it was worse than he said."

"I never understood," said Coulson, "why they made it so hard for pupils to find out when operations and *post mortems* were taking place. It was as if they had something to hide."

Thomas snorted. "Some of them do."

Coulson frowned. "Steady on. That's a bit strong."

"Is it? Take Lucas. I'm sure he doesn't want pupils to see how useless he is, nay dangerous."

"Pity. His father was a fine operator."

"But that's just it. He was appointed by his father. You must see how nepotism is holding back progress. Surely the best should get the jobs?"

"Dangerous talk!" laughed Coulson. "Of course you're right. But do be careful. If you want to get on in London, you've got to watch what you say."

As Coulson filled his pipe, Thomas picked up the latest issue of the *London Medical & Physical Journal*.

"They've added *London* to the title," laughed Coulson. "At least they've been honest enough to acknowledge the limit of their interests."

Thomas put it back down. "I've thought a lot about what you said, how the two medical periodicals aren't interested in what you do. It was the same with our lecturers. If they ever mentioned general practitioners, it was to denigrate them, tell us people like you and Phelps knew little."

Coulson nodded. "I know. So, tell me, why are you here? Can't believe it's just a social visit, delighted though I am you've come."

Thomas brushed his hair off his forehead.

"I don't know what to do. I thought some surgeon in London would want an assistant."

"Hm. What you mean is none of them advertised for one. My advice is, go and knock on their doors. Present yourself."

"Really? Very well, I'll try that." He paused. "There's something else."

Coulson was nodding slowly and smiling. "Thought there was."

"I want to do something to change things. Medicine's being held back. We could help people much more if we trained pupils better, if the best were appointed to hospitals, if doctors up and down the country could learn about the latest ideas, if we weren't afraid of judging each other, of speaking up when things go wrong so we can put them right. Trouble is, I don't know what I can do."

Coulson sighed. "I'll say this for you, Wakley, you're not one to shy away from a challenge. I'm not sure I can be of much help beyond cautioning you to take care. And don't try being a hero on your own. No-one ever changed the world single-handed. Find others who share your views and work together. For when you do take action... whatever that may be, you'll need each other's support."

Thomas gazed out of the window, lost in thought. When he turned back, Coulson was smiling at him. "Does that help?"

"Beyond measure. Not only by not ridiculing my ambition, but by making the impossible seem possible."

"Possible, maybe. But still an immense challenge. Don't take on too much."

"Tell me, where did you learn to be radical?"

Thomas had never heard Coulson laugh so loud.

"Wakley, I'm no radical. But after twenty years in this town, I've learnt how to get things changed. Small things perhaps – improved food at the workhouse, vaccinations for the poor, reducing miasma in the malthouses. Nothing gets done without persuading the powerful. And an army of supporters helps."

Coulson stood up. "Now, it's time for dinner, and the family all want to see you. You should have heard the commotion when they heard you were coming. Come on."

Upstairs in the parlour, Mrs Coulson, Caroline, and Louisa were waiting for them. He'd barely had time to greet each of them before Louisa, glancing at her sister, asked Thomas, "Are you going to come back and work for Papa?"

Thomas smiled. "I think there's already enough doctors here."

"It's why Robert had to settle in Wycombe," interjected Coulson.

At dinner, Thomas barely got the chance to eat, answering the barrage of questions about his life in London. He told them how, through an old school friend, he'd gone to concerts, and how the pupil he lodged with, who really wanted to be an artist, had taken him to exhibitions. He wanted to tell them about his plans to marry, but he'd given an undertaking to Goodchild that only their families should know for now. It was true he'd told Wiltshire and Freddy, but they'd sworn to tell no-one.

Thomas slept late the following morning after the long walk the previous day. Downstairs, Coulson was by himself at the breakfast table.

"Morning, Wakley. Sit yourself down. It's just us. The others were up and out earlier. Market day."

The bread rolls were still warm from the oven. Steam rose as Thomas tore one open.

"If I remember correctly," said Coulson, "you're rather keen on a spot of shooting."

"I am, or rather I was. Have to say, I was a pretty good shot years ago."

"Want to see if you still are? I've a spare gun for the shoot tomorrow on the Mongwell Estate."

Thomas was torn. He'd planned to set out, keen to get back to London. But the lure of a day's shooting was too much.

"If you're sure, I'd love to."

*

Traipsing between hides rekindled his love of the sport. By late morning, Thomas had already bagged several dozen pheasants, prompting Coulson, jokingly, to ask him to give the other guns a chance. Mid-afternoon, their host, Shute Barrington, invited them back to the house for dinner. Seated round a grand dining table, laden with food and drink, the men set about putting the world to rights. At least, the world of Henley. It was clear they governed the town.

"Splendid day's shooting, Barrington." The speaker was a large, jovial man who was tucking in as though he'd never eaten. "Indebted to you, as ever."

"Quite so, Golding," added another, as he refilled his wine glass. "What with all these riots and I don't know what, such a relief to get away from it all."

"Troubling times, indeed," said Barrington. "Least we're free of it round here."

"Not entirely," said Coulson.

Some of the men stopped eating and stared at him.

"What have you heard, Doctor?" asked one of them.

"No, no. I don't mean we're going to see rioting here. But we are seeing more seeking refuge in the workhouse. Some of the children are no more than skin and bones."

"We've got that volcano to thank for that," chuckled someone who was anything but wasting away. "You can send some of them to help get my harvest in. Barns are already filled."

"With due respect, Hulme, I don't think one good harvest is going to put everything right," said Coulson, "least not straight away. We need to enlarge the workhouse and more provisions are needed."

The whole table had quietened down as they listened to Coulson. Some were nodding and looking concerned, though others showed no interest.

"Well, if you say so, Coulson," said Barrington. "I'm sure the town can see its way to helping." No-one demurred. "Now, who's for some brandy?"

"And we must toast Wellington," chortled Golding, "for restoring its supply."

Much as he liked rural life, the meal just served to convince Thomas he could never live in a town like Henley, dealing with men like that.

"Did you plan that?" asked Thomas, as Coulson's carriage carried them home.

"Do what?"

"Get them to agree to more money for the workhouse."

"It's the way you get things done. Got to get their respect. It's like building a house. Quietly lay the foundations."

"And there was I thinking it was just a shoot," said Thomas.

That evening, before dinner, Coulson handed Thomas a letter.

"Introduction to a surgeon. Bampfield, William Bampfield. Got a thriving practice in Bedford Street. May well be in need of an extra pair of hands. We were pupils together and kept in touch. If he can't help you, he may know someone who can."

Thomas didn't want to be beholden to anyone, not even Coulson, who he knew meant well. He was determined to make his own way. But he didn't want to seem ungrateful.

"That's kind of you, thank you."

"It tells him what a damn fine doctor you are. Going places."

Thomas set out before sunrise the following morning to walk the forty miles to London. He wanted to get there by nightfall. The closer he got, the more he worried about finding a job. He couldn't bear to contemplate the consequences for him and Elizabeth if he were to fail.

*

The narrow stairs creaked as Thomas followed the proprietor of Gerard's Hall up to the third floor. The only light was from the oil lamp Ivatts was carrying.

"This'll be you, sir," he said. "Small but clean, as my dear old wife used to say. We take pride in running a tight ship. Can't help it, what with having spent years at sea. You learn to keep things neat."

Ivatts bent over the small table in the corner of the room and lit a lamp. When he straightened up, Thomas could see the pride on his face.

"There now. Fit for a king," he laughed, showing no sign of leaving.

The man clearly wanted to chat but Thomas was too tired for that.

"Thank you, Mr Ivatts. Need to get some sleep," said Thomas, standing back so the proprietor could get past him.

"Oh, right, sir. Martha will bring hot water at seven. And if you're hungry, can recommend the pies in our tavern."

Thomas closed the door and lowered his bag off his back. The last few miles of his walk had been a struggle. The bag seemed to get heavier and heavier. He sat on the bed, pulled off his boots and stretched out.

Next thing he knew, someone was knocking at his door. It took him a moment to work out where he was. Outside, a maid stood with a pitcher of steaming water which he gratefully took from her. His bag lay on the floor, untouched from the night before. He hated sleeping in his clothes. Reminded him of being at sea, when there was every chance of his clothes disappearing in the night.

An hour later, stepping out onto Basing Lane, he made his way round the corner onto Cheapside and dived into the first coffee shop he found. That morning's newspapers lay scattered around, abandoned. He spread *The Times* out in front of him and read it avidly as he devoured his breakfast. When he'd finished, he sat back and looked around. This was what he'd missed. He was animated by the energy. Through the misted windows he could see the street outside was packed, a constant stream of carriages and carts struggling in both directions. The cries of tradesmen, peddling their wares, could be heard. He finished his coffee then headed back to Gerard's Hall to prepare for the search he'd start the following day.

As he stepped into the entrance hall, Ivatts appeared, as if he'd been lying in wait.

"Morning, sir. All satisfactory, I trust."

"Fine, thanks."

"Just you let Ivatts know if there's anything you want," he added, with a wink, "and I mean anything."

Thomas started to head for the stairs, but Ivatts wasn't done. "So, what'll be your trade, sir?"

He'd known such a question was inevitable and had considered not revealing he was a surgeon, fearing it would attract unwanted interest. But with all his medical books upstairs, he knew the truth would soon emerge.

"Surgery," said Thomas, moving towards the stairs.

"Surgeon, eh? That's good." Ivatts leant forwards and lowered his voice. "My dear wife and I always preferred residents to be professional men if you know what I mean."

Back upstairs, Thomas unpacked his few clothes and laid his books and papers out on the small table. He propped his treasured charcoal drawing of Elizabeth against the wall. Although the window was quite small, being three floors up it let in a surprising amount of light. It was also quiet, being well above the street.

Before leaving London he'd taken the precaution of making a list of surgeons from the street directory he'd found in the library. He knew it may not be up to date but it would do.

First, though, he wanted to reacquaint himself with the Borough hospitals. He hoped he might meet someone who could help him. Two years earlier, when he'd registered as a pupil, the benefits of being an alumnus had meant nothing, but now he realised how useful it could prove. He could attend lectures, operations, *post mortems*, even visit the wards. Best of all, he remained a member of Phys Soc. Despite his misgivings about how the hospitals were run, they were his medical home.

✻

Samuel Lightfoot glanced up from his desk but said nothing when the maid showed Thomas into his consulting room. As he stood waiting, Thomas wondered if he behaved like this to his patients. From the richness of the furnishings, he imagined his fees were considerable. Eventually Lightfoot put down his pen and sat back, staring at Thomas.

"Wakley," said Thomas, bowing his head. "Thank you for seeing me."

Lightfoot grunted. "Looking for work, are you? Where did you train?"

"St Thomas's and Guy's, sir."

"Hmm. Damnable places. But where were you apprenticed?"

"Mostly in Henley."

"Mostly? What does that mean? Get thrown out?"

"No, sir. I spent time in Beaminster beforehand." Thomas had no intention of mentioning Incledon. For all he knew, his notoriety may be known in London.

"Damned if I've heard of it. But Henley. Fair town. Fine regatta. Do you row?"

Thomas wondered if Lightfoot was going to show any interest in his medical knowledge or experience.

"No, sir, I don't."

"Well, I don't need an assistant, what with two sons and no end of nephews, and their fathers pestering me for work."

Lightfoot stood up, making clear the conversation was over.

"If you want my advice, find a surgeon unencumbered by a family. We've got to look after our own, haven't we?"

Back out on Oxford Street, Thomas was once again clenching his fists. He stood on the pavement, waiting for his breathing to slow, oblivious to shouts of tradesmen and street hawkers cursing him for getting in their way. He retreated to a coffee shop, needing time to calm down before continuing his visits. Over a dozen surgeons seen and none had shown any interest in him. None were even interested in finding out how good a doctor he was.

An hour later, refreshed and having calmed down, he headed off to visit Burnet, a surgeon in Marylebone.

"Come in, Mr Wakley," said Burnet, a short elderly man who, unlike all the others, seemed pleased to see him. It soon became clear why that was.

"Always good to see a fellow wielder of the scalpel," he laughed, as he sat down behind his desk, gesturing Thomas to take a seat opposite. "Even we medical men fall ill, though have to say, you look remarkably well."

"No, I'm not here seeking your help – least, not as a patient. I'm looking for work."

A look of disappointment replaced his affable smile. "Oh, my apologies. Jumping to conclusions."

"I've just qualified and wondered if you needed an assistant."

"Assistant? Not while I've got my nephew. Can't your father or an uncle take you on?"

"They're all farmers."

"What? Surely one's a doctor?"

Thomas had to stop himself laughing. It was as if Burnet thought he might have overlooked one.

"See your problem," Burnet continued. "Not sure what you can do."

Thomas realised how naïve he'd been. Why had he imagined opportunities away from the hospitals would be any less dependent on who you knew? Knowledge and experience were irrelevant.

When he'd been faced with difficulties in the past, he'd always found ways of coping. On the farm, by keeping out of his brothers' way. At sea, seeking the sanctuary of the naval surgeon. With Incledon, simply avoiding him. But this time, he had no idea what to do.

*

He'd been up and down East Cheap three times, searching for the paint-stainers where Wiltshire worked, before he found the place. The owner led him through to a back room where his friend was leaning over a length of wallpaper, carefully applying a wooden block of print. He waited till Wiltshire lifted the block from the paper and straightened up.

"Wiltshire."

Wiltshire spun round and beamed from ear to ear when he saw Thomas.

"Wakley. What a surprise." He put down the block and wiped his hands on his apron. "What brings you here?"

"Looking for you. I'm back in London, living nearby."

"Been wondering what had become of you." He glanced at his master who was hovering, curious to know who the visitor was. "Look, I can't talk now. *King's Head* in Cannon Street at seven? You can't miss it."

Wiltshire was already there with two tankards of porter in front of him when Thomas arrived.

"Got you a small one," he laughed. "From their own brewery out the back."

Wiltshire watched him as he took a sip.

"What do you think?"

"Fine. It's tasty… and strong."

Wiltshire leant closer. "Special brew," he whispered. "You need to know to ask for it. I'm told the excise men don't know about it."

With that, he downed half his drink and sat back.

"Not sure I've ever thanked you for Elizabeth's portrait. Kept me going through the tougher times."

"Oh, had quite forgotten. Yes, not a bad resemblance I thought."

"So, how's the portraiture business going?"

Wiltshire smiled. "It isn't. Had a few commissions, but I know it's not going to happen. Strange thing is, since I accepted defeat, I've enjoyed paint-staining more and more. I'm starting to design as well as print. One of my designs is proving popular – four customers have ordered it."

"That's wonderful."

"If all goes well, I'll be able to propose to Sarah. We still might end up brothers-in-law."

"We might indeed."

Wiltshire stared at Thomas. "It's so good to know you're back. How about going to some boxing and cockfights?"

"Definitely."

"So, tell me, why are you back so soon?"

"Didn't work out. Doesn't matter why. The point is I've got to find work." Thomas cradled his tankard on the table. "There's forty surgeons in this city and I must have visited half of them. No-one's interested. They're polite, mostly, but I can see they can't wait to get rid of me."

He sat back, running a hand through his hair. "It's just like in the hospitals. If you're not a son, a nephew, even a godson, there's no chance."

"So, what will you do? What are you living on?"

"Still got some of my fight winnings. Don't worry, something will turn up."

He wasn't sure why he said that and, from Wiltshire's expression, suspected he hadn't convinced his friend.

"Wakley, I admire your optimism, but what if it doesn't? Don't want to come visiting you in the Debtor's Prison!"

Thomas sipped his ale.

Wiltshire was screwing up his eyes. "Come on. I know that look. You're not telling me something."

Thomas leant forward, interlacing his fingers. "I've got a letter of introduction to a surgeon in High Holborn. Someone Coulson knows. But if I use it, I'm no better than everyone else. Just another benefiting from connections, knowing the right person."

Wiltshire roared with laughter and slapped his hands together. "You are impossible. Your own worst enemy."

"What do you mean?"

"There's nothing wrong with a helping hand from your old master. God, you're so self-righteous. Should have been a priest."

Thomas was feeling light-headed, not having had a drink since his last night in Henley.

"True to my principles. That's how I'd put it."

"All right. So, what does Elizabeth think?"

"I haven't seen her yet."

"What! You've been back a fortnight and not seen her?"

Thomas leant forward and lowered his voice. "Because when I see her, I have to be able to tell her I'm in work, earning."

"And what if that takes months?"

"It won't."

"Right," said Wiltshire, speaking calmly and slowly. "That does it. You've got to go and see Coulson's friend."

They sat in silence for a while. Looking around the pub, Thomas was convinced no-one else had a care in the world. Drinking and laughing, flirting with the barmaids, smoking their pipes.

Wiltshire leant forward, speaking quietly. "She'll be wondering if you've lost interest."

"No!" shouted Thomas. He collected himself. "It's not like that."

"I know, but she doesn't."

"But without a job, she'll think I'm a failure."

"And you fear that more than her thinking you're having second thoughts?"

Thomas stared at his hands, angry at being corrected by his friend. "You don't understand."

They sat in silence for a while until Wiltshire said he was going to the bar. Thomas, still nursing his drink, put his hand over his tankard, muttering he was fine.

"I'm sorry," said Thomas, when Wiltshire returned. "I didn't mean what I said. I know you understand."

"Wakley, I wasn't sure whether to tell you, but for your sake, I must."

Thomas stared at his friend. "What? What is it?"

"Nothing, really. Least as far as I know. But I believe Elizabeth has attracted the attention of someone else."

"What! Who?"

"Wait. It's probably nothing, but I was in *The George* over in Borough one evening. There were these three men talking loudly, the worse for drink. I suddenly heard one mention a 'Miss Goodchild'. Well, you can imagine, I sidled closer and discovered it was Elizabeth he meant. He was quite well-dressed but rough-tongued. Looked like he'd been in the military. He starts telling them of his intentions. Means to find a way to meet her. He talked of what a fine match she'd make, what with her father's wealth."

Thomas sat back. "That's outrageous. How dare he?"

"Steady. It was probably just bravado, showing off to his friends. And we don't know if he has tried to pursue her."

"That's not the point."

"Forget it. You're back now, and you know you're Elizabeth's only interest."

"How can you be sure? This is all because Goodchild won't announce an engagement."

"You surely can't doubt Elizabeth? She probably isn't even aware of this scoundrel's interest."

Thomas sat, turning his tankard around on the table.

"For God's sake, Wakley. Why can't you be like everyone else? Accept help."

Thomas grimaced. "Seems like my future depends on Coulson's letter."

Chapter 7

1817

Thomas lay awake most of the night. Wiltshire had to be wrong. Using Coulson's letter would make him no better than those he abhorred, people who advanced through favours. It shouldn't be about who you know. Where would be the sense of achievement? You should have to fight and prove yourself. The very thought made him realise how like his father that made him. He was still haunted by Incledon's accusation about the privileges he'd enjoyed. The man may have been a rogue but what he'd said still rankled. Thomas knew he'd had opportunities others less fortunate were denied.

He'd no sooner convinced himself that he must keep to his principles than he found himself resenting having to abandon his dream. But far worse, he risked losing Elizabeth. Her father would never let him marry her if he couldn't support her.

The past two weeks had been agonizing, knowing she was living nearby but fearful of visiting until he'd secured a job. Maybe this once he should compromise. After all, he told himself, it was merely a letter of introduction, hardly the same as giving your son or nephew a job. And he'd readily accepted his brother-in-law's offer to go to Beaminster and then being recommended to Coulson. He promised himself it would be the last time he'd accept a favour. And no-one need ever know.

Bedford Street was a terrace of fine, new four-storey houses. As he approached Bampfield's front door, a well-dressed man emerged and doffed his top hat to Thomas before getting into his waiting carriage. Thomas brushed down the front of his coat as he went up the steps. He'd no sooner pulled the bell than a maid appeared.

"Please give this to your master," said Thomas, handing her Coulson's letter.

He was shown into a small elegant room where he was soon joined by an elderly, grey-haired man in a fine maroon frock coat clutching the letter.

"Bampfield," he said, nodding slightly.

"Good morning, sir. Wakley. Dr Coulson suggested I visit you."

"So I see," said Bampfield, as he scrutinised the letter. He took off his spectacles and scrutinised Thomas. "Thinks highly of you. So, you're looking to be an assistant? Well, I can't offer you anything permanent but if you'd like a few weeks' work, I need someone while I'm in Scotland. Like to know my patients are in safe hands, not exposed to the whims and fancies of any old practitioner."

Thomas knew to reassure him. "Quite so."

"Hmm. Coulson says you know what you're about. Can you start next week?"

Thomas beamed with delight, unable to conceal his relief. "Yes, sir. I'd be delighted to."

"Keen, aren't you?" He rang for the maid. "Can see why Coulson thinks you'll go far. Mary here will show you how we do things. She sees to the patients' comings and goings."

As he stepped back out onto the pavement, Thomas couldn't believe how simple that had been. Coulson's word, taken on trust.

*

The following week, when Thomas arrived just after dawn, Mary was still lighting the fires.

"Oh, wasn't expecting you so early, sir. This way."

He'd never seen such a plush consulting room, with its buttoned leather chairs and polished mahogany desk. Two rather forbidding landscapes hung either side of a grand white marble fireplace. Net curtains over the lower half of the large sash windows shielded the room from the carriages and pedestrians passing in the street.

It was the best part of an hour before Mary returned, giving him time to peruse the rather old and out-of-date medical texts in the bookcase. There was no sign of any current journals. As the clock on the mantelpiece chimed nine, his first patient arrived.

"Mrs Lindley is here to see you, Doctor," said Mary, holding the door wide open.

A short elderly woman, dressed in black, strode in.

"Hmm," she said, looking Thomas up and down. "So, Bampfield has deserted his post."

Thomas smiled. "Please, Mrs Lindley, take a seat."

Her rose-scented perfume filled the room.

"What can I do for you?" he asked.

She sighed. "Bampfield never has to ask." She paused, leaving Thomas wondering if she was going to tell him. "Very well, young man. My joints. Can hardly walk. Always worse in the damp. I need more of my medicine."

Even though there had been no sign her walking was limited, she was clearly someone used to getting what she wanted, even if it wasn't strictly needed.

"And what does Dr Bampfield usually give you?"

"You should know that. You are a doctor, aren't you? You tradesmen are all the same."

While Thomas had worried he may not be able to cope medically, he'd not considered having difficulty with how patients behaved. At Guy's, and even in Beaminster and Henley, he'd not been questioned by patients. They just accepted whatever they were told and were grateful.

Thomas ascertained the medicine Mrs Lindley was usually prescribed, gave her what she wanted and, relieved, saw her out.

Although some patients that morning were apprehensive on discovering Bampfield was away, most were not as difficult as his first one. Generally they were well-to-do, with such mild problems he wondered why they'd come to see him. Vague aches and pains, slight bowel problems, small skin blemishes. Despite him doing little, they thanked him for his time and were content if he prescribed the same medicines they'd been on for some time. The only exceptions were two well-dressed men he suspected of having venereal disease. They refused to accept the suggestion, became quite hostile, and threatened to report him to Bampfield on his return.

By mid-morning there were no more patients to see. Mary gave him the details of three who wanted to be visited at home. All were only a few minutes' walk away, so by early afternoon he had finished for the day. He still had an hour before he was expected at Tooley Street.

*

As he crossed London Bridge, the river was, as ever, shrouded in thick fog. Watermen were steering their wherries between river steps, carefully threading their way between the ships. The stench was so strong he kept moving. As usual, Tooley Street was clogged with carts.

The Goodchilds' maid curtseyed as she stood aside to let him in. Elizabeth must have heard his voice as she was already descending the stairs while he was still removing his hat and coat.

"Thomas." She took his hands then leant back inspecting him sternly. "I thought you were never coming."

"I'm sorry. Finding work has taken up all my time."

"Not good enough." She paused before a wide smile appeared. "I'm teasing you. You're here now."

She led him upstairs to the drawing room.

"Mr Wakley," said Mrs Goodchild, putting aside her embroidery. "Come and sit down and tell us all your news."

Sarah closed the magazine she'd been reading, as eager as ever to listen. Thomas glanced at Elizabeth, hoping she'd suggest they withdrew to another room, but she encouraged him to sit down. There was no end of questions, about his family, his travels and his new job. As time passed he became increasingly frustrated at not being able to talk with Elizabeth alone. It wasn't until four o'clock, when Mrs Goodchild announced she must attend to dinner arrangements and needed Sarah's help, that they were left in peace.

Elizabeth burst out laughing.

"What's funny?" asked Thomas.

"You. A picture of exasperation."

"Oh, was it obvious?"

"To me it was. I don't think Mama noticed, though Sarah will have."

They sat side-by-side on the settee.

"Well, you've heard everything I've done," said Thomas. "It's your turn. What have you been doing?"

She leant back against the cushions. "Oh, nothing much. We only came back from Mill Hill a week ago. After last year it was so wonderful to be able to garden again. Maybe it was having to survive no summer last year, but plants put on the most magnificent display I've ever seen. I so wanted you to see them."

Thomas smiled, any lingering fear of a rival suitor having vanished.

"It took being back in Devon for me to realise how much London has changed me," said Thomas. "Everything I want is here."

Elizabeth reached out and stroked his head. "Most of all, me?"

He took hold of her hand. "Of course, you most of all."

"I've so many plans for us this winter. Theatres, concerts, exhibitions. But first, you must talk to Papa. Stay for dinner and speak to him afterwards. Now you're working, he must announce our engagement."

He sat looking at her, their fingers entwined. "You make everything seem so straightforward. These past few weeks, all I've seen are difficulties."

"Then that's got to change."

He picked up the magazine Sarah had been reading.

"*The Lady's Magazine.*" He raised his eyebrows. "Are men allowed to look?"

She smiled. "Don't be silly, though I doubt you'll find much to interest you. It's not like your medical books or the newspapers."

He flipped through the pages, glancing at the articles. "Such variety – stories, poems, theatre reviews."

"That's why it's popular. You never know what you'll find."

He suddenly stopped and held it up. "And science. What's that doing here?"

"Why shouldn't it be?"

"Just wasn't expecting it in a magazine for ladies. I've never seen such a mixture in a periodical before."

"That's why it's successful. Just because ladies like novels and poetry doesn't mean we're not interested in other things."

The dinner gong sounded downstairs.

"Come on. I'll lend you a copy but you might not want to be seen reading it in your coffee shop."

*

He'd always woken early. While it was still quiet outside, he'd read by candlelight and annotate the notes he'd made the previous day. He rarely had anything of interest to chronicle from Bampfield's patients but plenty from his visits to the Borough hospitals. He'd also taken to writing short pieces, a paragraph or two, which helped him collect and organise his thoughts about the way patients were managed and how the hospitals were run.

After two or three hours, he went for breakfast, always to the same coffee shop on Cheapside where he could be sure of finding abandoned newspapers. There was rarely any medical news so he was surprised one morning to find that several were reporting an extraordinary twenty-fold rise in the number of cases of typhus fever in the hospitals. Throughout the morning he kept pondering how they could have made such a claim.

By midday he'd decided to investigate. Apart from going to the Borough hospitals, he'd visit the Middlesex and the Westminster. It was unlikely anyone would question what he was doing on their wards as he was still young enough to pass as a pupil.

He was astonished to discover numerous patients had indeed been diagnosed with typhus. Mostly young men, but none had the dull red rash and the dry hacking cough typical of the disease. Not only that. Invariably they'd been feverish for weeks; too long to be typhus. The more he saw, the more he was convinced this was synochus. He hurried home, composing in his head the letter he'd write to *The Times* questioning the typhus claim.

Two days later, when he opened the paper and saw it, he could barely contain his excitement. He'd never seen his name in print. He kept re-reading it, so pleased with his phrasing – '*I believe it is synochus which has been, by some practitioners, unthinkingly named typhus.*' Unthinking. It had taken him a long time to come up with a word that was both hard-hitting and polite. He imagined hospital doctors reading it and bridling at such criticism, wondering who *T Wakley of Guy's Hospital* was. He was pleased he'd gone on to explain why his observation was important. '*It will remove the groundless anxiety which exists with respect to the prevalence of typhus in this city.*'

Throughout the morning he struggled to concentrate on his patients' complaints, so elated was he by his letter. He felt it announced his arrival on the medical stage.

*

Thomas got used to Ivatts lying in wait for him. Whatever hour he returned to Gerard's Hall, the proprietor miraculously appeared. Maybe he did it with all the residents.

"Evening, Mr Wakley... sorry, Dr Wakley."

"Good evening," said Thomas, continuing towards the stairs.

"Another long day. And bless me, you start so early. What was it, four o'clock this morning?"

How did Ivatts know that? Did he stand outside, looking for candle light at his residents' windows? Did he never sleep?

Thomas hesitated at the foot of stairs. "Quiet at that time. Helps me concentrate."

"That's good, what with the important work you do."

"Good night then, Ivatts."

Thomas knew the man meant no harm, that he was just lonely. The first week of his stay, he'd told him of his wife's demise.

"Poor woman. Passed two winters back. Between you and me, the apothecary didn't help. No end of medicines. Cost me a fortune but did no good. Do you think a surgeon, like your good self, would've helped?"

"I'm sure the apothecary would have suggested a surgeon if he thought it necessary."

Thomas had no idea if that was true. Upstairs, he unbuckled his bag and took a sheaf of papers with that day's notes on the patients he'd seen and that evening's talk at the Westminster Medical Society. He added them to the growing piles on his table. He could do with more space, but for now this met his needs. Being on the top floor the only sounds he heard were the bells of St Mary-le-bow and, when the wind was from the west, St Paul's. And it was cheap. He needed to save as much as possible.

*

"Surely you, of all people, can see what's happening," implored Freddy.

Thomas had never seen him so incensed. Where was the quiet, thoughtful man he'd known? Freddy wouldn't settle constantly walking about the small sitting room while Thomas laid out the chessmen.

"I know lots needs changing," said Thomas, "but I can't honestly see that things are any worse than they've always been."

"What? Thomas, *habeas corpus* has been suspended. You know what that means, don't you? Sidmouth can have any of us locked up just because we disagree with him." Freddy sat down. "Goes against everything British."

Thomas leant back and tried to placate his friend. "It's only because the government believes revolution is brewing. Mob rule, like in France."

"That's ridiculous," said Freddy. "People just want enough to eat. They're not interested in bringing down parliament, more's the pity. And no-one wants what happened in Paris." He sat forward. "All right, let's play."

Within a few moves, Thomas lost a knight.

"Hey, not like you," said Freddy.

Thomas pushed his chair back. "You've changed, Freddy. What's happened? You weren't like this before I left London."

"Just never talked about it. I imagined it wouldn't go down well with Signor Clementi." He smiled. "Only the wealthy buy pianos."

"What about your uncles?" asked Thomas. "What do they think?"

"Who knows? They only talk about pianos and the business, though once or twice I got the impression they agree reforms are needed." He picked up a copy of the *Political Register* that was lying on a side table. "Wouldn't want them to see me with this though – not until I was sure of their views."

Thomas reached over and took it from him. "You read this?"

"Along with half of London," Freddy laughed. "Don't know for how much longer it will appear now that Cobbett's had to scarper to America, frightened of being locked up."

"I saw him speak once," said Thomas, as he thumbed through the periodical.

"Cobbett? How come?"

"When I was boarding at All Hallows in Honiton, there was an election. I didn't really understand what was going on, but for a schoolboy it was exciting. One evening, me and another boy crept out of the dormitory and went to the hustings."

He sat back, staring into space. "I remember it clearly. There was a wooden stage in the main street. It was pretty boring until Cobbett spoke. He was so rude to the Tory. Accused him of paying men to vote for him. When he told the crowd he wouldn't pay, they jeered and called him all manner of names."

"Ah, a potwalloper borough!"

"I couldn't understand why the Tory just stood there with a self-satisfied smile, unperturbed."

"Your first taste of politics!" chortled Freddy.

"Cobbett dropped out. Left it to the Whig to take on the Tory. Every evening that week, I sneaked out to see the results pinned up in the High Street. After three days there wasn't much in it but as the week wore on the Tory got more and more. He must have been bribing those who hadn't yet voted."

"Well, not sure when we'll hear Cobbett speak again. Mind you, there are plenty of others worth hearing."

Freddy got up to put more coal on the fire.

"I know I've always been a bit of a loner," said Freddy, "but now I can see that to get change, people have to join together."

"That's exactly what Coulson told me if I wanted to take on the medical establishment."

"The meetings are exhilarating. I always come away convinced reform is possible."

"Meetings? What meetings?"

"About how parliament must be reformed, getting rid of the Corn Laws, stopping the enclosures... Come and see for yourself. The MP Henry Brougham is coming next month." Freddy laughed. "He's so radical his fellow Whigs loath him."

Thomas stood up and clapped his hands together. "Count me in. Now, let's forget chess for today. I'm starving. How about some dinner?"

Being a Sunday, it wasn't busy in the chop house.

"You know, rabbit never tastes as good in London as it does in Devon," said Thomas, wiping his mouth with his handkerchief. "Best of all when you've just shot it yourself."

Freddy winced "Not my idea of fun." He put down his tankard. "So, when is your engagement to be announced? I've never been good at keeping secrets."

"Next week."

"Splendid. How come? What's changed?"

"I've got a job. Just got to persuade Bampfield to keep me on for a while."

The following week, when Bampfield returned, he looked grey and tired.

"Don't look so worried," said the elderly doctor. "It was just a bit gruelling. Eight days on the road, and nights in inns. I'm getting too old for it. Give me a few days, I'll be fine."

He gingerly lowered himself onto a chair. "Mary tells me patients speak highly of you." He spoke slowly, coughing at times. "Had plenty of time to think these past weeks. Decided it's time I took on an assistant. Are you interested?"

Thomas struggled to hide his excitement, fearing it might appear unprofessional.

"Most certainly am," he said.

*

"I haven't stopped thinking about that play," said Thomas.

He and Elizabeth were sitting in the Goodchilds' house taking tea. It had been Thomas's first visit to a theatre.

"Wasn't sure what to expect. Such a strange title. *A New Way to Pay Old Debts.*"

Elizabeth smiled. "What did you think of Mr Keen? Wasn't he wonderful?"

"I thought they all were. Couldn't believe they weren't real people."

"That's the magic. It's why I love the theatre. I was sixteen when I first went. *Romeo and Juliet.* Kept thinking about it for months."

"Have to say, at first I thought it was daft. The story was preposterous but then I realised I've met men like Sir Giles Overreach. I got so lost in it, I wanted to join in and argue with them."

Elizabeth burst out laughing.

"What?" said Thomas.

"Good job you didn't. 'Surgeon thrown out of Drury Lane Theatre'. Would never have lived it down."

"But at Medical Society meetings we join in, debate things. Least I do."

Elizabeth was refilling their cups.

"What puzzled me," said Thomas, "was Overreach was such a villain, destroying men financially, yet the audience liked him. How could people condone the way he behaved?"

"Oh, Thomas. What they loved was a newly-made man getting one over the old, landed gentry who were so self-satisfied, looking down on him. People sympathised because he was made to feel an outsider."

"But he was unscrupulous and deceitful. Men like that shouldn't be lauded like a hero." He paused. "So, what's the next play?"

She smiled. "Ah, hooked already. Shakespeare, *Henry IV*. But you have to promise me one thing."

"What's that?"

"You won't be tempted to join in!"

1818

That winter the fog seemed even denser than usual. Some evenings the buildings on the other side of Basing Lane were hardly visible as he left Gerard's Hall. Ivatts was convinced it was a sign of God's displeasure; an explanation he frequently cited and one that Thomas had stopped bothering to challenge. He gingerly made his way up to Cheapside where he was meeting Freddy for breakfast.

"Bit noisy in here," said Freddy, removing his hat and unwinding his scarf. "Why do you come here?"

"Aha," said Thomas, raising an index finger. "They bake their own Duchess of York biscuits, and customers leave their newspapers lying around. Never have to buy one."

"People like you will put the papers out of business."

"Nonsense. You said yourself the steam-presses had quartered their costs but I don't see any reduction in their prices."

"All right. Let's see what's so good about their biscuits."

The four men sitting at a nearby table who were shouting over one another, got up to leave.

"Thank goodness," said Freddy. "Couldn't hear myself think. Now, what news of Bampfield?"

"He's kept me on. Trouble is, I'm not sure how long I can put up with it."

"Really? He sounded fair and decent."

"Oh, he is. It's the patients. There's not much wrong with most of them."

"They must have something wrong, else why would they summon him?"

"Oh, they can always come up with something. Minor aches and pains, stomach gripes, stiff joints. I suspect they've been encouraged by Bampfield to keep coming back."

"Ah ha! Good for business," chuckled Freddy.

"Thing is, while it's providing me with an income, I rarely get to do any surgery and when I do, it's just simple stuff. Feel more like a general practitioner. Beginning to wonder if my plan is doomed to fail."

"Give it time. Can't expect to gain a reputation overnight. Took Signor Clementi years."

A maid appeared with mugs of coffee and biscuits.

"What did you make of the meeting last week?" asked Freddy, as he stirred sugar into his coffee.

Thomas's face lit up. "Brougham's some speaker. So clear and straightforward. Suppose that comes from being a lawyer, trying to convince jurists. Couldn't believe that a respected lawyer like him lives in fear of being jailed."

"Like I've been telling you," said Freddy, "we live in times when anyone who speaks out is at risk."

He pulled a rolled-up journal out of his coat pocket and leafed through it.

"Listen to this. '*Some men are deemed inflammatory by an establishment that openly defends the inflammatory conduct of those that give rise to it.*' Sums it up. If you question an aristocrat with an income of £24,000 a year, you're the one pilloried in the newspapers, not the rich person who's done nothing to deserve such wealth."

Thomas took the journal from him.

"*The Examiner.* What a great title. Not like the tired, boring titles of our medical journals."

Freddy roared with laughter.

"You know," said Thomas, "Brougham made me realise that the corruption, the nepotism, the unaccountability in medicine, is no different from other areas of life."

"Think about it. Why would it be otherwise? It's the same people in control, protecting their own interests. Look who your hospital governors are. Why would they run the hospitals any differently than the way run everything else – parliament, the church, the army, the government? It's all linked."

*

The short walk to Fleet Street that usually took him fifteen minutes took almost an hour. Every time Thomas tried speeding up, he collided with people who, like him, were blinded by the fog. Some apologised but others were quite threatening, blaming him as if he'd collided on purpose. Although he'd been to the London Medical Society several times, it took him a while to find the small alley leading into Bolt Court. The gas lamps over the entrances to buildings offered little help.

Upstairs, the room was packed. Several men acknowledged him with a slight nod or, in a few cases, a smile. When he'd first attended, he'd been ignored, subjected to dismissive stares. He'd decided that to get noticed, he needed to contribute to the discussion. The first time he'd tried, men looked at him as if he had no right to speak, even though he went out of his way to reinforce others' views. It amused him how easily they'd been hoodwinked. Now he'd been accepted, he intended to be far less restrained, saying what he really thought.

"Gentlemen, if you'd take your seats," said the president, Dr Sims, standing at the lectern, his chain of office dangling round his neck. "Tonight, Mr Cribb is to address us on abdominal dropsy."

At great length, Cribb told the tale of Betty Crane, a twenty-four-year-old with a distended abdomen.

"Tapped her and released 35 quarts of fluid."

The audience gasped, forcing Cribb to wait for them to settle down.

"Went on to bleed her, apply mercurial liniments, and prescribed diuretics and purgatives. A month later, she'd filled up again. Took twenty quarts this time. Gave her more diuretics, bled her some more and blistering on the abdomen, only for her to fill up again. Twenty quarts that time."

A man in the front row raised his hand. "Did you not think of sweating her as well?"

"I did indeed, sir. A sudorific twice daily for a week."

All around the room, men were nodding and muttering to one another.

"To continue, gentlemen. Another tapping produced twenty-two quarts, so I decided it was time to try something new."

He raised a finger and, clearly expecting to impress his audience, he announced he'd ensured the abdominal puncture wound remained open by deliberately induced inflammation of the peritoneum.

Thomas was mystified. He'd never heard of such an approach, but the audience were unperturbed.

"Although the case ultimately terminated fatally, I'm convinced my actions were not the cause."

Thomas's gasp was met with hostile looks from those around him, so he quickly pulled out his handkerchief and blew his nose, apologising for disturbing them.

When Cribb eventually finished, Thomas waited for someone to challenge him but the only question was about the bore of the tubing used. Thomas couldn't understand why no-one questioned the wisdom of what he'd done. The meeting would soon end. It was now or never.

"Mr President," said Thomas, rising to his feet, "might I ask Mr Cribb on what he bases his conclusion that his treatment wasn't the cause of death?"

Cribb's condescending smile incensed Thomas. "I can see you're early in your career. It's based on experience, something that you too will enjoy in a few years' time."

As Thomas sat back down he realised, with horror, that Cribb really believed that. As the meeting broke up he could hear men planning to copy Cribb and deliberately inflame the peritoneum. He remained seated as men filed past him, some offering him withering looks. Dejected, he went to retrieve his coat from the cloakroom. As he was winding his scarf round his neck, a clean shaven, youthful looking man, wall-eyed with gingery hair, introduced himself.

"Glad someone asked that," he said, in a broad Scottish brogue. "Though not much of an answer. Or maybe you don't agree?"

"Wakley," said Thomas, bowing his head. "Umm, no, it wasn't the answer I was expecting."

"Very diplomatic." There was a hint of a smile. "Don't believe I've seen you here before. Wardrop."

Thomas was distracted trying to decide which of Wardrop's eyes to look at.

"I only joined a few weeks ago."

"Don't be put off. The place needs men like you." With that, he wrapped a cape over his Spencer. "Next time." He turned and headed briskly for the door.

Thomas was intrigued, not least by his archaic clothes. He'd not seen anyone wearing a Spencer in London. Clearly a man who didn't care what others thought.

*

Since his engagement, dinner with the Goodchilds had become a regular part of Thomas's week. He was always warmly welcomed by Mrs Goodchild, while Sarah could be counted on to tease him, wanting him to describe the operations he'd seen, complaining if his account wasn't gory enough. Her fascination reinforced his frustration that all he ever did was remove a skin nodule or suture a small wound. He feared it would always be like this unless he could get his own practice and establish a surgical reputation. That was the only way he'd stand a chance of being elected an honorary surgeon in a hospital.

After family meals, Mrs Goodchild let him and Elizabeth withdraw to the small parlour at the back of the house, as long as they left the door ajar.

"It's a year-and-a-half, Thomas," said Elizabeth. "How much longer before we wed? I can tell from their looks, my friends are wondering if it will ever happen. And Mama tries to hide her worry but I know she's concerned."

"Soon, I promise. I'm trying. Even taken on extra work at St James' workhouse to earn more." He paused. "There's a practice in Camberwell which, if I borrowed some money, I could afford."

"Camberwell?" Elizabeth looked down at her lap, smoothing out the pleats in her dress.

"It's in a fine terraced house."

She looked back up. "But it's so far away."

"The great Dr Letsom lives there."

From her blank look he could see that had fallen flat.

He tried again. "There's a new road from Vauxhall Bridge."

"Can't you find a practice in the West End?"

He sighed. "Maybe, but even if I did I couldn't afford it. Not for years."

"I'm sorry, Thomas. It's just, I so want to get away from here. The stench of the river in summer, the fog in winter and all the time, the noise and grime of the factories."

"Well, we'd be away from all that in Camberwell."

She sat twisting the ribbons on the front of her dress round and round.

"Please say something," said Thomas. "The last thing I want to do is upset you."

She looked up. "I'm sorry. I just wish I could do something to help."

*

"Quite a conundrum," acknowledged Freddy when he next saw Thomas. "But given your wily skills on the chessboard, I'm sure you'll solve it."

"Can't see how."

"Is this the boy who got us out of so many scrapes at school? Remember that time Mr Clarke set us a translation of Ovid and we didn't do it because you insisted it was the perfect weather to catch fish in the Tone."

"You didn't need much persuasion, as I recall."

"Perhaps. But you told Mr Clarke we were not yet satisfied with our translation, needed an extra day. You remember how taken aback he was? Then you stayed up all night doing it."

"You've left out the end of the story. He thought it was the best translation he'd ever seen."

"True, he did. Now, I know just what you need," said Freddy, fetching a bottle and two glasses. "Madeira. Drink this while I set up the pieces."

As he sipped his drink, Thomas picked up an old copy of *The Examiner* and thumbed through it. He suddenly stopped and waved the journal at Freddy.

"Ah, Keats again. Did I tell you we were pupils together?"

Freddy looked at the cover. "December 1816. It's nearly two years old."

"It says here, he's one of the three most promising new poets," said Thomas.

"You should find out for yourself. You know, poets like him are just as radical in their way as Brougham and Cobbett."

Thomas gazed into space.

Freddy stared at him. "Tell me. I know that look."

"My friend Wiltshire said the same about some of the new artists. Turner, Constable."

"What have I been telling you? Reform is all around us. It's coming. Now will you believe it's not just doctors and hospitals that need turning inside out?"

1819

He feared the worst. A letter from Goodchild summoning him for five o'clock on a Wednesday afternoon. This was clearly not for a social gathering. If Goodchild was going to rescind the engagement, he wondered if Elizabeth knew. Maybe the man Wiltshire had overheard in the inn had asked permission to propose to Elizabeth. While he knew the idea was ridiculous, he couldn't get it out of his mind. He wanted to speak to her first but worried her father would think he'd gone behind his back. Better to just face him and try and make him understand that it wasn't for lack of effort that he hadn't yet saved enough.

Come the day, the dreadful weather seemed a fitting portent. Driving sleet added to the usual dense fog that enveloped the banks of the Thames. The only light visible in Tooley Street came from the furnaces, deep inside the factories. Thomas took extra care. Lose your concentration for a moment and you could be mown down by a cart. He'd seen plenty of victims in the admissions ward at St Thomas's, most of whom later succumbed to gangrene and fevers.

The maid showed him into Goodchild's office. The last time he'd been in there, two years earlier, was to ask for Elizabeth's hand. He didn't have to wait long.

"Ah, Wakley," said Goodchild, "sit yourself down."

The place was so crammed, Goodchild had difficulty squeezing through to get behind his desk. The way he scrutinised Thomas reminded him of his father. Thomas sat upright, determined to hold his gaze.

"Understand you've not got your own practice yet."

"Not yet. But I hope to afford one soon."

"That's as maybe." Goodchild lit his pipe and leant forward, his elbows on the papers covering his desk. "I've got a determined daughter who keeps pestering me to do something. Seems she can't wait to get married."

"I'm as keen as she is but the practices I've suggested aren't in places that Elizabeth would choose to live."

"Hm. So choose somewhere she favours."

"I would if I could afford it. Maybe in a few years if all goes well. Meanwhile, there's a practice in Camberwell with excellent prospects but she won't hear of it."

Goodchild sat back and roared with laughter. "That young woman. Always been like it. Must get it from her mother."

Thomas felt his whole body relax, slumping slightly.

"She's always made clear her feelings about living here," continued Goodchild. "I understand. No place for a young lady. Thought that getting out to Mill Hill for the summers would help."

Thomas felt some sympathy for this tough, down-to-earth man. He was like so many Devon farmers, accepting their lot despite the harsh conditions they endured.

Goodchild put down his pipe and stood up. "I'm a practical man. Believe in finding answers and moving on. Only way to survive in business. So, here's what I plan to do. I'll pay for the practice. See it as an investment. You'll have to find it as I haven't a clue about that sort of business."

The idea caught Thomas unprepared. He wondered if Elizabeth lay behind it. Whether or not she did, it angered him. It was the way Goodchild was telling him what was to happen, treating him like a child. The man hadn't even made a pretence of discussing it.

"That's most unexpected." Thomas paused, floundering for how to stall on making a decision. "It's very generous of you. If I accept, I'd want it to be a loan, paid back over time as the practice became established."

"If you wish but that's not required."

"I need to talk to Elizabeth about it."

"Very well. But don't dawdle. I can't take much more of her constant badgering."

*

Working for Bampfield continued to test Thomas's patience. Watching capital operations at the Borough hospitals – cutting for stone, amputations, removing cancerous tumours – just increased his frustration at having to deal with aching joints and skin rashes. He was still determined to become a hospital surgeon despite missed out on a dresser-ship. He longed to be centre stage in an operating theatre, watched by countless pupils, like the leading actor in a play, applauded at the end.

Freddy had invited him to a concert in Marylebone but Thomas barely listened to the music. Goodchild's offer was so tempting. His own practice would let him hone his skills and build up a name for himself. But he so wanted to maintain his independence. He heard his sister's voice:

"We all have to compromise, Thomas, throughout our lives. Do you think I haven't put up with things I didn't like?"

It wasn't until an hour after the concert when they were in a local chop house eating supper that Thomas finally got the chance to tell Freddy of Goodchild's offer.

"That's wonderful," said his friend, lifting his tankard to celebrate. "Here's to your good fortune."

"It's not that easy."

"Ah! Why aren't I surprised?"

"I don't want to be beholden to him; to anyone, in fact."

175

"Ah, yes, the old Thomas," laughed Freddy. "Just the same in Wivey. Like when my father offered to pay your coach fare back to your farm and you refused, insisting you'd rather walk."

"It's not like that. I'd be dependent on him for ever more. Elizabeth will think I'm not able to care for her."

"Thomas, you don't half talk nonsense for such a wise man. Why would she think that?"

"You don't understand. You're not married."

Freddy put down his tankard and sat back. "Is that how you see me?"

"Oh, Freddy. I'm sorry. That was a crass thing to say. Please forgive me and forget it."

Freddy slowly turned the tankard round and round on the table.

"If you want my advice," said Freddy quietly, "you gracefully accept."

*

Even as he was being shown into the first-floor drawing room, he still wasn't sure what he was going to tell her. Elizabeth rose, came over and put her arm through his.

"Thomas. I didn't know you were coming today. We've eaten, but I'm sure Mrs Spring could rustle up a meal for you."

He smiled. "It's fine. I've already eaten."

"Good evening, Mrs Goodchild." She was sitting by the fire, as ever, embroidering.

"Good evening, Mr Wakley. Elizabeth, if you want to retire to the small parlour, I believe there's a fire in there."

Thomas imagined Mrs Goodchild knew of her husband's offer and had anticipated Thomas's visit.

Elizabeth sat in one of the small armchairs while he took the settee.

"So, what brings you here? Is anything the matter?"

"No, no." Thomas cleared his throat and ran a hand through his hair. "I know how much you want us to live in the West End, and that you know I won't be able to afford that for some time. Well, your father has offered to pay. I need to know what you think."

"Oh, dear Papa. He can be distant and gruff at times but he always says yes eventually."

Either she was a good actor or her father hadn't mentioned the offer to her.

"So, you think we should accept it?"

She looked astonished. "Of course. Why ever not? It means we can wed at last." Her eyes narrowed. "Isn't that what you want?"

"Nothing I want more."

"So, what's the problem?"

Thomas sighed. "You'll probably think it stupid but I've never liked feeling dependent."

The way she was looking at him was so disconcerting. "Isn't that what marriage is all about? Doesn't dependence lie at its heart?"

Thomas had imagined they'd talk about the practicalities of accepting the funds, of her father owning the practice and their home. Instead, she had taken him onto territory he'd given little thought to.

"Of course but isn't that a different sort of dependency?"

"Is it? Are there different types?"

Thomas was relieved by a light knock on the door. It was the maid wanting to know if they required drinks. It gave him time to regain his composure. After the maid had gone, Elizabeth, not taking her eyes off him, waited for him to speak.

"Very well. I'll accept the offer on the understanding it's a loan that we'll pay back."

She rose slowly, came over and sat beside him on the settee.

"And I will tell Mama she can start arranging the wedding. She'll be so happy."

"It may not be for a while. I've got to find a practice and then the purchase has to go through."

"But it doesn't stop Mama and I starting to plan."

*

He lost no time in starting his search. He let his interest be known at the medical societies and revisited the more elderly surgeons he'd met when seeking work the previous year. The prospect of a purchaser being available might persuade someone to consider retirement.

For weeks he found nothing. Then, one morning Bampfield told him he'd heard that Malleson, a surgeon in Mill Street near Hanover Square, might be persuaded to sell up.

"I'll write and introduce you," said Bampfield.

Thomas lost no time. Malleson was in his sixties, wanting to retire and return to Northamptonshire where he'd spent his boyhood.

"Been unsure how to find the right person to take the practice on," he told Thomas, "so your interest solves that. If Bampfield recommends you, that's good enough for me."

Thomas was having difficulty restraining his joy.

"I'm not quite ready to stop," said Malleson. "One last summer. September would suit me."

Another five months working with Bampfield. How would Elizabeth take a further delay? But he'd found nothing else and it would give him and Elizabeth time to find a house. It would have to be nearby if he wanted to hold on to Malleson's patients.

There was a spring in his step as he strolled back down Oxford Street. He had to stop himself tipping his hat to passers-by. He headed straight to Tooley Street to speak to Goodchild.

Later, as he made his way home, it dawned on him that for a man who engineered two medical pupils to meet his daughters in Mill Hill on the pretext of his hospital subscription, this was all simply the final stage of his grand design. Thomas smiled to himself as he recalled Goodchild's final comment.

"After all, want a good home for my grandchildren."

Chapter 8

1819

Thomas now felt he was a Londoner; that he belonged. He loved the way the coachmen at the *Bell and Crown* in Holborn recognised him on his Sunday morning trips to Mill Hill. The journey had become so familiar, he anticipated every bend and deep rut, bracing himself as the coach lurched from side to side.

All week he longed for Sundays when he'd see Elizabeth, despite knowing that he'd disappoint her with his continued failure to find them a home. It wasn't until late July that he travelled bearing the news she longed for. The journey seemed to take longer than usual. He became convinced the coachman was deliberately going slowly to frustrate him.

Once up on the ridge, standing outside the Goodchilds' house, the fresh air was a tonic after the muggy oppressive heat of London. The maid showed him through the house and out onto the terrace where the family were sitting under the large awning. As Elizabeth leapt to her feet to greet him, her face dissolved into a broad smile.

"You've found somewhere," she said, clapping her hands together.

He was crestfallen. He'd wanted to be the one to break the news.

"Don't look so forlorn," said Elizabeth, taking both his hands. "It's just... it's written all over your face. So, tell me, where is it?"

"Let the poor man sit down," said Mrs Goodchild, pointing to the chair beside her. "He's barely arrived."

He heard Sarah calling for them to wait as she made her way across the lawn from the swing, which hung from a large oak tree. The maid returned with a jug of elderflower cordial and filled their glasses.

"Come on," said Elizabeth. "You know I can't stand suspense."

"I need a drink first," said Thomas, determined to make her wait. He took several gulps before putting his glass down.

"Thomas," said Elizabeth, crouching down beside him, "tell me."

"Argyll Street."

"Argyll Street." He'd never seen such a look of joy. "Oh! Perfect. How did you find it? Does father approve? It must be so expensive."

"Don't worry. He's agreed the rent with Thompson, the owner, who lives next door. The tenant, Woolaston, wants to give up his lease in December." He paused. "He's an archdeacon, so I think he can be trusted."

Everyone laughed except Elizabeth. "Not until December?"

"Oh, my love. It's not long."

She pursed her lips. "It's just, we've waited so long."

"But sister, it's such a fine street," said Sarah.

"Woolaston described the neighbours as 'persons of consideration'," said Thomas, "whatever that might mean."

Sarah started giggling until Elizabeth cut her a severe look.

"I expect he means they're reputable but not wealthy," said Mrs Goodchild.

"I thought the Earl of Aberdeen lived there," said Sarah. "I'm sure Mr Wiltshire designed wallpaper for him."

"Never mind the neighbours, tell me about the house," said Elizabeth. "What's it like inside? When can I see it?"

"It's huge. I lost count of the rooms as I went round. I'm told there are fifteen, though that includes the basement and the servants' floor at the top. There's a double drawing room on the first floor, with three tall windows overlooking the street, and on the floor above are two bedrooms. Downstairs, at the back, there's the perfect room for seeing patients."

"We're going to need so much furniture."

"Well, Woolaston was keen to sell much of his, so your father negotiated what he felt was a fair price."

"I wonder if the archdeacon felt it was fair," joked Sarah.

"Now, my dear, don't make fun of your father," said Mrs Goodchild, though unable to suppress a slight smile. "It sounds ideal, if a little too grand for me."

"I'll move into Malleson's house in Mill Street in September" said Thomas, "so I can take over his practice. I mustn't risk losing his patients. And Malleson wants to sell me his consulting room furniture and his stock of drugs."

"Now," said Mrs Goodchild, "it's one o'clock. Just because your father's not here doesn't mean we should have lunch late. Come along."

After lunch, he and Elizabeth stood arm-in-arm in the shade of the trees at the bottom of the garden looking out over the forested hills.

"What are you thinking?" she asked.

He continued to gaze into the distance. "About all that's happened to me. All the setbacks. At times I doubted I'd ever have my own practice, be in control of my destiny."

Turning, he gently took her shoulders. "You know what this means? I can establish my reputation as a surgeon and then it's only a matter of time before a hospital offers me an honorary post."

As she pressed against him, he wrapped his arms around her.

"We must talk to Papa and Mama about our wedding."

"But your father insists I prove myself first."

She broke away. When she turned back, her eyes had filled up. *What now?* he wondered. *Why couldn't she celebrate what he'd achieved?* He'd spent weeks searching for a house that would meet all her desires. He'd expected her to rejoice.

She dabbed her eyes with a silk handkerchief.

"I'm sorry. I know you're doing your best. Papa's always been like this. Has to be in control." She managed a slight smile. "Still, once we're married that's an end to it."

Not till they'd paid back the loan, thought Thomas.

*

He was in his room at Gerard's Hall, writing, when Ivatts' maid appeared to say Mr Collard was downstairs.

"Come on," said Freddy, standing in the entrance hall, being watched by Ivatts. He lowered his voice. "You can't miss tonight's meeting."

He clapped Freddy on the shoulder. "All right, I'll come."

"It's starting, Thomas," said Freddy, as they walked briskly along Cheapside. "At last, reform is in the air."

Turning into Great Queen Street, Freddy bustled Thomas into the Freemason's Tavern. The large room was already packed.

"You lead," shouted Freddy, pushing him forward.

Thomas smiled. "Ah, can see why you wanted me to come. Be your bodyguard."

"Just keep going. As close to the front as possible."

It was like being in the anatomy theatre at Guy's, squeezed in like herrings in a barrel. There were men from all walks of life and Thomas sensed the anger in the room. Men scowled and shook their heads as they engaged in heated discussions.

When the meeting started, and for over an hour, the crowd's anger was stoked up by speaker after speaker.

"The Prince Regent. What profligacy," thundered one. "Workers starving while he and his cronies feast on peafowl and pineapples."

Men booed and stamped their feet.

"Gentlemen, gentlemen," shouted the next. "Only one thing for it. Do away with the monarchy and all their hangers-on."

Freddy leant closer to Thomas. "And end up with Napoleon? No thanks."

Men reported anti-Corn Law protests all over the country, broken up by the military and the leaders imprisoned. The organiser was just preparing to close the meeting when someone rushed up to him with a message.

"Before we close, I'm told there's some important news from Manchester you'll want to hear. This gentleman's travelled all night to get here."

An elderly man, stooping slightly, stepped forward clutching his cap. The crowd fell silent, wondering what was to come.

"It's with a heavy heart I must tell you there was a massacre yesterday."

There were gasps as people turned to their neighbours, checking they'd heard correctly.

"Tens of thousands of us, gathered in St Peter's Field demanding parliamentary reform. A vote for every man. Then, as Henry Hunt addressed us, we were attacked by cavalry. It was a slaughter. Countless defenceless people killed." He struggled to keep going, gulping to get his breath. "Weavers just wanting to feed their families."

Men just looked at each other in disbelief. Then, defiant voices were heard.

"Enough talking, action now."

"String 'em up."

"Death to the Tories."

In vain, the organiser called for calm, pleading that violence wasn't the answer. But few were listening. Men were pushing their way out.

"Stand to the side," Freddy told Thomas. "We'll wait till they've gone."

When eventually they made their way outside, they found a large crowd milling around calling for a march on Parliament.

"This isn't the answer," whispered Freddy, his voice cracking.

Several Bow Street officers had gathered on the opposite side of the street, watching.

"Come on," said Thomas, steering Freddy away. They crossed Lincoln's Inn Fields and dived into *The Seven Stars*.

"Sit there while I go to the bar," said Thomas. Even he needed a drink tonight.

When he returned, clutching a large and small tankard, Freddy was leaning on the table, playing with the soft wax dribbling down the candle.

"It's odd," said Thomas, looking around. "None of this lot know anything about Manchester yet. It's as if time has stood still. Here in London, we're still in a time when the massacre hasn't yet happened."

"That'll change soon enough," said Freddy, "though the papers will probably blame Hunt."

"But he harmed no-one."

"That won't stop them. Shame Cobbett's not back yet. He'd have it round the country in days."

"What? He's coming back from America?"

"So I hear."

They both sat drinking for a while, lost in their own thoughts.

"I fear there'll be calls for an uprising," said Thomas, "but it's reform we need, not bloodshed."

*

When it came time to leave Gerard's Hall, Thomas was surprised by how upset Ivatts was.

"Been one of my longest, Dr Wakley. Always paid on time. You're a real gentleman."

Thomas had become quite fond of the proprietor. "My thanks to you, Ivatts. Keep taking those medicines I prescribed and let me know if you need any more help."

Malleson's house in Mill Street was far grander than anywhere he'd ever lived. And he inherited a housekeeper, Margaret, who agreed to stay on for a while. To his relief, Malleson's patients were prepared to give him a chance but Thomas soon discovered few were seriously ill and many, he suspected, were just wanting to check him out, to decide if they'd stay with him. Although he felt more like a general practitioner, he needed their custom to maintain a good income until he'd built up his reputation as a surgeon.

A few weeks later, the move to Argyll Street went without a hitch, largely thanks to Margaret. That first evening, when all was done, Thomas sat at his desk pressing his fingertips together, looking around. A bookcase housed the few works he'd accumulated and a small cupboard beside the couch contained Malleson's surgical instruments, though he'd need several more. He'd left behind the lancets and scalpels as they were so blunt. On top of the cupboard were five glass pots awaiting a delivery of leeches. His membership certificate from the Royal College of Surgeons hung on the wall, alongside a charcoal sketch of Guy's Hospital that Wiltshire had done years before. He'd never felt so content, no longer harbouring resentment about not having got a dresser-ship. He'd show them.

Stepping out into the hallway, the house was silent. He'd given Margaret the night off as she'd worked tirelessly all day making sure the porters didn't damage the furniture, organizing deliveries of coal and sorting through what Woolaston had left.

He went upstairs and stood at the drawing room windows watching carriages passing. The flickering light from the gas lamps in the street bathed the room in a soft, yellowish glow. He imagined coming up here after dinner and sitting with Elizabeth in front of the fire. He loved the way, when he'd shown her round, she'd immediately come up with ideas on how to decorate and arrange the furniture. He wished she could join him sooner than February but the date of their wedding was now set.

Having never hired staff before, he was relieved Margaret wanted to vet her successor. She was so demanding that it was two days before she ventured a suggestion.

"A couple here who I think might suit you. Daniel and Sarah Witcher."

When, after a few minutes' questioning, Thomas discovered Daniel had grown up in Devon, the die was cast.

*

Despite the pressure of work, Thomas kept attending Medical Society meetings. He no longer kept quiet when questions and comments were invited. The trouble was, it had reached the point where fellow members groaned slightly when he stood up. However, afterwards, one or two would discreetly thank him for saying what they'd been thinking.

To his relief, every so often he'd hear a talk that was truly scientific. One such was a treatise on how best to treat gout. He thought of Coulson and how general practitioners like him would love to read about what was said. As the meeting was drawing to a close, he got to his feet.

"President. Shouldn't our proceedings be published?"

Henry Clutterbuck, the president, smiled benignly. "Young man. You need to understand there are great benefits from our meeting in private. If our differences were aired in public, it could undermine the fine standing of our noble profession and simply cause distress among those with no medical training."

There were mutterings of approval and self-satisfied looks from members, delighted to see Thomas quashed. He was dumbfounded. Clutterbuck had always seemed to be a progressive, thoughtful physician.

Afterwards, as he was collecting his coat, he felt a hand on his shoulder and turned to find Wardrop, the man who had been so encouraging the previous winter.

Wardrop leant towards him. "Would you join me for tea next week?"

Thomas detected a slight smile and glint in his eyes. "Of course, be delighted to."

"Good. Tuesday, four o'clock. Number 2 Charles Street."

*

This is how our home might look, thought Thomas, sitting in Wardrop's first-floor drawing room. Velvet maroon drapes at the three windows, a gilt-framed mirror above the mantelpiece, deep-buttoned leather armchairs and settee, and two large oil paintings of mountains and a lake.

"Loch Lomond," said Wardrop, "most beautiful place in the world. You should go."

"I've heard say there's excellent hunting."

"Aye, so there is. There's nothing to compare to stalking a stag high above the loch." Wardrop put down his cup. "You're probably wondering why I invited you. I'll be frank. I can see you're not much enamoured by our profession. Am I right?"

Thomas stalled for time, sipping his tea. He knew so little about his host but couldn't believe this man had gone to the trouble of inviting him only to trap him.

"Is it that obvious? I've always tried to be careful what I say at Society meetings."

"Clear as day to me."

Thomas leaned forward, his hands on his thighs. "I can't believe so much of what I see."

"Aye, go on."

Thomas took a deep breath. "Take the other night. They were frightened to admit not knowing what's best for patients, what works." He paused. "It's not just that. When I was a pupil, most of them taught us nothing on their ward rounds. Just happy to take our fees."

Wardrop was listening intently, encouraging him to continue.

"And why is nothing done to stop incompetent surgeons? I've seen patients suffering in theatre and other surgeons standing back, just watching. No-one does anything. Not the hospital, not the College. Same with the physicians. Persisting with treatments that are doing no good, watching patients decline and die."

Wardrop's smile emboldened him.

"Can't something be done?" asked Thomas.

"Trouble is, most doctors don't think it's their job to do anything. They worry about rocking the boat, falling out of favour with the powerful."

Thomas felt the pent-up pressure he'd been harbouring for years being released. At last, a London doctor he could talk to openly, without fear.

"Can I ask you about Sir Astley?" asked Thomas.

"Go on."

"He's committed to scientific surgery and was such a brilliant teacher, even staying after lectures to answer questions. Why doesn't he advocate reform?"

"Ah, Sir Astley. An enigma if ever there was one. Quite a radical in his youth. Some say he was a Jacobin. Story is, the Guy's treasurer told him he had to disavow his beliefs to get appointed, otherwise the governors would reject him."

"So, he's propping up a system he doesn't believe in?"

"Wakley. We all have to compromise, be pragmatic."

"Do we? Have you?"

Wardrop said nothing as he stood up and went over to the mantelpiece. Having lit some candles, he turned to Thomas.

"Look at this house. Back in Scotland, I became a surgeon to help those less fortunate. Yet I sit here, in Mayfair, receiving a stream of Scottish nobility most of whom are worrying unnecessarily about their aches and bowels." He sat back down. "Why? Because their payments allow me to pursue my scientific interests. Pragmatism. The key to success."

"But that hasn't helped you get a hospital appointment." Immediately Thomas felt he'd overstepped the mark. "I'm sorry. I've no right to say that."

"Nonsense. It's why I wanted to meet you. A man prepared to challenge." He paused. "Truth is, there's nothing I'd like more than a hospital post, operating in a theatre." He sat forward. "Years ago, I had to accept it'll never happen." He laughed. "Not unless I set up my own hospital."

"I don't understand. Why on earth not?"

Wardrop smiled. "I'm not one of them. An outsider. Probably also doesn't help that in the past I questioned the way they treated some patients."

Thomas put down his cup and sat back, his head down.

"Are you all right?" asked Wardrop. "Gone quite pale."

Thomas looked up. "I've been pinning my hopes on establishing myself so I might get appointed to a hospital. Needn't be one of the big ones."

"Sorry. Didn't intend to upset you."

"I've been kidding myself. It's been staring me in the face. I saw not getting a dresser-ship as just another setback to be overcome. Thought I'd still succeed despite them. Defy the odds."

"Ah. Unfortunately, it's not like racing when an outsider sometimes wins. The medical establishment ensures that can't happen."

That evening, sitting alone in his large drawing room, Thomas knew Wardrop was right. The man himself was evidence enough. If a surgeon as able and accomplished as Wardrop couldn't win, how could he?

1820

It took several weeks for him to accept the hopelessness of his ambition. With his marriage coming up, he knew for the moment he had to just keep the practice going. There'd be time to decide what to do later.

What made it worse was he'd become convinced in the past few months that he'd put all past adversities behind him. He'd seen himself standing in an operating theatre, poised to start, his audience falling silent, spellbound, and later applauding as he stood back. He felt stupid, ashamed at having been so naive. He was too embarrassed to share such realisations with Elizabeth; least, not for now. He needed time to come up with new plans.

Just as he thought things couldn't get worse, a strange and unsettling letter arrived. Standing in his study, he had to steady himself against the edge of his desk. He clutched the letter so tightly, he crumpled it. Slowly lowering himself into his leather chair, he read it again.

'*Beware. Your house will go up in flames within the month. Jealousy is the cause.*'

He turned it over in search of a clue as to who the sender was. Nothing. The handwriting was competent without being that accomplished. He got up and summoned Daniel.

"Sorry, sir," Daniel said, wiping his hands. "Was just laying a fire."

"Who brought this letter?"

"Don't rightly know, sir. Not seen him before. Came that early, woke me. Did think it a bit odd he didn't want to wait for a reply."

Thomas looked back at the letter, unable to keep from reading it yet again.

"Will that be all, sir?" asked Daniel.

"Yes, thank you."

Thomas was perplexed. Who could want to harm him? Jealousy? Jealous of what? His practice, his good fortune to be helped by Goodchild, his upcoming marriage? He recalled Wiltshire's tale of the man interested in Elizabeth a year back but surely a passing fancy wouldn't drive a man to this?

It was the cowardice that angered him most. If someone wanted to harm him, for whatever misguided reason, they should at least confront him openly. He glanced down to see his hands were clenched, ready to do battle. But without an opponent he felt impotent.

As he read it yet again, he convinced himself it was an empty threat. Anyone intent on arson would just do it. No, this was the work of a weak coward. Thomas imagined him out there, watching the house. Well, he'd grant him no satisfaction. When he set out to visit patients later that morning, he'd give the air of a man unperturbed, full of confidence and bonhomie. It wasn't much by way of retaliation. Hardly a decisive left hook. But he smiled to himself at the thought of keeping the man waiting for hours in the freezing snow-covered street.

He knew he could tell no-one about it, least of all Elizabeth. With their wedding only weeks away, she'd be terrified of coming to live there, always fearing an arson attack. Disrupting

Thomas's life was exactly what the perpetrator wanted. No-one must know. Life must go on as if nothing had happened.

*

It was bitterly cold as Thomas and Freddy set out by cab one Saturday morning in February to make the short journey from Argyll Street to St James's Church in Piccadilly. Their progress was hindered by the heavy fall of snow overnight and the piles of rubble in the streets from the buildings being demolished to make way for a grand new avenue.

Thomas tried peering out, but the window was fogged up. "Do you ever feel events are conspiring against you?" he asked.

Freddy, wedged in beside him in the carriage, furrowed his brow.

"What a question on your wedding day."

"But do you?"

"Thomas, I've never met anyone who has overcome adversities as well as you. Whatever you've set out to do, you've succeeded. Once you put your mind to something, you do it."

Thomas sat quietly for a while, staring out of the window again. "We could get there faster on foot."

"Thomas, you're going to get married. You can't turn up on foot."

"All right. You know I've never been patient."

They sat in silence for a while.

"Is that how you see me?" asked Thomas. "Someone who always succeeds."

"What have you ever failed at? Tell me."

"Getting a dresser-ship."

"That was different. Sounds like you couldn't have done more. Without the golden connections, the dice were loaded against you."

Thomas gazed back out of the window. "You've helped me so much and I... I've done nothing for you. Not sure I'd be marrying if it wasn't for your encouragement."

Freddy laughed. "Well, that's true. You did need encouraging." He slapped his hands together. "Now, enough of this. We're almost there. Let's get you married before Miss Goodchild freezes to death waiting."

A pathway across the church courtyard had been cleared of snow. The sun suddenly appeared between the snow-laden clouds, making Thomas stop. The church seemed to be floating on a sparkling white carpet.

"Everything all right?" asked Freddy.

Thomas smiled broadly. "Today it most certainly is."

*

He leant back, transfixed by the flames illuminating the decorative fire back, resting his head on Elizabeth's shoulder.

"I can't believe how much you've done in a fortnight," he said.

She smiled. "I started planning months ago, right after that first visit. I don't think there's a store in London I haven't been to. And don't go thinking I've finished."

Every day, when he returned from his rounds, she insisted they take tea while she showed him their latest acquisition. Lined velvet drapes from France with a pink silk fringe, a sumptuous couch, rosewood cane-seats with brass ornaments. He made himself show some appreciation, though in truth, he was content as long as a chair was comfortable and a table sturdy.

He got up and put more coal on the fire, sending sparks up the chimney.

"I've only just started in here," she said. "Over there I think we need a what-not, and between the windows a card table. I need somewhere to take the ladies when we leave you men to smoke after dinner."

He sat back down. "Fine, though I might have to withdraw too, as I don't smoke."

She laughed. "One other thing."

He closed his fingers about hers, wondering what was coming.

"You look so worried." She paused. "You need some new clothes."

"New clothes? That's it? I thought it was something serious."

"Thomas, it is. Don't you see that to be taken seriously you must first earn the respect of the powerful."

"What? Become one of them?"

"No, of course not. But let them think you're no threat. That way you'll get their ear. You won't be dismissed as a man of no consequence."

He sat looking at her. "Where did you come by such insight?"

"Novels and plays. Countless stories of men rising up, of good overcoming evil."

"Stories," mused Thomas.

He went and closed the drapes. When he came back he leant over and kissed the top of her head.

"Very well. But you'll have to do it as I've no clue about clothes."

Over the following weeks, a stream of tailors, bootmakers, glovers and others visited. They measured him and showed him endless fabrics to consider. He failed to see the need for so much but Elizabeth assured him it was necessary. Pairs of trousers, black silk gloves, purple and green silk handkerchiefs. As far as he could see, her wardrobe was even more extensive, augmented by countless items of jewellery.

*

"You look exhausted," said Freddy as Thomas joined him in *The Seven Stars* one evening. This had become their meeting place, being midway between their homes.

"Malleson's old patients might not have much wrong with them but they aren't half demanding. Expect me to come running at all hours of the day and night. Trouble is they all want leeches."

"Why's that a problem?" asked Freddy.

"Can't get them. The farms say the hospitals come first but they're using more and more. Fifty thousand at Tommy's last year. Can you believe it? Twenty times as many as three years ago."

Freddy laughed. "Ah, the leech craze."

"Have had to start rationing them; even considering re-using them the way hospitals did when supplies from France were cut off."

Thomas pulled out a purple handkerchief to blow his nose.

"What's this?" said Freddy. "Silk, eh? Gone up in the world."

Thomas quickly stuffed it back in a pocket. "Don't. Not my doing. Elizabeth insists you only earn respect if you're suitably attired."

"And do I detect you don't agree?"

He sat looking at Freddy. "No. Reluctantly, I do. It's one thing she's taught me."

"Hmm? Only one thing?" teased Freddy. "You look most distinguished. A real gent."

"Maybe but it's purely pragmatic. If I have to listen to another conversation at dinner about the right width of collar for the season…"

Freddy guffawed. "I'd love to be there to see you."

"Enough of that," said Thomas. "What's been the fallout from the Peter's Field massacre?"

"Ah, Peterloo. That's what it's being called. Largely ignored. All the talk is about the Thistlewood Gang. Five of them are being done for high treason." He shook his head. "Such idiots. Managed to make people sympathise with the government."

Thomas sat taking it all in.

"What are you thinking?" asked Freddy.

"Never thought I'd find myself siding with a Tory government."

Freddy roared with laughter. "Welcome to the messy world of politics. We've no choice. People like Thistlewood are even less desirable than the Tories. He'd have us decapitate the King and destroy parliament so he can be our Napoleon."

"Heaven forbid," said Thomas. "And just when there's growing support for reform."

"Talking of which," said Freddy, "how do you intend to shake up the doctors?"

Thomas stared at the table. "Truth is, Freddy, I've been distracted."

"Ha. I warned you. Fine dining and soirees turning your head."

"No, no. It's not that." He looked at his friend. "Something else. If I tell you, you're not to tell a soul."

"Trust me, I won't."

Thomas took a deep breath. He leant forward and spoke quietly. "I'm being threatened."

"What? What do you mean?"

"Keep your voice down," said Thomas, glancing round to make sure no-one was listening. "Letters. The first was just after Christmas. Said they were jealous and would burn down the house."

"What!"

"Shh. Nothing happened, so I forgot about it. Then, two weeks ago, another letter."

He pulled a crumpled paper out of his inside pocket. Freddy took it and flattened it out. He read it out, quietly.

"*You are not forgotten. Your house will yet be burnt and you assassinated within the month.*" All the colour drained from Freddy's face. "Why would anyone do this?"

"Haven't a clue."

"Have you talked to your solicitor?"

"Lofty? He says to increase the fire insurance. But if I did, I can't tell them the reason. If that got out, Elizabeth would refuse to live there."

Freddy stared at him, narrowing his eyes. "You haven't told her? Thomas, she's entitled to know."

Thomas took back the letter, folded it up and stuffed it in his pocket. "It would just cause her to worry. Nothing's going to happen. Whoever it is just wants to frighten me, else he'd have acted by now."

"But you're still worried or you wouldn't have shown me."

"Not really." He clasped his hands together. "It's just, I can't put it out of my mind completely."

"Have you told Bow Street?"

Thomas opened his hands towards Freddy. "You should be a solicitor. Just what Lofty said. Actually, he insisted. Said it was important, just in case anything ever happened."

Freddy stood up. "Don't know about you but after that I need a whisky. Then I must be going."

*

The moment he got back from visiting patients, Thomas sensed something was wrong. Martha appeared, looking distressed.

"Oh, sir, my lady's in the drawing room. Asked if you'd go straight there."

He hurried upstairs to find Elizabeth pacing about, her eyes red, and clutching a lace handkerchief.

"Oh, my love," said Thomas, rushing over to her. "What's the matter?"

As he took her in his arms, her body shook and tears poured down her face.

"It's Mama. She's gone." She gulped, unable to go on until she'd taken a few deep breaths. "I only saw her a few days ago."

Thomas sat her down on the settee and she buried her face in his shoulder, sobbing. He was tongue-tied, unable to think of what to say. He'd never experienced anyone close dying. Everything he thought of saying sounded inadequate in the face of Elizabeth's overwhelming grief. He then realised that there was nothing to be said. He remembered how, at the end of a bare-knuckle bout, there had never been any need to say much to your defeated opponent. There was an understanding that transcended talk. A look, a nod, an acknowledgement was all that was needed or, indeed, wanted. So, he just sat silently while she wept.

For the next couple of weeks, they didn't go out at night. After dinner, she settled in front of the fire in the drawing room, reading, while he sat at a small writing desk making notes on that day's patients.

One evening, having finished and stoked up the fire, he joined her on the settee.

"Shelley," he said, picking up the book she'd been reading.

She smiled. "One of my favourites."

"Can't get over how much poetry you've been reading. Seems to be like a balm."

"Ah, spoken like a surgeon." She sighed. "Shelley embraces death."

"But my job is to stop people dying."

"Yes, but everyone will die and he thinks we should accept that and form a close relationship with death. That enhances life."

"How can death enhance life? It strips us of our life."

She took the book back from him. "But until then, our hopes of what happens afterwards should be united with our love for life."

Thomas wasn't sure he understood but could see the solace it gave her.

"Let me read you some," said Elizabeth. "This is called *Mutability*."

He closed his eyes as she read.

"'*We are as clouds that veil the midnight moon;*
How restlessly they speed, and gleam, and quiver,
Streaking the darkness radiantly! - yet soon
Night closes round, and they are lost forever.'"

As he opened his eyes, she closed the book. "Papa let me read him some."

As they sat gazing into the flames, she stroked his fingers.

"You never talk about your Papa and Mama."

He turned to her. "Don't I? I suppose not."

"Do you not want to see them? I can't imagine not seeing my family."

He sat forward. "It's different with mine. We've never been close; least, I haven't. Apart from with Anne, that is."

"But family is so important."

Twisting his head round, he looked at her. "Is it? I never felt part of life on the farm. I couldn't wait to get away. And then…" He hesitated. "When I left last time, I swore I'd never have anything more to do with my father. It was despicable what he was doing."

He felt her hand gently rubbing his shoulder.

"Whatever he'd done, you can't go through life never speaking to him again. And think of your poor Mama."

He sat back and ran a hand through his hair. "That's what Anne said." He paused. "Maybe, one day."

*

It wasn't until May that Thomas spoke to the Hope Fire Insurance Company. He made no mention of the threatening letters but said he was doubling his insurance because of all the plate, china, jewellery and clothes they'd acquired.

A month had passed since the second death threat, reinforcing his belief that the perpetrator had no intention of carrying it out. How he longed to know who the man was so he could confront him and put an end to it.

Not having seen Wiltshire in a while, Thomas was delighted when he received a letter suggesting they go to a prize-fight.

"And I know the perfect place for dinner beforehand. Best scalloped oysters and potted rabbit to be had in London."

Despite the inn being packed, the landlord found them a table.

"A little influence and a coin or two works wonders," chuckled Wiltshire.

Wiltshire was one of those men who Thomas could start talking to as if they were just carrying on their last conversation.

"So, how's the paint-staining going?"

"Splendidly," said Wiltshire. "You wouldn't believe the number of commissions my designs have been getting. I'm hoping Goodchild will agree to Sarah and I marrying next summer."

Their food arrived. After a few mouthfuls, Wiltshire wiped his mouth and leant forward.

"I must tell you about the Newgate executions. Thistlewood and his accomplices."

"You went! Too gruesome for me."

Wiltshire laughed. "A squeamish surgeon. Wonderful." He looked around to make sure no-one was listening. "I was some way from the scaffold. Wasn't going to pay two guineas to get a place up front. There were lots of unsavoury types mingling with the crowd, handing out leaflets calling for everyone in the Lords and Commons to be executed."

"Damn revolutionaries," said Thomas, shaking his head.

"Crowd was so large they needed Life Guards to hold it back. They hanged the five of them, one by one, then left them swinging for half an hour before cutting them down."

He leant closer.

"Now, what happened next is what I wanted to tell you. This man appeared, black mask over which he'd tied a coloured handkerchief. Wore a hat, slouched down to complete his disguise. Well, as he stepped forward wielding a scalpel, the crowd started yelling and hissing. Have to say, he did it so deftly and speedily, seemed he'd done it before. *The Times* reckoned he was a surgeon. Lots in the crowd thought so, too."

"Well, it's of no consequence. Good riddance. Revolutionaries like Thistlewood set back the cause of reform." Thomas slapped him on the shoulder. "Come on, or we'll not get ringside."

*

Thomas and Elizabeth didn't get back from her brother Joseph's wedding until midnight. Heavy rain meant the road from Hendon was almost impassable in places. The Witchers met them in the hallway and took their coats.

"Kept the fire stoked up in the drawing room, ma'am," said Daniel.

"Shall I bring you hot toddies?" asked Sarah.

"Please do, and some of those delicious rout cakes," said Elizabeth.

Upstairs, she knelt by the fire to dry her hair.

"It's so sad Mama didn't live to see Joseph marry."

Thomas looked up from that day's letters that lay on his lap. "Sorry. What's that?"

She glanced at him over her shoulder. "Can't they wait till the morning?"

He dipped his cake in his drink. "Just checking there's nothing urgent."

"Not to see your only son get married." She ran her fingers through her hair, parting the locks.

Thomas put his letters aside. He could feel the toddy warming his cheeks.

"Papa's lost so much, so quickly. First I left, then Mama died, and now Joseph leaving. No wonder he's so withdrawn and deflated."

She leant back against Thomas's legs, rested her head on his lap and closed her eyes. "I could just go to sleep here."

He reached for the magazine on the settee beside him and flicked through it.

"Another bizarre collection."

She opened her eyes. "Oh, *The London Magazine*."

"Theatre reviews, politics, poetry, philosophy," he said, flicking through the pages. "Even medicine. The dangers of people treating themselves for illnesses." He turned the page and stopped. "Oh no, not Keats again. Why does he get so much attention?"

Elizabeth sat up. "Because he got harangued in *Blackwood's*."

"*Blackwood's?*"

She smiled. "It's another magazine; very traditional. They dismissed him, calling him a member of the Cockney School of Poetry."

Thomas frowned. "Why's that so awful?"

"It's insulting. *Blackwood's* thinks he's a fraud. For them, you can only be a romantic poet if you live in the countryside, at one with nature."

"It shouldn't matter where he's from. Question is whether he's any good."

"Truth is, they don't like him because he advocates reform."

Thomas put down the magazine. "Reform?"

"Yes. Poets can be political. Just like doctors can."

He smiled. "Hm. Just what Freddy said."

She sat looking at him for so long he wondered what she was thinking.

Finally, she asked, "Why did you want to be a doctor?"

"Why?" He paused, despite knowing the answer. "It started with Davis. A naval surgeon."

"What? A surgeon aboard a ship?"

Thomas smiled "It's a long story but when I was eleven, I went to sea; a midshipman."

As he told her of his journey, she sat barely moving, occasionally her mouth dropping open as she gasped.

"Davis provided a sanctuary, the chance to escape from the brutality and the struggle to survive."

She turned and stared at the fire. "You were only eleven. No more than a child."

"Yes but it was my choice. All I wanted to do."

"So, you've always been strange, even as a boy."

"You think I'm strange?"

She got up and sat beside him. "Not strange. Different. Not like most men."

"It wasn't just Davis. What really did it for me was when I first saw a surgeon operate in a hospital. It was in Taunton. Everyone watching and assisting was in awe of him. He had complete control. His assistants did exactly what he said." He paused, gazing at the fire. "His confidence pervaded the room." He looked at her. "To me, he was a hero, and I so wanted to be him."

She took his head in her hands and kissed him. "Come on, that's enough revelations for one night."

*

As he climbed out of a cab at the entrance to Guy's hospital he could hear distressing shouts coming from St Thomas's across the street. He pictured a dresser in the admission room trying to immobilise a fractured leg. Picking his way past some beggars on the pavement, he headed into Guy's, determined not to miss the *post mortem*. The room was crowded and instead of the usual quiet whispers, there was a hubbub.

"What's happened?" he asked the man standing beside him.

"You've not heard? A surgeon got attacked last night, right outside in Maze Pond."

Next to him, a tall, bearded man was holding forth. "Tom Davies. He and I were pupils seven years ago."

"Has a practice over in Vauxhall," someone added.

"They tried to cut off his testicles," added another, though Thomas wondered if that was true as it was met with laughter.

"Gascoigne, the chap with him, says they accused Davies of beheading the Thistlewood gang."

"Why did they think that?"

"He had a head in a bag. Just collected it from Tommy's to take home to dissect."

"Hang on," said Thomas, joining in. "How did his attackers know that?"

"Obvious, isn't it? Someone in the dissection room blabbed."

It was quite possible, thought Thomas. He could imagine a porter might sympathise with Thistlewood.

"Means none of us are safe," someone said. "If they've done it once, they'll probably try again."

"Not good for the hospital having their alumni being threatened," said the man standing beside Thomas. "Probably why the surgeons have given Davies fifteen guineas."

"Gentlemen," said the pathologist, tapping his scalpel on the metal dissection table. "Your attention, please."

*

Thomas could barely contain his rage as he left the patient's house. A forty-year-old haberdasher who'd had a hernia repaired at the nearby Middlesex Hospital, now suffering such dreadful abdominal pains he was wasting away as he'd more or less stopped eating. What had the surgeons done? This wasn't the first time he'd wondered what was going on at the hospital. Only a fortnight earlier he'd been called to see a woman who'd had a breast removed and been left with half her chest wall suppurating. And then there had been the boy whose amputation stump had never healed and now the skin flap was gangrenous.

He doubted the hospital surgeons had any idea what happened to their patients. Or if they even cared; simply interested in their patients leaving hospital alive. After all, that seemed to be all that the governors wanted. That way they could cling to the belief that all was well. Bad news would harm their ability to attract more subscribers.

He felt guilty that, as a pupil, he'd never thought about what happened to patients after they left the Borough hospitals. Maybe if he was working near there, it would be the same.

Intrigued to see what was happening at the Middlesex, he decided he'd slip into the hospital to watch some surgery. As he approached the operating theatre, he nodded to the porter guarding the door.

"Good morning," said Thomas, "fine weather at last."

The porter, so taken aback at such a well-dressed man addressing him, just stood aside.

"Oh, morning, sir," he said, bowing his head slightly.

Thomas strode purposefully in. He'd learnt that an air of entitlement worked wonders. One of the three surgeons, John Joberns, was to operate on a hernia. From the course he'd taken at the Great Windmill Street School, Thomas recognised Charles Bell, one of the two other surgeons, sitting to one side.

"Gentlemen," said Joberns, wearing a filthy, spattered apron. "As you can see, this man's got a large inguinal hernia. Wouldn't reduce manually despite several hot baths over the past two days."

His assistant lifted a sheet and revealed a hernia the size of a football, purplish in colour. Thomas was aghast. Hours had been wasted and now it was clear the loop of bowel trapped inside was gangrenous. Even if Joberns managed to get it back in the abdomen, it probably wouldn't survive.

With the patient almost unconscious, having been plied with endless amounts of alcohol, Thomas watched as Joberns started incising the skin and underlying muscle. Despite his assistant trying to stem the flow, blood spurted out, drenching his apron. Minutes went by with little progress being made. Thomas couldn't understand why Joberns was picking away, making small cuts, when what was needed was a large decisive incision that would let him shove the loop back inside. Then, to Thomas's horror, he saw faeces pouring out of the wound. The surgeon must have nicked the gut and, being so friable, it had split.

Joberns looked dreadful, pale and sweating, looking around for help. Bell came over and spoke quietly to him, indicating with his hands what needed to be done. It seemed to Thomas that it would now make little difference. Even if Joberns could repair the gut and return it to the abdomen, that loop was destined to die – and with it, the patient. All around him, Thomas could see distressed looks on the pupils' and dressers' faces. Then he suddenly realised, they didn't seem surprised. It was as if they expected something to go awry. He'd seen enough.

"What's happened?" asked Elizabeth, when Thomas got home. "You look like you've seen a ghost."

Thomas grimaced as he slowly sat down on the settee. "In a way I have."

"Tell me," she said, putting aside the book she'd been reading.

"Such incompetence," he said, leaning forward, staring at the floor.

He looked up. "After all that I've seen over the years, I'm not sure why this one has upset me so much. A man at the Middlesex with a huge hernia. They left him to suffer for two days. They should have operated sooner. Would have given the poor man a chance. Mind you, in that surgeon's hands I somehow doubt that." He paused. "As usual, the other surgeons watching did nothing. I could see what was going on, so they must have."

"Why didn't they help?"

"Honour among surgeons, I suppose. Never criticise a brother surgeon."

Elizabeth sat silently, waiting for him to compose his thoughts.

He looked up. "Odd thing is, I'm glad I went. It made me finally realise, despite dreaming of being a surgeon all my life, I couldn't now join their ranks."

"What do you mean? It's what you've always wanted to do."

"Not if it means being part of that world, of turning a blind eye to others' incompetence, keeping quiet, or worse, defending them." He paused. "Even great men like Sir Astley seem to feel the need to collude. I just couldn't do that."

He sat back, ran his hands through his hair and smiled to himself.

"It may sound strange, but I feel liberated. As I was coming home today, I suddenly realised why I haven't been able to resolve how I can be a surgeon and yet devote myself to reform." He stood up. "The answer was obvious all along. Doing both was impossible."

He went over and gazed out of the window. "It had to be one or the other. And now the answer is clear." He turned back to her. "What I saw today convinced me that I can do more, save more lives, confronting and exposing all that is wrong, than I could ever achieve treating a handful of patients."

Elizabeth remained impassive, giving Thomas no idea as to what she was thinking.

"Don't worry," he said. "I'll go on running the practice in the mornings, ensuring we have a good income."

She smiled. "I'm not worried."

"Really? You don't think I'm being reckless."

She got up and went over to him.

"Thomas. You've never hidden your passion, your desire to change the world – least, not from me. As a girl, I read stories of men like you, single-minded, committed to changing the world. Living in Tooley Street, I never imagined I'd meet one. But when I did, I was intrigued, excited."

"It was that obvious?"

She laughed. "For such a brilliant man, you can be quite naive."

He smiled. "You realise life won't be easy. I'll make enemies, determined to stop me at any cost."

"Oh, I know. I've thought about it a lot."

"You have?"

She took his head in her hands and kissed him. "Oh, yes. Just been waiting for this day to arrive."

Chapter 9

1820

Slowly, he opened his eyes. He could just make out a doorway on fire. Why was he on the floor? He tried pushing himself up but started coughing so violently he collapsed back down. He grasped his chest to stop the spasms of pain. Looking at his hands, he saw they were covered in blood. He struggled to keep his eyes open, as they smarted from the heat and smoke. He was on the point of giving into the temptation to lie there, close his eyes and rest, when he heard Incledon screaming at him. "Get up, fight." A burning timber crashed down, showering him with sparks. He frantically brushed them off and, clutching the sleeve of his shirt to his face, started crawling away from the burning doorway.

From the cold stone floor, he knew he'd reached the kitchen. His head hit something. A chair. He used it to push himself up until he was standing, holding onto the sink. Above him, it sounded like hailstones hitting the roof. He was trapped. Looking up through a skylight, he could see flames high above. He clambered onto the table, reached up, and shattered the glass with his fist. Splinters rained down, cutting his hands. Gripping both sides of the opening, he hauled himself through, out onto the roof. Dollops of molten lead were cascading down from the roof of the house as he staggered over onto the roof of the neighbour's kitchen.

Stamping on their skylight, he smashed it, and lowered himself through, landing heavily on the stone floor. Gasping, he lurched through the scullery, supporting himself along the walls. In the distance, the front door lay open, through which he could see a silhouetted figure. As he stumbled out onto the street, the figure turned.

"Wakley," shouted Thompson, grabbing him.

Clutching him, the two men staggered through the crowd that had gathered to watch the blaze. Beyond them, men were running in all directions shouting orders. Thomas could just make out a line of fire engines.

"Why aren't they doing anything?" he said.

"No water," shouted Thompson.

Flames poured out of the windows of his house. There were loud crashes as burning joists fell through the building, sending great clouds of sparks into the night sky. Parker, another neighbour, was ordering men to rescue what they could but it looked hopeless. Only the most intrepid were willing to try. Parker suddenly saw him and hurried over.

"Thank God. We thought you'd perished. Let's get you inside. Where's Mrs Wakley?"

"Mrs Wakley?" said Thomas, staring vacantly up the street.

"Your wife, is she still in there?" Parker was now shouting and shaking him. "Answer me."

A young man, clad only in a nightshirt, hurried up to them.

"Oh sir, you're alive. Thought you were in there still."

"What? No."

"It's Daniel, sir, your servant."

"Daniel. Yes."

"Mrs Wakley weren't at home," Daniel told Parker.

"Come on," said Parker. "Let's get him into my house."

Parker and Thompson each took an arm and walked Thomas across the road. As they mounted the pavement, someone rushed up and grabbed Thomas's watch from his waistcoat pocket. In a flash, Thomas grabbed the thief by his collar.

"Didn't mean no harm, mister," squealed the man, half choked.

Thomas tried to tighten his grip but the pain in his hand was too great. Then he was being pulled away.

"Let him go, Wakley," shouted Parker. "The constable will deal with him."

Thomas was struggling to see clearly, blood and sweat running down his forehead into his eyes. As they reached Parker's front door, Thomas stopped.

"No, no. My house. I must get my instruments, my books."

"It's too late, Wakley," said Thompson. "Come on, we need to get you seen to."

"Seen to?"

"You're bleeding, man."

Thomas persisted in trying to free himself. "No. I'm fine, that's nothing. Had worse than that."

"Come on," said Parker.

They forced Thomas indoors and sat him down in the front parlour.

"Here," said Parker, handing Thomas a glass of whisky, "drink this. Dr Luke is on his way."

Thomas sipped the drink, then went to get up.

"Hang on, Wakley. Need to get those wounds sorted out."

"Later. I need to check my study." As he tried heading for the door, Parker grabbed hold of him.

"Get your hands off me," shouted Thomas. "No-one tells me what to do in my own house."

"It's not your house," said Parker, beckoning Daniel to help restrain him.

As they forced him back, the door opened.

"Ah, Luke, thank goodness." Parker lowered his voice. "He's quite delirious."

Luke put down his bag and took Thomas's wrist. "What's under the bandage round his head?"

"No idea," said Parker, "already had it on."

"Wakley, I'm your neighbour, Dr Luke. Need to have a look at you."

Thomas stared at him. "Best be quick as I need to go to my study."

A maid brought in a bowl of warm water and some towels. With Daniel's help, Luke slowly peeled off Thomas's blood-soaked waistcoat and shirt. He stood back, shaking his head.

"I don't understand it. Looks more like he's been in a fight than a fire." He pointed at two cuts. "Stab wounds. And there's bruising all over, front and back."

He leant over to examine Thomas's severely swollen right ear, filled with dried blood.

"What on earth happened to you, Wakley?"

Thomas, struggling to stay awake, said nothing.

"Looks like you've gone twenty rounds in the ring."

At this, Thomas managed a wry smile.

"Now, what's with this bandage?" asked Luke, as he unwound it.

When it fell away, Luke gasped. "What on earth? Leeches." He shook his head. "Can't make head nor tail of it."

Suddenly Thomas was roused, throwing off the blanket Daniel had wrapped round him.

"Elizabeth. Let me out, I must talk to Elizabeth."

Luke, who'd added laudanum to Thomas's whisky, handed it to him.

"You're to drink this, all of it. It'll take away the pain." He turned to Daniel. "He'll calm down in a while, then put him to bed. He should sleep for a good few hours. Let's see if we get more sense from him later."

*

Thomas awoke to see sunshine streaming into the room. He looked around, unsure of where he was. His head was throbbing and his whole body ached. As he lay there, piecing together a series of images, he heard voices outside. Then, a knock on the door and Parker crept in.

"Ah, you're awake. Did you get much sleep?"

"On and off," said Thomas, rubbing his eyes.

"Brought you some clothes. Might be a bit small but better than nothing. Plenty of food downstairs when you're ready. I'll send your man up to help you."

Even with Daniel's help, it took some time to dress. Navigating the stairs sent waves of pain through his body.

It wasn't until he was sitting in the dining room, before a fine spread of dishes, that Thomas realised how hungry he was.

"Let me help you," said Parker, sitting down opposite him. "Jugged veal, turbot, calves' liver."

Thomas watched as his neighbour loaded up a plate. He had to turn his head to hear Parker, as he was deaf in his right ear.

"Have to tell you," said Parker, "we all thought we'd lost you. It was ages before you appeared. Didn't think anyone could survive that long."

He placed the plate in front of Thomas and poured them both cups of coffee. Thomas struggled to hold his fork but refused help from Parker, insisting he could manage.

"Shows how easily a spilt candle can play havoc," said Parker.

Thomas continued staring at him, expressionless.

"Must have had a fair bit to drink last night," chuckled Parker, "to sleep through the commotion."

Still Thomas said nothing.

"Luke was surprised by your bruises. Fumbling in the dark, you must have fallen a lot."

Thomas sat back and took a deep breath. "I was attacked."

Parker put down his cup, his eyes widening. "What? What do you mean?"

Thomas spoke slowly and quietly. "A man came. I was in the bedroom. Had dimness of sight all evening so I'd decided to apply some leeches."

Parker said nothing, waiting for Thomas to continue.

"Damn things wouldn't take so I was still up after midnight. There was frantic knocking at the door. Staff were all in bed, so

I bandaged my head and went down. When I asked who it was, a man said Ivatts had sent him. That he was sick and wanted me."

"And you opened the door? At that time of night?" asked Parker. "Bit dangerous, wasn't it?"

Thomas looked at him. "Ivatts is a good man. I said I'd come in the morning. Was in no state to go out. The man said he was parched, would be grateful for some cider."

Thomas paused, trying to make sure he got it right. "I went downstairs to get it but as I came back, there was an almighty crack on the side of my head." His hand went up to his right ear. "There were three of them, I think. They just kept kicking and stamping on me, then one stabbed me."

"My God, Wakley, most men wouldn't have survived."

"I must have passed out. Just as well, as they must have thought I was dead. Next thing I remember is choking."

Exhausted from reliving the events, Thomas slumped in his chair and closed his eyes. The grandfather clock in the hall chimed two.

"Why's it so light at two in the morning?"

"It's Sunday afternoon," said Parker.

Thomas opened his eyes and peered at his neighbour. "Was everything lost?"

"So Mr. Tarrant, the magistrate, says."

Thomas grasped the edge of the table, pulling himself forward. "Elizabeth. I must get to her before word reaches her."

"Of course."

"Kensington. She went to visit her brother."

"All right, but first Luke needs to see you."

Right on cue, there was a knock at the front door and a few moments later the doctor came in, accompanied by Thompson.

"Afternoon, Wakley," said Luke, putting down his bag and taking hold of Thomas's wrist. "Good, good. Strong and regular."

"I must go to Elizabeth," said Thomas.

Luke examined his head. "All in good time, my fellow."

Having checked the stab wounds, he asked Thomas to take some deep breaths. He then pressed on each rib in turn. Several times, shockwaves coursed through Thomas, but he refused to flinch, determined not to give Luke a reason to stop him leaving.

"Going to be sore for some days but no lasting damage. My carriage is outside. We can go in that."

*

"Thomas," said Elizabeth, putting down her book and standing up, "what are you doing here?" Suddenly she froze, her mouth wide open. "Thomas! What's happened? Your face..."

As she moved towards him, her arms outstretched, he took a step back, worried that if she hugged him he wouldn't be able to conceal the pain. He kept his hands hidden deep in his pockets.

"Thomas, you're frightening me. Talk to me. Tell me," she pleaded. "Whose voices were those I heard downstairs?"

"Our neighbours, Luke and Thompson. They were passing this way and offered to bring me." He paused. "I need to sit."

She stood back to let him pass. As he lowered himself onto the settee, he had to put out a hand to steady himself.

She gasped. "Your hand. Look at it."

She went to take it but he drew it back. He'd spent the journey toying with how best to break the news to her but there was no way of cushioning the blow.

"There was a fire last night. Our house. It's destroyed, all gone, everything." His eyes filled and he struggled to speak. "I am so sorry."

"No, no. It can't be."

She staggered backwards, clutching the back of an armchair.

"That's not possible," she said, struggling to get her words out. "It's... it's our home."

She seemed to be pleading with him to say it wasn't true. He tried to stand up, to go and comfort her, but was unable to get up. Slowly, she sat down beside him.

"What happened?"

He recounted all he remembered, leaving nothing out. When he'd finished, she gently unbuttoned his shirt and looked with horror at his bruised body. It had turned deep purple. Her look of disbelief reminded him of the shock he'd felt when he'd first seen a sailor flogged.

She stood up to look at his back.

"Oh heavens," she exclaimed. "There's the print of a boot. They stamped on you."

She sat back down, her hands covering her mouth. "They could have killed you."

"They thought they had. That was all that saved me."

"So Ivatts is behind this," said Elizabeth. "Have you told Bow Street?"

"I don't believe it. Daniel's gone to speak to him."

Resting his head against her shoulder, he closed his eyes as she gently stroked his hair. "You smell of wood smoke."

There was a light tapping on the door. Elizabeth helped Thomas pull his shirt back on.

"Please ma'am," said Martha, "Mr Witcher's here. Says he needs to speak to Dr Wakley."

"Good," said Thomas. "Show him in."

Daniel came in sheepishly, bowing his head to each of them in turn. He stood, just inside the doorway, twisting his cap in his hands.

"Please, sir, Mr Ivatts says it weren't him. Says he's fit as a fiddle. He were right upset to hear about the fire. Wants to know what he can do to help."

Thomas slumped back. "Thank you, Daniel."

"Other thing, sir, is servants and cabbies in Argyll Street say there was a rumour that the man what behe'ded them five Thistlewood men what were hanged, 'e were a young surgeon in Argyll Street."

"What?" shrieked Elizabeth. "That's nonsense, it's a lie. Why would they say that?"

Daniel looked alarmed. "Sorry, ma'am."

"That's all right," said Thomas. "Go and get some rest."

"Oh," said Daniel, fumbling in a pocket. He handed Thomas his watch. "Found this in the street last night."

"That's something, I suppose. Thief must've dropped it when I grabbed him." He paused. "When you've rested, find out as much as you can."

As soon as Daniel had gone, Elizabeth stood up, shaking her head.

"I don't understand. Why would they think it was you?"

"No idea. They just pick on someone. Say it often enough and people believe it."

Elizabeth gripped her hands together, all colour drained from her face.

"When they hear you're alive, they'll try again."

His head dropped. "No, they won't. Cowards don't hang around. They'll have scarpered, left town."

"How can you be so sure?"

He wasn't but he wanted to convince her it was true. He looked up at her.

"I need to sleep."

She came over and gently stroked his hair. "Not until you've had a hot bath, and then I'm putting arnica on the bruises."

He smiled. "You sound like my Mama."

∗

The following morning, as he lay in bed, he could hear Elizabeth moving around quietly, trying not to disturb him. She was already dressed and was laying out a shirt and breeches that she must have got from her brother. Through a gap in the drapes, he could see dawn was breaking.

"You're awake," said Elizabeth, sitting on the edge of the bed.

He could see how red her eyes were. He pulled his arm out from under the bedclothes and took her hand.

She sniffed. "I couldn't sleep. All I could think was how I could have lost you."

She leaned down and kissed his forehead. "I kept picturing you lying there, injured in the burning house, fighting to get out."

She lay down alongside him, carefully sliding an arm under his neck. He turned his head, burying his face in her hair. His eyes filled and, try as he might, he couldn't stop tears pouring forth. He knew she, too, was crying.

"You were restless all night," she said, gulping. "And shouting out. I didn't know if I should wake you."

"Shouting? What did I say?"

"I couldn't tell but you sounded so distressed, terrified."

"I'm sorry."

She leant up on an elbow looking at him. "You're to stop apologizing. It wasn't your fault."

As she lay back down, he wondered if that was true.

"We do have some good news," she said.

He stared at her. "What are you talking about?"

She smiled. "I'm expecting."

"No!" He tried to sit up but the pain prevented him. "That's wonderful." He managed to lean towards her and they kissed.

They lay in each other's arms, both smiling.

*

With Elizabeth's help, Thomas dressed. As she helped him down the stairs, there were sharp pains in his back.

"Come and sit down," said Harriet, as they entered the dining room. "You poor man. I can't believe anyone would do that."

Thomas gingerly sat down at the table.

"Joseph's already left," said Harriet. "He wanted to stay and help but had something to sort out at the works that wouldn't wait." She turned to Elizabeth. "Said he'll let your father know."

"Ah," said Thomas, picking up the *Morning Chronicle*, "Let's see what they have to say." A moment later he slapped it down, shouting, "Balderdash."

Elizabeth laid a hand on his arm. "Thomas, you're frightening Harriet."

Thomas looked at his sister-in-law. "I'm sorry. That wasn't called for."

"It's all right," said Harriet. "You've got every reason to be furious."

"What's the problem? What does it say?" asked Elizabeth.

"They say the fire engines had water when there was none. Then, yesterday afternoon at Parker's, I'm meant to have bled myself. And they make out we're rich, that we had an immense quantity of guineas, and we've gone to our country residence."

"Thomas, none of that matters," said Elizabeth.

Thomas snorted and picked the paper back up. Out of the corner of his eye, he saw Elizabeth and Harriet exchange glances. A moment later he gasped, folded up the paper, and put it to one side.

"What now?" asked Elizabeth.

"Nothing. You were right. I over-reacted."

She was scrutinizing him. "Thomas, you're white as a sheet. What does it say?"

"I'll tell you later. Let's finish our breakfast."

Harriet put her napkin back in its ring. "I'm afraid I must get moving. Visiting a friend. Ask the maid for anything you need."

As the door shut, Elizabeth came and sat beside Thomas.

"What's it say in the paper?" she asked.

"Nothing important."

"I must know everything. You mustn't keep anything from me."

Thomas pushed some locks of hair off his face. "It's just, it seems our disaster has become a great mystery. That's all. People have got nothing better to do than speculate on who the perpetrators were."

She reached over him for the paper but he startled her by grabbing it first.

217

"Thomas. I want to read it."

He sighed. "All right, but before you do, there's something I need to tell you."

He couldn't bring himself to look at her.

"Last Christmas, I got a letter threatening me. No idea who it came from or why. Sender said it was out of jealousy. Thing is, he said he'd burn the house down."

"What?" exclaimed Elisabeth, leaping to her feet.

"Then another letter came in March."

Her eyes narrowed as she leant on the table glowering at him. "You never told me." She took a moment to compose herself. "Didn't you think I deserved to know?"

"Please, Elizabeth. I lay awake night after night struggling to decide whether to tell you or not."

She stood up. "So why didn't you? Thomas, I need to understand. It's important."

His head dropped as he felt his eyes filling up. "I feared you'd not want to marry me if you knew."

"What? How could you think that?" She started pacing around the room. "Thomas, as man and wife we share everything. I want to help you when you're in difficulty and expect the same in return." She stood at the window staring out. "What else haven't you told me?"

"Nothing, I promise. I thought I was doing what was best, protecting you."

"Protecting me. Is that how you see me, in need of protection? Do you think I can't cope?"

"No, it's not like that."

"Sounds like it is."

Thomas leant forward, his elbows on the table, his head in his hands.

"I can see now that I got it wrong. I'm sorry. But you must believe me, I only ever had your happiness in mind."

She remained standing at the window for a long time before slowly coming back and sitting down beside him.

"You must never, ever do that again, do you understand? I won't be treated like a child."

"Oh, my love. I am so sorry."

She spoke slowly and calmly. "We'll get through this but you have to trust me. I'm a lot stronger than you seem to think. I believe in you, that you can do great things, but you have to let me help you."

He held out his hands to her. "Please forgive me."

"Of course I do. I love you."

She leant towards him and kissed him.

"Now. Who knew about the letters?"

"Only Lofty, and he insisted I tell Bow Street." He couldn't bring himself to mention he'd confided in Freddy.

"So, the newspaper either got it from Lofty or Bow Street."

"Won't have been Lofty." He sighed. "No, it was Bow Street. Plenty there would take a few shillings from a newspaper man for some information."

*

Thomas couldn't understand why, three days after the assault, he still felt so weak. It had never taken that long after a fight, even a long, grueling bout. Confined to the house in Kensington, the same question went round and round in his head. Why did the gang think it was him? He thought back through everything he'd done and said but could find nothing that could explain them picking on him.

Daniel brought news that their silver plate had been found in the ashes, repudiating those who still suggested the motive had been theft.

"Thieves don't murder people," he told Elizabeth.

"So," said Elizabeth, "all we know about them is they knew you'd lived in Gerard's Hall and had treated Ivatts."

"I suppose so, but anyone staying there could have known that."

Over the next few days, Thomas had all the London newspapers delivered. He sat in the garden in the late summer sunshine, scouring them for reports of the fire. Nonsense and wild suggestions no longer surprised him, though they still riled him.

"I don't know why you go on reading them," said Elizabeth. "Why don't you speak to the magistrate, set the record straight?"

"You think the truth will stop the rumours and innuendo? Newspapers want fanciful stories full of intrigue and mystery."

"Maybe, but talking to the magistrate can do no harm."

That evening a tall, lugubrious man dressed entirely in black arrived.

"Tarrant," he announced, bowing his head deferentially to Thomas and then to Elizabeth. "Magistrate. Glad you're feeling well enough to help us, Dr Wakley."

He clutched a black leather case that, when opened, served as a portable writing desk. Having given his coat to the maid, he sat facing them with the case on his lap.

"Right. Describe what took place. Don't leave anything out, however trivial you perceive it to be."

Thomas smiled to himself. The last time he'd been spoken to like that was at school in Wivey. As he recounted the events, the images he conjured up were so stark, it was like reliving them. He was relieved whenever Tarrant interrupted, seeking more details, as it broke the spell.

"Well, Dr Wakley," said the magistrate when, after an hour, Thomas concluded his account. "Seems those first reports were wide of the mark."

Thomas was about to regale Tarrant with his views of the press when he felt Elizabeth's hand on his arm.

"I'm sure Mr Tarrant doesn't want to hear what you think of the newspapers," she said.

Tarrant closed his case. "We're continuing to consider two possibilities. This man who sent you letters out of jealousy, and the remnants of Thistlewood's mob."

"It can't be the letter writer," said Thomas.

"And why's that?" asked Tarrant.

"Stands to reason. Why would he wait so long if he was so incensed? Nine months. No, it must be the gang. Question is, why did they pick on me?"

Tarrant stood up. "I'm told there'd been talk for a couple of weeks that the be-header lived in Argyll Street. No idea why. Best we keep our minds open, but I agree the gang seems more likely. We know they'll stop at nothing. Goodnight, Mrs Wakley. Goodnight, sir."

*

"Well, that's something," said Thomas, folding up the *St James Chronicle* next day. "First correct report I've seen. Looks like you were right about talking to Tarrant."

A moment later, his mood changed as he sent *The British Gazette* flying across the room. "Such rubbish."

Elizabeth shook her head, exasperated. "Thomas."

"Well, they now say there were six, not two, threatening letters."

"Ignore it. You know they print whatever they want; the more sensational the better."

"They shouldn't be allowed to get away with it."

Elizabeth sighed as she put down the book of poetry she'd been reading.

"I thought we'd agreed that we had to start thinking about the future. Leave it to Tarrant and Bow Street."

There was a knock at the front door, and moments later the maid appeared. "Please, sir, ma'am, Mr Lofty's here."

"Show him in, show him in," said Thomas, standing up.

Lofty entered, smiling weakly. "Good morning."

Short and rotund, he shuffled over to the writing desk and put down the sheaf of papers he'd been clutching. He bowed slightly to Elizabeth.

"Come and sit down," said Thomas. "What news? Out here, all we have are the newspapers."

"Talk of the town, Wakley. Never seen anything like it. Even my partner, Mr Fairthorne, whose seen it all over the years, can't remember a case attracting so much interest."

"But why?" asked Elizabeth.

"To be honest, not best sure. Seems everyone harbours a view. Only thing people are talking about in the inns and coffee houses."

"So, what are they saying?" she asked.

"Well ma'am, those who go for the jealous writer are speculating on why he was jealous." He turned to Thomas. "Rather unsavoury, some of it. Best not repeated, sir."

"For God's sake, man, we must stop it."

Lofty fidgeted in his seat and cleared his throat. "I think it best we concentrate on a more pressing matter."

"What can be more pressing?"

Lofty coughed and took a page from his papers. "The Hope Fire Insurance Company are refusing to pay."

"What? Why?" asked Thomas, getting up.

"They won't say. Just claim that the circumstances mean you're not entitled."

"They can't," said Elizabeth, shaking her head. "We lost everything."

"I know, Mrs Wakley, which is why I recommend we issue a writ against the directors of the company. Should be enough to make them back down."

Thomas went and gazed out the window. After a while, he turned round. "You realise what this means, don't you? They're intimating I started the fire, that I deliberately burned down our home. It's preposterous. How dare they? And on what grounds?"

"Dr Wakley, I agree. Which is why, if necessary, we'll fight this all the way to the Court of the King's Bench. Have to say, I've never encountered such flagrant injustice. Try not to worry. We won't let them get away with it."

Thomas was nodding vehemently. "Issue the writ immediately. We'll make them regret this."

*

Next morning, Thomas rose early, invigorated by the prospect of a battle. Sitting at the writing desk in the drawing room, he was so absorbed he didn't hear Elizabeth come in.

"Up so early," she said. "You must take it slowly till you're better."

He turned and looked up at her. "There's much to be done."

"I know but it can wait."

He smiled. "No. It can't. There's a swirl of hostility gathering around me. People are convinced I beheaded those men. Others are saying I burned down our house." He paused. "I'm being condemned from all sides and I've no idea why. What have I done to deserve this?"

"Nothing, you've done nothing." She stood silently for a while. "Thomas, I don't understand what's going on but don't do anything precipitate."

"The longer we sit here, the worse it will get. We've got to strike back."

They were interrupted by Joseph and Harriet. As the four of them sat over breakfast, their hosts wanted to know their plans.

"As you know, I'm a simple, practical man," said Joseph, "who likes to get things done. Step by step. So, first things first. A new house and some work."

"It's only been a week," said Harriet, "give them a chance to recover."

Thomas nodded to Joseph. "No, no. You're right. Lofty reckons if it goes to court, it could take months. Already arranged to go and see someone today who might be able to help with getting work."

"Excellent, because I might have found you a house. Just so happens a customer told me of a place in Kentish Town."

Thomas's face lit up. "That's so good of you but I can't go till tomorrow."

"I can go today," interrupted Elizabeth, glancing at Thomas.

"If you're sure," said Thomas hesitantly, surprised and irritated in equal measure.

"I think I can judge the suitability of a house," she said, smiling.

"Excellent," said Joseph. "I'll take you this morning. Don't have to be at the works till later."

Elizabeth went off to prepare for her outing, leaving Thomas mulling over why her offer had annoyed him. The more he thought about it, the more he regretted his reaction as he realised it was her determination, the way she thought so clearly, knew her own mind, that had caught his attention in the first place. It was why he loved her.

*

"Terrible business," said Wardrop, as he offered Thomas a seat in his consulting room. "As if a surgeon would have anything to do with be-headings. Word is it was Grainger's man, Tom Parker. Runs his anatomy school."

"Doesn't stop people being convinced it was me."

"It'll pass. As soon as the rabble find another *cause célèbre*, you'll be forgotten."

Thomas fingered a button in the upholstery of the chair. "I wish I could believe that."

"So, how can I help you?"

He found Wardrop's Scottish lilt calm and comforting.

"The fire insurance company have got it into their heads that I started the fire deliberately to defraud them."

Wardrop almost spilt his coffee in his haste to put it down. "What! Why would they do that? Are you meant to have beaten yourself up as well?"

"I've no idea. All I know is, until it's sorted out, I haven't the money to buy another practice. I need an assistant post but with all these stories circulating, not sure any surgeons in London will offer me anything."

"Nonsense. Don't go thinking that. Some of our brethren are not so gullible as to accept any of that hogwash. I'll ask around. I'm sure we'll find you something."

"Can't say the same about our much-lauded colleagues in Guy's and Tommy's," said Thomas. "I'd expected their support, the way they helped Davies when he got attacked. But I've heard nothing."

Wardrop shook his head and smiled. "That doesn't surprise me."

"But I'm an alumnus, like him. They talk of a lifelong affiliation. Once a Guy's man, always a Guy's man."

"Oh, Wakley," laughed Wardrop, "you've a lot to learn." He went over to his desk and looked at his diary. "The London and the Westminster societies are meeting this week. I'll get them to publicly declare their support for you."

*

A few days later, he and Elizabeth were sitting in the parlour of their new home in Kentish Town while Daniel brought in the trunks of clothes that Joseph and Harriet had lent them.

"My love, it'll be fine," said Thomas. "It may not have the grandeur of Argyll Street but it's quite big enough. It won't be for long. Lofty still hopes the company is going to back down."

He went and wrapped his arms around her. Leaning over, he kissed her forehead.

"I know," she said. "As soon as we get what's rightfully ours."

The early morning coaches from *The Bull and Last Inn* in Kentish Town whisked him into Holborn and a short walk took him to Hatton Garden, where Wardrop had found a surgeon needing a replacement for a month. Picking his way through the crowded streets, he kept losing his temper with men blocking his way. On two such occasions he was forced to apologise when the men retaliated, threatening to lay him out.

It wasn't just frustration at being forced once again to work as an assistant but also not being able to start devoting time to his pursuit of reform. Any hope of a swift end to this situation was quashed by Lofty reporting that the Insurance Company wasn't backing down.

"They're determined to continue this charade," he told Elizabeth, slapping the letter down. "And they refuse to say why they suspect me."

She picked it up and read it.

"How can they get away with this?"

"They won't," said Thomas. "If it's a fight they want, they've picked on the wrong person."

He leant forward, stroking his clenched right hand. They sat in silence, the only sound being the wind rattling the windows.

"Ah, nearly forgot," said Elizabeth, getting up and retrieving a letter from the mantelpiece. "This came at midday."

Thomas turned it over, studying the writing. "Hmm... don't recognise the hand."

As he read it, his face brightened up.

"Well, someone believes me. William Gardiner. Says he's a journalist and teacher of elocution."

"What's he want?"

"Maybe rid me of my Devonish accent?"

Elizabeth's furrowed brow made him burst out laughing. "Only joking. He says he has a passion for justice. Is so incensed how I've been slandered, he's offering to publish a pamphlet exonerating me."

"Do you think it's genuine? Can you trust him?"

"Only one way to find out."

Two days later, Thomas met Gardiner in *The Ship Tavern,* off Holborn. Tall, with long sideboards and brown hair tied back from his face, Thomas had never encountered someone so animated.

"Pamphlets," said Gardiner, waving around his ink-stained hands as he talked. "Best way to spread the word. Look at Queen Caroline. It worked a dream for her. Made a farce of the

King's witnesses who alleged she's been unfaithful. Showed they're all affidavit men."

"Affidavit men?" asked Thomas.

"False, every one of them. All been bribed by the King."

Thomas cleared his throat. "So, what would you put in a pamphlet?"

Gardiner glanced around before answering quietly. "Sworn statements from all who witnessed the fire. Yourself, your neighbours Thompson and Parker, your manservant, and the doctor who saw the wounds."

Thomas was impressed. He'd clearly done his homework.

"Best if your solicitor also contributed," continued Gardiner. "I'll add a foreword on how the company's claims have no foundation and are just vindictive."

"But who'd print it? And how can you sell it?"

Gardiner laughed. "My uncle's a publisher. Reckon it'll be about thirty pages, so will take a couple of days to print."

"Is that all?"

"Joy of the steam press," chuckled Gardiner. "Luddites might not like them but we pamphleteers couldn't live without them. Means we only need charge a shilling."

"I had no idea it was so easy... and cheap." Thomas paused, studying Gardiner. "Why would you do this for me?"

"Dr Wakley, my problem is I can't stand injustice. My reward will be seeing you demolish those unscrupulous men in the full glare of the press. They're no better than common thieves."

"How much would you want for doing this?" asked Thomas.

Gardiner held up both his hands. "Not a penny. I know. You're thinking what my wife thinks. Tells me to stick to my proper job, earn more money, but you know what? Pamphlets are what I love."

Thomas nodded as he weighed up Gardiner's offer.

"Even if this pamphlet doesn't get the insurers to back down, it'll tilt the case in your favour when it comes to court."

Thomas sat forward and clapped his hands together, grinning. "Let's do it."

Gardiner raised his tankard. "Here's to our success."

*

"It's so late," said Elizabeth, helping him off with his coat. "You've got to take it easier. It's only three weeks since you were almost killed."

He took her in his arms and kissed her. "Don't worry. I wasn't working. I went to see Freddy."

"Well, you can tell me what he had to say over dinner. I'm starving."

She led him into the dining room. "Mrs Witcher's cooked your favourite, jugged veal, followed by apple crumble with bramble berries."

"Ah, last chance to eat them!" said Thomas as they sat down.

"What do you mean?"

"Devil spits on the berries after St Michaelmas Day."

Elizabeth gave him a despairing look. "For a man of science, you come out with some nonsense."

"Mama wouldn't have them in the house after the 29th of September."

Smiling, she shook her head. "What a strange childhood you had."

"Didn't seem so at the time."

"Enough of that. What did Freddy have to say?"

"Not good, I'm afraid. Told me he was still hearing men talk of how I was the be-header. And these were well-to-do men who should know better. Bizarre part was, it makes me some sort of hero in their eyes."

"There's got to be someone who'll help, who recognises the truth of what you've said." She paused. "What about your medical societies?"

"They refused."

"What!" shrieked Elizabeth. "Your fellow doctors?"

"They refused. Something about awaiting the outcome of the court case."

"Are you telling me they think you might be guilty? They doubt your word?"

"Seems so." His voice cracked as he struggled to speak. "The one time I asked for my profession's support and… nothing."

Elizabeth got up from the table and came and wrapped her arms round his shoulders.

"They should be ashamed of themselves."

Thomas smiled weakly. "Don't worry. I won't forget."

As she was returning to her seat, she suddenly stopped. "When there were thefts from the works, Papa always said how helpful the Sheriff was."

"Sheriff of London? Parkins?"

She sat down. "It's worth a try. You've got to put a stop to this…" she hesitated, searching for the right words, "this multitude of malignant slanderers."

Thomas was astonished. "Perfect, the very words I'll use."

"Well, go and write to him now."

*

He was alone at breakfast when Gardiner's pamphlet arrived. He turned the pages, amazed at how quickly it had been produced. True to his word, Gardiner had detailed accounts, all making clear there had been intruders who'd attacked him and started the fire. Other people's servants described how they'd seen three men run off when the watchman had whistled, escaping in a waiting carriage.

Thomas rushed up the stairs two at a time, waving the pamphlet at Elizabeth, who was still in bed.

"He's done it. Completely scotched the accusations."

She sat up and took it from him. As she read Gardiner's foreword, she couldn't stop smiling.

"What a way he has with words. *'The viper Slander, whose venomed shape is matured in human distress, has lifted her hideous head and, flattered by the misery of its victim, charges him with being the incendiary in order to complete the sacrifice of his ruin.'* He should be a poet."

"And look at how he ends," said Thomas, taking it back. *"'The public have only to peruse these statements to rectify the delusion caused by the rapid and foul propagation of slander.'* "

She reached forward and hugged him. "Oh, my love. At last, people will know the truth."

"He's extraordinary, like an angel, appearing from nowhere to save us."

Over the next two days, Gardiner kept him informed of how well sales were going. Best of all was when Thomas got a note from Freddy telling him of two customers who'd come in carrying copies and talking about it. He wondered if, as sales mounted, the insurance company would back off and settle.

But nothing happened. Once again, Thomas realised how naïve he'd been to think the pamphlet was the answer. It may help the court case, as Gardiner had suggested, but there seemed no prospect of a more immediate impact.

A week later, he and Elizabeth were settled in front of the fire after dinner when Daniel came in.

"Just been delivered," he said, handing Thomas a letter. "Man didn't wait for a reply."

Thomas broke the sealing wax, unfolded it, and read.

"It's… it's… from Parkins," said Thomas, spluttering to get his words out. He leapt up, gripping the letter with both hands, beaming from ear to ear.

"It's just what we hoped. Apparently, it was his deputy, Turner, who procured the be-header. Says he was only five foot six, a resurrection man who worked for some surgeon. Just like Wardrop told me." He laughed. "Listen to this. The man told Turner he was in the habit of 'cutting off nobs to obtain knackers'."

"Let me see," she said, stretching out her hand. He waited while she read it. "Perfect. It's impossible anyone could mistake

230

you for the man. Oh, Thomas, you must get this in the papers straightaway."

"Gardiner. I'll get him to visit all the newspaper offices in the morning. He'll know who to talk to."

*

The next day, four national newspapers published Parkins' letter and the rest agreed to do so over the following few days. Excited by finally turning the tables on his accusers, Thomas resented the distraction of having to attend the trial of Henry Heald, the young man accused of stealing his watch.

Thomas had never been in a court before. The way the room was divided up into sections and levels intrigued him. Everyone seemed to know their place. Across the room he could see Heald, who was cleanly dressed and had brushed his hair. He looked terrified, barely able to raise his head, and when he spoke, the judge had to tell him to speak up.

As the prosecutor described the events of that night, no-one was questioning the notion there had been intruders who had attacked him and set fire to the house. Thomas kept expecting the judge or the defence barrister to object, but no-one did. It suddenly dawned on him. The trivial incident of his watch being stolen was providing him with an official record – from the Old Bailey no less – that vindicated him, scotching the notion that he himself was the arsonist.

How had he or Lofty not spotted this possibility? Then it dawned on him. Neither had the insurance company's lawyers. He felt as though he'd won the Golden Lottery.

When, inevitably, the jury found Heald guilty, the boy crumpled, collapsing to the floor. Instead of feeling satisfied, Thomas could only think how scared Heald must be, his prospects ruined. Without another thought, he stood up and addressed the judge.

"Your Honour. As the victim of this crime, please show clemency. He's clearly a hard-working son from a respectable family. I can see he regrets his foolish act, and I hazard he's learnt his lesson."

"Mr Wakley," said the judge, peering over his spectacles. "Admirable as your sentiments are, his behaviour was too aggravated for the court to accept leniency. It cannot condone such a blatant act of theft."

Thomas felt crushed. What sort of justice was that?

"It was wrong," said Thomas, as he recounted the events to Elizabeth that evening. "They've destroyed that young man's life for a trivial mistake."

"But you yourself said he was guilty."

"I know but if you'd seen him. It seemed so vindictive."

Elizabeth smiled. "That's why you're a doctor and not a lawyer, and why I love you."

*

Thomas spent the autumn working for a surgeon in Albermarle Street. Being back in Mayfair meant his work often took him past the burnt-out remains of the house; a painful reminder of all they'd lost.

Wardrop insisted he visit him regularly. They'd settle down in his consulting room and talk about all that needed changing. While it helped keep alive and burnish his enthusiasm to do something, Thomas was no clearer what it was he should or could do.

One afternoon, Wardrop couldn't wait for them to sit down before handing Thomas a thick new journal.

"*Medico-Chirurgical Review*. Never seen this before," said Thomas.

"Only started three months ago. Edited by some naval surgeon, name of James Johnson. Two hundred and fifty pages of accounts of the latest scientific thinking on all sorts of common conditions ordinary doctors have to deal with."

"More like a book," said Thomas, flicking through it. "Still, it's a start." Thomas thought of Coulson. This could be just what men like him craved. "I wonder what the hospitals and colleges think."

"They probably won't be bothered, as there's not a word about their mendacity and corruption."

Despite the grandfather clock striking every fifteen minutes, Thomas always lost track of time, never wanting to curtail their conversations. Inevitably, he ended up having to race back to Kentish Town, willing the cabbie to go faster as he pictured Elizabeth alone, waiting to eat dinner.

"I'm so sorry," said Thomas, struggling out of his long, heavy coat in the hallway. "Lost track of time."

"You always do," sighed Elizabeth, as he gave her a peck on the cheek. "I'm getting used to it. Come and eat, or dinner will be cold."

Martha filled the soup bowls and carefully carried them to the table.

"Ah, ham and pea," said Thomas. "Perfect."

They drank their soup in silence, Thomas unable to stop thinking about what he'd been discussing with Wardrop. He could see Elizabeth watching him.

"What?" asked Thomas.

"When you've been with Mr Wardrop, you're different."

"Different? In what way?"

"Lost inside your head, in a different world."

Thomas put down his spoon. "He's extraordinary. I've never met anyone like him. He makes me think in new ways, helps me develop my ideas. I don't know how he does it."

"And do you do the same for him?"

"Oh, certainly not. He's much wiser than I could ever be."

Elizabeth sat looking at him, saying nothing.

"What?" he asked, unnerved by her silence. "Not sure what that look means."

"I'm not there, of course, but I wouldn't be so sure. If you feel so strongly, I'd wager he gets the same out of it."

Thomas scoffed at the idea. "I may contribute the occasional thought, stimulate the odd idea, but nothing more."

Martha came in to remove the soup bowls and serve the meat.

"Despite being away from noise and dirt and the smells of London, I do miss the bustle of life there," mused Elizabeth.

"I tell you, it gets worse every day. It's not helped by all the building work for Regent Street."

"Hmm. Now he's King, shouldn't it be King Street?"

Thomas laughed. "Suppose so. You should hear what Wardrop has to say about him as a patient."

"He looks after the King?" asked Elizabeth.

"He's a Surgeon Extraordinary."

"I thought he wanted a republic. Bit hypocritical, isn't he?"

"Don't worry. It hasn't reduced his zeal for reform." He chuckled. "He revels in the way his appointment annoys the leading hospital surgeons. Getting back at them for not supporting his appointment to a hospital post."

Elizabeth shook her head. "What a strange world. All these pompous men and their petty squabbles."

Thomas guffawed. "You know what? Someone should write a play about them."

*

Throughout the autumn they'd visited theatres but with the first snows of winter, Elizabeth, now six months pregnant, no longer wanted to make the journey into London. As Thomas had stopped attending the medical societies since they'd refused to support him publicly, they spent every evening at home. He'd come to accept there was nothing more he could do until the court case in the new year.

Then, one evening, a letter arrived.

"Quite extraordinary," said Thomas. "It's from William Cobbett."

"Cobbett? I thought he was in the debtors' jail."

"Not since October. Says he's appalled at the way I've been treated and wants to meet me."

"Be careful. Isn't he seen as dangerous, stirring up revolt? If people find out, it could jeopardise the court case."

"He wants reform not revolution," said Thomas, flattered that Cobbett had written to him. "If you want, I'll ask Wardrop what he thinks."

The following day, Wardrop made light of Elizabeth's worries.

"Can't understand your hesitation." He laughed, clapping Thomas on the shoulder. "Who knows, could change your life."

Chapter 10

1821

His hair had turned grey, almost white, and he was now quite portly, but Thomas had no trouble recognizing him. Cobbett was sitting in a gloomy back room of *The Garter* in Whitehall, nursing a tankard of ale. As Thomas approached, Cobbett put aside the pamphlet he'd been reading.

"Wakley. Only just got settled so won't get up."

As Thomas sat down, Cobbett shouted through to the bar for service.

"Hope you didn't mind meeting so close to the Houses of Corruption."

Thomas presumed he meant Parliament.

"Thing is," he continued, not waiting for a reply, "it's one of the few pubs in this ghastly city where you can get Barrett's ale." He raised his drink. "Farnham's finest."

"I'm sure it is, but I drank quite enough over Christmas," said Thomas, turning to the serving maid and ordering coffee.

"Alien stuff. You don't want to drink that," said Cobbett, blowing his nose on a large blue handkerchief and then stuffing it back in a jacket pocket.

As Cobbett lent forward, light from the one small window revealed how pale and pasty his face was.

"The Thistlewood mob," he said quietly. "Read all about your troubles. Been threatened by them myself, though they've never attacked me – least, not yet."

"Why would they want to harm you?"

Cobbett glanced around the room but the few men at other tables were deep in conversation.

"They're convinced I work for the government. Me? Clearly never read my views of that pack of war-mongers down the road, lining their pockets and now demanding we pay for their corruption and incompetence." He sat back and folded his arms. "Now, you're probably wondering why I wanted to meet you. Simple really. The shocking way the newspapers keep defaming you."

Unsure how open to be, how much to divulge, Thomas decided to play for time.

"Years ago, I heard you give a speech. In Honiton."

"Honiton? Must be fifteen years ago." He paused, scrutinising Thomas. "How old were you?"

"About ten. I remember being spellbound. The way you took on your opponent."

For the first time, Cobbett smiled. "Really? My first forage into parliamentary elections. Naively thought I could compete with some despicable Tory bribing people for their votes." He picked up his tankard and took a swig. "What's so amusing?"

"Sorry. It reminds me of the way physicians and surgeons get their hospital positions. I hear say, unless they've got a father or uncle to insist on their appointment, they bribe the governors to vote for them. The person who manages to bribe the most, gets elected."

"Doesn't surprise me. Whole system's corrupt. Isn't just buying votes if you want to get into Parliament. When I stood in Coventry a few months back, the establishment got me another way. Lots of electors claimed to live in London."

"Why did that matter?"

Cobbett shook his head. "Tory government has decided candidates have to pay travel costs of those who vote for them. I had to pay hundreds of them. Bankrupted me. Only just been released from confinement for my debts."

Thomas sat wide-eyed. "That's appalling."

Cobbett drained his tankard and called for another.

"It is. They come up with all manner of means to ensure only rich landowners can win."

As the maid put his tankard down, she spilt some.

"Whoa!" shouted Cobbett. "Clumsy girl."

No need for that, thought Thomas, but managed to hold his tongue.

"So, you're from Honiton?"

"Near there. Grew up on a farm."

"Ah ha. Excellent. A fellow son of the soil. So, you've seen what's happening in the countryside. Landowners getting richer, driving hard-working people off the land."

Thomas immediately thought of the Pullens.

"It's one of the reasons I came back to London," said Thomas. "Fell out with my father over it."

"I see." Cobbett cradled his tankard in both hands, rotating it slowly. "I've met lots of surgeons and all they talk about is operations and bleeding and I know not what." He paused and smiled. "Oh, and money. But you seem different."

"Different? How do you mean?"

"Well, it's not normal for a boy of ten to be fascinated by a hustings, to fall out with his father over land enclosures and, to cap it all, take on a fire insurance company."

The way Cobbett was wagging his finger at him reminded Thomas of his teacher in Wivey.

"You may not want the advice of someone who's been in gaol, gone into exile, failed in elections... I could go on." Cobbett finished his drink. "Get Thomas Denman to represent you when you take on the insurance company. Fearsome. Destroyed the King's case against the Queen. He'll make those unscrupulous vermin of directors wish they'd never heard of you."

He stuffed the pamphlet he'd been reading into a pocket. As he pushed himself up and out from behind the table, he leant over to Thomas.

"I'll be keeping an eye out for the case."

*

Thomas had come to expect delays so wasn't surprised when Lofty told him they wouldn't go to court for another four months. As he travelled home with the news, freezing rain battering the windows of the coach, he worried how Elizabeth would take it. Meant they wouldn't be back in London before their child was due.

He put off telling her until after dinner. When he did, she looked away, gazing at the fire for a while, her hands cradling her pregnancy, then looked back.

"If it's to be June, it's June. It's not what I wanted but we'll manage."

"I thought you'd be upset."

She laughed. "You keep forgetting, I grew up in Tooley Street."

Right on time, in early March, Elizabeth went into labour. The sound of her cries distressed Thomas far more than those of the women he'd assisted in childbirth in Beaminster and Henley. Then, he'd been preoccupied with delivering the baby. He so wanted to help but knew he had to leave everything to the midwife. When, in the afternoon, all fell quiet and the midwife appeared beaming with delight, he rushed upstairs. Elizabeth lay exhausted. As he stroked her hair and kissed her forehead, they both burst into tears.

"It's a boy," said Elizabeth. "Our son."

Thomas turned and looked into the cradle. As he lifted him up, the dying rays of the winter sun lit up the baby's face.

"He's perfect," said Thomas.

"He's Thomas Henry," said Elizabeth, "after you and your Papa."

"Thomas Henry. When did we decide that?"

"We didn't," said Elizabeth, smiling, "but I did, months ago, when you said you were too busy to discuss names."

＊

It took Thomas some time to find Denman's chambers. He'd never been in one of the Inns of Court before. It was like another world, an island of calm in the heart of the city. Fine terraces surrounded manicured lawns. He was reluctant to ask for directions from the men rushing past, heads bent down, clutching sheaves of paper. Eventually an elderly porter saw he was lost and directed him to a five-storey building, its doorway adorned with the names of dozens of lawyers.

Upstairs, Lofty was already briefing the barrister who just nodded at Thomas and waved at Lofty to keep going. Shelves lined the walls, crammed with boxes and paper scrolls. In one corner a man sat scribbling as Lofty spoke. Thomas sat down and watched as Denman, behind a large oak desk festooned with bundles of documents tied with red ribbons, occasionally made notes.

When Lofty finished, Denman put down his pen.

"Just to be clear, Dr Wakley. Why did you increase your insurance cover in May?"

"To cover my wife's possessions and acquisitions," said Thomas, glancing at Lofty.

"No other reason?" asked Denman. "I need to know. Don't want any surprises in court."

The lawyer returned to his notes. "Now, these threatening letters. What was the sender jealous of?"

"All I can think is, he was a disappointed suitor. You see, my wife's father is a wealthy man."

"I see. You say they came in January and March, long before the fire."

"Yes, that's why by May, when I increased the insurance cover, I no longer took them seriously."

"Hmm. Best we allude to it and dismiss it as irrelevant before the defence tries using it."

Denman looked back at his notes. "They're going to claim two things: you overestimated the value of your property and you deliberately started the fire. Adolphus, what do we have on the valuations?"

The man in the corner looked through the papers on his desk. "We can document £1050. Mr Malleson and Archdeacon Woollaston have both been most helpful, as has a Mr Ashelford, an upholsterer. When we add in estimates of the value of items not included, comes to £1764."

"Good," said Denman, "well above the £1200 you're claiming."

He returned to his papers, tapping his pen on the desk. "With all the witnesses we've got, it's hard to see how they'll mount a case of arson."

"Might they resort to affidavit men?" said Thomas, immediately worried he'd made himself look foolish.

"Indeed," said Denman, a broad smile appearing. "I see you're familiar with unscrupulous practices."

"Sorry," said Thomas, "spoke out of turn."

"Nonsense. Wouldn't put it past Hope Insurance directors to resort to such measures. Don't worry. If they dare, we'll make them regret it."

Denman closed his file. "Right. I've got all I need. I'll see you in court."

As Adolphus showed them out, he put a hand on Thomas's shoulder. "Try not to worry. Denman's long wanted to take an insurance company down a peg or two."

Thomas wasn't worried. He was in awe of the way Denman had cut through all the detail and minutiae, making the arguments so clear and decisive. He loved the way the lawyer dismissed opinions and conjecture, just focusing on the facts, the evidence. It was so different from most medical lectures and Society meetings. He couldn't wait for the case to come to court, to see Denman in action. Unless he'd got it wrong, he was a man who relished a fight, he was sure of it. For the first time since the terrible night, he felt elated and optimistic.

It was early afternoon when he got back to Kentish Town. Elizabeth was sitting in the garden in the sunshine, feeding young Thomas. He went over and kissed her.

"I've just had the best day ever," he said, taking a chair at the small garden table. "We have this incredible lawyer. He can't wait to destroy the insurance company's claims. My love, I think we're almost there."

Elizabeth finished feeding and handed the baby to Martha to take away for a sleep. She poured them both a cup of tea and sat back.

"You sound wonderstruck by him," said Elizabeth. "So, tell me everything."

*

With Elizabeth on his arm, Thomas walked through Westminster Hall to the Court of the King's Bench. He felt her tighten her grip on his arm. Looking at her, he could see she was more composed than he was.

He leant towards her. "You're remarkable."

"Have you only just noticed?" she laughed.

Once in the courtroom, Elizabeth joined her father and the other witnesses.

"Morning, Wakley," said Adolphus. "Attracted plenty of interest," he added, pointing to the public gallery.

"Too much. It's been like this these past nine months."

"The tall lawyer over there," said Adolphus, indicating a group of men in black gowns and wigs huddled together talking quietly, "is Marryatt, their lawyer." He laughed. "As ever, defending the establishment."

In the public gallery, several newspaper men sat clutching notebooks and pens. Denman glanced up and acknowledged Thomas before returning to the sheaf of papers before him, like an actor reminding himself of his lines before going on stage.

Suddenly the court fell silent and everyone rose as Lord Chief Justice Abbott entered and took his seat. Thomas still couldn't fathom why his case was deemed worthy of being presided over by the most powerful judge in the land.

With the jury sworn in, Denman was called to present his case. Adjusting his wig, he rose.

"Your Honour. This case should never have come to trial." He turned to the jury. "We will show it is a travesty of justice the way the directors of the Hope Fire Insurance Company have impugned the plaintiff, Dr Wakley, a highly respected and respectable surgeon with an unblemished past. You will hear from many who know him well, what a fine man he is." With that, he bowed his head to Thomas.

"The insurance company's refusal to pay him is based on wholly false grounds. First, that he fraudulently overestimated the value of his possessions and second, even more outlandish and without a shred of evidence, that the plaintiff brought this calamity upon himself by setting his own home on fire."

Over the next hour, the true value of Thomas's property was established. Malleson and Woollaston testified to the items they had sold to Thomas. Ashelford reported the cost of his upholstery services, and Goodchild confirmed the size of the dowry he'd given his daughter. When Elizabeth took the stand, Thomas's anxiety proved unfounded. Calmly and with great clarity and assuredness, she went through a long list of china, books, silver plate, clothing, and linen she'd purchased. She ignored Marryatt and the Fire Insurance directors as they became restless and irritated.

"Gentleman of the jury," said Denman, "I now turn to the outrageous claim that the plaintiff started the fire. It is on public record that a court at the Old Bailey... the Old Bailey, no less... accepted without question that the plaintiff had been attacked and that his assailants then set fire to his house."

Marryatt leapt to his feet, so incensed he struggled to get his words out. "Irrelevant. Your Honour, I demand that be ignored."

"On what grounds?" asked the judge.

Thomas clenched his fists. Denman had floored their opponent. A perfect uppercut. Marryatt, who was bent over talking frantically with his team, had clearly not been made aware of the earlier trial.

"Your Honour," said Marryatt, "we weren't informed."

"Mr Marryatt. It is your job, not the plaintiff's counsel, to appraise yourself of all the facts. Objection dismissed."

There was some cheering from the gallery. Denman glanced round at Thomas and winked. A string of witnesses then proceeded to corroborate Thomas's version of events. Thompson, Parker, Dr Luke, the Witchers, as well as servants from neighbouring houses. At the end, Denman walked over to the jury.

"Gentlemen. Aside from all this evidence, consider for a moment what motive Dr Wakley could possibly have had. Why would a successful surgeon, recently married, want to destroy his home and his practice? And if he was trying to defraud the insurance company, why insure his property for £1200 when, as you've seen, it was worth at least £1600? This isn't a man in need of money. Both his father and father-in-law are wealthy."

Thomas smiled to himself. He'd never ask either of them for more money but he could see how it helped his case.

Denman turned and pointed at the defendants. "These men should be ashamed of themselves trying to destroy the life of a fine young surgeon, committed to helping his fellow man."

Thomas couldn't imagine what Marryatt could say in response. Surely Denman had seen off every line of attack.

Marryatt, apparently undaunted, strode into the well of the room and swirled his gown around him.

"Members of the jury, if only it were that simple." He smiled, shaking his head. "My honourable colleague has conveniently failed to tell you the whole story. So, let me enlighten you. This supposedly fine young surgeon conveniently increased his insurance cover just weeks before the fire."

Denman was back up on his feet. "Your Honour. We have already shown that he increased it three months before, following the addition of his wife's property. There was nothing suspicious about such a wise, responsible action. Indeed, the Hope Fire Insurance Company entreats people to do just that."

There was more laughter in the public gallery, and the judge had to call for order.

Unperturbed, Marryatt continued. "In which case, why were Dr Wakley's claims as to the amount of silver plate twice that which was found in the ashes?"

Once again Denman rose. "Your Honour, the defence chooses to ignore the evidence you've heard from witnesses, that men were seen entering the building during the fire and running out with bags. I suggest that those bags contained silver plate. Or perhaps Mr Marryatt wants to suggest it was books of poetry."

Guffaws of laughter and the sound of foot stamping reminded Thomas of a fight crowd. Not what he expected in a court. The way Marryatt wouldn't give up was like a fighter who was clearly going to lose, insisting on carrying on, despite the punishment he would suffer.

It wasn't until six o'clock that the judge called proceedings to a halt. He advised the jury that in the absence of any motive, it wasn't credible that the plaintiff would have started the fire. As for over-estimating the true value of his possessions, they needed to consider the evidence each side had presented.

Thomas didn't have to wait long. It took the jury only thirty minutes to state their belief in him. The judge immediately instructed the insurance company to pay the full £1200. Thomas rushed over and hugged Elizabeth, his eyes filling up.

"Thank God that's over," he said. "No more innuendo and accusations."

"Come on," said Elizabeth. "Home. We need to tell Thomas Henry!"

*

It was years since he'd heard the dawn chorus. As a boy, he'd often get up before everyone else and go and sit in the field above the farmhouse, on the edge of the woods, watching the first rays of the sun strike the hills on the far side of the valley. He perched on a small wooden bench in the garden and was smiling to himself when Elizabeth stepped out of the house. She tightened her dressing gown and came and sat on his lap.

"Do you hear them?" he asked. "The wood pigeons. 'Take two cows, Taffy.'"

"What? What are you talking about?"

"It's what the woodies are saying. Listen."

She cradled his head in her hands and kissed him. "Something else from your strange childhood, I suppose."

They sat listening, watching the sky turn pink.

"I couldn't sleep," said Thomas. "Just want to get into town and start looking for a practice."

She closed her eyes, rocking slowly in his arms.

"The money we got," he said, "won't be enough for a practice in the West End or as splendid a house as we had. And fighting it has cost over £140."

"As long as we're back in London," she said. "Just promise me it won't be like Tooley Street."

He pushed a ringlet of hair off her face. "I promise. Away from the river and factories. And even if it takes a few years, we will get back to a house like Argyll Street."

Just as he had a couple of years before, he set about visiting surgeons who might be thinking of retiring and selling up. With reports of his legal success in the morning newspapers, he expected a warm welcome and maybe even an apology for not supporting him. But while everyone was polite, most claimed they had pressing business to attend to and couldn't talk. As the morning wore on, he was horrified to realise many doctors still questioned his innocence. He started imagining what they said to one another. No wonder the medical societies hadn't supported him. By the afternoon, having traipsed all over town, he'd found nothing.

As he travelled back to Kentish Town, the joy he'd felt that morning had gone. He'd been foolish to think the trial would be the end of their problems. At home, he found Elizabeth sitting in the garden with their son. She looked up, shading her eyes with her hand.

"How did it go? Did you find any practices?"

He sighed. "Not as such. But now word is out, won't be long before something comes up."

She transferred Thomas Henry from one arm to the other, looking at Thomas quizzically.

"What's the matter?" he asked.

"Thomas, I love your optimism but you've got to be realistic. What if there aren't any practices for sale?"

He sat, staring across the garden. A pair of blackbirds were hopping about on the freshly dug soil.

"I'll find one. Just got to be patient."

Several more days enquiring and still nothing. He was becoming convinced that he was being ostracised, that even if there were a practice available, he would not be welcome. To lift his spirit, he decided to take a break and visit Freddy. Making his way along The Strand, the bells of St Mary's were chiming as he passed. He stopped to listen to them. Across the street, his eyes alighted on a druggist's shop, *Butterfield's*, its distinctive large carboys of coloured water standing out from the grey, drab shop fronts all around.

"Why not?" he heard himself say, then laughed as it reminded him of how he used to talk to himself in the street when he'd first arrived in London as an anxious pupil.

He picked his way across the road, avoiding the carriages and wagons, and went in. The walls were lined with countless pots and boxes. From the number of customers, it was clearly doing well.

"Can I help you, sir?" asked a tall man, stooping slightly.

"Mr Butterfield?" asked Thomas.

"Indeed so, sir."

"Thomas Wakley," he said. "Tell me, are there many surgeons around here?"

"Surgeons? Well, only old Paternoster down Norfolk Street, near the river." He lowered his voice. "But if it's a surgeon you need, sir, I think you best look further afield."

"Is that what your customers do?"

Butterfield looked about him to make sure no-one could hear. "Indeed, they do. Not convenient but, probably shouldn't say this, it's for the best."

"Most grateful to you, Mr Butterfield." He paused, looking around. "May I say, what a fine shop you have."

"Thank you, sir. It's been a good life here, but all good things, as they say."

Thomas stopped and went back to the counter.

"You're leaving?"

"Unfortunately, sir, have to. Sixth one is on its way and my wife insists we find somewhere bigger."

Thomas was barely aware of what Butterfield went on to say, so lost was he in a wild idea he was having.

"Mr Butterfield," said Thomas, doffing his hat, "thank you. Can't tell you how helpful you've been."

Once outside, he stood looking up at the property. A sturdy if unspectacular four-storey house. Being on a corner, he imagined there were fine views both along The Strand and down Norfolk Street. As he made his way back towards Charing Cross, all thought of visiting Freddy having gone, he had a spring in his step. His mind was racing. The idea was outlandish but he was already convinced it could work.

Back in Kentish Town, he rushed in and went to find Elizabeth.

"I've seen our future," he said, pacing around the parlour while Elizabeth sat, gently rocking Thomas Henry.

"Thomas. Please, quietly. I'm trying to get him to sleep."

He pulled up a chair beside her. "I'm sorry. It's just... I've found the answer." He paused. "Establish a new practice." He sat back, beaming. "Don't know why I didn't think of it before. There's a druggist selling up in The Strand..."

"A druggist?" she exclaimed. "Thomas, we're not becoming shopkeepers."

"Of course not. Listen. The owner, Butterfield, says there are no competent surgeons round there, and plenty of his customers need one. So, there'd be plenty of patients for me."

"But what about the shop?"

"I'll employ a druggist to run it for us. He can get an apprentice to help him. And it's a fine house. We'd have three floors and the basement."

He'd learnt not to panic when she said nothing. Just wait, give her time to think. But her silence was so prolonged, he became convinced this time he'd gone too far.

"What are the neighbouring shops?" she asked.

"What? You want to know about the neighbours? Well, on The Strand there's a chart and map seller. Down Norfolk Street I think it's a saddler."

She nodded slowly. "When can we visit?"

His mouth dropped open. "You mean, you'd consider it?"

"Thomas, you're ingenious."

"I know it's not Argyll Street, but I reckon with the income from the shop, I won't have to work all hours seeing patients."

*

As he approached Samuel Parker's house in Argyll Street, he wondered why he'd been invited.

"Wakley," said Parker, getting up to greet him. "So good to see you. Didn't get the chance to talk after the trial."

"Elizabeth whisked me away." He ran a hand through his hair. "You know, you and Thompson were crucial to our victory."

They sat down and a maid served them coffee.

"No doubt you're busy, so won't keep you long," said Parker. "Thing is, I was approached by Ivatts. He hears a lot in his tavern." He paused. "Pains me to say it, but despite everything, he tells me a fair few people still think you set fire to the house."

Thomas stared out of the window. So, it was not just his medical brethren harbouring doubts.

"I don't understand," said Thomas. "The Old Bailey trial supported me, Gardiner's pamphlet had all the evidence, and the Lord Chief Justice couldn't have been clearer."

"I know. Which is why I want to hold a public meeting. We can use Ivatts' tavern. What do you say?"

"A meeting? Why would you do that?"

"Wakley. Lots of us are outraged about the way you're being pilloried. I got Gardiner to make enquiries and the newspapers promise they'll report it."

Thomas shook his head. "Can't believe you'd do this for me."

"Least we can do. And we're going to ask people to contribute to your legal costs."

Thomas couldn't wait to tell Elizabeth.

"Isn't it wonderful? Some people still have trust in us."

She sat, stoney-faced, looking at him over the dining table.

"What's the matter?" he asked.

"It might just fan the flames, putting it back on the front pages. People might think there's still some doubt."

"What? So, I'm meant to give up?"

She put down her fork. "No, but there are different ways of fighting. Ignoring people, saying nothing, can be as effective as rising to the bait. Think of Hamlet. 'The lady doth protest too much'."

"But she was guilty. I'm not."

He got up from the table, wrenching his napkin out of his waistcoat and threw it down.

"Why can't you be more supportive like Parker and Ivatts?"

He could see her eyes filling up. "Supportive? What do you think I've been doing these past months? So, I have to agree with everything you decide to do, is that it?"

"No, I didn't mean that."

Elizabeth got up from the table.

"Thomas. What's happened has affected me as much as you. Women I meet are distant and not as friendly as they were. I hate it, but knowing you're innocent, I won't let them upset me."

He tried to take her in his arms but she stood stock still, looking away.

"I'm sorry," said Thomas. "I shouldn't have said that. Please forgive me."

She said nothing for a while, then looked at him. "Of course I do, but please, I don't want to spend years embattled, fighting. We must put what happened behind us. Unless we do, we can't expect others to forget about it."

Two weeks later, over breakfast, there on the front page of *The Morning Chronicle* was a full account of the meeting. He hesitated to tell her but knew she'd read it later.

"Parker's meeting. On the front page."

Elizabeth sat with Thomas Henry on her lap but said nothing.

"Parker didn't hold back. *'Malicious reports totally destitute of truth'. 'Cruel and unmerited oppression'*."

Elizabeth put the baby in his crib and came and stood behind Thomas, wrapping her arms around him.

"I hope you're right that this will stop the gossip but please, don't expect too much. People love scandal. They don't want to be told it's not true."

He put the paper down and took hold of her hands. "I just can't let them think I've given up, that they've beaten me."

✳

It wasn't until after midnight that The Strand quietened down and then, only for a few hours. After a year in Kentish Town, they'd forgotten how noisy it was living in the centre of the city. Before dawn, carts started rumbling past, laden with produce for Covent Garden, their drivers shouting to one another. While Thomas had spent the first few days downstairs setting up a consulting room, Elizabeth, with Daniel's help, rearranged the furniture they'd bought from Butterfield.

"I know it's not what you'd hoped for," said Thomas, as they sat in the first-floor drawing room after dinner. "Shouldn't be for too long. Then we can move."

"We'll be fine," she said. "So close to the theatres. I've already booked tickets for all the plays at Drury Lane and Covent Garden this autumn."

He'd no difficulty finding a druggist to run the shop. *Butterfield's* had such a good reputation, there was no shortage of people wanting to take it on. He'd chosen Patchett because he was enthusiastic about combining the shop with a surgical practice. It quickly proved successful. Within a week, every day five or six customers were asking to see the new surgeon.

Late one afternoon, with no more patients to see, Thomas decided to pay a surprise visit to Cheapside.

"Heavens," exclaimed Freddy, "I thought you'd left London."

He clutched Thomas's arm as they shook hands.

"Right. That decides it," he said, locking the door. "I'll close up."

They went upstairs to his lodgings. As Freddy was making tea in the kitchen, he called through. "So, tell me, how's your baby?"

"Thomas Henry? Oh, seems to be thriving."

Freddy poked his head round the door. "You don't sound very certain."

"No, it's not that. I leave him to Elizabeth. Not much for me to do till he's older."

Freddy sighed but said nothing as he came back with a tea tray.

"I can see nothing's changed here," said Thomas.

"Ha. That's where you're wrong," he chortled, "because the changes that really matter can't be seen."

"What do you mean?"

"Clementi. All he wants to do now is compose and perform. Oh, and travel. We haven't seen him for about a year. The business is now really in the hands of Uncle Frederick and Uncle William."

"So," said Thomas, "the Wivey brothers make good."

"Indeed. Full partners now. Little did they know when they left Somerset they'd end up rich and renowned."

"And where does that leave you? Still the prodigal son?"

"I'll be honest. They want me to take over when they've had enough. They both dream of going home."

"Signor Freddy, piano king of Cheapside," sniggered Thomas. "You'll soon be a pillar of the establishment."

"Never," said Freddy, raising his voice.

"I'm sorry, I was only jesting."

"It's all right," said Freddy, as he refilled the cups. "I know you didn't mean it but the prospect of being comfortable, even rich, troubles me. The more I hear about what's going on across the country, the angrier it makes me."

Thomas could hear the passion and determination in his voice.

Freddy was staring into space. "I'm starting to feel a fraud, spending my days being polite to customers who I know oppose reform. But I don't want to let down my uncles who have been so good to me."

He looked at Thomas. "All these," he said, waving at the piles of pamphlets and periodicals, "are rousing people, showing them they don't have to put up with being exploited and impoverished, but I don't know what I can do."

Thomas nodded slowly. "I wish I knew as well. For now, I spend my time visiting hospitals hoping for inspiration. That and finding like-minded doctors. But everyone is so cautious, frightened of being ostracised."

"Can't believe that would happen."

"It's true. They're right to be worried. I saw it when I spoke out at Society meetings. The annoyance and hostility it created. And it did no good. No-one cared what a surgeon who can barely support his family has to say."

They sat in silence, drinking their tea.

"Do you have time for a game?" asked Freddy, eyeing the chess board set up on a side table.

"You know me. I'd never turn down the chance to beat you."

They hunched over the board, concentrating, trying to work out what the other was up to. It was Thomas who broke the spell.

"You know what angers me most about the past year? All the time I've wasted on this legal stuff." He paused, smiling. "But I'll let you into a secret. Courts are amazing places."

"Never been in one, thankfully."

"They're like a cross between a theatre and a political debate. You know how we long to capture the public's attention, make them aware of what's wrong, what needs to change? Maybe the answer is public trials. Gets it onto the front page if it's juicy enough."

"So maybe some good might come from the fire," suggested Freddy.

Thomas reached out and took one of Freddy's bishops.

"Hang on. Were you deliberately distracting me?" asked Freddy.

"Never. Meant every word of it."

*

"Can't tell you how grateful I've been for your support," said Thomas, as he once again settled into a deep leather armchair in Wardrop's study. "You've been the only doctor to stand by me. Was over at Guy's yesterday and I could see the looks, pupils pointing me out to one another."

"Wakley, that's only because you're famous."

"Infamous more likely."

"So, will you stop going?"

"Damn, no," said Thomas, almost shouting. "Sorry. No, that would be as good as accepting the false accusations. They'd love that."

"Ah, that's the spirit."

It was getting dark outside and had started to snow. Wardrop got up, lit some candles, and went over to a small sideboard.

"Would you take a wee dram, warm you up?" he asked, picking up a decanter.

"Not my usual but, yes, thanks."

"Now," Wardrop said, as he handed Thomas a tumbler and sat back down, "haven't seen you at the Medical Societies this season."

Thomas swirled the whisky round in his glass. "No, I've not set foot in those disgraceful places."

"Oh, steady. They're not that bad."

"Wardrop, they failed to support me. As good as connived with my accusers."

"But you can't have been surprised. They're only interested in preserving themselves and their arcane rituals."

"Maybe, but I can't forgive them."

"Hang on. You're happy to spend time at Guy's, despite their lack of support." He sipped his whisky. "You've got to keep your eye on the true goal. Can't let this setback deflect you. Remember, to beat your enemy you must understand them first."

Thomas sipped his whisky, feeling the warmth suffuse through his body.

"If you don't appear at the Society meetings," continued Wardrop, "people may conclude they were right to question your integrity. If you want my advice, get back out there. Show them you are unbowed."

Thomas stared into his tumbler, thinking of how defeated fighters who refused a rematch were written off as losers.

"All right. I'll give it a try."

"Good. Oh, I saw Cobbett recently. You impressed him." Wardrop chuckled. "That doesn't happen often, I can tell you."

"Really? I decided he thought I wasn't to be taken seriously, bit of a lightweight."

"You? Even your supposed enemies don't think that." He paused. "You won. Get back out there and fight."

Thomas raised his glass. "You're right, as ever."

1822

Although it was March, the city remained enveloped in thick, damp fog. The sound of the bells of St Mary's and of

St Clement's could be heard but, despite each being only a hundred yards from their home, neither could be seen. In the shop, Patchett could barely keep up with the demand for cough medicines and inhalations.

While there was plenty of demand for his service, few people living in that neighbourhood could afford to pay Thomas much. It wasn't like in Argyll Street. If it wasn't for the profits being made from the sale of drugs, they wouldn't survive. More than once he'd wondered if he was any better than Incledon. But he was determined not to work longer hours and have no time to visit hospitals and to read and write.

When they weren't at the theatre or a concert, Thomas and Elizabeth spent their evenings at home. Despite heavy drapes at the windows, a cold draught could still be felt when the wind got up.

"I went over to Tooley Street today," said Elizabeth. "I'd forgotten how dreadful it is. No place to live."

"How are they all?" asked Thomas, looking up from the *Evening Chronicle*.

Elizabeth sighed. "Not good. Papa's still not interested in the business. Leaves it all to Joseph. And when Sarah and Mr Wiltshire marry in August, there'll only be Ann to look after him."

She picked up her embroidery and he resumed reading. After a while he put the paper down and sat watching the flames flickering in the fireplace. When he glanced up, he saw she was watching him.

"What?"

She smiled. "I was just remembering the first time we met. I'd never met a man who seemed so self-assured."

"Self-assured? Can't tell you how nervous I was."

"Well, it didn't show. Most men were terrified of Papa but not you. When I saw that, I was yours." She raised her eyebrows. "Just had to make you notice me."

Thomas got up and put more coal on the fire. When he came back, he crouched down and took her hands.

"Over that first lunch," he said, "you wouldn't smile or acknowledge me. Made me determined to get your attention. As I made my way back to London, I thought it was a hopeless task. But at that party a few weeks later, I couldn't believe you seemed pleased to see me." He kissed her hands and looked up at her. "That was the best night of my life."

"The best night? Not our wedding night?"

"Ah. Second best then."

With tears in his eyes, he reached out and stroked her cheek.

"Don't forget it's Drury Lane tomorrow night," she said. "*The Castle Spectre*."

"Not a ghost story."

"Wait and see. It's set in Wales. A gothic drama."

"Hang on. That's the play Wiltshire was telling me about. He only went because there's an exhibition of actors' portraits on show."

"Did he enjoy the play?"

"Don't know. Didn't ask him."

"Thomas!"

"Well, we mostly talked about the prize fight he'd been to."

The following evening, they got to the theatre early. As they looked at the portraits, Elizabeth delighted in telling him the actors' names and what she'd seen them in. Until they came to one she didn't know.

"Who on earth is Henry Betty?" she said quietly to Thomas, but not so quietly that a woman standing alongside didn't hear.

"He was a famous child star a decade ago," said the woman. "Never made it as an adult."

"But deserving of a fine portrait nevertheless," said Elizabeth.

"Do you think so?" the woman said.

Thomas could see she was blushing. "Are you the artist?"

She bowed her head slightly. "Yes, I am."

Thomas craned his neck at the picture. "But it says here, John Onwhyn."

The woman looked around then spoke quietly. "My husband. They won't allow women to exhibit."

"What?" said Thomas.

"Shh, keep your voice down," said Elizabeth.

"But that's not right," said Thomas.

"It's how it is," said Mrs Onwhyn.

Thomas left Elizabeth talking to her and continued on round the exhibition. When the bell went announcing the start of the show, he and Elizabeth made their way to the dress circle.

"I can't believe it," said Elizabeth. "Fanny's love of the theatre is even greater than mine. They live nearby, so I invited her to come for tea next week. Her husband's a publisher."

*

It wasn't until May that the fog finally lifted, and the sun appeared. As the days grew warmer, the stench from the river sometimes drifted up to The Strand. Thomas agreed that Elizabeth should take Thomas Henry to spend the summer in Mill Hill. As Sarah and her father were there already, she'd have company. And Thomas would visit at weekends.

With Elizabeth away, he devoted all his time to work. The Witchers became used to the unusual hours he kept. Up before first light, they'd bring him coffee and rolls in his study downstairs, where he'd spend a couple of hours reading and writing before seeing patients. From midday he was out, watching operations. He perfected a way of getting past porters and into theatres in all seven public hospitals. In fact, after a few visits the porters actually welcomed him, doffing their caps. Handing out small retainers to surgical men ensured they let him know when a capital operation was taking place. And once a week he'd visit Wardrop.

"It just gets worse," said Thomas, striding into Wardrop's study and throwing his bag into a chair.

"Good afternoon, Wakley," said Wardrop, smiling. "Slow down and I'll order tea."

"I thought I'd seen everything." He pulled a sheaf of paper out of his bag. "I've documented it all. They can't deny it."

"Go on. Tell me. Where was it this time?"

"The Westminster. Fit, strong man with a deep gash on his head. Three attempts they made to trephine his skull. Three! What started as a two-inch wound became six inches and bleeding copiously. As ever, the other surgeons just watched. Did nothing."

"You know fellow surgeons can't intervene."

"So, patients carry on suffering."

There was a knock at the door and Wardrop's maid brought in a tray of tea.

"And Mr Lawrence is here, sir."

"Splendid. Show him through." Wardrop turned to Thomas. "Finally, you two get to meet."

It had been seven years since Thomas had seen Lawrence speak at Phys Soc.

"Wakley," said Lawrence, bowing his head slightly. "Heard so much about you from this fellow."

Any trepidation Thomas had about meeting such a renowned surgeon vanished.

"Sit down," said Wardrop. "Wakley was just telling me of the latest display of surgical acumen at the Westminster."

Lawrence turned to Thomas. "Wardrop tells me you're not enamoured by the way our profession behaves."

Thomas took a deep breath. "Don't know where to start. Apprentices are exploited. Doctors aren't interested in teaching on the wards. Lectures aren't disseminated around the country. Oh yes, and London medical societies don't publish their discussions."

Thomas looked at the two men whose looks of concentration gave him confidence to carry on.

"It's as if our profession believes medicine has to be closely guarded. The hospitals, societies, colleges seem to fear scrutiny. No-one is interested in finding out if their patients get better. Meanwhile, the public are to be grateful for anything they do, even if it kills them."

259

Lawrence and Wardrop exchanged looks. Then Lawrence started clapping. "Magnificent."

"Sorry, rather went on."

"For heaven's sake," said Lawrence. "First rule of a reformer, don't apologise."

"Don't get me wrong," said Thomas, sitting forward. "I've seen some great doctors - Sir Astley, Charles Bell. Strong advocates of scientific surgery, but for some reason they don't speak out."

Wardrop fetched the whisky decanter and three glasses. All the while, Lawrence was studying Thomas.

"Let me ask you something," said Lawrence. "The medical establishment won't hesitate to punish you if you take them on. I've had to withdraw my criticism of vitalism, and the College is ending my appointment as professor. So, my question is, how far are you prepared to go, knowing you'll be subjected to unfounded assaults not just on your professional position but your personal life as well?"

Thomas looked him in the eye. "After what I've been through, that doesn't frighten me." He paused. "It's simple, really. I've no choice. Maybe it's what saints say is a calling."

Lawrence, his elbows on the arms of his chair, steepled his fingers. "You're a warrior, me thinks."

"That's all very well," said Wardrop, "but what to do? How do we shake the establishment out of their complacency and confidence?"

"He should talk to Cobbett," Lawrence said to Wardrop. "He'll soon be back from gallivanting around the shires."

"I did, last year," said Thomas.

"Well, meet him again. See what he suggests."

*

Summer was over, and with their second child due soon, he was so pleased when Elizabeth returned home. For weeks he'd only seen her at weekends, and even then he didn't have enough time to tell her all he wanted to share. Her absence had made him realise just how much he'd come to rely on her clear, considered thoughts as a counterweight to what he knew was his tendency to be impulsive and, if left unchecked, reckless.

With autumn, Thomas started attending Medical Society meetings again, where the frosty, suspicious reception he'd received the previous spring had abated. He took care to make his contributions less hostile, only challenging the most unfounded suggestions. Elizabeth would be proud of how he'd become more diplomatic.

Taking Wardrop and Lawrence's advice, he arranged to meet Cobbett again. He'd read most of the morning newspapers left abandoned in *The Garter* before Cobbett came bustling in, his boots caked in mud.

"This damn town. Traffic hardly moves. Took me two hours from Kensington."

With some effort, he pulled off his outer coat, before sitting down heavily and calling for a tankard of Barrett's.

"Setting up a plant nursery in Kensington," he said, but offered no apology for being late as the maid handed him his drink.

His florid complexion, a legacy of his recent rides around the home counties, reminded Thomas of childhood pictures of Old Testament prophets. Having immediately half-drained his tankard, Cobbett leant back, scrutinising Thomas.

"So, you're still determined to sort out the medical profession. It'll be as tough as my battles with landowners."

"That's why Wardrop, Lawrence, and I want your advice. What should we do?"

"Ah, that's indeed the question."

He snorted some snuff as he thought about it. "I can tell you what not to do. Three of you, or even a dozen, can achieve nothing. You'll be made examples of, and all those who you thought were behind you will melt away."

He took a swig of ale and leant forward across the table. His breath was foul, but Thomas needed to hear what he had to say.

"No general won a battle without troops. So, who are your troops, your foot soldiers? Who are you trying to help?"

"Pupils, apprentices, and general practitioners up and down the country."

"Right. While they accept their lot, nothing will change. So, you've got to raise their hackles, get them demanding more."

"But how? They're spread all over the nation." He thought of the travelling Cobbett had just completed. "I can't leave home, go around holding meetings, speaking to them."

"Maybe not, but you can send your message in print."

Cobbett sat back, smiling. "When I started the *Register,* had no idea the appetite there would be. Then the *Tupenny Trash* put that in the shade. Forty thousand copies a week. Go into any inn in England or the dingiest back streets of our cities, you'll find people spouting ideas from it. We wouldn't have seen the uprisings without it."

"You think we should start a periodical?"

"I do. Like nothing that's ever been seen. Make people sit up and take note."

Thomas rubbed his right hand though his hair, resting it on the back of his head. "Trouble is, I know nothing about publishing."

"From what I've seen and heard about you, you can do it. And when you decide to do it, I'll help you."

Chapter 11

1823

The sun rose as he reached the Serpentine. The trees, encrusted with hoar frost, sparkled. The only sounds were of someone coughing in the guard house by the bridge and the Egyptian geese grazing on the frost-covered grass. A pair of grey herons swooped down and dived into the water. How he missed the countryside. While Hyde Park was hardly unbridled nature, it reminded him of striding out from Land Farm before sunrise to watch kingfishers on the River Otter.

Every night since meeting Cobbett, he'd lain awake wrestling with his suggestion. Last night was no different. Elizabeth had been up twice to feed Elizabeth May. Knowing she'd want to sleep as long as possible, he'd dressed quietly and let himself out, telling Martha he'd be back for breakfast.

He stood on the bridge over the river, gazing at a pair of swans floating towards him from Kensington Gardens, every so often dipping their long necks to feed. Beyond the bare trees, the night stagecoaches from Oxford and further west rattled past. For a moment he wondered what he was doing here, in London. They could leave the noise and filth of the city for a country town where he could ride every day and hunt. Leave others to reform the medical world. But he knew that was no longer an option, if it ever had been.

"When you do it, I'll help you." Cobbett's certainty that he would indeed establish a periodical had filled his thoughts over Christmas and New Year. Several times he'd caught Elizabeth looking at him quizzically, clearly aware he was distracted. At Christmas dinner, when they'd been joined by Sarah and

Wiltshire, she'd lost patience with him, berating him for not being more festive.

He knew why he was still dithering. It was fear. Cobbett's challenge had rekindled a feeling from boyhood he thought he'd banished forever. But here it was again. And on top of that, the horror of the venture failing and being left bankrupt, his family ending up in the Marshalsea. It was why he'd not dared broach the idea with Elizabeth and yet, he knew in the end he'd be guided by her.

*

"Never been done before." Freddy laughed. "Is that the best reason you can give me? Is this the fearless schoolboy, the bare-knuckle fighter, the man who takes on stalwarts of his profession, who takes an insurance company to court? Thomas, listen to yourself."

Once again they were in his small sitting room above the piano shop, huddled over a coal fire, drinking tea.

"You don't understand," said Thomas. "You need the backing of a Society or College to set up a periodical. I'm just a nobody, practising from the back room of a druggist's shop, barely making a living."

"Isn't that all the more reason to do it?" said Freddy. "You said yourself, if you couldn't be a hospital surgeon, you certainly weren't going to settle for being a general practitioner. Dabbling in surgery. That's how you described it."

Thomas sighed. "True. I did."

"Anyway, there's a more important reason. I know you well enough to know you won't be able to live with yourself if you don't take the plunge."

Thomas sat staring at the fire.

"So, what is it that's stopping you?" asked Freddy.

Thomas gripped the arms of the small chair he was sitting in, pulling himself forward. "So many things. First off, I don't think I can write well enough. Only ever published one short letter."

"Hang on," said Freddy. "You've been writing for years. Those diatribes you gave me to read, they're magnificent. Probably get you in all sorts of trouble but, by God, some excoriating turns of phrase."

Thomas laughed. "Exactly. Couldn't possibly let people see that. It was just to help me think things through. Not the sort of stuff medical journals publish."

"You mean those journals you describe as dull as ditchwater?"

Thomas roared with laughter.

"You've a real talent," said Freddy. "Your writing has all the energy and fury of Cobbett but, have to say, much more fun to read, though I don't suppose your targets will agree! If what you say is true, thousands of doctors out there will love it."

As Freddy stoked the fire, he turned to Thomas. "Describe it to me."

"What do you mean?"

"Don't pretend you don't have a vision for this periodical."

Thomas put down his cup. "Well, it has to be weekly. Monthly or quarterly is useless for generating debate. Trouble is, doctors have never subscribed to a weekly." He paused. "It has to be like a young stallion, not like an old carthorse."

Freddy clapped his hands. "Excellent." He sat down, beaming. "Go on. I want to hear more."

"It's got to rouse and excite. Show doctors they no longer have to accept the way hospitals and colleges and societies are run. Challenge corruption and nepotism, poor education and incompetence. Doctors have got to be held to account for what they do."

Freddy waved an arm in the air. "Hoorah. A call to arms. The end of deference."

"But not like this," said Thomas, picking up the *Political Register*. "This is too heavy going. Fine for those already committed to reform, but it wouldn't appeal to doctors. No, it's going to have to be…"

He struggled to find the right word.

"Entertaining?" offered Freddy. "Or is that too demeaning for the noble profession?"

"Be serious, will you? It's got to offer... variety."

"Variety? What on earth do you mean?"

"I'm not sure, but it wouldn't be entirely medical. Maybe theatre reviews or some literature."

Freddy picked up a notebook and pen. "All right. Enough of the contents. Let's talk money and business; something I know about. How much will you charge?"

Thomas stared into the distance, picturing Coulson and Phelps. "No more than sixpence if it's going to be every week."

"Right. How many pages?"

"Goodness, I haven't thought that far ahead."

"Well, you've got to. Let's say, like the *Register*. Thirty-two. Now, how many subscribers can you get in the first year?"

"Freddy! I've no idea."

Freddy shook his head. "I can see I'm going to have to turn you into a businessman."

"All right, all right. There's nearly ten thousand doctors out there."

"Do you think a thousand is expecting too much?"

"If I don't get that, it's not going to foment reform and frighten the establishment."

Thomas sat waiting while Freddy scribbled.

"I reckon if you can print and distribute for tuppence a copy, in the first year you'd have an income of nearly a thousand pounds."

"And if no-one subscribes?"

Freddy looked back at his pad. "A loss of over four hundred pounds."

"So, we could lose our home."

"But if you're right, and there's a hunger for something like this, you'll have thousands of subscribers within a few years."

"If I'm right. That's what it all comes down to."

Freddy sat staring at him. "What if someone was prepared to lend you enough to cover your losses if the worst happened? You'd pay them back when you could afford to. And if you never could, it would be their money that was lost not yours."

"An investor? And where would I find such a guardian angel? No rich doctor's going to do that."

"I wasn't thinking of doctors. Someone who believes in you and the journal."

"They couldn't have any say on what I published. No interference."

"Don't worry. They'd only do it because they trusted and believed in you."

Freddy got up and placed a guard in front of the fire. "Think about it. But now, I must away. Concert at Grosvenor House, no less."

*

"What took you so long?" chided Cobbett. "It's been two months."

Thomas unbuttoned his coat. As he sat down, the serving maid brought him a coffee.

"Still drinking that diabolical stuff," scoffed Cobbett.

Thomas ignored him and spooned some sugar into his cup.

"So," said Cobbett, "as you're here, I take it you're going to do it?"

"That's the plan. Still a lot to sort out."

"When would you start?"

"If I'm going to publish hospital lectures and Medical Society meetings, it's got to start in October."

"Right. Well, that gives you several months to prepare. Should be enough."

"Doesn't feel long to me, but then I know nothing about publishing."

"Do you think I knew anything when I started *Porcupine's Gazette*."

"*Porcupine's Gazette*?" laughed Thomas.

"You'll not have heard of it," said Cobbett, dismissing it with a wave of his hand. "Years ago, in America. I wasn't much older than you. Only lasted two years but taught me a lot."

"It's not just not knowing anything about publishing. I've got to find someone to fund it."

"Ah, good. Glad to see you've already learnt the most important lesson – risk someone else's money. Cost me a fortune, almost my liberty."

He leant forward, lowering his voice. "You'd be surprised how many rich men secretly want to see reform. You'll find one, I'm sure."

"Don't know how. Can hardly advertise, let everyone know what I'm planning. Plenty out there who'd go out of their way to prevent me even starting."

"I don't doubt it," said Cobbett. "Have you at least got a publisher?"

"For the same reason, I haven't started looking."

"You need one who publishes radical works, who's not easily intimidated when the writs start coming in. They'll handle all the printing and distribution."

"You make it sound so easy."

Cobbett wagged a finger at him. "Key man your publisher, so choose carefully."

As Thomas sipped his coffee, he could see he was being scrutinised.

"Come on," said Cobbett, "what's on your mind?"

Thomas put his cup down. "I've thought a lot about my court case last year. Not the case itself but how the courtroom is like a public forum, perfect for holding the establishment to account. The public watching, joining in at times, and the newspapers reporting it all."

Cobbett was nodding, which encouraged Thomas to continue.

"My lawyer, Denman was so eloquent. The way he cut to the chase and tore apart Maryatt. Showed everyone what nonsense he was spouting. Made me think, what if doctors and hospital governors could be scrutinised in that way? Forced to answer for what takes place in the hospitals. Same with those doctors who run the colleges and societies. I remember thinking how like a theatre it was, but with real people being taken to task."

Cobbett was smiling. "I sense you have a plan."

"What if we deliberately libel people, inciting them to take us to court? We can then force them to try and justify their nepotism and corruption and incompetence."

Cobbett sat back. "You're even smarter and wilier than I took you to be. Took me years to realise being prosecuted for libel is a veritable badge of honour. The greater the truth, the greater the libel. But a word of warning. If you choose the wrong case, you'll end up in the debtors' prison."

"Don't imagine I haven't worried about that," said Thomas. "It's why we must be scrupulously fair. Everything backed up with evidence. But as we'd be the ones choosing who and when it happened, we can make sure we win."

Cobbett ran his fingers up and down his pewter tankard, deep in thought. When he looked up, he was smiling.

"Do it, but use the best lawyers. You've seen Denman in action. Excellent man but the person you really need is Brougham, Henry Brougham. Finest Scotchman I've ever met."

Thomas sat forward. "I've heard him. At the *Freemasons'*. He was magnificent. So clear and persuasive."

"Aye, that's him."

"I want to turn the courtroom into a lawyers' boxing ring," said Thomas. "Capture the public's attention and the newspapers' interest."

"Wakley, you fill me with fresh hope. But now," he said, pushing himself up and out from behind the table, "I must get back to my desk. As you'll discover, there's no let-up producing a weekly. Every day is precious."

✳

He'd always found it easy to make decisions, scornful of those who dithered, unable to make up their minds. But now, poised on the brink, Thomas didn't know what to do. Encouraged by Wardrop and Lawrence, Freddy and Cobbett, he knew with their help he could do it, establish a new periodical. And he wasn't concerned about the risk to his own reputation among doctors. No. It all came down to the risk to his family.

Time was running out if there was to be any chance of publishing in October. As he and Elizabeth settled down in the drawing room after dinner one evening, he couldn't settle, barely able to concentrate on the pile of evening mail on his lap. Elizabeth, who'd just opened her book, glanced over at him, closed it, and put it aside.

"Come on. What's troubling you? You've been agitated for days now."

"Is it that obvious?"

"Do you not think I see it when your mind is miles away? Like at the theatre the other night. Were you even listening, following the play?"

He looked at her and took a deep breath.

"I can't decide what to do. It's funny. All the adversities I faced in the past seem like nothing compared with this. I suppose that was always about coping with what was happening. Working out ways to protect myself from what others were doing to me. But now, it's about the future, our future. It feels much more difficult. If I get it wrong, make the wrong decision, it'll be my fault."

"Thomas. What are you talking about? What decision?"

"Oh, I'm sorry." He put his mail to the side. "You know what I think of my profession, the way hospitals are run, and how patients are treated. How I've been searching for a way I can do something to change all of that."

The way she didn't react gave him no clue as to what she was thinking.

"Well, I'm thinking of starting a periodical."

She tried to speak, but he raised his hand. "Hang on, please, hear me out."

He saw her shoulders drop as she retreated.

"A periodical unlike anything that has ever been published. One that rouses the thousands of doctors out there to stand up for their rights, that gives them all a fair chance, that considers patients and what they want."

"Thomas. That's all fine. Noble, worthy ambitions. But you know nothing of publishing."

"That was my first thought when Cobbett suggested it."

"Cobbett! Hardly the best man for advice. I thought he'd been jailed and forced into exile."

"It isn't just him. Wardrop agrees it's just what's needed."

"It's all very well them encouraging you but it's your life, our life, that will suffer if it goes wrong. We'd be bankrupt."

"Freddy thinks there is a way."

"Freddy? What does he know about medicine? And it's not him who'll be at risk."

"True. True. Which is why my plan would be to find someone else to pay for it for the first year, so if it fails, we lose nothing. We're no worse off and I go back to practising."

"And where are you going to find this person? Papa has made it clear there's no more money and I can't see you asking your father."

Her anguished look told him all he needed to know. This was what he'd been fearing. She'd not tolerate him being so reckless. And he knew she was right.

They sat in silence for a while.

"I'd never do it if it risked our family, our home."

She sighed, got up, and came and sat beside him on the settee.

"Let's just assume you did find a benefactor. Why would doctors subscribe?"

"Sorry, what? So, you don't think it's absurd?"

"Describe it." Her left hand was playing with her necklace, one of the few pieces of jewellery she'd had with her on the night of the fire. "I need a picture of what it would look like."

Thomas smiled. "You sound like Freddy. Well, it'll mostly be medical but I intend it should be unlike any existing periodical. There'll be all sorts of other things of interest to doctors."

"Ah, that's why I've caught you reading *The London Magazine* so often." She laughed. "I've corrupted the surgeon."

He smiled. "Not corrupted, taught me, opened my eyes. How about theatre reviews?"

"Theatre reviews?"

"Why not? All I have to do is write down what I think of the plays we see." He paused. "You could do some."

"Thomas, I've never written anything."

She took his hand. "You really are the most brilliant, imaginative man."

"What? You agree?"

"Thomas. I love adventures. Why do you think I read novels and go to the theatre so much? With you, it's like being in our own play."

"So, if I can find a benefactor, you think I should do it?"

"No." She paused, studying his face. Then she smiled. "I insist you do it."

*

Wardrop got up and went over to a mahogany cupboard, returning with two glasses of whisky. He handed one to Thomas.

"This requires a toast. To Wakley's Weekly!"

"So, you still think I should do it?"

"Aye, I do." He put down his glass. "The more I've thought about it these past weeks, the more convinced I've become that this could be the key we've been looking for to unlocking reform. Now, tell me, what are you planning to include?"

"Aside from the usual accounts of cases and essays on diseases, I want to provide word for word reports of pupils' lectures. Think of all those out there who never get the chance to hear men like Sir Astley or Charles Bell lecture."

"Let me get this right. You'd publish lectures given by the leading physicians and surgeons? What makes you think they'd agree? They earn a fortune from their pupils' fees."

"I know, but the way I see it, they lecture in public hospitals so I reckon the public own them."

"Ha. I'm not sure they'll see it that way."

"How can they stop me? Take me to court? Fine. The world will get to hear how much they earn, and I bet the newspapers would be interested in hearing from pupils about how often some lecturers don't even turn up, leaving it to their assistants."

Wardrop couldn't stop himself laughing. "Clever. But they'll never give you their lecture papers. Don't tell me you'll steal them."

"Of course not. I'll attend and take notes. Surrounded by pupils doing the same, no-one will know what I'm up to."

Thomas shuffled forward, perching on the front of his chair.

"I'll start with Sir Astley. He can easily afford it, and imagine, instead of preaching to a few hundred we'll give him an audience of thousands, doctors who trained years ago who'd never come to London and pay again."

Wardrop swilled the whisky around in his glass, breathing in the fumes.

"Aye, he's probably your best choice. We've all long suspected he supports reform. Just too entrenched in the establishment to say so." He smiled. "Secretly he might welcome it."

"That's what I thought. And he's the best lecturer I ever heard, wedded to science and the need to find out what's best for patients."

"So, what else?"

"Reports of Medical Society meetings."

Wardrop, who'd been about to take a sip of his drink, stopped.

"What? You know they're against that. You've only just been accepted back by them. Do you want to stir things up again, put their backs up?"

Thomas stared into the distance. "I'll take that risk."

"And who's going to do all the writing?"

"To start with, I will."

"All of it? Lectures, Society reports?"

"I can't expect others to take the risk until it's established." He paused. "I hope you'll contribute, but I must make clear I don't intend holding back. It's about exposing all that's wrong with our profession."

Wardrop smiled. "Wakley. I'd only help you if you do that. And talk to Lawrence. He won't want to be left out."

*

Lawrence welcomed him like an old friend. As he sat back in his armchair giving nothing away, he listened to Thomas's plans. When Thomas finished describing his vision, Lawrence sat drumming his fingers together, saying nothing.

As Thomas waited, he was distracted by the dust particles floating in the shaft of sunlight that streamed in through a high arched window. He was jolted out of his reverie by his host suddenly clapping his hands together.

"Perfect. Just what's needed."

"You think so?" said Thomas, struggling to contain his excitement that a fellow of the Royal Society, a man who'd challenged a fundamental belief of the medical and clerical establishment, was praising him.

"I do and I most certainly want to be part of it."

A maid appeared and placed a tray of coffee on the table between them. Thomas leant back and crossed his legs. Lawrence stirred some sugar into his drink then looked up.

"One benefit of no longer being professor at the College is I can speak freely without fear of being reprimanded." He stroked his mop of dark hair off his large forehead. "Exposing incompetence in the hospitals is all well and good but what about all the quackery outside the hospitals?"

"We'll go after them as well. Beauty of doing that is, however much the establishment detest us for exposing their failings, they'll have to support us attacking the quacks."

274

"Excellent. Can see you've thought this through," said Lawrence.

"And our strong advocacy of science will also make it difficult for them to attack us," said Thomas. "They'll hardly want to be seen opposing practice being based on scientific knowledge."

Lawrence clapped his hands together again. "You're a canny operator, Wakley. Don't know how you learnt all this but your plans are a joy to hear." He paused. "Have you thought about including news from abroad – Paris, Vienna, Italy?"

Thomas's face lit up. "I hadn't but we should. We can take it from foreign journals."

"Exactly. Not much they can do to stop it. Just have to pay translators. Mind you, I imagine that'll be the least of your costs. So, how are you going finance this?"

Thomas rubbed his chin. "That's all that's stopping me. I've got to find a benefactor or there'll be no journal."

"You know what?" said Lawrence. "I've seen enough of you to think you'll find one."

Thomas wished he shared everyone else's confidence.

*

Despite the cold weather, once again Elizabeth wanted to take the children up to Mill Hill for the summer.

"Otherwise, Papa will be there alone," she said. "Sarah's staying in London, as her baby's due next month, and Ann's looking after Tooley Street."

Thomas knew he had to let her go but he'd come to depend on her so much these past few months. She helped clarify his thoughts. Often, she'd come up with solutions he'd never have considered. She made him see things differently. Mind you, he'd balked at her latest suggestion.

"Poetry! You're forgetting my readers will be men."

"Thomas. Don't shout at me just because you disagree."

"Oh, my love, I'm sorry. It's just... men don't read poetry. It's... it's not a manly thing."

"Is that so? Then how come most poets are men? You knew one yourself – poor Keats. He clearly made an impression on you."

"But that was about his presence. He had a certain aura. Someone you couldn't ignore."

"Men like Byron are fighting the establishment and tradition, too," she continued. "Keats and Shelley did right up until they died. Can't you see it's the same battle? They're your allies. If doctors don't know this, it's your job to enlighten them."

Thomas rubbed the back of his neck, reluctant to accept her argument but knew she was right.

"You're not suggesting I include poems, are you?"

"Not poems, no. But the disputes. They're like your battles. Look at how Southey and Byron are sparring."

He laughed.

"What's funny?" she asked.

"Sparring. Have you been listening to me and Wiltshire talking about prize fights?"

She smiled. "Just because I don't join in doesn't mean I'm not listening, taking it all in. Helps me understand men."

"So, what's this dispute?"

"All right. Byron can't forgive Southey, who used to be radical but is now an arch-monarchist, a high Tory. After the old King died, Southey wrote a paean praising him. *A Vision of Judgement*. He dismissed Byron for criticising the King. Denounced him as belonging to a satanic school of poetry."

"Satanic?" Thomas laughed. "Is that worse than the cockney school?"

She laughed. "Ah, so you have been listening."

"Always."

"Anyway, the point is Byron wasn't taking that. Last October he hit back with *The Vision of Judgement*, ridiculing Southey. Some reckon it's destroyed the laureate's reputation for ever."

"My God. Makes doctors' disputes seem quite tame and polite." He rubbed his hands together. "I'm still not sure doctors would be interested."

"Only one way to find out." She raised an eyebrow. "Not like you to spurn the chance to be adventurous."

Thomas laughed. "Ah, that trick. Trapped me again." He paused. "You're getting more reckless than me."

"Not reckless. If readers don't want it, you can stop. But who knows, it might get you more subscribers."

He raised his hands in surrender. "All right, I give in. At this rate there won't be much space for medical matters."

He stood up and went over to the window, watching carriages and wagons making their way up and down The Strand.

"The trouble is, all these ideas are worthless unless I can find funding."

"I know," said Elizabeth. "I wish I could help. But meanwhile, have you found a publisher so you'll be ready when you do get funds?"

"Ah," he said, turning round, "that's another problem. I'm worried about talking to publishers as the more people who know the plan, the more chance word will get around, including my identity."

"What about Mr Cobbett's publisher? Surely he could be trusted to keep it confidential."

"I tried but he can't take on more work. The *Tupenny Trash* is so damn successful."

"Why not ask Mr Onwhyn? From talking to Fanny, he sounds like someone who'd take it on. After all, he's published Byron."

"Onwhyn? Do you think I could trust him to keep it secret?"

"From the times I've met him with Fanny, I'd say you could."

*

It had been three years since he'd gone to a concert with Freddy. Sitting in the Argyll Rooms, near his old home, he found it hard to concentrate on the music. Even when he'd visited Wiltshire and Sarah that afternoon and they'd told him they'd named their baby Thomas, he struggled to feign interest. The nagging thought that the journal might never happen was so dispiriting. It confirmed something he'd always known. He was a bad loser, unable to cope with defeat.

He was so distracted, it took the audience's applause to make him realise the concert was over.

"Come on," said Freddy, taking his arm as they made their way along Oxford Street. "For a man who doesn't drink much, I can see that's just what you need."

He guided Thomas into *The Clarendon* and while Freddy got the drinks, Thomas found a table in a quiet side room.

"Thought this would do the trick," said Freddy, handing Thomas a ruby rich drink. "Finest tawny port. Now, tell me. How's your grand plan going?"

"Grand plan? Most days I feel that's all it's ever going to be. Without finance, it'll just be a chimera."

Freddy smiled. "Always were one for the mythological."

Their candle started guttering, molten wax dripping down onto the well-worn table.

"The good news," said Thomas, "is Wardrop and Lawrence are keener every time I see them. And Cobbett couldn't be more helpful. His belief in it has kept me going at times. That and Elizabeth's enthusiasm."

"Elizabeth? She's in favour, despite the risks?"

"I know. Surprised me, too. Don't think I'd understood how committed she is to reform. Gets it from her father I think. He can't abide gentlemen landowners who look down their noses at men like him."

"Hm," said Freddy, "or maybe her support stems from her love and loyalty."

Thomas put down his drink. "You really are a romantic, aren't you?"

"All music lovers are, hadn't you noticed?"

"Best news," continued Thomas, "is I've found a publisher. Well, strictly, Elizabeth found him. John Onwhyn in Catherine

Street. He's sworn to secrecy." He paused. "But as I said, all this amounts to nothing without money."

Freddy finished his port and ordered another, having failed to persuade Thomas to drink more.

"Well, my news should cheer you up." He moved his empty glass aside and leant forward, his elbows on the table. "After we last spoke, I thought a lot about your plans. Did some more calculations, then bided my time until an opportunity arose to tell Uncle William."

"What!" shouted Thomas, bringing his fist down on the table. "I told you, no-one must know. You promised. I thought I could trust you."

Freddy sat back, startled. "Steady. Wait a minute. Let me finish."

Thomas looked down, shaking his head. "I can't believe you did that. Might as well have written to the newspapers."

"Thomas," shouted Freddy. "Enough."

Thomas froze. He'd never heard his friend raise his voice before. Men at another table had turned round, agog.

"You know," said Freddy, lowering his voice, "you can be so pig-headed at times."

Thomas, chastened, took some deep breaths but couldn't bring himself to look at his friend.

"Just listen," said Freddy. "I was well aware of the need for confidentiality. Didn't tell him who you are. Just explained that I'd known you all my life, that I trusted you and felt your criticisms of doctors and hospitals was well justified."

"So, what did he say?"

"I'm coming to that. As a governor at Bart's, he knows all about the ways hospitals are run and how incompetence is tolerated. Turns out he's as keen for change as you are. Quietly detests the privileged class. I suppose I shouldn't have been surprised. After all, he's the son of a clothier from Wivey who never got to go to grammar school. Earned his fortune through sheer hard work."

Freddy paused while a serving maid handed him his port.

"I told him I couldn't tell him more about you or your plan, suffice to say it was a weekly medical journal for the thousands of doctors currently ill-served, like those in Wivey. That seemed to strike a chord. Told him I was confident it would be commercially successful. Indeed, it could turn out to be highly profitable."

"Steady on. I'd be happy if just paid its way."

"Hmm. Anyway, then I mentioned you'd need a thousand pounds over the first year to get it started."

"Yes?" said Thomas. "And…?"

Freddy sat back, a huge smile across his face. "He agreed."

"He agreed?" Thomas leapt up, went round and hoisted Freddy out of his chair and hugged him, unable to find the words he wanted. When he finally released his friend, Thomas pulled a handkerchief from his pocket to mop his eyes. He had to hold the table as he lowered himself back into his chair.

"I'm sorry. I can't believe it. I've been worrying for months. I was convinced it would never happen. And now…"

Having readjusted his neckerchief, Freddy placed his hands on the table.

"Uncle William doesn't want anyone to know. He worries if it got out he was supporting a radical periodical, it could harm the business. There's to be no paperwork and the money comes through me, so if it ever came to light he wouldn't be involved."

Thomas sat shaking his head. "Sorry. Still can't believe you really mean it."

"Of course I do. Stop worrying."

"Freddy. This is the best news I've ever had."

"Better than the midwife's? Better than Elizabeth accepting your hand?"

"All right. There I go again, exaggerating." He laughed. "Definitely better than beating you at chess."

"Ah, that reminds me. I've had an idea for your journal. Lots of doctors play chess. Well, how about a chess column, reporting interesting games?"

"A chess column? Would people want to read about chess? Play it, yes, but read about it?"

"I know, maybe it's nonsense, otherwise it would have been done already. Think about it. Would give me a way of contributing."

"That, my friend, is reason enough!"

Chapter 12

1823

Despite it being August, it was chilly at night. Thomas asked Daniel to light a fire in the dining room and Sarah to cook something hot. Just after eight, his guests – Wardrop, Lawrence, and Onwhyn – arrived. This was the occasion he'd often dreamt about. Finally, the periodical was to become a reality.

"Wonderful news you've found a benefactor, Wakley," said Wardrop, as they went into the dining room. "Don't suppose you'll tell us who it is."

"I won't," confirmed Thomas. "They don't want anyone to know."

The four of them settled round the table and Sarah served the soup.

"Second issue of the *Medico-Chirurgical Review* is out soon," said Wardrop. "We'll soon know how successful it's proving with our provincial colleagues."

"Two hundred and fifty pages. I'd be surprised if they sell many," said Lawrence. "More like a book. Doubt it will get more than a few hundred at best. More to the point, should we be worried about that weekly that started in February?"

"For a thin pamphlet, it's got a long title," said Wardrop. "*Medico-Chirurgical & Philosophical Magazine,* if I remember rightly."

"I've looked at a few copies," said Thomas. "It's entirely medical. No criticism or calls for reform."

"I don't think you need worry unduly," said Onwhyn. "Their publisher, Cox, tells me it's not selling. He reckons it'll fold before the end of the year."

"So, I say we hold our nerve," said Thomas. "Keep to our vision. Let others worry about us."

"Damn fine mushroom and beef soup, Wakley," said Wardrop. "Must get your cook to tell mine what's in it."

"Now, Onwhyn," said Thomas, putting down his spoon and wiping his mouth with his napkin, "timings. When will you need material if we're to get it out and across the country on Saturdays?"

"Got it all worked out." He pulled a sheet of paper out of his pocket and spread it on the tablecloth in front of him. "Working backwards, I'll need the checked proofs by Friday morning at the latest. That means we can start printing in the afternoon and have a thousand copies by nightfall, ready for the midnight stagecoaches."

"So, when do you need the manuscripts?"

"Early as possible. Latest will be Thursday morning, as long as you can be sure to check the proofs on Thursday night."

"That's a problem, isn't it, Wakley?" ventured Wardrop. "Sir Astley's lectures finish at nine on Wednesday nights."

"Don't worry," said Thomas. "I'll manage. I'll work through the night if necessary."

"Rather you than me," quipped Lawrence, wiping his soup bowl with a chunk of bread roll.

Sarah came in, collected the bowls, and placed a large stuffed haddock in the middle of the table.

"Will you manage that, sir?" she asked. "Or do you want me to serve it?"

"Mrs Witcher, I think three surgeons should be able to cope," laughed Thomas.

Lawrence reached forward and picked up the large fish knife and fork.

"Watch carefully, Wardrop," he chortled, "you might learn something."

"From a Bart's man? Hardly likely!"

Thomas sat back and looked at his companions in arms. He still couldn't quite believe it was really happening. Sitting there with two of the country's finest free-thinking surgeons. Together, they would soon unleash an assault on the medical establishment the likes of which had never been seen.

They fell silent for a while as they all tucked into their food.

"Delicious," said Wardrop. "Now, tell us, Wakley, what you want Lawrence and me to do."

Thomas put down his fork.

"All right. I propose we don't start exposing botched and bungled operations until we've published a few issues. Keep the hospitals guessing what our intent is. Just like in a prize-fight. Don't provoke your opponent straightaway. Always the best strategy during the first few rounds."

From the confused looks on his companions' faces, it was clear they didn't share his interest in boxing.

"Never mind. There's a practical reason, too. We'll need reporters in each hospital. I'll only have time to attend the Borough hospitals."

"Bit risky, isn't it, finding reporters?" asked Lawrence.

"Sound more like spies," added Wardrop.

"I'd like to think of them as revealers of the truth. But you're right, Lawrence. Can't just advertise for them. What I'm hoping is, when pupils see my reports from the Borough hospitals, some of them in the other hospitals will contact the periodical, in confidence, offering to help. We can assure them we'll preserve their anonymity."

Wardrop clapped his hands together. "Brilliant. Can see you've thought it through."

"So, there'll be no case reports at first?" asked Lawrence.

"Not quite," said Thomas, leaning forward. "This is where you two come in, selecting cases reported in other medical journals."

Wardrop and Lawrence exchanged glances.

"I know what you're thinking," said Thomas, "they'll be reports by self-serving doctors claiming how clever they'd been."

"Even when the patient died," added Lawrence, sending the three doctors into gales of laughter.

"Sorry, Onwhyn," said Thomas, noticing the publisher looking shocked. "You'll have to forgive us doctors our strange sense of humour."

"All right," said Wardrop, looking at Lawrence. "I reckon we can find enough for a few weeks."

Lawrence nodded. "I guess that with Sir Astley's lectures taking up a fair few pages, we should have plenty to fill the first issues."

Thomas passed round the decanter of red wine. "More than enough as we've got to leave enough space for the other items."

"Other items?" asked Lawrence, raising his eyebrows. "What items?"

"Well, first of all, the editorial. I've already written several attacking all our *bête noires*. Got enough for the first few issues."

"Knowing you, Wakley, you won't have pulled your punches," chortled Wardrop.

Thomas smiled, amused by his companion's lack of awareness of how fitting his boxing comment was.

"Fine. What else?" asked Lawrence.

"Elizabeth's convinced me we need variety. After all, our readers will have interests other than medicine."

"No doubt, but we don't know what they are," said Lawrence.

"And they'll all be different," added Wardrop.

"So, we try things and find out," said Thomas. "If it's not wanted, we'll try something else."

"What are you thinking of including?" asked Wardrop.

"To start, theatre reviews and chess."

Lawrence, who'd just put a forkful of fish in his mouth, almost choked. "Chess!"

"Think about it," said Thomas. "Most doctors play chess. So, we report interesting games. Maybe set them challenges."

Lawrence, having pulled his napkin out of his waistcoat, had just about stopped coughing. "Wakley, you really are extraordinary."

"Have to be honest, it was a friend's idea, and he wants to write it."

"Anything else?" asked Wardrop, looking quite anxious.

"Table Talk."

"Table Talk? What, like we're having now?" asked Lawrence.

Thomas pushed back his chair. "We all hear stories or read snippets of news which we pass on to our friends in the coffee house. They may be entertaining, shocking, amusing. My idea is we publish a page or two of them."

"What, medical tales?"

"Not necessarily. Anything that embarrasses the powerful, the establishment. Best of all, if it exposes lies and deception."

"That's no better than gossip," said Wardrop.

"But think about it," said Thomas. "People love gossip, even doctors."

Lawrence was shaking his head. "You really do mean it to be very different, to shake things up."

"I do. That's not all," said Thomas, enjoying milking his audience's incredulity. "We need our profession to understand that the problems we face are not unique to medicine. We're not special. And most important, we're not alone. In all walks of life, reform is needed."

"You've been talking to Cobbett too much," said Wardrop.

"No. I don't just mean parliamentary reform or the Corn Laws." He paused. "Painting, novels, poetry."

Both Wardrop and Lawrence put down their cutlery and stared at Thomas.

"I've learnt a lot these past couple of years," said Thomas. "I'd had no idea that poets are engaged in as robust a battle as we are. A staid, conservative establishment is being assailed by the radical romantics. Does that sound familiar?"

"Had never thought of myself as a medical romantic," laughed Lawrence. "Rather like the idea."

Onwhyn, who had said nothing for some time, clapped his hands. "You're right, Wakley. I love it. Show the doctors they're part of something much wider."

"Exactly," said Thomas, beaming with delight. "If they understand that, I believe they'll be braver, readier to stand up to the establishment and demand change."

Thomas looked at his medical companions. Their earlier look of bemusement was passing as they gradually smiled.

"My God, Wakley. You've really got this all thought through, haven't you?" said Wardrop, shaking his head slowly.

"I'm all for it if it raises hackles in the College," added Lawrence.

The relief Thomas felt. "Have to say, I've been pretty anxious at times that I was getting carried away, that you'd not agree, you'd want to walk away when you heard my plans."

"Nonsense," said Wardrop. "Quite the opposite." He pulled his napkin out of the top of his waistcoat and sat back. "I'll be honest. From the start I saw in you a fellow traveller, someone who'd want to join in working for change. But at no point did I have an inkling it would come to this. Leading us forward."

"Hear, hear," said Lawrence.

Martha came in and cleared away their plates while Thomas passed round a decanter of port.

"There's something else you need to understand. I intend to use the Court of the King's Bench to air our concerns."

"What? Thought we feared them taking us to court?"

"We do. Which is why we take control. We make them think they've got the upper hand, but we'll be the ones choosing the targets. We criticise and expose the most clearcut incompetence, forcing them to take on hopeless battles they can't hope to win."

All three of his guests still looked worried, glancing at one another.

"Bit risky, isn't it?" said Wardrop.

"As I say, not if we select examples where we have clear evidence of incompetence. We just need doctors and pupils who are prepared to testify what they witness. Won't be easy initially but once people see there are no repercussions, I believe men who are so incensed will volunteer. If we can interest the national press, they'll spread our stories far and wide. They can reach audiences we can't hope to. And best of all, it won't cost us a penny."

"Let me get this clear. We'll be guilty of libelling people but on good grounds with irrefutable evidence of incompetence or ineffective treatments."

"Exactly. At times we'll have to pay fines for harming their so-called reputations but the lawyers I've talked to assure me the amounts will be derisory. So small it should embarrass them, ruin their puffed-up reputations."

No-one spoke for a while as they took in what Thomas was suggesting.

"Hospital governors will be furious," said Lawrence. "They'll be so confused. Wakley, it's a masterstroke. And those accused won't know whether to keep quiet and avoid risking public humiliation or sue us for libel!"

"I can see this promises to be a rumbustious journey," said Wardrop. "Just leaves one thing. Do you have a title for this blunderbuss of a periodical?"

Thomas stood up, wanting his announcement to have maximum effect. He'd spent weeks wondering how his suggestion would go down.

"I want something so different to the stodgy titles medical journals have always had. Something short and dramatic that captures people's attention. Like *Tuppenny Trash, Black Dwarf, The Examiner, The Scourge*."

He could see his audience looking increasingly apprehensive.

"Come on, tell us, man," implored Lawrence.

Thomas smiled. "I intend to call it *The Lancet*."

"*The Lancet*," repeated Wardrop.

"Like a lancet window," said Thomas, "shining light on the dark, murky recesses. And like a surgical lancet, we'll cut out the dross and corruption."

Lawrence started clapping. "Wakley. It's perfect." He leapt to his feet, raising his glass. "Gentlemen. *The Lancet*."

*

After living alone all summer, Thomas couldn't get used to how noisy the house was again. There was rarely a quiet moment, least not until the evening, and only then if Elizabeth May was sleeping. During the day he retreated downstairs to his study. He was now turning away most patients, knowing he had to concentrate on writing. It was vital to get the preface to the first issue right, to convey *The Lancet's* ethos and ambition. Over the years he'd written copiously about what he'd seen, about best practices, the atrocious way hospitals were run, and how incompetent some doctors were. But that had been for himself; not for others to read. The challenge of compiling a clear manifesto was proving more difficult than he'd imagined. Endless versions filled his wastepaper basket.

Every evening, he welcomed the sound of Daniel's footsteps coming downstairs as it meant he could stop agonizing over intractable problems.

"Sir, Mrs Goodchild asks if you're ready for dinner?"

"Yes, yes. Tell her I'm coming."

Grabbing a notepad and pen, he made his way through the shop and upstairs. As they took their seats at the table, Thomas saw the latest version of his editorial on pupil education he'd given her to read, lying on the table.

Martha came in and placed a dish of ox tongue in a thick, brown gravy on the table. Having served herself, Elizabeth told him she'd read it but didn't give away what she thought of it.

"Come on. Tell me. What did you think?" asked Thomas.

She smiled. "I can see why change is needed. How do senior doctors get away with it? Not turning up, not letting pupils ask questions. Why don't the governors do something? I know you've told me how dreadful it is, but the way you describe it…"

"So, you liked it? You think it's all right to publish?"

"Thomas. It's more than all right. Those guilty should so embarrassed. Surely it will make them change?"

"That's our hope. Let's see."

She picked up her fork but before starting to eat she looked across the table at him.

"One thing puzzles me. How did you learn to write so powerfully?"

"Don't know. Just practice, I suppose."

"I love the way you're so direct. You don't leave any doubt in the reader's mind. It must be wonderful to be able to write so easily."

"Easy? Oh, it's not easy. Got a basket full of previous versions downstairs. Just ask Daniel!" He paused. "I've found it gets easier. Two years ago, I'd not have shown anyone what I wrote. But now, some days I can get it right first time."

She laughed. "Just as well if you're going to fill *The Lancet* every week."

"That's my worry. That I'll not be able to keep up. It's easy to get the first issue filled but it's going to be unremitting, week after week. Never a chance to take a break."

Elizabeth smiled. "You know what? You'll find a way."

"Wish I shared your confidence." He paused. "Onwhyn tells me most periodicals last a matter of months, at best a couple of years. I keep thinking we'll be just the same."

She fixed him with a look he had come to recognise. "I won't let that happen."

He knew she couldn't possibly guarantee that but, nevertheless, the way she smiled filled him with belief and optimism.

At the end of the meal, as Elizabeth rolled up her napkin, returning it to its silver ring, she asked him what he'd been grappling with that day.

"Everything happening on a Wednesday evening."

"What do you mean? Come on, explain."

"Covent Garden and Drury Lane both start their seasons the week of the first issue, and both open on Wednesday, same night as Sir Astley starts lecturing."

"You're not thinking of abandoning the reviews are you? You've got to have them. Marks you out from the other journals."

"But I can't be in three places at once."

Thomas could see Elizabeth eyes weren't focused, just gazing into the distance.

"You've thought of something, haven't you?" said Thomas.

"Promise to hear me out before you say anything."

He nodded.

"It doesn't have to be you. I could write a review of a play."

"You? But you've never done one."

"What, and you have?"

"No but I've done lots of writing, of other things."

"And I've read dozens of reviews. Doesn't strike me as being so difficult. After all, after a play, we always discuss it. Instead of telling you what I think, I'll write it down."

He leant forward, his elbows on the table, his hands together. "Why didn't I think of that?"

"Hmm, I wonder, too," she said, laughing. "I'll go with my sister."

She picked up her knife and fork and carried on eating.

"If you go to *The Rivals* at Drury Lane," said Thomas, "what about *Much Ado* at Covent Garden? We need someone else."

"Well, I know someone who's seen even more plays than I have."

Thomas raised his eyebrows and waited.

"Fanny Onwhyn. She could come back here afterwards and we'll help each other."

He pushed back his chair, went round and leaning down, kissed her. "Perfect."

"Me or the idea?" she asked.

"Both." He stood back up. "Just one thing. I'll need the reviews by dawn."

She smiled. "Let's hope our daughter sleeps that night."

Later, in front of the fire, as Elizabeth sat reading the new issue of *The London Magazine,* Thomas saw she was twiddling with a lock of hair on the right side of her neck, a sure sign she was deeply absorbed. He put aside the evening mail he'd been reading.

"What's so interesting?"

She looked up. "You remember I told you about the contretemps between Southey and Byron?"

"I do. Love to see a radical landing a knockout blow the way Byron did."

She looked taken aback.

"Sorry, didn't put that very well. But you have to admit, that was some lashing Byron handed out."

"Well, another letter's appeared admonishing Southey."

She handed him the magazine.

"Elia," said Thomas. "Who's that?"

"Charles Lamb. He's an essayist. Read it."

When he finished all eight pages, he looked up. "Are you suggesting...?"

"It's perfect," interrupted Elizabeth.

"It's so long, though." He paused. "Could you help me identify an extract?"

Elizabeth smiled. "Just what I was hoping, Mr Editor."

*

With only three weeks to go, as those around him became increasingly excited, Thomas's concerns grew. What if he failed, let them down? Younger, when he'd faced adversities – as a midshipman, in the boxing ring, getting away from Incledon – he'd only had to consider himself.

As he made his way through Charing Cross on his way to meet Cobbett, he imagined the hostility he'd have to put up with when people discovered he was the editor. He knew he'd be able to preserve the anonymity of the others but not his own. And then it wouldn't just be him who'd suffer. Elizabeth would as well. And after all they'd suffered in the wake of the Argyll Street fire.

At night he lay awake, fearing she hadn't understood the extent of the risk they were taking, how it could end their opportunity to be accepted in London society. He even started wondering if Wardrop and Lawrence were only encouraging him to be so reckless because they knew they'd be safe, hidden from view. Could they have been manipulating him the whole time? Was he foolish to trust them?

As he headed down Whitehall, he had to stop while a carriage going into Craig's Court crossed his path. He stood there, in the autumn sunshine, watching people going about their business, none of them aware of what he was planning. If he told them, they'd probably not think much of it. Maybe he'd fooled himself into expecting too much, exaggerating its importance.

Although his way was now clear, he remained standing as people bustled past. He stared into the distance, remembering how so often before fights he'd doubted his ability, at times terrified, and how he'd learnt that if he gave into such fears, he was sure to lose. And how afterwards, having won, he'd wonder how he could have harboured such fears, determined never again to doubt his ability. But it was always the same next time. Was it the same pattern repeating itself – doubting, fearing the worst?

"Watch out," shouted a porter shouldering a huge load, almost knocking Thomas over. As he regained his balance, he heard the hour bell on the nearby Admiralty Building. He was late for his meeting.

Cobbett's fervour soon dispelled his doubts and misgivings.

"You know," said Cobbett, "the more I've thought about it, the more I'm convinced periodicals like yours, aimed at particular occupations, are the way forward. *The Register* can only do so much. Perhaps yours will be the first of many."

He gulped down some ale then wiped his mouth with the back of his hand. "So tell me, how are you letting people know about it?"

"A few adverts in the newspapers, but mostly by Wardrop and Lawrence spreading the word, claiming to have heard a rumour. Seems to be working as yesterday, at Guy's, someone told me of the rumour. And people keep pestering Onwhyn to find out who the editor is and what organization is behind it."

"That's a start but not enough," said Cobbett. "You've got to whip up more interest and curiosity. People love some mystery. If it were me, I'd start spreading false rumours as to who the editor is."

"Really? But spreading falsehoods goes against all we stand for. Openness, honesty. I'd rather wait for doctors to see the power and truth of what we publish…"

"Honourable I'm sure but not enough," interrupted Cobbett. "Too slow."

"So, what do you suggest?"

"Scandal. Ask any newspaper man. That's what sells papers."

"Before long, we'll publish plenty of that. Surgeons' incompetence, corrupt hospitals, nepotism, …"

"No. Not vivid enough for the ordinary man and, let's face it, underneath it all doctors are just ordinary men." Cobbett leant forward and lowered his voice. "You say one of your aims is to root out charlatans, rogue doctors?"

Thomas nodded.

"Right. I've got the perfect one for you. William Bengo Collyer. Evangelist preacher who claims to be medically trained. He's been molesting young labourers in some public baths." He winked, nodding knowingly. "Claims he was checking them for hernias."

"Collyer. There was something about him in *The Morning Chronicle* last month."

"That was just the start. I've a lot more in *The Register* next week, revealing salacious details from the young men. Thing is, I've got even more and you can have it. It's perfect for a periodical committed to rooting out and exposing quacks. Not only that, and you'll like this, Collyer hates radicals. Forever preaching about the licentiousness of Byron and Shelley."

Thomas sat trying to take it all in. "Exposing quacks is one thing but this wasn't the sort of thing I was thinking of including. But... it seems too good to be true."

"Exactly. The man's an abomination. Mind you, hard to call him a man given his proclivities."

"Would certainly help us establish our moral rectitude. Be hard for the establishment not to agree and support us," said Thomas.

"I can see you're getting the hang of it. We'll make a newspaper man out of you yet. Now, in your first issue, only announce you're going to reveal more about Collyer in the second week. That way, readers will come back and you'll drum up lots more interest."

Thomas sat rubbing his chin. "I can see I've got a lot to learn."

"From what I've seen of you, that won't take long."

*

The days leading up to publication were frantic. As planned, on Wednesday night, while Thomas sat in his study writing up Sir Astley's lecture, Elizabeth and Fanny worked upstairs at the dining table. Around midnight, he went to check on their progress, still not convinced they'd be able to do it.

"How's it going?" he asked.

"Well, after several false starts, we think you have two first-rate reviews, don't we?" laughed Elizabeth.

"Well, I suppose that's for the editor to decide," said Fanny.

"And how are you getting on downstairs?" asked Elizabeth.

"I'll be honest. Taking longer than I'd imagined. But I'm determined to get it right, show Sir Astley the respect he deserves. I'll be a few hours yet."

It was three o'clock when he finished, bundling up his manuscript and tying it with a ribbon. Upstairs, he found the theatre reviews. With some trepidation, he sat down to read them. He needn't have worried.

The following night it only took until two o'clock to check the proofs. By then he was too fired up to sleep. The prospect of seeing and handling the first issue was only hours away. With the proofs dispatched to Onwhyn, he sat in the drawing room imagining all the mistakes he'd missed, questioning if he'd made the right choice of articles and becoming convinced his preface hadn't captured *The Lancet*'s aims. But his biggest fear was whether he should have taken on the Collyer case.

Soon after dawn, Elizabeth appeared carrying Elizabeth May.

"You're still awake. You've hardly slept for two nights."

"I'm going to have to get used to it, unless I can persuade Sir Astley to start his lectures earlier."

She put Elizabeth May in her crib and joined him on the settee.

"I know I said I'd have no worries about reviewing the play," she said, "but I really struggled at first. Strange thing was, once I'd got going, it got easier."

"Just as well, because with Sir Astley lecturing twice a week, and evening meetings of the medical societies, I'll need you to do more reviews, at least over the next few weeks."

She sat looking at him. "You really are as remarkable as I thought when I first laid eyes on you."

"Well, I hope you still feel that when irate doctors, hospital governors, and colleges come after me."

"Thomas. I've always known the risk but I also know you can stand up for yourself. Anyway, it's not as if I could have stopped you. Not that I would have wanted to. That day you came home and told me what Mr Cobbett had suggested, I could see the die was cast." She paused. "Whatever happens, I'll never regret what you're doing."

Thomas stared into the distance. "I once read that in everyone's life there comes a moment when they have to make a momentous decision, one that will determine their whole future, their whole life."

He looked at her. "This is mine. All those decisions I've made so far, they seemed so important at the time. But now I can see they were nothing compared to this."

She took hold of his hands. "Now you're to go and get some sleep before your meeting this evening."

*

To his surprise, he managed to sleep soundly. It was already dark when Elizabeth woke him.

"Come on, they'll be waiting for you."

It was only a few minutes' walk to Onwhyn's office on the first floor above his printworks. Wardrop and Lawrence were already there and they were soon joined by Cobbett.

They squeezed into the small office and Onwhyn passed round glasses of whisky. The steady throb of the printer downstairs could be heard.

"I tell you, Wakley," said Onwhyn, "I've never seen such interest in a new periodical and I've published a fair number."

"There was lots of talk at the medical societies this week," said Lawrence, "and I'm told it's the only topic of conversation in the College. People can't believe no-one knows who's behind it."

"It's the title that's really got people puzzled," said Wardrop. "Nearly everyone saying it can't be a serious periodical with a title like that. And as for it being weekly, it's being dismissed as worthless."

"Up on Paternoster Row," said Onwhyn, "publishers tell me it'll fold in weeks, convinced a medical periodical has to be quarterly or, at most, monthly."

"They'll not say that when we have hundreds of subscribers and are outselling the opposition," said Lawrence.

"If the other periodicals really believed we'll fail, they wouldn't be attacking us before they've even seen it," said

Wardrop. "Did you read what Johnson said? Described us as *'having the baleful influence of a private spy and public informer'.*"

"Same with *The London Medical & Physical*," said Lawrence. "Mcleod already accuses us *'of a monstrous breach of professional etiquette'*!"

"And the fight hasn't even started yet," said Thomas, "still just bobbing and weaving. Imagine what they'll say when the fists start flying. Then we'll give them good reason to fear us."

Suddenly it went quiet. Downstairs, the printer had stopped. Then Thomas heard slow steady footsteps on the stairs. His heart started racing and he could feel goosepimples on his arms. The door opened slowly and an elderly man with ink-stained hands, wearing a long leather apron, handed a pile of copies to Onwhyn.

"The moment's arrived, gentlemen," said Onwhyn, standing up and handing each of them a copy.

As Thomas laid it on his lap, his hands were shaking so much he could barely turn the pages. It was still warm from the printer. Against all the odds, he'd done it. He felt his eyes filling up. He so wanted to hug Elizabeth.

Then the spell was broken by Wardrop, who'd stood up and raised his glass.

"*The Lancet*. The future of medicine."

Epilogue

Within two years *The Lancet* had 4,000 subscribers and two years later, a staggering 12,000. It continued to thrive, becoming the only journal of its time to survive into the second half of the nineteenth century. Today it is one of the four leading medical journals in the world.

Thomas Wakley's desire to conceal his identity as editor lasted only a few days. When William Collyer sought legal means to stop publication of the second issue, the only person he could indict was the publisher, John Onwhyn. To protect him, Thomas was forced to identify himself and transfer to a new publisher. The exposure and denunciation of Collyer went ahead and he never proceeded with his legal action against Wakley.

His plan to use the Court of King's Bench by libeling carefully selected doctors proved as successful as Wakley had hoped. Over the first few years, six leading London doctors rose to the bait and accused *The Lancet* of libel. Of the £8000 reparations they demanded, the court awarded a paltry £155. As he had intended, several cases gained considerable publicity in the national newspapers.

The Lancet's success, combined with the vitriol of its criticisms of the other medical journals, incited their editors to attack Thomas ferociously. They even continued to assert he was an arsonist who had set fire to his own home to defraud the insurance company. James Johnson labelled him "an outcast of medical society" and pronounced that publicising doctors' failures was a "cruel and demoniacal torture". Loving a fight, Thomas thrived on the attacks, vindicated by *The Lancet's* soaring number of subscriptions. Within a decade, most doctors across the country were reading it.

His earlier altercations with the leading London medical societies was heightened when he started including first-hand reports of their meetings. He was denounced as a "literary pirate and disseminator of moral garbage". The hospitals were equally hostile. Less than a year after starting *The Lancet,* Thomas became the first alumnus to be banned from the Borough hospitals for daring to publish critical accounts of the care they provided. Governors viewed public hospitals as their's, not the public's.

Thomas's criticism of the way apprentices and pupils were treated was denounced as a "vampire presence chilling the current of communication between the preceptor and the pupil".

The establishment were so fearful *The Lancet* would put off provincial doctors sending patients to London, thus damaging their income, they established a rival weekly journal, *The London Medical Gazette*, which looked uncannily like *The Lancet*. Dedicated to attacking Thomas as "a populist agitator" and "champion of the ignorant and illiterate", it failed. After two years, having attracted a derisory sixty-six subscriptions, wealthy London hospital doctors were forced to pay for it to be given away for free.

With publishing success came financial success. In 1826, three years after its start, Thomas and Elizabeth, now with four children, moved into a fine house in prestigious Bedford Square. Frustrated by the slow pace of medical reform, Thomas decided he needed to get into Parliament. In 1835 he was elected Member for Finsbury (London), and four years later also became the first medically qualified coroner in London (having argued that non-medical lawyers couldn't judge whether a death was natural or not). For the best part of the next twenty years he, in effect, had three full-time jobs – editor, MP, and coroner.

Sadly, their daughter Elizabeth May died in 1838, aged only sixteen, but their three sons had successful careers. The eldest, Thomas Henry Wakley, became a surgeon and later also a journalist; Henry Membury Wakley was a lawyer; and the youngest, James Goodchild Wakley, also trained in medicine. In 1852, at the age of twenty-six, James joined his father in editing *The Lancet*, succeeding to the post following his father's death in 1862. Elizabeth had died five years earlier.

Both Thomas and Elizabeth were interred in the catacomb at Kensal Green Cemetery (north-west London), where they lie forgotten. Despite arguably being the most important initiator of reforms to the medical profession and to hospitals, heralding the start of modern health care, there is little recognition of his contribution. In many ways, he was as important to medicine and hospitals as, a few decades later, Florence Nightingale was to nursing and health care. Yet there is no statue to honour him, no museum, no authoritative biography. A tall price to pay for defying the establishment.

Acknowledgements

Researching my first novel, *The Honourable Doctor*, I came to recognise just how pivotal the establishment of *The Lancet* in 1823 was in initiating and paving the way for modern health care. Until then, doctors enjoyed complete autonomy, not even accountable to their peers let alone the public and their patients. Its significance cannot be overestimated.

Hence, I was intrigued as to why more attention has never been paid to why it was Thomas Wakley, and not one of thousands of other doctors, who was the harbinger of such monumental change in the medical profession and the hospitals. Why him? What motivated and enabled him? And even, why did he chose medicine?

Historians lack of interest in his life before 1823 may have simply been because there are no personal records, such as diaries or letters. Wakley was notorious for refusing to talk about his past even, apparently, refusing to cooperate with John Saunders when, in 1840, he was compiling memoirs of the twenty-seven most eminent living political reformers.

The brief accounts of Wakley's formative years contained in his three biographies (Squire Sprigge 1897; Charles Brook 1945; John Hostettler 1993) plus John Fernandez Clarke's memoir (1847) of working for Wakley, repeat many claims that I found couldn't be substantiated by official records and documents.

This offered the possibility of constructing a fictional account, based on the few events in his life that are beyond dispute, weaving them together to gain a plausible narrative as to why, at the age of twenty-eight, he embarked on a venture that in all likelihood would lead to ostracism from the medical establishment if not the whole profession.

In investigating his early life, I am grateful for the help of many local historians: Jenny Beaman, Membury Historical Society; Bryan Drew, Membury; Sharon Mason, Chard Grammer School; Margaret Lewis, All Hallows School; Sue Farrington, Wiveliscombe Book Group; Graham Edwards & Liz Grant, Somerset Heritage Centre; Mike Davidson, Taunton & Somerset Hospital; David Feary, Henley Archaeology & History Group; Valerie Alasia, Henley Society; Miles Derverson and Julia Haynes, Mill Hill Historical Society.

A highlight of my investigations was a visit to Wakley's boyhood home, Land Farm in Devon, where the current owners, Margaret and Stephen Bulpitt, not only showed me round but provided afternoon tea. At the nearby Axminster Medical Practice, the practice managers Sharon Giles & Donna Walsh showed me the portraits of Thomas, Elizabeth and Henry Wakley, which are on display for today's patients.

Historical fiction depends on archives which in turn depend on the invaluable work of archivists. Thank you to Janet Payne (The Society of Apothecaries), Colin Gregory (The Worshipful Company of Glaziers) and Gemma Hollman (King's College, London). And to Emma Burton for her forensic genealogical help to piece together Thomas Wakley's family and descendants.

I benefited from the insight and wisdom of many academic experts, among them: John Barnard, Wolfson College, Oxford; Paul Craddock, University College London; James Grande, King's College London; Sally Frampton, University of Oxford; Mike Brown, University of Lancaster; Bill Bynum, University College London. I also learnt from correspondence with others with a lifelong interest in Wakley: David Sharp, James Butcher, David Evans and Clive Wakley. And particularly, Carolyn Paul,

University College London, whose excellent research on Thomas's period at sea I drew on heavily.

Of the many books and articles consulted, these were of particular value: Edwina Sherrington, *Thomas Wakley and reform*; Debbie Harrison, *All The Lancet's Men: 1823-1832*; Brittany Pladek, *"A variety of tastes": the Lancet in the early-19th century periodical press*; Carolyn Paul, *Wakley at sea*; Michael Brown, *'Bats, Rats and Barristers': The Lancet, libel and the radical stylistics*; John Fernandez Clarke, *Autobiographical recollections of the medical profession*; Squire Sprigge, *The life and times of Thomas Wakley*; Joan Lane, *Apprenticeship In England, 1600-1914*; Roger Jones, *Thomas Wakley, plagiarism, libel, and the founding of The Lancet*; Charles Brook, *Battling surgeon*; John Hostettler, *Thomas Wakley*; David Sharp, *Thomas Wakley (1795-1862): A biographical sketch*; Nicholas Roe, *John Keats*; James Grande, John Stevenson, Richard Thomas, *The opinions of William Cobbett*.

Once again, I've been fortunate to have a perceptive alpha reader, Pippa Gough, who not only provided valuable critical feedback on my first draft but whose enthusiasm for the tale reinforced my belief there was a story to tell. Along the way, Max Eilenberg provided a creative, challenging sounding board. Thank you to my beta readers for their comments: Emma Burton, Jeremy Snape and Diane Elbourne.

For help turning my manuscript into this book, thanks to Melanie Bartle, Christine McPherson and Julie Scott at Grosvenor House Publishing.

When I started writing in early 2024, I was disappointed to learn that Susan (Suzette) Sprague, who at the time I believed was Thomas and Elizabeth's only living descendant, had died the previous year. However, in summer 2024 I was delighted to discover that Susan had had four children, the great, great, great grandchildren of Thomas (and there are four more in the subsequent generation). It was a pleasure to meet and spend time with three of them - Serena Hayes, Denis Sprague and Delia Gilbert. From the start, they (and their sister, Karen Mathews) have encouraged me in this venture. I hope they find Thomas's extraordinary story as gripping as I have in imagining how their remarkable ancestor came to be the most important and effective reformer of British medicine and who, arguably, kickstarted modern health care.

www.ingramcontent.com/pod-product-compliance
Lightning Source LLC
Chambersburg PA
CBHW021207250626
47155CB00008B/2704